75p

About the author

Sally Worboyes was born and grew up in Stepney with four brothers and a sister. She now lives in Norfolk with her husband and three children. She has written plays broadcast on Radio 4, various East End sagas, and has adopted her own play and novel, WILD HOPS, as a musical, THE HOP-PICKERS.

SALLY WORBOYES

Girl from Brick Lane

CORONET BOOKS
Hodder & Stoughton

First published in Great Britain in 2002 by Hodder and Stoughton
A division of Hodder Headline

A Coronet Paperback

2 4 6 8 10 9 7 5 3 1

A CIP catalogue record for this title is available
from the British Library.

ISBN 0 340 81894 8

Typeset by Palimpsest Book Production Limited,
Polmont, Stirlingshire
Printed and bound in Great Britain by
Clays Ltd, St Ives plc

Hodder and Stoughton
A division of Hodder Headline
338 Euston Road
London NW1 3BH

For Gladys Stiff who lived and loved the twenties and now quietly enjoys the 21st century.

My thanks as ever to my Editor, Sara Hulse.

I

April 1905. Beaumont Square, Stepney

There was little to suggest anything significant about this lovely spring morning, except that it was Saturday and Grace Wellington was wearing a Sunday outfit. She had chosen soft colours in silk and fine lace, magnolia and powder pink with pale blue trim – shoes and hat to match. She was, however, in a far from sedate mood.

Hidden from the outside world, with a fine view from the drawing-room window, she was fussing with a perfectly good flower arrangement. The idea of joining her husband, Tobias, had come to her during the night, while she lay awake, tortured yet again by doubts. Having taken stock of all the Saturday excuses, she had come to the conclusion that it was time to find out the truth. In her twenty-sixth year and having been married for just five years, she could hardly believe that she was having to spy on her husband. Had she been born plain and grown dowdy she might have blamed herself, but this was not the case and she knew that men found her attractive. Her thick gold hair, pale complexion and light blue eyes set her apart from most other women in her circle. Her natural ways and love of conversation did sometimes annoy her husband. He had expressed, more than once, that he would prefer it if she would not behave so childlike.

Wondering what his response might be, now that she had finally summoned the courage to be strong and to confront him, she found herself smiling. After all, this act she was about to play out would give him a clear message: I do not trust you and I believe you to be a liar. Never before had she dared to challenge anyone, let alone her domineering husband.

From the window, Grace could see beyond the tall garden gates and into Beaumont Square where the trees reflected dappled rays of sunshine and around which, other houses towered. She was waiting for the hansom cab to turn into the Square. Tobias, at that moment was downstairs, in the library, watching from the window, also waiting for the cab. Grace's timing would have her stepping into the seat next to her husband *after* he had given the destination address to the driver.

Directly the hansom drew into the Square and before it had come to a halt, Tobias was out of the house and waiting to climb aboard and be away and Grace lost no time in joining him as planned. The look of horror, as she slipped into the seat next to him was enough to prove his guilt. She smiled and spoke quietly, 'I thought I would join you, Toby. It's a perfect day for a drive.' Before he could protest, the cabman was driving his horse onward bound.

'This isn't amusing, Grace,' he growled quietly. 'I have a meeting with a very important client.'

very brave. I would love to have the courage to do something as worthwhile. Can you imagine what it must feel like to break new ground?'

'It's no more than a flash in the pan, thankfully, a passing fashion. Why they should want to make a spectacle of themselves by charging through the streets waving banners—'

'Not always charging towards a cause, Toby. We do have quiet, serious, meetings too. More often than not in fact. One day we'll surprise the world and women will be given the freedom to vote.'

'Grace, please . . . I'm in no mood for this.' Not wishing to go on with that line of conversation, Tobias turned his attention to the outside world, his mind on other matters, his own silence betraying him. He looked every bit the guilty man trying to fathom a way out of a tricky spot. He couldn't think of anything to say to get himself out of this predicament.

A tense silence filled the cab as they journeyed through the East End and into the filthy backstreets, passing ragged children and rough-looking men and women. When the cabman pulled up in Brick Lane and in front of a run-down tenement house, Grace was mortified. Could this be it? Could *this* be where his mistress lived? Surely not.

'I hope you'll be satisfied,' said Tobias, placing the blame at her side, with those few curt words. With no intention of helping her down from the cab, he spoke with the driver, asking him to wait.

'Here?' whispered Grace, peering into his face. 'This is where you come every Saturday?'

'Yes, but this was to be the last. *Is* to be the last. You'd best brace yourself, and remember, those who look through keyholes are never satisfied.'

'What am I about to find out, Toby?' she said, now worried and frightened by it all.

'You're here now so see for yourself.' He knocked twice on the front door of the run-down back-to-back, terraced house. 'You needn't worry, it's a clean family, you couldn't catch anything if you tried.' Still he wouldn't look at her and Grace felt as if she were standing next to a complete stranger instead of her own beloved husband.

The door opened slowly with a long whining creak and there stood a woman, older than herself, who appeared tired but happy until she saw the anxiety in Tobias's eyes and especially when she saw the expression on Grace's face. 'What's this then?' she said, her worried voice tinged with suspicion.

'Mrs Brown, this is my wife, Grace. She insisted on coming with me—'

'Oh, did she now? Well you'd best come in.'

Stepping into the short and narrow passage, Grace was totally bemused. She could not make head nor tail of this. 'I hope I'm not intruding . . .' she said, still puzzled. She was beginning to think she had made a terrible mistake and this was perhaps a very old skeleton out of her husband's family cupboard that he had tried to keep under wraps.

'You're not in the way, you might 'ave bin 'ad you come a week or so earlier, but not today 'cause we're moving out.' The woman looked at Tobias hoping for an explanation as to why he had brought his wife along but he avoided her searching eyes.

'Well I would offer you a cup of tea but they've cut the gas off on account of us moving out.' The woman waved a hand over a pile of bulging cardboard packing cases. 'One more cart load and we'll be away. My daughter's gone on ahead to clean up the place properly for when we get there, me and the husband, that is. He's in the backyard, in 'is shed, packing his tools and that.'

She looked from Tobias to Grace. 'So you found out at last.' She spoke in a sort of caring way. 'I wish I could make it more bearable for you dear but I can't. Love's a very strange thing.'

'Love?' said Grace, hardly able to believe it. 'Love between my husband and . . .'

'My daughter,' said the woman, cutting in. 'The proof's in the front room.' She nodded towards the door leading in, 'You'd best go in and see for yerself now that you're 'ere.'

Turning away, Grace eased the door forward and froze. There, lying on two wooden crates which had been pushed together, was a small basket-woven cradle. In that cradle lay a baby girl, a baby girl who looked almost identical to Grace and Tobias's two-year-old daughter, Sarah, when she had been newly born. Grace could neither move nor speak, she simply stared at the face of the sleeping baby, realising what this meant. She could hear murmuring from the passage. The woman and Tobias were whispering together and Grace was clearly the outsider. Stunned by it all, she clenched her hands and forced herself not to break down. She had to get through the next few minutes. Once outside in the fresh air and spring sunshine she would be able to breathe properly again.

'It's your own fault, Grace. You needn't have put yourself through this.' Tobias had come into the room. 'I did try to stop you.' He lowered his eyelids, showing a wounded face.

She could do no more than gaze at him. As always, he had the nerve to lay the blame at her feet. But not this time, even he couldn't find a way out of this, surely? She hoped he was about to tell her that he had been trapped by a cheap whore whom he had come to pay off.

'This is the last thing I wanted.' His voice was gruff and there was a tinge of remorse. 'I intended to break it to you, bring it all out into the open in a week or so. Once the girl was settled in the new house and—'

'The *girl*? Settled in the new house?'

'Yes, she couldn't stay here, not now. It's not the best of places to bring up my daughter, which I know you'd be the first to—'

'*You're* moving her? To a better house?'

'Yes. It's hardly a palace, just somewhere better than this dreadful place. She doesn't belong here and neither do her parents. It's excellent rented accommodation that comes with employment—'

'And you,' said Grace, cutting into his babble, 'will you be moving in there too?' Had this not been so serious it would have been amusing. 'Shall you be moving out and into a slum, with no bootboy to see to your every need?'

'Not now, Grace, not here. It's hardly the place, it wouldn't be right.'

'You have the temerity to mention *right*?' She pulled herself to full height, eyes blazing, shoulders back. 'You scrape the bottom of the barrel and talk to me of what is right? You . . . who've been sleeping with a whore and made her with child. That is, of course, if it *is* your child. How on earth would you know – a family like this? Do they know you're married with two children . . . have they no shame?'

The door opened with a crash. The woman stood there, arms akimbo, glaring at Grace. 'Get out of my 'ouse now! Before I say something I might regret.'

'Oh, don't let me stop you, madam, give me the whole sordid, if not amusing, story'

'It ain't sordid and it's not a joke. He's bin coming 'ere for a couple of years now and we fink of 'im as one of us, just posher that's all.'

'And wealthy, let's not dismiss that little fact,' said Grace, pushing her face closer to the woman's. 'I'm sure you've all been very good to him, but I'm afraid he already has a family.' She tilted her chin, raised an eyebrow, saying, 'I wish I could make it more bearable for you, my dear.'

Before all hell let loose, Tobias put a caring arm round the woman's shoulders and walked her out of the room. Grace could not help but hear him say, 'Well, there we are, now you can see what I have to put up with.'

Allowing a few minutes to compose herself, Grace knew she had to be tough to get through this nightmare. Here, in this God-forsaken part of London, lay a newly born child, the sister of her own children and yet nothing to do with herself. In the passage was the grandmother who, by all accounts, knew Tobias and knew him well. They were on intimate terms, sharing secrets of which she had no part. Gazing down at the innocent baby, she clasped her hands together and forced herself to be strong, but the overwhelming sense of being an intruder in this place proved too much.

Close to tears, she summoned the courage to join her husband in the passage and managed to speak, albeit with a broken voice. 'I would like us to leave, Toby.'

Engrossed in a quiet conversation with Mrs Brown he hardly heard her. Then, gently squeezing the woman's arm, he smiled at her and turned away to let himself and Grace out. Pausing for a moment, Grace looked into the face of the woman with one question in her mind: How could you allow this to happen? They held each other's gaze in silence until a broken Grace turned slowly around and left the house.

Once the street door was closed between them, Mrs Brown reached for the banister and gripped it to steady herself. This ordeal had not been an easy one, it had taken every bit of her strength not to drag her daughter downstairs from where she was hiding and let her learn from her mistake of messing with a married man. To her mind this kind of thing belonged to the next generation. Change was in the air and it did not sit right with this woman. She could see nothing but misfortune coming from this business of the upper classes flirting with the lower. She blamed the Boer War. All sorts of people from all walks of life had been thrown together and had stood united, and this was one of the consequences, which would no doubt be just a flash in the pan but with a trail of illegitimate children as a keepsake.

Treading noisily on the staircase, deliberately crashing the worn heels of her boots on each tread, Mrs Brown called out to her daughter. 'Flora, come down here and see to your baby! Your married man's gone and for good if I'm not mistaken!'

Sheepishly coming out of her bedroom, the lovely nineteen-year-old Flora, who had been shedding a tear, fixed her gaze on the floorboards and murmured, 'Did he leave anyfing for me?'

'A cheque for a hundred pounds, think yerself lucky. Another man would 'ave walked away and not left you a farthing.'

'It's not for me,' she said, 'it's for baby, for Beanie. I won't touch a penny of it for myself.'

'We'll see. You can't live on fresh air. Flinging decency aside doesn't bring rewards it fetches a lifetime of regret. No one's gonna 'ave you now, Flora Brown, not with the shame over your 'ead. You'll die a spinster with a terrible secret, and that poor little baby'll 'ave to go through 'er life living a lie.'

'He said we'd be jest like man an' wife only wivout the certificate,' murmured Flora, 'he said I'd be 'is mistress and that he'd always be there for me. He said—'

'I'm sure he did. But words are cheap and a smile costs nothing, and that's what he's bin giving you for the past two years.'

Flora swallowed hard, trying her best not to cry. 'You're talking like he's never coming back, like I won't ever see 'im agen.'

'Of course you won't see 'im agen. He brought his wife wiv 'im, did he 'ave to spell it out any more than that? You've bin left high and dry.'

'That'll do, Violet,' said Flora's father, Willie, as he came in from the backyard and stood in the passage. 'You've had your say, now leave it be.' He climbed a few of the stairs and looked into the face of his daughter, their one and only child. 'You're not on your own, pet. Your ma and me'll look out for you and the wee bairn. Don't fret, bonny lass, some young lad'll be more than happy to take care of you and the little one. You're a pretty girl, mind, and lovely with it, so you'll not have to get down on your knees.'

'So you do fink he's gone away for good,' said Flora, her eyes pleading with him to say that her beloved would be back.

'I cannot tell you that, lass,' he said, slowly shaking his head and climbing the stairs until he was by her side. Pushing his fingers through her long, curly black hair, he managed a smile. 'We none of us can tell, pet. He's fair decent, mind, compared to most, found you a place to live and paid a month's rent up front, so you've no need to fret over that.' He kissed her lightly on the cheek and winked at her. 'Your da will always be here for you, lass.'

'I know,' she said, leaning forward and brushing a kiss across his cheek. 'I love my baby as much as I love you and mum, so even if he doesn't ever comes back, it won't matter, will it? I've got you, I don't need an 'usband, I'll be all right.'

'Aye, I think you will, little lass. You'll have to work at it, mind and you'll do no worse than getting proper training. Five guineas is what it'll cost but it'll be money well spent, it'll not make such a hole in the hundred pounds. That it won't.'

'At the Whitechapel Domestic School.'

'Aye. Your ma'll take care of the bairn while I'm earning a living and I'll look out for the bonnie lass on Sundays. She'll want for nothing, pet, for nothing.' He laid a hand on Flora's shoulder and smiled broadly. ''Ee you'll make a right good cook, lass, aye, you were born to it. Turned out a cracking jam tart before you could write your name.' He turned from her smiling face to his wife at the foot of the stairs. 'She'll be educating fledglings before she's thirty gone, if I'm not mistaken.'

Shrugging, Mrs Brown turned away to see to the baby who had started to cry. 'That's as may be but she can't start no lessons till baby's off the breast, that's one fing I can't do for 'er!'

'Well, there we are then, Flora lass,' said Willie, his blue eyes sparkling. 'Your ma agrees. So you'll get your training.'

*　　*　　*

On the journey back to Beaumont Square, the aggress-
ive silence which filled the cab was unbearable. Grace,
filled with the worst emotions: jealousy, hurt and self
degradation, was beginning to blame herself for her
failing marriage. Questions were racing through her
mind: Where had she gone wrong? Had she paid
enough attention to her husband's faraway moods
and creased foreheads? How long had he been putting
on a brave face? How long had he been living a life
of deceit?

In a pensive mood now, she said, 'What do you want
to do about this, Toby, should we file for a divorce,
with as least scandal as possible?'

Taken aback by her sudden remark, Tobias turned
his attention to what was going on outside the cab.
'Don't be ridiculous,' he mumbled.

'Am I to take it then, that you've no intention of
seeing the girl again, or the child?'

'She's not a girl, Grace, she's a woman, a young
woman. It was a misfortunate and very stupid mistake.
I've seen to it that she and the child will not go hungry
and will have a dry roof above their heads, now let that
be an end to it, please. Had you not meddled in my
private affairs all of this would have blown over and
you'd be none the wiser.'

'Meddled? In your *private* affairs?' snapped Grace,
her temper up. 'We are man and wife, how dare you
accuse me of meddling, how *dare* you!'

'The trouble with you, Grace,' returned Tobias,
shaking his head blandly, 'is that you have to know
everything. Well now that you do, perhaps we can

now pursue a pleasant, contented life.' He finished with a drawn-out sigh which fuelled her anger.

Pleasant, contented life . . . Is this all they had, in his view? To Grace, it sounded very much like a loveless marriage, a marriage of convenience. 'I shall speak with the family solicitor first thing tomorrow, your whore will not get one penny of my inheritance . . . and neither will you for that matter.'

'May we never forget self-respect, my dear,' he droned, an air of self-conceit about him. 'I believe that was something you once said when in your elitist mood. Well, I'm being the thorough gentleman, wouldn't you say, looking after the "whore's" welfare?'

Fuelled with anger she was all but ready to strike this man who was suddenly like a stranger. But she would not rise to his baiting, she would not lose her dignity. Giving herself time to relax she spoke quietly, reciting an old proverb. 'When Adam delved . . . and Eve span . . . who was then the gentle man?'

His answer was another of his infuriating long-drawn-out sighs. All feelings of self-pity fast fading, she made a vow there and then to probe further into his private world and find out more of this husband who was living a double life. She would check *everything* no matter how long it took and she would choose her time well to go through his most private files and especially the file into which she had not once glimpsed, the one marked: Bank, Stocks and Shares.

With nothing but silence for company on the drive home, she allowed Tobias to take her hand, knowing he would pat it gently, as if she were his pet dog. His words went above her head. 'It's over and done with, my dear. I went there today for one purpose and one purpose only, to give them the cheque and be done with it.'

She didn't believe him, nor did she care. She had, however, registered his damning confession. He had given her a cheque – not cash but a cheque. The woman, therefore, had a bank account and there was no doubt in her mind who had opened that account and who might be paying more cheques into it, in the future.

Grateful that her husband had gone quiet, lost in his own thoughts, Grace wondered whether this girl from Brick Lane had been the *only* other woman in his life. She no longer knew this man sitting beside her.

'What are you thinking about, now?' said Tobias, coming out of his private world.

'Our children, Herbert in particular. I was wondering what your son would make of this. What Sarah might be like, once she's twenty and single. It would be soul-destroying if she sank so low as to let a man fuck her out of wedlock and a married man at that. She has your blood in her after all, how can I be sure she won't be promiscuous? Then of course there's Herbert. Will he take a leaf out of his father's book—'

'Grace, please . . .'

'Of course, by the time Sarah reaches eighteen, your other daughter will be sixteen and probably be on the streets at night in Whitechapel. I mean, what else can the poor bastard-child expect with no father around to see that bills are paid and that she does not starve to death? The poor child certainly has something to thank you for. Never mind that young mother whose life you have ruined.'

'They are good hard-working people, and as for the child, not all of the lower classes go down that road, my dear.'

'And how would you know, the only thing that separates that family from us is money. Finance provides education and all else that allows decent people to move in the circles that we are lucky enough to enjoy. *You* of all people should know that.'

'Oh, not that swan song again, Grace, please. The girl has benefited from our knowing each other. She no longer sees herself as a wretched low-class person for whom there is no hope, she now has a passion, ambition.'

'Oh, dear, it's worse than I thought,' groaned Grace.

'It was all a hideous mistake, a terrible blunder,' he said looking away, fed up with her sarcasm. Things were bad enough for him as it was. It was going to be a while before he could dare take the risk of seeing his lovely young Flora again. He wondered if Grace imagined him to have no feelings at all. Wasn't he the victim here?

'God forbid any man should see a child of mine as a terrible blunder,' said Grace, as they pulled into Beaumont Square. 'Now, let this be an end of it,' she continued, straightening her new hat. 'We have our lives to get on with. That girl is, from now on, consigned to history.' She turned to face him again,

but this time looked him straight in the eye. 'Her name
will not go into my diary.' That said, Grace climbed
down from the cab before he could be there to assist
her. She had not forgotten that he had seen fit not to
help her off in Brick Lane. A new pattern had been cut
by himself and now she would keep to it. She would
also spend more time at meetings, drinking tea and
having cake with her lady friends. She would march
and shout for the rights of women until her throat was
sore, running through the streets with them, waving
their banners . . . and she would have her husband to
thank for it all. He had shaken her to the core and
in the long run, it would do no harm. Again her
mother's words ran through her mind: *It is so much
easier once one knows. Doubts destroy the soul.* She had
been referring to Grace's father, who had also strayed
and more than once.

Some weeks later, arriving home from the office much
later than usual, Tobias looked not the worse for drink,
which had been his tired excuse for being late, but
the better for something else. Something or someone
had put roses into his cheeks and a sparkle into his
eyes. It was not whisky so much that Grace sniffed
as he passed her, but perfume. This time, instead of
waving if off as she had done in the past, *before* the
Brick Lane revelation, she locked it in her mind but
said nothing. The one thing she had learned out of
the torment he had caused her, was to keep quiet,
stay charming, find out more. Inside, however, she
was deeply troubled and doubly hurt. For all of his

promises and talk of adoration, he was still making love to other women.

She began to lay the plan to look into his files – finances being uppermost in her mind. That he was seeing more than one woman, she had no doubt. Whether it was the mother of his bastard-child or someone else she had no idea, but the most important thing now was to see that he was not draining his or her bank account. Grace had to make certain he was not spending her inheritance from her beloved grandparents, on cigars, whisky and women. She had, after all, her own two children to think of.

For all the right reasons, when Tobias returned home late one night, with similar excuses and heady fumes on his breath and scent on his clothes, Grace played the game of having no idea what he'd been getting up to. Together in the snug, her every emotion stretched to the limit, she listened to his tales of work at the office and staff who were incompetent, offering false-hearted words of sympathy now and then. She also topped up his glass of whisky each time it fell below a certain level and put less and less iced water into it. She wanted him fully-clothed but out for the count. Which is exactly what happened.

Her heart beating rapidly, her slender fingers trembling, she slipped her hand inside his jacket and into the pocket of his waistcoat, carefully withdrawing a silver keyring. With it clutched tightly in her hand, she looked anxiously at her husband, fearing that he might suddenly wake and catch her out, even though he was out for the count, slumped in his favourite armchair, his cheeks a high colour, his mouth open and snoring.

Creeping out of the room and closing the door silently behind her, she went into his study and to his bureau. Listening intently all the while, she turned the small key in the lock and drew open a deep drawer in which his files were neatly held. Then, in the silence of that room, she extracted the equities file.

Seated on his desk chair, desperate to overcome the fear that he might walk in on her, she expeditiously scanned page after page of his accounts. Debits and credits, until her worst suspicions were confirmed. Tobias was drawing a regular sum of fifty pounds a month beyond their requirements, and substantial amounts had been debited from their account since they had married. Not only was he a womaniser but worse than a thief in the night. He was stealing from her and in effect from his own children, whose inheritance could have turned out to be little or nothing had she not found out now before it was too late. Saddened by it all and very tired after hours of examining and double-checking figures, with the desk lamp up as high as she dare turn it, she was ready for her bed. The bed which she sometimes slipped into when she was having trouble sleeping; the bed which was in one of the guest rooms and hardly ever used other than by herself. Here she could toss and turn, cry and curse. Here where she could think and contrive a way out of this trap she had allowed herself to be caught in, the worst trap of all: Silence. This sickening revelation could not be told to anyone. She couldn't think of a single friend on whose absolute trust she could depend. After all, what Tobias had been doing was, in effect, a criminal act. Friends and family would certainly see it as such. The shame of them finding out would be as bad as the discovery itself. There was only one person who could bring a stop to all of this and that was Grace, herself. She had never felt so alone in her entire life.

However, the next morning she awoke after fits and starts of sleep through the long night, fresh and resolute to act straight away. She would tell Tobias that, from then on, she would not burden him with her finances but would take care of her own personal banking.

Tobias's reaction at first was outright refusal to change anything, but on this, Grace had stood firm. She was playing him at his own game, acting the meek lamb while keeping the mind of a fox. When guilt did creep in and his sorry face bit into her conscience, she brought damning lines from his journal to mind: *Today, my lady from Brick Lane and I sat in Victoria Park smoking Turkish cigarettes as a brass band played in the distance. Heaven-scented days.*

Grace once again began to take up her earlier hobbies that Tobias had despised: drawing and painting. She went back to her classes in Bloomsbury and to an entirely different set altogether. She changed her style of dress from demure and soft shades, to flamboyant deep rich colours of blood red, shimmering gold and silver satins, beaded emerald greens, midnight blue, purple and black. She was introduced to the very latest cocktails and aromatic cigarettes. She attended soirées in the afternoons and gay parties in the evenings and took to the new dance like a duck to water. Grace, in short, was enjoying her second flush of youth. She enjoyed the attention of attractive men and she enjoyed the occasional drift into promiscuity. Tobias despised his wife for it all but said nothing because her preoccupation left him free to continue with his latest secret affair – a beautiful dark girl of the stage who loved him and sang like a bird in the music-halls and who lived in the backstreets of Shoreditch. The backstreets of the East End of London were a lighthouse for Tobias, homing in a stray ship of the night. His penchant for cockney girls was in his blood and in his roots.

When Grace had first met him, he had been playing the lead in an end-of-term stage play, *The Taming of the Shrew*, at a private school in Chigwell, Essex. She had been in the audience purely by chance since a friend of a friend was also in the play. Backstage she had met Tobias and it was a case of love at first sight.

Although the family house, in which Tobias lived at that time, was fairly grand, both his parents had been born and bred in Bethnal Green, the heart of the East End. Before his birth and after, his mother had worked from dawn till dusk, cleaning first thing and then going on to a factory where she had been employed as the tea lady, pushing her trolley along corridors and going from one floor to the next.

Tobias's father had filled his every waking hour, labouring in a small tailor's shop as a machinist at first and then a pattern cutter. In the evenings and on Sundays he would work at home for a few private customers and his reputation as a bespoke tailor brought him more customers from the City. After two years he could afford to rent a spacious room in an old warehouse and employ two apprentices. Tobias's mother became his right hand, cutting cottons, threading machines, sewing on buttons, steam pressing and generally helping to keep things shipshape. Their ambition was to see their one and only son through private schooling. By sheer tenacity and hard work, this was achieved – this and more. The Wellingtons had risen from low working class to middle class with an adequate bank balance.

The long hours and hard work did, however, have sad consequences. Tobias's father, at the age of fifty-five had suffered a massive heart attack and died soon afterwards. Mother and son continued to enjoy a comfortable living after the business was sold and up until Mrs Wellington, tired and lonely without her lifelong partner, gave up her lovely house and went into an exclusive retirement home in Brighton. Her one and only son, Tobias, having achieved good results at school had moved on in life, visiting her only twice a year, once at Christmastime and once in midsummer. Gradually her son broke her heart, for she knew that he had grown ashamed of his parents' background; ashamed of his mother who still spoke with a cockney accent; ashamed of their story of hard work, labouring over sewing-machines and scrubbing other people's floors.

When Alice Wellington lay on her deathbed, surrounded by her friends at the home, she bore no malice and had no regrets. She and her husband had seen their dreams come true: their son had been educated by the finest masters, he had been employed in a City bank. Their Tobias had married into the upper middle classes – it had not been for nothing. At peace with her memories, Alice slipped quietly and comfortably into her last sleep.

2

1925

There was a feeling of a backwater about St Mary's Courtyard, which was vastly different from the run-down house in Brick Lane, where Flora Brown had grown up and her illegitimate daughter, Beanie, had been born. Coming up to her fortieth birthday, Flora was no less attractive but her curly black hair was now streaked with light grey and was always pulled back tight, into a French pleat. Her plain clothes and lack of face make-up or jewellery gave out a message: I am past my prime and settled to being an old maid. I have loved and lost which is better than not being loved at all.

Beanie was the light of her life and Flora would lay down her life for her precious child. But Beanie was now a young adult and though devoted to her mother, did sometimes go against her wishes and lived life to the full when she could and in her own modest way. She was fun-loving and there had never been a shortage of admirers. At twenty years old, she looked the image of her mother when she had been as young and almost as carefree.

Other than the regular tradesmen, only those who lived in St Mary's Court, or visiting relatives and friends, entered the long archway leading into this small, quiet, flagstoned area, which was enclosed by an ivy-clad brick wall and terraced houses. In the centre of the paved courtyard a flowering apple tree had been planted and was a picture when in bloom and a feast once the fruit was ripe for picking. In winter, however, with just one gas light the court was a dark place at night, especially when the fog was low and thick. Even so, those lucky enough to live there never wanted to leave.

But Flora and Beanie were going to have to move out of their cosy two-up, two-down with the pretty back garden. When the news broke that the clay-pipe factory, where mother and daughter were employed, was to close down, it was the worst thing. They had loved working in the family-like atmosphere and were practically running the factory canteen and kitchen. Flora as cook and Beanie as kitchen maid and waitress in the directors' dining room. Now, the only alternative open to them was to go into service, in one of the big houses, as live-in staff. Devastating though it was, they were going to have to face facts and move out of their little haven, tucked away in a quiet part of Limehouse in the East End, where they would no longer be able to afford the rent.

Flora was by now resolved to the fact that she would not find a husband. There had been suitors throughout the years and one or two had asked for her hand in marriage, but the moment she confessed that Beanie was not in fact her orphaned cousin, as she led most people to believe, but her own child, they withdrew to disappear without trace. The consideration received from Beanie's father, soon after her birth, had been generous enough, but spent over the years. A hundred pounds seemed like a fortune in 1905 and even though Flora had managed to train and work as a qualified cook, she had been unable to put anything aside for emergencies. All of her furniture, when she moved into the courtyard had come from second-hand shops as did most of her daughter's clothes. But still, with her careful use of material resources, post office savings were something she could only dream of.

And so it was decided that Flora would apply for a post as live-in cook and once she was settled in, she would recommend Beanie for kitchen duties. The fact that they were mother and daughter would be kept secret. In the court the neighbours knew the circumstances and had turned a blind eye and between them had given little treats to Beanie when she was small.

Flora's modest furniture was going to have to be sold and from the return, Beanie was to buy a set of smart clothes from a good second-hand shop. She would be ready for interviews, when the time came. Meanwhile, she would lodge with her doting grandparents in their tiny terraced cottage which belonged to Charringtons, the local brewery, where Flora's parents were now employed as part-time bottle washers. Beanie with her lovely looks and personality would always find temporary work and didn't mind what she did so long as the company was good.

The saving grace was that capable women, as live-in

maids and especially trained cooks with a good refer-
ence, were in demand. Flora could choose in which
part of London she would prefer to live and work.
Her daughter's only plea was that they applied to
those houses which stood tall and elegant in a grand
square. Happy to oblige, Flora began to study the list
of situations vacant.

'So,' said Flora, as she and her daughter sat drinking
tea in their tiny back garden, 'you want to live in a
posh square. Well then, I've marked all of those
beginning with the letter B so you can be Beanie
from Beaumont Square or Bedford Square or Berkeley
Square.'

'Beaumont,' said Beanie, waving a hand. 'Let's
go for the first one, where is it, somewhere nice
and posh?'

'Yeah, Beaumont Square off Beaumont Place, right
in the heart of Stepney.'

'That don't sound much fun, can't we go for one
of the others?'

'We'll try 'em all, sweetheart. Come on, pen and
paper – best 'andwriting.'

'Mine?'

'If nothing else, you can write lovely. We've got a
new life to find, Beanie love.' She raised her cup of
tea and Beanie clinked it with hers.

'I know your game, muvver. You wanna marry me
off to a rich bloke.'

'Only if he's as 'andsome as your dad was at your
age.'

'And a royal prince. Me dad was a royal prince wasn't

he?' said Beanie, smiling and teasing her mother. Flora didn't think she was that far off the mark.

Having secured an interview with all three applications, Flora decided, in the end, to stay in the area where she felt most at home: Beaumont Square. She was to start immediately she had worked her notice at the clay-pipe factory. Expecting Beanie to be disappointed that she had chosen Stepney Green, Flora treated them to a fish and chip supper and broke the news while she poured them both a glass of cider.

'You wouldn't know that you was in this part of the world, Bea, honest to God. The people living in that Square are just as posh as them living in the rich areas. They're wealthy businesspeople who need to be close to the City and most of 'em, if not all, 'ave got a residence in the country.'

'Well that'll do us, then,' said Beanie, breaking off hot crispy batter from her succulent piece of fried haddock. 'Did you ask about a parlour maid?'

'No, love, it's too soon. But I had my wits about me and I can tell you now that position won't come up. The young lady's been there from school and sees it as 'er home. But, scullery maid that's another kettle of fish. The girl's as daft as a brush and don't know a thing about blacking a stove. She won't last long.'

'Oh right, that's it then, 'cos I do . . . and brass polishing. What else will I 'ave to do?'

Flora leaned back in her chair and popped a chip into her mouth. Thinking about it, she ran through the list: 'Clean and whiten the doorsteps, clean and light fires, polish brass and copper, scrub kitchen tables, clean and polish, wash up, prepare vegetables. And we shall be at their beck and call, make no mistake.'

Beanie's eyes widened with an expression of horror. 'How many hours' sleep am I s'posed to 'ave?'

'Depends 'ow early you go to bed. Get your chores done, leave nothing to the morrow, and you'll 'ave a nice life. You'll 'ave to be up early mind, six o'clock, like me.'

'That early?'

'Yes, Beanie,' smiled Flora, 'fires 'ave to be made up. Mind, you wouldn't 'ave to worry too much there. Most rooms 'ave got gas fires. I'll let you lie in till half past six.'

'You will?'

'Oh, yeah. Cook's the boss,' she said, pleased as punch.

'That can't be right,' said Beanie, 'you're making all this up.'

'No I'm not. They don't 'ave a butler at Beaumont Square so I'll be in charge. Why d'yer think I chose to work there?'

'So, why's the cook leaving then,' said Beanie, wrapping a slice of buttered bread round a handful of chips, 'if it's that good?'

'That's her business and I'm thankful for it. She said that her employers Tobias and Grace Wellington are the best,' said Flora, topping up their cider. 'They've got a place in the country and when they go, so do the staff. The bootboy, parlour maid, scullery maid and the cook. It's in Suffolk by all accounts . . . Laversham Hall. And not too far from the coast either.'

'What about kids?'

'A son, about five years older than you, and a daughter who must be somewhere around twenty by all accounts. Before you ask I never set eyes on either of 'em, and before your mind starts turning over, don't even consider it – above and below never mix. It'll be more than both our jobs are worth if you so much as smile at the lad.'

'Wouldn't dream of it, muvver,' said Beanie, sipping her cider.

'I mean it, Bea, you stray across the line and I'll have you sacked.' The tone in Flora's voice said it all. 'This is a chance of a new life for both of us, so long as they don't clock that we're mother and daughter, we'll be all right.'

A vague expression passed across Beanie's face which did not go unnoticed. 'It'll be hard for the both of us, Beanie, but we shall have to keep up the pretence.'

'Why . . . why can't we be honest from the start, what's wrong with us working together?'

This was not easy for Flora. How could she tell her child that she had been lying to her all these years and that, not only had she no idea where her father was, she had never been married. 'It's not done, that's all. Besides which, an unmarried cook with no ties is what most domestic advertisements ask for. Once we've proved ourselves, after a couple of years or so, should it come out, we'll stand more chance of keeping our jobs.'

'Just as well I'm a bit of an actress then. That's what my music and drama teacher always said anyway. I bet you slip up before I do.'

'Maybe so, but as long as we always bear it in mind, we can't do no more than that. The fact that you've inherited my hair won't matter so much, now that I'm going grey. Luckily you've got your father's eyes. It's always the eyes that give you away.'

'It wouldn't matter anyway, they won't be looking for things like that. We'll be all right, if you can get me in there, that is. It's not certain, is it?'

'Oh, I'll get you in, Bea, make no mistake.' The tone in Flora's voice was positive. Beanie meant the world to her and no employer was going to keep them apart. The most she wanted from life now was as little heartache as possible. She loved her cooking and she loved to grow things in the garden and, as luck would have it, Lenny the gardener had been only too pleased to have someone take an interest in his work.

Showing her round what he considered to be *his* garden, he'd given a running commentary on what grew where and when. Walking briskly along the paved path up the centre, he'd shown off the rose beds which were now sleeping. He pointed out his favourite summer climber, the sweet-scented white jasmine which covered almost the whole of the old brick wall to the back of the garden. He told her of the wide open yellow crocus in early spring and the tulips that stood to attention and the primulas and the bluebells. Then, and most important for a cook to see, were the fruit bushes and the vegetable patch. The mulberry tree, apple and plum, which produced prime fruit for pies. This was indeed a little oasis in the heart of the East End, to which birds and butterflies paid homage. Flora Brown was happy again, as happy as the day when she first went to live in St Mary's Court. In Beaumont Square she and Beanie would be quite content.

The kitchen, where the staff ate their meals, was quite large, with an old couch and two small armchairs placed round a glowing coal fire. The scullery, just off the kitchen, housed the double gas cooker as well as the copper, and a large wooden mangle. The sink overlooked the garden which made washing up more pleasant than it might otherwise have been. The staff toilet was outside adjacent to the kitchen.

Had Tobias Wellington not been so astute, all those years ago, as to use a pseudonym and say he lived in Westminster, Flora Brown would never have attended this interview. As far as she was concerned, her sweetheart of long ago was called Charles and who very soon after their first meeting was nicknamed, Prince Charlie. This, Tobias had found amusing and was flattered by it. Flora had, since their final parting, given up any notions of him coming back to her and the love which had burned for so long in her heart had gradually turned to resentment. He was the furthest person from her mind when she had stepped into that luxurious grand hallway of the house in which they would both now be living. He above stairs and she below.

*   *   *

Soon after Flora was settled in at number ten and had observed that Bridget the scullery maid was quite hopeless in the kitchen, she bided her time and waited for someone else to say something. It was obvious that the girl did not want to be here in England but back home in Ireland. She had been sent from Dublin by her family to get away from all the troubles but she cried continually and talked non-stop about her boyfriend whom she feared to be in danger. She had seen the terrible consequences from the guerrilla warfare when brother fought against brother and father against son. She had seen Dublin when it had been a city of smoke and fire and heard tales from all parts of the country, of battles, ambushes, kidnappings and murders. And yet all she wanted was to go back home to her family and her sweetheart – this wish was soon granted. It was Fanny Baker, the parlour maid, who plucked up the courage to say something. Often working from dawn to dusk herself, she had to have someone she could rely on to pull her weight else her workload would be twice as hard. It was for this reason that Fanny had gone above stairs to speak to Grace Wellington. She liked Bridget, they all did, but facts were facts. Grace Wellington, however, was quick to give Fanny peace of mind. To remove the burden of guilt from her parlour maid, for telling tales, she expressed her own feelings on the matter; that she had seen enough incompetence from Bridget and knew she would not settle in England and that she herself was ready to buy her a ticket to Ireland. This was not done out of malice, she had always taken an interest in the welfare of her staff. The result of which was a well-run house with no bad feelings or unrest.

Once Flora had had the story related to her, she was quick off the mark, recommending a hard working young lady who would fit the bill. And, so, Beanie was given the job of scullery maid on a month's trial after sailing through her interview with Grace Wellington. Now, on her first day, having been shown round, Beanie was in the tiny snug below stairs, with her mother, Flora, having a so-called run down on her timetable and daily duties.

Albert, the valet-cum-bootboy, a thin young man with a pale face and freckles sat staring into the flames of the small fire in the scullery, thinking how lovely this new girl was, with her dark blue eyes, raven hair and sweetheart lips. His thoughts were quickly shattered when the basement door crashed open suddenly.

'Gawd, that's wicked out there tonight,' said Fanny Baker, coming in and forcing the door shut against the wind. 'Gave me a worse lashing than my old man ever did with 'is belt. It's howling round the Square, I'll tell yer that much.'

'You never was belted as a kid was yer, Fan?' said Albert, pushing a hand through his coarse sandy hair.

'Only when I deserved it.' Lifting the lid off the large pot, Fanny sniffed the aroma of beef stew. 'Ooooh that's got me juices goin', spoon some into a dish for us, Albert. I wanna get these cold clothes off me back.'

'Wot, all of 'em?'

'No, not all of 'em, time and place for everyfing. God that frost could fracture a rock, slipping all over the place I was.'

'Shouldn't 'ave gone out then should you?'

'If I never went out on me half day off I'd be a bit on the sad side. Don't ask me 'ow me sister is, will yer?'

'How's yer sister, Fan?'

'All right, thanks, so's me little niece and nephew,' she said, peeling off her long black coat. 'The fog was much thicker over Clapham Junction. Good job she gave me a stick, I 'ad to rap along the railings till a friendly policeman saw me to the station. Did the fruit-and-vegetable man come?'

'Nope. Cook 'ad to serve an all meat dinner. It's the sack for you, me gal.'

'Was Cook pleased?'

'Nope. Upstairs 'ad limp and mouldy veg, so did we for that matter. The carrots was as soft as an old man's wotsit and the onions was yucky in the middle. Some of the fruit 'ad to be chucked away.'

'So it was all right then, good. What's the new scullery maid like?'

'Lovely, nice big arse.'

'So where is she?' demanded Fanny, making herself comfortable by the coal fire where she unlaced her ankle boots. 'Come to that, where's Cook?'

'They're both in the backroom goin' over fings. Cook said she, Beanie that is, 'as gotta lot to learn, but she finks she'll be all right.'

'Yeah and what would she know, not bin 'ere five

minutes 'erself. Soon got her feet nicely under the table.'

'I thought you thought she was all right?'

'She is all right. A bit above 'erself that's all. First time I've known a cook not to want us to call 'er by 'er name. Daft if you ask me.'

'No it's not, I've worked below stairs since I was nine, don't you forget.' His eyes glazed over as he remembered and began counting. 'Six 'ouses altogether I've worked in and from memory I would say that four out of six cooks were called "Cook". So there's nuffing unusual about it. Unless of course she's got a past . . .' said Albert, teasing her. 'Perhaps she's been in prison for poisoning a parlour maid, one who was a bit like someone I know and I mention no names.'

Showing him no response whatsoever, Fanny leaned closer to the fire and rubbed her hands together. 'As it 'appens I don't mind calling 'er Cook. I might ask to be called "Parlour Maid" in the future instead of Fanny. That way they'd be no mistaking who's who round 'ere.'

'Anyway,' said Albert, 'I put 'er straight about one or two fings.'

'Did you now, and what exactly did you put 'er straight about, Albert Henry? Not me, I 'ope. You better not 'ave bin gossiping about me.'

'I just told 'er what you got up to on your evenings off that's all. She threw her 'ead back and laughed, said she liked a sailor now and then as well.'

'You never did say such a thing!'

'I implied it, that's all, I mean I couldn't say for fact

could I? Wot do I know of wot you get up to when you go out? Getting yerself done up like lady muck. It's the only time I see you wearing lipstick and powder. Wot's a bloke s'posed to fink?'

'None of your blooming business, anyway, I might 'ave gone to my sister's and I might not 'ave done, that's for me to know and you to wonder, Albert my boy.'

'Tripe. I've got better fings to fink about. D'yer want yer stew scalding 'ot or lukewarm?'

'In between the two as you well know, put it in the bowl and leave it to stand. So, is she pretty then?'

'You could say that and then again . . .'

'Well is she or ain't she!'

He placed an arm round her shoulders and kissed the top of her head. 'Nowhere as near pretty as you, Fanny, but then, no woman is.' Cupping her face he looked into her almond-shaped green eyes. 'One of these days you're gonna be my missus.'

'Is that right . . . well pull off me boots for me then.'

'First fings first,' he kissed her gently on the lips. 'You gonna let me warm the cockles of your 'eart tonight?'

'No. No more till I've got to know the new girl, she might be a spy. I don't want 'er running upstairs and telling tales out of school now, do I?'

'I s'pose not. She seems all right though, a bit . . .' he wrinkled his nose.

'What, a bit what?'

'Dunno. Not posh exactly . . .'

'Posh? I should bleedin' 'ope not; she must be a spy

if she is. How can a flippin' scullery maid be posh. I am, granted, but then *I* am a parlour maid. There's a difference.'

Thinking about it, he scratched his ear. 'Anyway, she don't sound 'er Ts or that, but . . .'

'But what, gimme an example, the sort of fing she'd say.'

'All right, let me think. Yeah . . . I asked if she fancied a cup of tea and she said, "That'd be lovely, fank you."'

Fanny raised an eyebrow and pulled a face. 'Well she's not daft then, picked that up from Cook straight away. Keepin' on 'er good side already.'

'Nah, she ain't a bootlicker, she's all right. You'll like 'er.'

'Well, all I know is that Cook says fings like that all the time: "That'd be lovely, Fan, thanks."'

Getting down on his knees, Albert grasped the heel and toe of Fanny's boot and caught a whiff of talcum powder. Slipping a hand under her skirt and petticoats and up to the soft fleshy bit beneath her corset, he groaned with passion. 'Oooooh . . . lovely, shall we go for a lie down, Fan?'

'Excuse me, Mr Henry, but you're talking to a good Christian girl, thank you very much.'

'Oh yeah,' he said, leaving his hand right where it was. 'When was the last time you went to church, then?'

'On the last Sunday I got off, which admittedly was two months ago, but that's not my fault, is it now?'

'No, sweetheart,' he said, giving her a wink and

tickling her fancy a bit more. 'So you want me to stop then do yer?'

'Not now . . . no, you're 'elping me to thaw out.'

'My little Fanny is a bit on the cold side, then?'

'No, I've got two pairs of drawers on,' she said, grinning.

'I know,' he said, beside himself, 'I wanna be in there, Fan . . .'

'Well if you must, gotta keep you 'appy, ain't I. Be quick though, before they come in.'

Shocked by her sudden change in character, he pulled his hand away and leaned back on his heels. Not that they hadn't played around in bed but he usually had to work on her more than this. 'What . . . 'ave a little bit, 'ere, in the scullery?'

'Cosy enough, ain't it?'

'Yeah but . . . What if Cook comes in with the new maid?' he said, pushing a hand up her leg again and stroking her thigh.

'Well, if you stop in that position, Cook'll think you're praying or proposing.' She gave him a saucy grin. 'Shall I unbutton yer flies for yer?'

'Fanny Baker, wot ever's come over you?'

'All right,' she said, clenching her legs and gripping his hand. 'Don't then, I can go without.'

'I don't know wot to say, but I can't leave me 'and trapped there all day so . . .'

'Oh, so you're not strong enough to pull it free then?' she said, grinning at him.

'Course I am but then agen you 'ave got the thighs of a wrestler.'

'Blooming cheek,' she said, releasing her grip.

'You sure you ain't got a mechanical grip tied to yer drawers?' he said, nursing his hand. 'No, don't answer, I'll take a look for meself.' Pulling up her skirt and petticoats he lowered his head to the sound of Fanny laughing, which might easily have drowned out the approaching voices, had she been less alert.

'Get up!' she said kicking him away and sending him sprawling across the floor just as Flora Brown and the new scullery maid came in from the back room.

'Not feeling well, Albert?' said Flora, amused by the sight.

'Er ... I'm absolutely fine, Cook, I slipped on somefing or other,' he said, nodding and smiling at Beanie.

'Did you now, well, I hope it wasn't something nasty been dropped on the floor and not cleaned off,' she said, eyeing Fanny.

'No it wasn't. I know I'm not the scullery maid, but still I wouldn't leave food to feed the mice. You could eat off that floor it's that clean.' She glanced at Beanie to see her hiding a smile.

'I was only teasing you, Fanny, don't get sassy now.'

'Anyway, it's not my responsibility no more, it's yours, Beanie.'

Flora, pleased that things seemed to be going well, realised that Albert had filled Fanny in on the new girl. Now it was her turn to add her ha'penny worth. 'This is Fanny Baker, Beanie, the parlour maid. Her duties are upstairs and you'll be under her. If she needs something you must see she gets it, we must work as a team, all four of us. If we manage to do that we'll be like family, which is how it should be when you're living under the same roof. Any questions?'

'No, Cook,' said Albert, back on his feet. 'Well, maybe just one.'

'Well, spit it out, I don't eat bootboys for breakfast.'

'I was just wondering, since it's Beanie's first day . . .'

'Call me Bea,' said Beanie, amused by the scene of her mother in charge.

'Since it's Bea's first day and since it's evening and upstairs 'ave bin seen to . . .'

'Oh for goodness' sake, Albert, what?' Flora was not one to suffer the long-winded gladly.

'Well, maybe me and Fanny could take Bea up West since it's 'er first day.'

'I beg your pardon, sir, you'll do no such thing. Do you want to see us all out on the street? A half day off each week for all three of you is what I was told, I got the gist of that straight away. No skiving.'

'Daft idea if you ask me,' said Fanny, keeping on the right side of Flora. 'I'm just about to 'ave a bit of hot stew if anyone else cares to join me.'

'I would,' said Beanie, 'it smells lovely.'

Seeing that her daughter was fitting in, Flora said, 'Well then I shall leave you to it. I've a recipe book to study before I turn off the lights. And don't be reckless and go against my word. If anything *can* go wrong it will: Murphy's Law.' With that she left the kitchen, in need of solitude where she could thank the good Lord for making everything go well. This was a good house, even though the bedrooms were cold, with just a tiny gas fire in each. More to the point, none of them had noticed any likeness between mother and daughter.

'Right then,' said Beanie, once Flora was out of earshot, 'what's there to do before we turn in?'

Looking from Albert to the new girl, Fanny stared at her, unblinking, until she said finally, 'You can scrub the floor agen if you like, as for me and Albert, we'll probably sit at the table and play a board game.'

'So there's no chores to be done then?'

'Like I said, you can scrub the floor, clean out the cupboards, clean and polish, fetch in the coal, or more importantly, get the range ready for Cook to make breakfast, it's muffins tomorrow. Or if you really wanna make an impression, go out there and scrub the front doorstep in the dark and freezing cold.'

'What about them upstairs, will they ring for us for anything?'

'Only if there's an emergency. Why don't you go up and ask if there is one?'

'And Cook don't come down once she's gone abed?'

'That's right, gonna write it down in your notebook are yer?'

Taking a few seconds to think things through, Beanie shrugged and splayed her hands. 'So no one'd know if we went out then – up West?'

Roaring with laughter, Albert slapped his knee.

'Luv a duck if she's not bin 'aving you on, Fanny.'

'You've not bin in service before, 'ave you?' said Fanny, wondering where this girl was from.

'No, but I'll soon pick it up from you two lovebirds.' She winked and grinned. 'An' don't tell me you're not sweethearts, I don't miss a trick, but then I've worked in a factory. So what d'yer reckon then, shall we bunk off? I've got half a crown. We'll fill our bellies with stew before we go so all we need is the fare and a few coppers each for a beer or two in a tavern. What d'yer say?'

'I say we go,' said Albert. 'We'll blame you though if we do get caught,' he said, half meaning it.

'That's right. Say I wouldn't stop crying 'cos I was homesick or plain scared to death. That way you'll be heroes and I'll be pitied.' She looked from Albert to Fanny and waited while each of them weighed up the pros and cons. 'I know a smashing little jazz club in Soho. The drinks don't cost much for ladies, if anyfing, they need us to lure in the men, we can afford a few pints for Albert between us. What d'yer say, Fanny? You and Albert dancing up close to a Louis Armstrong or Jelly Roll Morton or, stop in and play a board game?'

'A bit of charleston'd do me,' said Fanny, lifting her skirts and warming her rump by the fire. 'It's all right for the likes of you, you're a factory girl and used to doing what you please, me and Albert are up the from the country.'

'You lying cow,' said Albert, chuckling. 'Take no

notice of 'er, Bea, she's from South London and I'm from Tottenham. Bin too long in service that's your trouble, my girl, all above yerself.'

'Is that right, well you can just go wivout me then, can't yer, I'll stop 'ere and 'ave an early night.'

'Oh well, if you don't want to break the mould,' said Beanie, 'I s'pose me and Albert'll 'ave to go—'

'What and leave me by myself?' snapped Fanny. 'I don't reckon so. Go and put on yer Oxford bags, Albert, while I doll meself up. And I'll say this and then I'll say no more – don't fink I'm gonna take the rap if we get caught out 'cos I'm not.'

Coming up from Tottenham Court Road underground station and caught up in the high-spirited mood of the crowds around her, Beanie's infectious laughter helped both Fanny and Albert to relax and stop worrying about this dangerous game of playing truant. There was a buzz in the air, for the cocktail and cabaret age had begun in London. Linking arms, the three of them walked gaily along the pavement, weaving in and out of the small happy groups and courting couples. Passing a doorway with stairs leading down to a jazz club, Beanie sang along with those enjoying themselves below and Fanny and Albert were quick to join in. Singing and swaying, with arms linked, they continued on towards Oxford Circus, stopping in a tavern or two on the way. Happy enough in their own company and with the contagious happy mood of others around them, they were content to walk arm in arm and simply soak up the atmosphere. It was only when thcy heard the sound of a particular number coming from inside one of the clubs that they stopped. The jazz band was playing the charleston.

'I don't know about you two,' said Beanie, dancing and cavorting, showing off her skills, 'but I'm going down there.'

Fanny was dubious but there was no stopping Albert, who led them down dark red and blue carpeted stairs towards red and gold lights. Arriving at the entrance they were enthralled, until that is, Fanny, to her horror, saw her employer's daughter, surrounded by four or five loud young men. This was not her first visit to the Blue Note. She seemed very much at home in these surroundings; in her bohemian clothes of blood red, black and rust, she looked quite stunning. Flirting madly she was carrying an amber and gold cigarette holder and smoking a French cigarette.

'Oh Gawd,' murmured Fanny, gripping Albert's arm. 'It's Sarah Bernhardt, do a quick about turn or we're sunk.'

'Sarah Bernhardt . . .' said Beanie, '. . . it can't be, she's dead.'

'Not the *real* one, silly drawers, one who swans about as if she's a blooming actress.'

'All right then, girls,' said Albert gingerly, 'don't draw attention. Just turn around and walk back up them stairs as casual as you like.'

'I said we shouldn't 'ave come . . .'

'Not now, Fanny, love. Just do as you're told, there's a good girl.' But it was too late for them to make their casual exit. The Wellingtons' attractive and fashionable daughter had spotted them.

'She's seen us,' said Beanie. 'I don't know who she is but she's scaring the wits out of you two. I'll take the wind out of her sails.'

'You don't understand, Beanie,' said Albert, his words trailing off as Sarah Wellington came closer. 'Oh Gawd . . .'

'I say chaps,' said Miss Wellington, taking a draw of her cigarette, 'doing a bunk are we? What a lark.' Her glazed eyes were focused on Beanie. 'I don't think I've seen you before, our Albert's not your *geezer*, is he?' She looked slyly at Fanny for a reaction. 'Can't be sugar daddy to the both of you, surely not?'

'I always thought that sugar daddies were old, rich and wrinkled,' drooled Beanie. 'Albert's young an' poor, a bootboy.'

'Mmmm . . .' she purred, raising an eyebrow and giving Beanie the once over. 'Bees around the honeypot tonight, I should think.' Smiling, she flicked a finger towards the group she had left. '*They* adore the cockney slang, pity you can't stop.' She turned to Fanny, her expression one of amusement. 'Does my mother know you're out?'

'No,' said Fanny, casting her eyes down. 'I s'pose you'll 'ave to tell her though, that would be only right and proper.' She was hoping that her subservient act might get her off the hook.

'Good heavens, I wouldn't dream of it, power to your elbow is what I say. You might want to find another little haunt, mind. My charming brother

Herbert is over in the corner with his chums, he might just deem it fit to split on you.'

'So we can take it you won't say anything, then?' said Beanie, realising exactly who this was.

'Of course I shan't say anything, silly. Live and let live, okay, we none of us were here.' She winked at Beanie and then squeezed her cheek, playfully. 'Get yourself out of here before one of the rogues pounces on you.' Chuckling, she went back to her arty friends and linked arms with a fashionable young man wearing a green velvet casual jacket, black shirt and colourful necktie. His loose gold hair almost reaching his shoulders.

Once outside in the fresh air, Albert burst out laughing and the other two joined in. 'What a bunch of prats they are,' he said.

'Just thank your lucky stars for it,' said Fanny. 'Fank Gawd we're in vogue, us cockneys; few years back and she'd 'ave spat on us.'

'Now, now,' said Albert, 'don't be like that. She's all right is Miss Sarah.'

'Yeah, but you can't always tell. She might not be so chummy wiv you, Albert Henry, once you've bedded 'er. She wants you to give 'er a going over, make no mistake.'

Coming out of the dark place and on to the street again, Beanie left Albert and Fanny to their silly banter. Her eyes were on someone else – a young man who had obviously come out of the Blue Note and was having trouble getting his car started. This was Mr Charles Savage, a medical student at Oxford, home for the weekend. Struggling with his motor car, a gift from his grandfather, he was trying to fathom why he could not make the engine turn over. He gazed at the beast more in despair than anger. Beanie found him attractive but was more interested in the car, and she fancied a ride in it. Everything about him spoke wealth, he was wearing a light camel coat, white neck collar and a not-too-jazzy tie.

'It ain't gonna go of its own accord, mate,' said Albert, pleased to have the opportunity of speaking to a gentleman of means, without having to be subservient. Here in this public place they were equals. 'You've gotta wind it up, mate,' he said, smirking.

'There's no need to be sarcastic,' came the disgruntled reply. 'I've been trying to turn the bloody thing.' He turned round to face the three of them and looked Albert in the eye. 'Here, see if you can do better.'

'I will if you say, please.'

'Please.'

'Didn't sound to me as if he meant it, honey-bun,' said Fanny, 'I wouldn't 'elp 'im unless he sounds as if he means it. You're not 'is paid servant after all said an' done.'

By now, this stranger was feeling embarrassed and a little out of his depth, Beanie came to his rescue once she saw his cheeks redden. 'Stop tormenting 'im, Albert, get the car going and you never know, he might give us a ride.'

'Of course I will, a lift home perhaps?' He returned Bea's smile. 'So long as I can find my way back home again.'

'Oooh, I dunno about that, cock,' said Fanny, 'I mean to say, we live in the slums you know, in the backstreets of Stepney. You could get yer throat slit for that motor car. All the worse rogues live in our part of the world. Don't you read the newspapers?'

'Well,' said Charles, accommodating her sense of humour, 'I'll just have to take that risk.' He leaned towards Fanny, smiling, and looked into her eyes. 'We don't take notice of all we read in the press, you know.'

'Come on,' said Albert, 'enough of this. Give us that crank, I'll soon get this fing going. I take it you've not run out of juice?'

'No, I filled it up before I set out.'

'Yeah, but where did you set out from, Australia?'

'No, from my home in Hampstead.'

With raised eyebrows, Albert conveyed that he was impressed. Hampstead was the place where rich folk lived, no mistake. With the crank in place, he began to wind up the car and after three or four attempts he had the engine running. To the sound of their cheers of jubilation, Charles Savage slipped proudly into the front seat of the soft-top green motor car and Beanie was in quick to be by his side. With its luxurious interior of highly polished wood panelling, gleaming brass and soft leather seats, the three of them could not have wished for a better ride home. After a few bangs from the engine, they set off along the road to the sound of Fanny singing 'California Here We Come'.

Arriving in Beaumont Square, Fanny gave her

instructions for Charles Savage to stop three houses short of number ten. It would not do for them to be seen from an upstairs window. If they were to enjoy other secret outings such as this one, they must not be found out. Beanie, however, having had a taste of the good life, was not ready for her cocoa nor her bed. So while Fanny and Albert stole quietly out of the car into the silent Square, she whispered in the driver's ear, 'We could go on to the Ship's Anchor, down by the river, if you really *do* want to see a typical cockney pub.'

'I don't recall saying so,' he whispered back, enjoying the attention. From the moment he had clapped eyes on Beanie he had been intrigued. She spoke in broad cockney and yet there was something about her features, especially those striking blue eyes. Gently he brushed a few strands of her lustrous dark hair off her face. 'No. I don't remember saying so, but if it pleases you . . .'

'No touching till you own the goods,' she said, pushing his hand away. Winding down the car window she motioned for the other two to go on in without her, which did not go down too well. The look of panic on their faces said everything. For one, if found out, she would lose her job and secondly, here was a complete stranger they knew little about.

'Don't you be so stupid,' snapped Fanny. 'You just get out of that car straight away, we could all end up in trouble here!'

'Course we won't,' said Beanie. 'Don't bolt the

basement door and leave a bit of a light on for me or I'll fall arse over 'ead trying to find my way through.'

'I will not leave anyfing unbolted if you don't mind. Me and Albert need this job and we need the roof over our 'ead – even if you don't care about your own welfare, we care about ours! Now come on out of that car and don't be a troublemaker.'

Raising her eyes to heaven, Beanie motioned for her companion to pull away. She then turned to Albert. 'Don't let Fanny lock me out, I'll return the favour one day, you see if I don't.' With that she started to laugh and left them on the pavement staring after her as the car trundled off.

'Stark raving bonkers,' barked Fanny. If truth be known, she was jealous of the way in which this new girl flirted with danger.

'Not quite right in the head, I'll grant you that, love,' said Albert, scratching his chin, ponderously. 'Not sure what to do about this one, Fan.'

'Nothing that'll detriment us. I dunno where she's from but I fink I know where she's heading for – trouble. Come on, the sooner we're in bed with the light off the better.'

'Oh, d'yer think we should, Fan? I mean with all this going on, I don't know if I could—'

'In our own beds!' snapped Fanny. 'How you can expect me to be loving when there's trouble in the air I do not know!'

'Sorry, dear,' said Albert, mollifying her. When she was in this mood it was best not to ruffle her feathers. 'I wasn't thinking.'

'No, you wasn't. I should never 'ave agreed to all this in the first place. It wasn't my idea to come out tonight, and it's freezin' bloody cold,' she puffed.

'Ne'mind,' said Albert, placing an arm round her shoulder, 'soon be tucked up warm. Gimme the key, we'll be all right after a hot cup of cocoa, eh?'

Fanny was no longer listening to him, she groaned inwardly in fear of worse things to come. 'We did leave a light on, Albert, didn't we?'

Gazing below at the dark scullery, he murmured, 'We did, Fan, yeah. We definitely did.'

'An' it's not on now, is it?'

'No, love, it's not.' He flicked the air and shrugged. 'We eat plenty of carrots so who needs a light to see by?'

'That's not the point. The question is, Albert, who turned off the light? Whoever it was, did they bolt the door as well?'

'Ah,' said Albert, 'now then . . .' He scratched the back of his head and deliberated. 'I s'pose it's gonna 'ave to be the larder again, Fanny me darling.'

'No it's bleedin' well not, I'm not squeezing myself through there agen. Besides, we don't even know if the window's open.'

'Well, let's not get in a twist yet, let's try the door first and see if it 'as bin bolted.' He stepped down into the dark area, masking his worry by quietly whistling a jolly tune. His whistling, however, was followed by a few cross swear-words once he turned the key to find that the door would not budge. Looking up at Fanny who returned his ardent gaze with a hardened frown, he shrugged helplessly, hoping his little boy act would melt the ice.

'Don't you come the old willy-nilly with me, Albert Henry,' snarled Fanny, quietly. 'Get yer arse through that window, double-quick.'

Gallantly he held up his hands in submission and walked round to the side of the house and studied the size of the window and reckoned it was just about possible – if he went in head first and thought of himself as a worm. Since there was no one around other than Fanny to give him a leg up, he was going to need something to stand on. The wooden crate which was there for those times when the greengrocer delivered at the crack of dawn, would do nicely. Placing it carefully beneath the larder window, he tested it for strength, it seemed fine. He then motioned for Fanny to come down into the area to give him a leg up.

Pushing the window open as far as it would go, he secured it, and then squeezed his head and shoulders through, inching the rest of his lean body inside. He gripped an iron meat hook hanging from the ceiling of the large storage cupboard and gradually eased himself through until he was lodged at the hips, then with a determined shove from Fanny he moved forward a fraction more until he was well and truly wedged.

'We're done for, Fan,' he said, terrified. 'I can't move.'

'Oh, yes, you can,' she said, shoving the top of her head into his rump and gripping a leg in each hand. 'I'm gonna steer you through this come rain or shine. I'm freezing to death 'ere!'

To his muffled cries of pain, she squeezed and pushed and eased for all she was worth until his rump was through and the rest of him followed and he went flying and crashing down on to the floor of the larder room. Pots, pans, jars of jam, and more, also went crashing to the floor as his arms flailed in his descent.

'Are you all right, Albert?' whispered Fanny through the open window. All the poor girl could hear were the moans and groans of her beloved. 'Albert . . . ? Answer me then.'

Mumbled sounds of reassurance followed as he tried to ease himself up from the floor without making a worse din. Satisfied that he was in the land of the living, Fanny gave him orders to unbolt the back door and be quiet about it. The sound of pots and pans clanking as he scrabbled in the dark was awful. To make matters worse, a light from somewhere above stairs came on. Urging him to get a move on, Fanny shifted the box away from under the window and crept to the door and waited impatiently to hear the bolt being pulled back. Seconds ticked by slowly and the street seemed eerily silent. 'Come on, Albert . . .' urged Fanny in a whisper, '. . . come *on*, for once in your life act like lightning . . . please . . .'

Grace Wellington, on her way down to see what the ruckus was about, was armed with a wooden truncheon which she would use on cat or man, depending what was in her scullery. This wasn't the first time a cat had got in through the larder window. Fearing nothing, Grace pushed open the door of the kitchen, switched on the light and headed for the pantry, from where she could hear the sound of movement. Pulling open the door, her heart leapt. She really had expected to find a stray cat in there. Once she recognised the man sprawled on the floor, surrounded by broken jars of jam and pots and pans and lids all over the place, she was relieved rather than cross.

'I hope you've a good explanation for this,' said Grace.

'I came in for some goose fat, Mrs Wellington, I gave my knee a real knock on the end of my bed and—'

'Albert, you are wearing your coat,' said Grace, 'and the window is open. Now if you would be so kind as to adjust yourself and come into the kitchen and explain what is going on . . .'

Leaving him to himself, Grace poured herself a glass of water and waited. She had not to wait long for Albert, looking sheepish, presented himself. 'I never did come down for goose fat, Mrs Wellington, though I think I might be needing some now,' he said, standing there as if he were a soldier on parade. 'I told a white lie to cover for myself. I went out for a stroll and although I locked the door behind me with my key, I couldn't of course bolt it from inside. Everyone else had gone to bed. I suppose you could say I was in a melancholy mood and wanted to be alone. Then I remembered one of Cook's sayings: *After dinner rest awhile – after supper walk a mile.* It did do me the world of good, that I will say.'

'I see. No doubt one of the others came down after

you'd gone out and bolted the door. Well, it could have been worse, I should get yourself to bed. You'll need to be up at the crack of dawn and before Cook sees the mess you've made of her larder.'

'Yes, Mrs Wellington and I'm very sorry. Very sorry, indeed. I shan't ever go out again unless someone else is up to let me back in.'

'I'm pleased to hear it, Albert.'

Not entirely convinced by his story, Grace went back to her bedroom, wondering whether he had been outside with Fanny or had been familiarising himself with the new girl with the silly name. 'Beanie indeed,' murmured Grace as she took off her robe and glided silently into the bed next to her snoring husband. Five minutes later, she glided out again, put on her robe and headed for her favourite guest room. She had a busy day ahead of her and needed her sleep, more than that she longed for silence and an empty bed all to herself.

Closing the bedroom door behind her, she came face to face with Fanny, followed by Albert. Throwing them a look to melt ice, she went back into her chamber. At least it was Fanny that Albert had been with and not the new girl. Tomorrow she would have to give them both a good dressing down in the library. Slipping back into bed next to her noisy husband, she closed her eyes, wondering what it would be like to live alone in a small house with just one live-in help or none at all. Drifting off to sleep she imagined herself with just a daily help coming in to clean, shop and prepare an evening meal. Life would be easier having to only think of herself. Was it possible for someone to turn their life around? Change things? Her mind went back to those heady days when she did change her lifestyle, her time in Bloomsbury had been wonderful and so had the lovers. Could she do it all over again? Smiling to herself, she settled down with that magic word drifting across her mind, *change*.

After all, Tobias, her deceiving husband, was still playing the Casanova, believing that she had no idea of it. That first time of daring to look into his private files those years back had not been the last, it had become, not so much a habit, as a pastime – a pastime which brought her much pleasure. His diary made interesting reading, not only did it keep her up-to-date on his behaviour but one step ahead of him. At least it was his own money that he was now spending on his mistresses and not hers. The trouble with Tobias was that he was too handsome for his own good. Not only a handsome man but excellent in bed, and this, Grace made the very most of. She was using him the way he used his whores and felt not the least bit guilty. The important thing in this charade was that she no longer loved him. It had taken a long time to kill off her devotion, but once it had truly gone, she felt a free woman, whereas Tobias continued to trawl his burden of guilt. The foolish man was forever having to hide his secrets and forever having to concoct lies to cover his movements.

When the sound of creaking on the landing stirred her from her slumber, she simply turned over and went back to sleep, believing it to be Albert creeping up to

Fanny's room and as far as she was concerned, what the eye didn't see the mind should not grieve over. In fact she was wrong, it was Beanie returning from her rendezvous with Charles Savage – a little tipsy and a little dizzy. She had had a marvellous time.

By six o'clock the next morning, Flora, having summoned the three of them to the kitchen, was not best pleased. Shamefaced, they sat round the table and a more subservient trio she could not have asked for. 'Leaving the door unbolted is unforgivable!' said Flora, thumping her fist on the table. 'All it required was for a burglar to slip a piece of tin between the catch, and what a different story it would be this morning if that had happened!' Again she thumped her fist on the table, causing the salt and pepper pots to tip over.

'I'm sorry, Cook,' said Albert, sheepishly. 'It's my fault. I should 'ave bolted it before I went up—'

'Sorry could see us all damned, I should think you *are* sorry, Albert.' She paced the floor. 'I dread to think what might have happened should Mrs Wellington have had reason to come below stairs and see that the house was not sound and secure.'

A hush spread through the guilty party. They couldn't tell just how clued-in Cook was. 'How did you know about it, Cook?' said Beanie, a little too familiar for a scullery maid. 'The door was bolted when you came down this morning, wasn't it?' She knew it was since she had been the last one in and had bolted it behind her.

'How did I know? Because *I* threw the bolt when I

came down for some effervescent last night, once you had all turned in. And what's more one of you had left a light on down here!' She was still pacing the floor and wringing her hands while the guilty three looked at each other, a touch relieved. Cook didn't know the half of it. Here she was, scolding them because she believed them to have gone to bed without locking up properly. 'We would have all been sacked for it, make no mistake, there's no shortage of domestic staff. I dread to think what could have been.'

'Well, Mrs W seemed all right about it,' said Albert, gently. 'She's left it up to you to give us a good dressing down. She knew you'd be mad once you'd seen the state of yer pantry.' A daunting silence filled the kitchen. He had put his foot in it.

'State of the pantry?' said Flora. 'Don't tell me you had a midnight feast, Albert.' A frown appeared on her brow, this was worse than she thought. 'You had a midnight feast and Mrs Wellington came down and caught you? Is that what you're trying to tell me?'

'Not exactly, Cook, no.' He pursed his lips boyishly and looked into her face, appealing to her good nature. 'I 'ad to squeeze through the window. A few jars smashed to the floor and Madam wouldn't let me clean it up, she wanted you to see what I'd done.'

Flora was aghast as the truth sank in. 'Are you telling me that you were out gallivanting when I came down to find a light on and the door unbolted, is that what you're telling me?' She looked from Albert to the shamefaced Fanny and Beanie. 'Good gracious me, we shall all be sacked for it.' She flopped down on to her kitchen chair and fanned her face with a hand.

'No we won't, Cook,' said Fanny, standing up and taking control. 'It's not as if the door wasn't locked, it just wasn't bolted, that's all. Things are not that bad, I'll pour you a nice cup of tea and you'll see it in a different light.'

'I very much doubt that, my girl.'

'Course you will,' said Fanny, a touch too confident. 'I mean to say, this was the first time it's ever 'appened and I'll be more'n 'appy to go and explain the way it was to Madam.'

'Well perhaps you wouldn't mind explaining to me first exactly the way it was.'

'Well,' said Fanny, 'poor old Beanie was homesick, wasn't she? Wouldn't stop crying for 'er mum and dad and little bruvver. So we took 'er out for a nice brisk walk to lift 'er spirits.'

'Lift her spirits, by walking out on a freezing cold night?' said Flora.

'It wasn't so bad once that cold wind had dropped. The smog cleared an' all,' said Albert, adding his pennyworth. 'Yeah,' he continued, slowly shaking his head. 'Poor cow, she was that upset, we 'ad to do something. We wasn't gone that long so you can imagine how shocked we was to find that you'd bolted us out.'

'And that's why you had to climb through the window, and the crashing woke Mrs Wellington.' Flora thought about it and then said, 'So I'm to tell her that you were only out there for ten minutes or so, walking Beanie round the block to help soothe her sorrow. Is that right?'

'That *is* right,' said Beanie. 'It seemed to happen all of a sudden. I thought about my granddad and then my nanna, and I come over all sad. Then I started to cry for my little baby brother and my mum and dad and—'

'Yes, all right, Beanie,' said Flora, giving her daughter the evil eye. 'Don't go overboard with the theatricals, I wasn't born yesterday. As far as I'm concerned you went out when I told you not to. I dare say you went to the West End.' The room went silent as she looked from one to the other. Not one of them could hide their guilty eyes from her. 'But there,' she said finally, 'I expect your story is the one which Mrs Wellington would prefer to hear and I dare say the true one would never 'ave come out in the wash. Your white lie saved us all from being turned out on to the streets. But I will say this—'

Her words of warning were interrupted by the jingling of one of the servants' bells above the kitchen door, it was a summons from the master bedroom. 'There we are,' said Flora, concerned. 'A troubled mind wakes early. Go on up, Fanny, and best foot forward. I expect they're ready for early morning tea.'

'Oh, can't you go for me, Cook?' said Fanny, going pale. 'If she starts asking me questions about last night I'll be that close to crying . . .'

'Stuff and nonsense, where's your mettle, girl?' The bell jingled again.

'Oh for heaven's sake, I'll go up myself, but mark my words all three of you. You are gonna have to please me today. Every bit of brass and polish in this house will gleam by nightfall!' With that, Flora stormed out of the kitchen and went upstairs to face the music.

Grace was taken back to see Cook coming into the room instead of the parlour maid. 'I trust this doesn't mean that the rest of the staff are still in bed, Cook?'

'No, madam. I've been giving them a good ticking off for the trouble they caused, and I thought it best to leave them to think about the error of their ways. I have them in the kitchen; their penitence is to be silent and to go without breakfast.'

'I see,' said Grace, covering a smile. 'Well I think that's an excellent exercise for them. Although, *we* should like breakfast earlier today, Mr Wellington has an early appointment.'

'How soon would you like breakfast, madam?' said Flora.

'In twenty minutes?'

'Very well, madam, I'll see to it. And I must apologise for—'

Grace waved a hand. 'No harm came of it, I should think the lesson they are learning this morning will teach them not to disobey house rules.'

'They're like naughty children at times,' said Tobias, his face hidden by the morning newspaper which he was reading. 'You'll have to take a cane to them, Cook.'

'Yes sir, but they are adults and I shall see they behave like adults,' said Flora, wringing her hands a little. 'They should respect your trust and—'

'Oh I'm sure they do,' said Tobias. He raised his eyes from the newspaper and glanced briefly at her through his reading glasses before going back to his financial pages.

Rooted to the spot and seized with shock and horror, Flora felt the blood rush to her face. Could it be possible or had her eyes been playing tricks on her? But what of the voice? That voice she would recognise anywhere – anywhere. This man sitting before her, hidden by his newspaper was, without a shred of doubt, Beanie's father. She had stepped across his threshold in total ignorance. But he had been referred to as Tobias Wellington and her sweetheart's name had been Charles. Prince Charlie. Her Prince Charlie. Had he moved his family from Westminster to the East End? Surely not? No . . . This could not be Charles from Westminster. It was impossible!

'I think you might be overreacting a touch, Cook,' said Grace, smiling at her. 'There's really no need for you to be so deeply embarrassed.' She was referring to the high colour of Flora's face and neck.

Tobias, behind his newspaper, sighed with a touch of frustration. 'If the breakfast arrives lukewarm then there may well be cause for embarrassment.'

'Oh, I'm sure that would never happen,' said Grace giving Flora a polite nod for her to leave. But Flora could not move. Every muscle in her body seemed to have contracted. It *was* him. To be unsure of his voice the first time was excusable – to mistake it on the second hearing, foolish.

Excusing herself with a nervous smile, Flora backed out of the room, praying that she would not be put upon to speak. Silently beseeching the good Lord to see her out of that room before her legs crumpled beneath her. Her stomach was churning.

Once outside the master bedroom, where fate had deemed fit to send her, she gripped the banister rail and used every bit of strength and will-power to control her breathing. It would not do for anyone to see her in this state.

It was no fault of hers that she had walked into the house of the man she once loved and whose name she believed to be Charles. The man who swore he loved her and would never go away. The man who had made her pregnant.

Going back into the kitchen where three sullen faces looked up at her from their place at the table, she went to the chair by the fire and sat down. If there was a time when a woman desperately needed to be by herself, this was it. The others took her silence to mean that she had had a dressing down from above stairs. With her back to them she stared into the flames of the small kitchen fire. Albert and Fanny looked at each other, puzzled. Their employers had always been fairly lenient and they couldn't imagine them upsetting Cook so much.

Beanie had eyes only for her mother. She was studying her face and before she realised what she was doing, she was up from the table and on her knees beside her. 'You all right?' she said, just managing to stop herself from being over familiar.

'I'm fine,' said Flora, avoiding her daughter's eyes. 'Upstairs are all right about what 'appened, no need to worry. I've a headache that's all, brought on by the worry I dare say.'

'Oh, Cook,' said Albert, sorry to see her like this. 'It'll come out in the wash. They don't bear grudges.'

'Course they don't,' said Fanny. 'You go up and 'ave a lie down and we'll manage between the three of us. Albert'll cook their breakfast and I'll—'

'No,' said Flora, firmly. 'Give me a minute, there's good children, I'll be fine, a glass of water would be very nice. Get the bacon from the pantry, Beanie, there's a good girl.' Still she couldn't look at her; she was feeling guilty. Guilty that Beanie had grown up believing that her father had been killed in action during the war, when in fact he was very much alive and a wealthy man. A wealthy man who wanted nothing to do with his own sweet child who had grown into the lovely young woman that any father would be proud of.

It was Fanny who finally brought a hint of a smile to Flora's face. While the other two busied themselves, she put a caring arm round her and whispered in her ear, 'I'm sorry we broke the rules. We won't ever get you in trouble agen.'

She smiled and squeezed Fanny's hand but inside she was crying. Crying for what might had been if her true love had not already been married way back, when they were so very much in love. She believed now as she had believed twenty years before, that she had been the only other woman in his life. Tobias Wellington was a true romantic and could be very convincing when making love.

Catching a glimpse of her reflection in the small mirror above the fireplace, she felt suddenly ashamed of her looks. Compared to Grace Wellington, who was seven years her senior, Flora looked older than her age – and very plain indeed. She wallowed in her self-pity: *Where are you Flora? Where's that face that turned so many heads? Where's the cheeky smile that won more than one heart?* She looked at her hands and the third finger where a cheap gold-plated wedding ring had been placed by her own father once she had started to show, when she was expecting Beanie. Glancing back into the mirror she turned her head one way and then the other, examining for wear and tear. She could hardly remember the last time she had worn lipstick and powder, never mind eye make-up. At least she hadn't lost her hourglass figure. Yes, it had filled out a little but was none the worse for that.

Taking a grip of herself she felt herself shiver and go cold. It wouldn't do to be melancholy with so much to attend to. Back on her feet, she took a deep breath and looked forward to bedtime when she could be alone and think about those good times with her Prince Charlie. Relive those wonderful two years when he treated her as if she was the most beautiful girl in the world. After all, thinking about him was all she had now and no one could take that away. But she would make certain that their paths would not cross again. Fanny was the parlour maid and it was her duty to attend above stairs. Flora would not cross the line unless she knew that the master of the house was away on business.

These had been her thoughts at the beginning of the day but as time wore on and night fell, she found that anger was building in the pit of her stomach. All day long little snippets of things he'd said and done came back to her, those which had obviously been lies – all lies. He had lied about the area in which he lived. He had been covering his tracks for the day when he was tired of her and ready to walk out of her life. As walk out on her he did – and now the father of her child was living in the same house. The father who Beanie believed had been killed in the war as a hero, was a lying, cheating, deserting, swine. Too many nights had been spent reliving her time with him whispering the words: *Blue are the hills that are far away.*

Whether Flora wanted redress or not, she had to keep her mouth shut. And so too did Mr Tobias Wellington, should he ever recognise his lovely Flora of long ago in the face of his lovely daughter, Beanie, whom he believed to be no more than a scullery maid.

3

With just one week to go before Christmas, below
stairs at number ten was a busy place. Flora, having
turned out excellent meals for the Wellingtons and
their guests during this festive season was not finished
yet. This evening there was to be a family reunion
and she was preparing a five-course meal for twenty.
Needless to say, all hands were to the fore. Lenny
the gardener had been called upon to peel the root
vegetables which were now soaking in cold salt water
while he and Flora enjoyed a quick Christmas drink
of sherry. Lenny liked this new cook, he liked her very
much indeed but kept it to himself. A touch bashful
at being alone with her and sharing a special moment,
he swallowed his drink too quickly and almost choked
on it. Flora was touched by Lenny's sensitivity. The
poor man had spent most of his life at someone's
beck and call and hardly knew how to relax when
off duty. Making his excuses of having to rush off,
he backed out of the kitchen and out of the house.
In truth, he had nothing to rush away to. His lodging
room in Three Colts Lane was a place to sleep and
no more. To Lenny, number ten was his home, his
reason for living. Here was a man who had come to

the conclusion that he had been born to serve and no more. And serve he had, from the age of twelve years old he had been fetching and carrying. Having now reached fifty, he was too used to the idea that every waking hour was meant for labouring one way or another.

Shaking her head, Flora finished her drink and went back to her chores, resolved that in the new year she would make more of an effort to encourage the gardener to relax in her kitchen, with the rest of the staff. He was far too subservient for her liking. Glancing at the kitchen clock she shook her head. Time always slipped by far too quickly.

Above stairs, Beanie and Fanny had completed their task of setting the banquet table with gleaming silverware and the very best blue, red and gold china. They were taking a few minutes to admire their work. The dining room was lit up by two exquisite cut-glass chandeliers high above the dining table and in the far corner of the room, towered the Christmas tree, aglow with twinkling white lights and sparkling tinsel. Baubles, colourful wooden soldiers and delicate porcelain angels clothed in pale gold silk adorned the tree which filled the room with the heavy scent of the pine needles. The crowning glory was the magnificent illuminated silver star.

By six o'clock, the room was ready and a fire burned in the brass grate of the marble fireplace. The dining table, laid fit for a king, was decorated with holly, white Christmas roses, and silver and gold painted branches from Harrods. Decanters and glasses sparkled under the lights. The white linen and lace tablecloth had been pressed until every tiny crease had been ironed out. All of this enhanced by the rich wallpaper, gold drapes and dark red and blue carpet was a sight to behold. And behold it the girls did. No one could have blamed them for standing longer than they should have, in the doorway, admiring their work of art. The only sound was the tinkling of small glass bells as they moved gently on the branches of the tree, a barely discernible current of fresh air circulating the room.

Meanwhile, below stairs, Flora was basting one of the loins of pork while Albert, whistling while he worked, was wiping down the kitchen table ready for his next chore. 'Them two are taking their time up there, Cook, better not be skiving.'

'There's a lot to do, Albert, if they're doing it properly.'

She leaned across from her worktable to check he'd crushed the garlic and salt to her liking. He had. 'I 'ope them balls are nice and firm.'

'Dunno, Cook. I ain't got me hand in me—' he said, giving her a saucy grin.

'Don't be disgusting. Did you put all the herbs in that Lenny fetched?'

'Course I did, best meatballs yet they are, I could eat one raw.'

'You might 'ave to if I forget to put them in the range,' she said, patting the sweat from her brow with the hem of her apron. 'Open a window, there's a good lad. It's like an oven in here.'

'Aye, aye, captain.'

'And then put the jar of redcurrant sauce in the dumb waiter and send it upstairs.'

'You sure, Cook? I thought the girls weren't s'pose to put out the—'

'It's not for the main course!' she snapped as she shoved the roasting tray back into the oven. 'It's for the duck pâté.'

Her sharp retort was a sign for Albert to keep quiet. Her earlier display of calm was obviously a show and who could blame her for being on edge? This was the first time she had to cook for a dinner party of twenty in a private house. Pretending he hadn't picked up on her anxiety, he managed to feign a dry cough.

'Ooh, I don't know about you, Cook, but I couldn't 'alf do with a cup of tea, be all right if I brew us a pot?'

'Make lemon tea, it's more refreshing. The heat from that oven—'

'Did I 'ear someone mention tea?' said Fanny coming into the kitchen.

'You did,' said Flora. 'Where's Bea?'

'Stargazing,' said Fanny, flopping down into the armchair. 'It looks beautiful up there. Go and 'ave a butcher's, Cook, you'll be that proud. Everything's bright as if the full moon's shining on it. And the table, well . . .' Overcome by it all, she swallowed against a lump in her throat. 'I ain't ever seen it looking that lovely.'

'I don't know why,' said Flora, 'everything came out of cupboards and from the attic room.'

'Ah, but it's not what you've got but what you do

wiv 'em. It was your idea to put the tree in that corner
and you who chose the table linen. Last year they put a
red cloth on just 'cos it was Christmas. Didn't look 'alf
as lovely as it does now. Them white candles all over
the place look smashing. Wasn't born in Buckingham
Palace was you, Cook?'

'Might 'ave been. I heard say there was blue blood
in our family. So what's that scullery maid doing up
there then?'

'I told you, gazing at the Christmas tree wiv tears
in her eyes. She'll be dahn in a minute. Gawd Cook,
there're some lovely smells coming out of that stove.'

'I should think there is. Four loins of pork spitting
at each other. Two legs of lamb and a rib of beef big
enough to feed an army.'

'Good. We'll be all right tonight then,' said Fanny,
rubbing her belly. 'Can't wait.'

'Well then you must learn how to, my girl,' said
Flora. 'All good things come to those who wait. By
my reckoning there'll be plenty left over to feed tcn
for lunch tomorrow and that's how many are stopping
over. We may 'ave to make do on a dumpling stew.'
She said this knowing that a chunk of leftover rib of
beef would go into it. She wasn't daft and had good
reason to overload the table upstairs; the leftovers were
tastier than anything she could buy from the below-
stairs shopping allowance. The main thing with Flora
was that she knew how to shop and where to shop for
the best meats and the best bargains. If she and her
Beanie were going to be fetching and carrying for the
rest of their lives, she would make certain they ate well.

'Ah, but,' said Fanny, still thinking of her stomach, 'what if they decide not to stop over?'

'Should ifs and ands be pots and pans, there'd be no work for the tinker's hand,' replied Flora, nodding at a basket of oranges in a corner.

'Oh,' said Fanny, affecting a scholarly tone. 'I always thought that the devil *finds* work for idle hands. Wasn't that wot you once said?'

'Probably,' sniffed Flora, amused by the girl's talent to bend accuracy when it suited her. 'And God sends meat but the devil sends cooks to work their fingers to the bones. Oranges . . . Fanny?'

'And lemons said the bells of St Clement's . . . You called me a lemon once, didn't yer? I was very hurt over that, til my sister told me it was a compliment. The lemon tree's very pretty with a sweet flower. So wot you gonna do wiv all them oranges then?'

'Not me, Fanny, you. You're gonna squeeze every drop of juice out of 'em.'

'That'll take ages!'

'Exactly,' said Cook, ending it.

In the dining room, Beanie was staring at the Christmas tree. Transfixed, she was in her own little world. Imagining this to be her house, with her husband, their little children and her mum all living together. She fancied herself wearing the style of clothes that Sarah Wellington wore and her mother in fine silks and satins just like the mistress of the house. So absorbed in her imaginary world she didn't hear Digby Morton, Grace Wellington's cousin come into the room. His polite and poignant little cough brought her back to the real world. Spinning round she was embarrassed to be caught daydreaming.

'I was just looking . . . to make sure it was all perfect, sir.'

'Well it would all seem to be perfect,' came the toneless reply. This young man was not smiling, not even a polite hint of a smile. There was a certain air of importance about him.

'Yes it does,' she said, echoing his manner. 'But then so does a rosy red apple, till you cut it through the middle.' She gave a hint of a curtsy and backed away towards the door.

'Not all rosy red apples, surely?'

'No, not all of 'em.' She arched one eyebrow, a trick she learned as a child. 'Which is why we must cut 'em through the middle.'

Walking gracefully down the wide staircase she continued with her previous fantasy, before the dour young man had interrupted her. Here in this house, she could be the girl from below, where others were concerned and the young lady from above whenever she felt like it. She could live in two worlds, the real one and the imagined, and no one could stop her. Hearing quiet laughter coming from the drawing room, she quickened her pace and slipped back into her other skin, Beanie the scullery maid.

'Oh, the wanderer returns,' grinned Albert, enjoying his beverage. 'Got lost did yer, Bea?'

'Yeah, lost in my own thoughts. I think you'll be pleased with the dining room, Cook,'

'I already told 'er,' said Fanny.

'Well, that's all right then,' she pulled a face and then asked Flora if there was time for a little rest break. A ten minute lie down.

'I should say not!' She shook her head disdainfully. 'Twenty guests to serve and she wants to lie down.'

'So would you if your feet was killing you. Aching from my toes right up my legs from all that standing.'

'Oh,' purred Fanny, 'so you'll be in too much pain to slip out this evening to 'ave a kiss and cuddle with Mister Charles Savage in 'is lovely motor car.'

Heaving herself up on to a pine side table, Beanie shrugged. 'I jacked 'im in, too boring. Worse than that though, is, he's always got a bit of snot trickling out of 'is left nostril. Puts you right off it does.'

Chuckling with the rest of them, Flora shook her head. 'No sense, no feeling. Or did he wipe it clean all the time?'

'Nah. Never knew it was there or didn't care. He smelt an' all. Of unwashed shirt and armpits.'

'Urghhh . . . you're disgusting at times Beanie, you really are,' Albert said, while furtively sniffing his underarms.

'He *was* good looking, Bea,' said Fanny, 'and rich. Snazzy dresser, wot more d'yer want?'

'Appearances are deceptive,' said Flora, 'it's what's underneath that counts.'

'Don't be rude, Cook,' said Fanny, chancing her luck.

Beanie leaned back in her chair and thought about it. The visitor upstairs came to mind. Dark hair, black eyebrows, light brown eyes, serious, rigid, strong . . . dangerous. With him she could play cat and mouse. With him she could be herself – speak her mind – fight her side.

'Well tell us,' said Albert, 'we might all learn a thing or two.'

'What?' Beanie had forgotten the question. Before Flora had time to say, rest break over, one of the bells over the door jingled.

'Number six,' said Albert. 'The library.'

'I'll go.' Beanie knew by instinct that it was going to be him.

'Legs all right now, are they?' Fanny wondered why she was eager to answer the bell.

'Be all the better for a good stretch.' Beanie grinned at Fanny and then gave Albert a wink.

'I think we're going to have some house rules around here.' Flora was not best pleased. 'There's been too much swearing and too much filth. If any of them upstairs heard some of the things you come out with, they'd be shocked by it. And we'd all—'

'Be sacked for it!' chorused the three of them.

Leaving Fanny and Albert to tease Flora, Beanie went upstairs and into the library to find Grace Wellington's cousin looking out of the window on to the garden. 'You rang, sir.'

'Yes I did.' He spoke without turning to face her. There was a mixture of tease and impudence to her tone, which he found interesting.

'So you'll be wanting something then?' She waited while he pondered. 'A nice cup of tea was it?'

'I should like you to give a message to Cook with regard to this evening meal.'

Nice broad shoulders, thought Beanie.

'I don't want any fuss made over my food. It's a simple matter. I don't eat meat.'

'Oh . . . you have shocked me.'

'Why?'

'Well, you're not skinny, are you, sir? Albert could do with some of whatever it is you do eat.'

'Albert?'

'The bootboy down below. Calls 'imself the master's valet. So what would you like cooked up special then?'

'That's the point of my ringing for you. I should like no fuss whatsoever. Vegetables from the table will do very nicely.'

'What about the roast potatoes and parsnips?'

'What about them?'

'They will have been roasted in dripping – from the meat.'

'That's absolutely fine.'

'Oh. You are sure? 'Cos Cook'll be more'n happy to do a little tray of roasts for you, cooked in margarine instead of dripping.'

Spinning around he glared at her, his face taut. 'I'm obviously not making myself clear. I ask you again, please pass on the message to Cook, so that I may eat with the rest of the guests, without fuss or embarrassment.'

'There's no need to raise your voice, sir. I'm not deaf. You don't want any pork or beef or lamb. Simple.

I'm in for a good supper.' Her relaxed manner broke the ice.

After a pause, he said, 'I apologise if I did raise my voice.'

'That's all right. It must drive you mad. Being interrogated every time. I bet most people try and change you. It'd get on anyone's nerves.'

'You're new here,' he said, after another of his silent pauses. 'I haven't seen you before.'

'I've bin working below for a good two months now. I used to work in a pipe factory, in the directors' dining room. They closed it down so I applied for this job.'

'Well, you seem settled?'

'It's all right. Nice family. Not that I've ever seen 'is lordship. Mrs Wellington's a lovely woman. Kind.'

'And your family?'

Her imagination vivid, she spoke in a quiet voice. 'I ain't got no family. I was brought up in Dr Barnardo's after being found as a tiny baby wrapped in newspaper. Someone thought I was hot tripe'n onions. Someone else said I must 'ave been dropped by the Germans in the war who couldn't tell the difference between a bomb and a baby.'

'And your family?' he repeated, hiding a smile.

'Was a bit pathetic wasn't it. Well, sir . . . I'm really a boy.' She could hardly believe her own audacity but neither could she stop herself. There was something about this cousin of the Wellingtons that was to bring out the worst in her. 'I couldn't get work down the dock 'cos I was all skin and bone. Dad used to thrash me something rotten with 'is belt and mum was on laudanum. She was a Lady something or the other who married beneath 'erself. So I ran away and tried to fend for myself. Wearing a frock's easier when you're looking for employment.'

'You're a terrible liar. It's just as well you didn't want to go on the stage. Any part you played would be totally unconvincing.'

'I'll tell Cook you don't want any meat, full stop, then, shall I, *sir*?'

'I would appreciate it . . . *madam*. Thank you.'

'My pleasure.' With that she curtsied and left the library having piqued more than his curiosity.

'No meat? I've never heard the like! And from a grown man! I can't set up a man's dinner with no meat!'

'You won't be setting it, Cook,' said Beanie. 'Me and Fanny'll be serving don't forget and I'll be more'n 'appy to give the chap what he wants.'

'Oh . . . you never say that to me now, do yer?' said Albert, always the joker.

'He wants no fuss and nothing special. He'll eat spuds and parsnips cooked in the meat juices. I can't see what's wrong with that.'

Flora was thoughtful, maybe the poor man wore false teeth and couldn't chew with them. 'I suppose I could grind some meat into a paste for him and shape it like a pork chop . . .'

'No. He doesn't want that! He'll be more'n happy with everything else but meat! I'll give 'im an extra Yorkshire pudding.'

'There'll be no Yorkshires thank you, Beanie. I can't

turn out a good Yorkshire to serve twenty people and most like two of mine as you well—' she stopped in her tracks, almost slipping up yet again and being too familiar with the scullery maid. She would have to speak to her daughter later as to *her* raising her voice. 'Well no I don't suppose you do know, your not having been here five minutes.'

'Two months, actually, Cook.'

'Maybe so, my girl,' said Flora, 'but you're still wet behind the ears. Now then . . . sprouts. Albert . . . stoke up the stove please. No more wasted time. I take it the dining room is finished properly?'

While Fanny ran through everything they had done, Beanie tipped a basketful of sprouts into the butler sink, her mind on the young man in the library. He seemed to suit the room, as if it was *his* room. She could imagine him sitting in the luxurious padded leather armchair by the fire, reading. His glass of wine on the small, mahogany table, a pile of books by the side of him selected from the crammed bookcase. The plants in the library were just right for him: tall, strong leafy plants that surrounded a bronze statue of a naked woman.

'So what's he like then?' said Fanny, breaking into her thoughts. 'White and puny is he?'

'No. Tall, dark and mysterious.'

'Is he now? Well I shall just 'ave to go and 'ave a butchers, shan't I? D'yer fink he'll still be in the library?'

'No,' said Beanie, lying. 'He followed me out and went to 'is room.'

'And you came down to the kitchen? Bit slow on the uptake there Beanie, girl. He took a shine to you, I reckon,' she said, ripping off the outer leaves of the Brussels sprouts. 'Was 'oping you'd go wiv 'im to his chamber if you ask me.'

'Would you have done that then? Followed him?'

'Was he handsome as well as mysterious?'

'Attractive is what I'd call 'im.'

'Mmm . . . I can't wait to serve 'im at table.'

'It was his manner, really. Aloof . . . with a question always in 'is eyes. Soft brown eyes.'

'That's enough of that, you two,' said Cook, having heard enough. 'Get them fingers working a bit faster if you please.'

Fanny raised an eyebrow and chuckled, 'Which bedroom is he in?'

Taking no notice of their skylarking, Flora fancied herself serving in the dining room this evening. Not the main course but the very last. By that time, plenty of drink would have been supped and Tobias Wellington would most likely be too tipsy to focus properly, let alone recognise her. He hadn't before, so why would he now? She looked no different from when she first saw him at number ten, in the bedroom. She hadn't been above stairs since that day. She shuddered at the memory of seeing him with Grace Wellington in their lavish bedroom. She could still see the four-poster bed as if it were only yesterday. Sipping her glass of stout, she felt a little daring and it felt good, but the present was not the time to take chances. No. She would wait, bide her time before presenting herself and when she did, she would be dressed in her best clothes and wearing make-up. She often fantasised about the day and if nothing else, it kept her in good spirits. Maybe he wouldn't recognise her, even with her face close up to his, but she had a voice and she would remind him of his visits to Brick Lane and of herself before he left her holding the baby.

The dinner party was not the last during Christmas week and by the time Christmas Eve came round, Flora, the girls and Albert, were dog-tired. Tired but thrilled at having the house to themselves during this festive season. The Wellingtons were spending the Christmas holiday with the cousins in Newmarket.

Alone in her room, gift-wrapping a scarf and glove set for Beanie, Flora was remembering a very special Christmas Eve spent with Tobias Wellington, when they had sat together in her parents' front room and talked of the future that never was to be. Before they had settled themselves by the fire, they had been in Flora's bedroom for the first time, making love, while her parents were at the local pub enjoying themselves. Usually it was a small hotel in Marylebone he took her to, which had not been as cosy as being under her own roof and it was probably because of this that Flora had given herself to him more lovingly than ever before – and more than once. This chance happening had been the reason she had conceived. In their passion they had not been cautious the second time round. Beanie was a Christmas conception. A present from the Yuletide Angels.

Snapping herself out of this mood, Flora shook off

the resentment which had crept in. It was, after all, Christmas Eve and she had three days rest to enjoy and didn't want Tobias Wellington spoiling it for her. He had gone like a thief in the night once their baby was born, after he had promised to stand by her. His cost had been a hundred pounds and hers torment and misery waiting for him to come back . . . and her little Beanie had had to grow up without a father.

Back in her kitchen Flora's heart was soon lifted by the sight of the Christmas tree in the corner of the room, brought in by Lenny the gardener. This was laden with decorations made by the girls from silver and gold paper from the wallpaper shop, Christmas crackers from Woolworths and small gifts purchased in Petticoat Lane. From Flora there was a Chinese figure of a nodding mandarin for Beanie; a painted silk fan for Fanny and a new tie for Albert.

Once supper had been taken, Flora was ready for her bed. Shopping in the markets on Christmas Eve was wearing. But she had done well . . . A bird, figs and dates, fruit and nuts . . . all out of the below stairs budget. All she wanted now was be up bright and early so as to slip Beanie's Christmas pillowcase into her room at the foot of her bed. This was one tradition that she was not going to give up.

Soon after she said goodnight, the girls and Albert, already tipsy from the sherry given by Grace Wellington, crept upstairs and into the drawing room where they helped themselves to all kinds of alcohol from the drinks cabinet. Then, settling themselves in the silky armchairs in front of a flickering gas fire, Albert, who had dimmed the lights began to tell them a ghost story. The girls were all ears and the time flew by. Before they knew it, the grand clock was striking midnight.

'You'll 'ave to bring the end forward, Albert,' said Fanny, 'otherwise Cook'll come and chuck us out before you've got there.'

Obliging and by now merry from the drink, Albert finished his tale, his voice more hushed as he went on until the finale, when he suddenly made them jump and cry with fright. He loved it. They were a perfect audience. Laughing, he went to the window and drew back the drapes enough to see out. The moon was almost full and snow was drifting down. 'Must be a good few inches deep, girls,' he said, admiring the square and the snow covered trees glistening in the moonlight.

'Let's go outside and have a snowball fight,' said Beanie, quite tipsy from their drinking bout, 'or build a snowman!'

'No. I wanna get Albert into bed before he's had too much too drink to make me 'appy.' There was a winsome expression on Fanny's face. 'I want a cuddle.'

'Oh, do you now?' said Beanie, wishing she had someone to give her a hug. 'Well then . . . push out the boat and sleep in the master bedroom. I dare you to. Go on, be daredevils,' she said, stretching out on the long soft couch.

Fanny grinned at her sweetheart. 'Shall we?'

'No,' laughed Albert. 'They'd smell us when they

climb back in. Mrs W wears different scent to you, Fanny my love.'

'I'll 'ave a bath first then. In their bathroom. Wash away me perfume.'

'People like us are not meant to sleep in luxury,' sniffed Albert, a touch of pride in his voice.

Slowly turning her head to peer at him, Beanie rolled her eyes. 'Stop being a servant for five minutes. Your blood's the same colour as theirs and we're all of the same flesh. They're not gods you know. Just got more money, that's all. If you don't go in there – I will. I fancy . . . a bit of luxury.'

'Well, go in Sarah's bedroom then.'

'No . . . not good enough, Albert. If you're gonna do it – do it prop'ly, is what I say.'

'And I couldn't agree more!' Fanny was on her feet in a flash. 'Come on. We'll 'ave a bath together.'

Albert looked quite confused for a moment but then shook his head. 'No. That's goin' too far.'

Waving a hand at them, Beanie pulled herself up from her comfortable place. 'I'm going abed. Do what you want.' Swaying slightly, she left them to it and went to her own room and sat on the edge of the bed feeling a little on the sad side. This time last year she and Flora were in their lovely little two up two down with colourful paper chains across the ceiling and brightly wrapped presents under the tree ready for the next morning. Sorry now that she and her mother hadn't gone back to the courtyard for the carol singing, a tradition always kept, she began to sink. Their lives had been turned upside down overnight and she didn't want to be in someone else's home at this special time of year. She regretted having agreed to it now. She would much rather be in the little cottage with her grandparents.

'That's what happens when you get caught up in other people's euphoria, Beanie,' she sighed. Fanny had talked up the idea of having a Christmas in Beaumont Square without having to fetch and carry. It had seemed an exciting thing at the time. Looking around her small plain bedroom she recalled the way her granddad had decorated hers, first washing the walls in pale yellow and then hand painting birds and flowers everywhere. It was so lovely and it was hers and now someone else was enjoying it . . . or worse still had whitewashed it – as they had done here in this room. At least she had a gas fire, and the guard in front, on which she hung her white towel, was brass, so she had it shining. The bedcover was also white and on the polished floorboards was a small rug. The curtains on the tiny window were plain but thick and kept out the draught. On the wall was a picture of a child angel.

Tired but thirsty, Beanie went below stairs to fetch herself a glass of water and was surprised to see her mother sitting by the fire all alone looking at a tiny photo of herself and Beanie, taken at Christmastime, a few years back. She too was remembering a proper family Christmas.

Placing a hand on her mother's shoulder, Beanie spoke quietly. 'Granddad took that – clever devil. I reckon he could be a famous photographer one day, if he wasn't so old.'

Undisturbed by her daughter's arrival, Flora nodded, gazing at the picture. 'We'll pay them a visit after breakfast and then go back again after Christmas Dinner. That way we'll be getting the best of everything.' Her voice did not hold conviction and Beanie knew that she too was wishing she had never agreed to stay at number ten for the festive season.

'I think that's a lovely idea.' She kissed Flora lightly on the cheek. 'Can I sleep in your bed with you tonight, Mum?'

Patting her daughter's hand, she nodded slowly. 'Course you can. It'll be lovely, Bea. You and me and no one else in the world to come between us.'

'Good,' murmured Beanie, ''cos you know what, I love you very much.'

'And I love you too, Bea,' said Flora.

The house was dark and still when the Wellingtons' twenty-six-year-old son, Herbert, turned the key in the lock of the front door. Accompanying him, Gerald Fairweather, his lover, was only just able to stand. They had arrived from Stratford-upon-Avon two days previous and had kept their coming a secret, not so as to give a pleasant surprise but to have it their own way. Grace Wellington had written to say that the family would be congregating at her cousin's house in Newmarket for the holiday and Herbert saw this as a stroke of luck. He had written back saying that he was in a production which was scheduled to run over the holiday and would not be home. He imagined that he and Gerald would have number ten to themselves over

Christmas. He had not bargained on the arrangement which had been made of the staff staying over.

Going directly into the library and helping themselves to a tipple before bed, he and his friend toasted themselves for the umpteenth time that night. They had been on a pub and club crawl and had had a wonderful time, drinking the finest champagne and the strongest ale. Showing his friend to the master bedroom where they would sleep, he had no sense whatsoever of there being anyone else in residence. When he opened the bedroom door to find the room candlelit and Albert and Fanny rolling about under the sheets, he was, to say the least, shocked. So caught up in their lovemaking the passionate pair did not hear the door open.

'*Mater* . . . ?' murmured Herbert, rigid. '*Pater* . . . ?' He turned to his companion who simply shrugged, not really sober enough to know quite what was going on or care.

Backing out of the door, with his friend in tow, Herbert quietly turned the handle. It was all too humiliating! He would rather die than be found catching them in the act.

'Good God. I thought they were past all that,' he said, leaning on the banister, 'I feel quite ill, old chap.'

Gerald pulled his gold watch from his waistcoat pocket. 'Never mind. It's Christmas Day.'

'Christmas Day,' sighed Herbert, shaking his head forlornly. 'I need a drink.'

'Sorry old boy . . . lids are drooping. Must have a

kip. Lead the way there's a good fellow. See me to bed and then you can do what you bloody well like.' Lowering his head to one side, he studied his friend's face. 'I suppose it is a bit tricky . . .'

'No,' said Herbert, concentrating. 'Not so much tricky as odd . . . now that I've time to collect myself. Do you know what I think? I think that whoever it is in there – it is *not* my parents.' Turning back towards the master-bedroom door, he paused and pushed it open, with Gerald close behind. The startled look on Fanny's face, as she straddled her beloved, who was now on the floor, was rewarding if nothing else.

'What the fuck are you doing in my parents' room?' was Herbert's stunned reaction.

'Pretty obvious I'd 'ave thought,' said Fanny, glad to have shocked the horrid Wellington junior. 'We're trespassing.' She pulled herself together and stood up, stark naked. 'I 'ope you're not gonna give us away?'

'Why – are – you – here? It's Christmas for *God*'s sake! You are not supposed to *be* here!'

'No, Mr Wellington and neither are you. In a Christmas play is what I heard.' Fanny then looked over his shoulder and smiled at Gerald. 'First time you've seen a lady starkers, is it?'

'Yes, actually,' he replied, giving her a second once over. 'You've got a few bits missing,' he pointed a finger and then wiggled it. He then looked from her to the stunned and naked Albert who was still on the floor, knees bent to hide his privates. 'Sorry to spoil your fun, old chap,' he grinned.

Stern faced and seething, Herbert jabbed a finger

into Fanny's shoulder. 'Don't you *ever* do this again. Now get out of here! And thank your stars that I'll not tell tales out of school!'

'Tales out of school . . .' purred Fanny. 'Well now wouldn't that be a lark if we all did that, eh?' She grinned and winked at him before leaving, with Albert sheepishly following.

Shuddering, Herbert Wellington showed his disgust at the common girl from below stairs. 'Close the door, Gerald, before they find a reason to come back in. God how I loathe the working classes.'

'Really . . . ? Well. You could have fooled me, luvvy. Seemed very much at home in the taverns with your working class chums.'

'That's different.'

'How so?'

'Oh shut up, Gerald, and take that silly smug grin off your face. You really are a top-class prater with your idle chatter. Well . . .' he continued, gazing at the turmoil in the bedroom, '. . . I'm not sure I want to sleep in this room now. Bloody clothes all over the place, not to mention soiled linen.'

'Well,' said Gerald, pulling off his tie, 'sleep where you like my love. As for me, it's the nearest bed for my poor head.'

'Don't be churlish. Come on. We'll sleep in my old room. The bed's big enough for two.'

'No,' said Gerald, his mind made up. 'I am sleeping here . . . come what may.' He peeled off the rest of his clothes and climbed into bed, drunk and exhausted. Herbert, however, was having none of it. He stormed out of the room and didn't bother to close the bedroom door after him, quite deliberately. He hoped the disagreeable swine would be woken at the crack of dawn by the staff as they made their way below.

'Mum . . .' whispered Beanie, 'Mum, someone's come into the house.' The only response she received from Flora was a sleepy acknowledgement which was inaudible. Hearing the door to Herbert's room opening and shutting Beanie presumed that the family had decided to spend Christmas day at home after all. Believing this, she only managed to drift into a light sleep. If they *had* returned they would have to work through Christmas Day and not be able to visit her grandparents. Too tired to reason things through sensibly, she closed her eyes and drifted off to sleep. In a more alert state of mind, she would have realised that the family would hardly change their mind and return to a house unprepared for them. The chicken would not cut to that many people and the Wellingtons were more used to goose or turkey.

Lying in his bed and wide awake, Herbert reproached himself for not giving the bootboy a thrashing with his belt for daring to go into his parents' bed, especially since he would rather be there himself, with his chum. But then of course it could have been worse. Had the tables been turned and the plebeians caught sight of himself and Gerald in bed together, the hand of blackmail might now be gripping his neck. Somewhat relieved by the narrow escape, he plumped his pillow wondering why the staff had not gone home. He hoped that lady luck would be on his side once again and that the common couple would be gone by the morning.

Lady luck was either Herbert's best friend or worst enemy, depending on how things went. She was most certainly against him when his parents had chosen to send him to All Saints School which was meant to prepare him for later entry into public school. Here, corporal punishment was enforced and as he soon discovered, it was essential, where life in the dormitory was concerned, to be strong and wakeful. Bullies were always on the lookout for boys weaker than themselves. His good looks attracted not only the bullies but homosexual masters who took pleasure in giving sadistic beatings. But All Saints did at least introduce him to a new world of the dramatic society where it became apparent not only to himself but others, that he had a natural ability for acting and recitations. Later in life he auditioned at the Central School of Speech and Drama, in secret. His father, Tobias, was fiercely against a son of his going on stage, especially since he had heard of the eccentric woman who taught at the school. Former actress, Elsie Fogerty, a frumpish but masterful lady who specialised in natural speech and voice production and who, although unorthodox, was an excellent tutor. Her large plumed hats and array of mismatched costume jewellery and colourful petticoats boldly creeping below her hemline were a case of once seen never forgotten. Herbert had everything to thank this woman for but in so far as he was concerned, she taught him nothing that he did not already know.

*   *   *

Waking to the sound of church bells with the moonlight coming in through the gap in the curtains, Flora,
having dreamt of a Christmas long ago, when she was
a young woman and Beanie a baby, was daunted by her
surroundings. It took several seconds before it dawned
on her that she was not in her bedroom in the house
in Brick Lane but in Beaumont Square. She lay very
still to the sound of her daughter breathing softly and
allowed herself the privilege of remembering better
times. This was something she would not usually do.
Dwelling on the past was not one of her pastimes.
Bringing Tobias Wellington's younger face to mind
she felt lonely. Sad that someone who once loved
her had so easily shed her from his life. Someone
who now lived in the same house and had no idea
as to who she or Beanie was. He hadn't recognised
her. She had, as always, swept her emotions under
the carpet, frightened in case the hurt would be too
much to bear. She glanced at her lovely daughter's
face as she slept peacefully on this Christmas morning and told herself that it didn't matter. She had
Beanie.

Slipping carefully out of the bed, she pulled her
faded housecoat on and left the room. Before going
below stairs and seeing the library door open, she went
inside. An overcoat had been thrown over a low table.
The snobby, arrogant, rude son of the Wellingtons
seemed to be in residence – and so too was one of
his actor friends, for there was also a long black cloak
in the room and an overly large black hat. She had
had the pleasure of a confrontation with Mr Herbert

only once and once was enough. Well, if he thought any one of them was going to wait on him hand and foot he was very much mistaken. And as for Christmas dinner, he could have the parson's nose and share that with his pal.

Once in her kitchen with the range going and a small fire lit, Flora sat in the armchair and enjoyed her early morning cup of tea, drinking it from her saucer. If it was good enough for Queen Victoria it was good enough for her. She recalled the royal funeral in 1901 of that wise, strong woman and raised her cup as a mark of respect.

On hearing another set of church bells in the distance, she cheered up. It was Christmas Day! A day when families were together and together hers would be. Her daughter would be at her side for dinner and her ma and pa for high tea. The one thing she was determined never to do was compare Beanie to her half brother, Herbert, or half sister, Sarah. Not even in her weakest moment. The only way to go on living under the same roof was to push from her mind the fact that the three of them were related. If she started to compare their lives there was no saying what she might do. Flora was no different from any mother in that she wanted the best for her girl. But she couldn't give the best and Grace Wellington could. Sarah dressed in silks and lace while Beanie wore second-hand clothes. No, thought Flora, I shall think of Grace Wellington's grown children as just that. Her children are hers and my Beanie is mine. She would face the consequences of her decision come the day when the truth might come out. Beanie would not hold against her the fact that she had kept the secret, she felt sure of it.

Without thinking she began to sing quietly to the sound of the church bells: 'You owe me five farvings, said the bells of St Martin's. When will you pay me, said the bells of Old Bailey . . .'

'I say, cook . . .' the voice of Herbert Wellington spoiled her festive mood. 'Couldn't pull an egg nog together for me, could you?'

'Well now, since you ask so politely I most certainly can. Bit of a hangover is it?'

'No. I've a headache. Fetch it up to my room. Oh and fetch my morning tea in a couple of hours. It'll be a full breakfast for two. I've a friend stopping over. We'll eat in the morning room.'

'Haven't you forgotten something, Mr Herbert?'

'No . . . ?'

'Happy Christmas?'

'Oh that. And yes . . . speaking of which . . . why are you here? Haven't any of you got homes to go to?'

'Yes we have, sir, but Madam warmed to the idea of us staying over the holiday to house mind. There've bin that many burglaries of late. I wish you'd written to say you'd be coming . . . I've only shopped for the four of us.'

'Oh . . . you expected us to sit down to Christmas dinner with you?' he smirked. 'Don't bother that old head of yours. We'll be dining at the Ritz. A supper of cold meats and cheese in the library will do. I should think we'll be back around midnight. Make certain that all the servants are in bed by then . . . if that's not too much to ask?' With that he strode out of the kitchen, leaving Flora to stare after him. At least he had confirmed one thing – her first impression of him had been right. He was despicable. She thanked the Lord that there was not the slightest resemblance between him and Beanie. She had seen certain similarities in Sarah but not enough that anyone else would see a likeness. The eyes were the only give-away.

Begrudgingly, she went to the pantry to collect and put to one side the food she would need for his breakfast. Staring at the shelf on which she kept the spices she wondered if there might be a dried herb she could add to give him the runs.

Grown men preferring each other's company to that of beautiful women was something she couldn't begin to fathom or concern herself with. The worst of it was, that although it was against the law, more and more of his type seemed to be crawling out of the woodwork and behaving in a flamboyant manner. Not only proud of what they were but deliberately rubbing in the salt. Flora wasn't old fashioned by any means and had made a good friend at the factory who was very feminine by nature. A nicer person she couldn't have wished to work beside in the kitchen. The difference between this man and Herbert Wellington was the former's wish to simply get on with life and let others get on with theirs. No flaunting, no bitching, no nonsense. The man who had just gone upstairs had the worst traits of his type.

Pushing him from her mind she stoked up the range just enough so it would be perfect for when she put in the bird. There would be more than enough to feed the extra two guests, their chicken being a fat capon, but she had no intention of having them at her table on this special day. Just as well you are going to the Ritz, she mused, Too much loving care has gone into the making of our plum pudding.

Reminding herself to fill a hamper for the lamp-lighters who would be round as usual, she pulled the small wicker basket from under the old Welsh dresser and gave it a wipe. She ran through the items to go in: a small tin of peaches, a chunk of Christmas cake, some cold meat left over from the Wellingtons' previous dinner party and a chunk of their finest cheddar and a few of Flora's mince pies.

Wrapped in her thoughts, she didn't hear Beanie come into the kitchen. 'Happy Christmas, Mum,' she said, rubbing her eyes.

Flora held out her arms and hugged her daughter close. 'Happy Christmas, love. We'll make it a good one, you'll see.'

'Do you want your present now?' yawned Beanie.

'No, we'll have a nice cup of tea first.' Flora couldn't wait to see the expression on her daughter's face when she unwrapped her surprise present – a sky blue coat with glass buttons that she'd purchased from the best second-hand clothes shop in the area. The rip in the hem she had managed to invisibly mend and a stain on the front make disappear with her home made spirit cleaner. 'Did you peep into your pillowcase yet?'

'Course I did, Mum. Thanks. I've got everyfing I wanted. Scent, gloves and chocolates . . .'

'And the scarf?'

'Oh Mum, it's lovely. Really soft and my favourite colour.'

'It's proper chiffon, you know, and the lining's silk and it wasn't from a second-hand shop.'

'I know. You don't 'ave to tell me. You always say that. Anyway, nor was your present – from a second-hand shop that is – I didn't pay much for it though,' she grinned. 'Bought it off the rag-and-bone man.'

'I don't care if you did, Bea. It's the thought that counts.' Smiling to herself, Flora wondered what thoughts were going through her Prince Charming's mind when he gave her that silk scarf all those years ago. Wrapped in tissue paper, it had never seen the light of day, until now. She was in no doubt that Mr Tobias Wellington would not recognise it. Gifts such as this would probably have meant nothing to him.

'I'll give you yours at breakfast then,' said Beanie, matter-of-fact, 'when we'll all be exchanging gifts.' Underneath her mask she was excited about her find in a tiny pawnbroker shop in Black Lion Yard. The pretty blue crystal necklace, linked with 9ct gold had cost no more than a florin. It had been in a tin with other bits and pieces and was very grimy until she washed it in warm water and Sunlight soap, bringing it back to its former sparkling glory. She imagined her mother's face when she opened the small box. Flora cut into her thoughts.

'You were right by the way,' she said, 'we did have visitors during the night and they're still here, more's the pity. Herbert Wellington and one of his lot. They're not staying for Christmas dinner though. They're off to a posh hotel. Here . . .' She handed Beanie a cup of tea.

'I wonder why he came home? He knew the family had gone to Newmarket, didn't he?'

'Don't tax your brain over it. You'll never fathom this family, not in a million years. Sit yerself down and I'll fetch the biscuit tin.'

Beanie raised an eyebrow. 'I'm not up properly, *yet*. I'm taking this back to bed wiv me – and then I'm gonna sleep a bit more. We're not on duty are we?'

'Oh please yourself what you do,' said Flora, her mind still on Herbert and what effect it might have on Beanie if she were to realise his sexual preferences.

'You're not cross wiv me are you, Mum?'

'Of course I'm not. Go on – up you go. I'll give the three of you a call at eight. That's a decent enough time to rise on Christmas morning. I'll have breakfast ready and we can all open our gifts.'

Pointing to a colourfully wrapped gift under the tree, Beanie said, 'Gran wants you to open that first thing. That smaller red parcel's from granddad. You can open that when you like.' With that, she left the kitchen, excitement welling inside. They weren't in their old house but it felt homely, especially with their employers away.

By herself again, Flora lifted the presents from her parents from under the tree, sat by the fire and opened them. From her mother there was a sparkling white apron on which she had beautifully embroidered her name, the date, and a tiny bunch of forget-me-knot

flowers. From Willie, her doting father, a box of chocolates and a lovely handmade red and gold Christmas
card sprinkled with glitter.

Yes, thought Flora, as she gazed into the flames of
the fire, we'll have a lovely day . . . all of us.

After breakfast and in the kitchen the three young
people exchanged presents, cracked nuts and sipped
ginger wine to the peal of church bells. Flora hadn't
given Herbert Wellington and his friend another thought
and when he appeared later in front of her to announce
that they would be in for Christmas lunch after all,
she didn't really mind that much. A few more roast
spuds, parsnips and Brussels sprouts to peel was no
hardship. Beanie was quite taken with the idea. A party
atmosphere was building.

'Where's your friend, then?' she said, addressing
Herbert as if he was her equal.

'Primping himself in the bathroom.' He floated a
hand through the air in a theatrical manner. 'Take
from him the mirror and he would shrivel and die.'
He glanced at the modest dining table, impressed. It
was covered with a perfectly pressed white damask
cloth and set with gleaming poor man's silver (polished
chrome), red Christmas crackers and a centre display
of evergreens, holly and clusters of red berries.

'I think a little wine from the cellar is called for.
What say you, Cook? A couple of bottles of Pater's
special for we poor things who must stay in London
while they wine and dine in the country?'

'If you say so, Mr Wellington, who am I to argue?'
They exchanged polite smiles with a certain optimism

that this festive dinner with its mix of guests *might* turn out to be something to remember.

'Well, I think you should pull the stops out, Herbert,' said Beanie, not giving a toss about decorum. 'Fetch a bottle of bubbly as well. Your old man won't miss one bottle now would he? Two even.'

'Mmm . . . we'll see,' he said, warming to the cockney.

Fanny glanced from Herbert to Beanie, hoping to catch her friend's eye. She knew this young man and knew him well. He could turn in a second and sting with a look. He could reduce a person to a quiver and finish them with a barbed remark.

'We wouldn't want you to get into trouble, Mr Wellington,' she said, deadly serious. 'Your father don't like anyone goin' into 'is cellar.'

'What the eye doesn't see my dear – the heart cannot grieve over,' Herbert tapped his nose and winked at her.

Too chummy, thought Fanny. Too good a mood. There's trouble ahead.

Christmas dinner, contrary to what Fanny imagined, went exceedingly well. Flora, wearing her pretty blue crystal necklace and Sunday frock, turned out an exceptional four-course meal, beginning with clear chicken soup and ending with a modest but tasty cheeseboard. Crackers had been pulled and jokes told. Now, with their bellies satisfied and ready for coffee made from ground beans which were usually kept aside for upstairs, the conversation was flowing.

Much to Herbert's delight, he was the centre of attention.

'So, why didn't your dad want you to go on stage?' asked Fanny, sipping a brandy. 'I'd 'ave thought that any dad would want their son to be an actor. I mean, it's not as if you're not a proper actor is it?'

'Indeed,' said Herbert leaning back in his chair and sighing dramatically. 'Would that he saw it through your eyes, Fanny my love.' After a calculated pause, he said, 'Not that there's anything *wrong* with the bit part player . . .'

'Why thank you, dear boy,' said his friend, Gerald, managing a grin to suit the tone in his voice. 'At least us "bit parters" get regular work, thus enabling us to pay our rent on time.' He tipped his glass and looked straight into Herbert's face, adding, 'Touché?' A stony look from his friend was his answer.

'I thought that all actors were well off enough to pay their rent,' said Beanie. 'Working all them unsociable hours 'aving to learn lines, playing to people who boo and chuck old tomatoes at yer. They should pay you double what they pay the man who comes to take the rubbish away.' Whether it was intended, and it possibly was, Beanie had just given the actors the worst put down possible.

'My sweet, innocent girl,' purred Herbert, leaning forward and looking into her face. 'We professional actors do not play to bawdy audiences. Well at least *I* do not,' he sniffed, glancing at Gerald.

'I always fancied myself as an actress,' said Fanny, dreaming. 'My mother was always saying I'd end up on stage. Used to call me Drama Lil. It was my accent that stopped me from taking it up. Only you lot get in, and then learn 'ow to talk like us for when it suits the play. Bloody daft.'

'You could 'ave taken elocution lessons, Fan,' said Albert, admiring her lovely face. She always looked six times as lovely to Albert when he'd had a drink.

'Good God, no!' exclaimed Herbert, covering his face with one hand and shaking his head painfully. 'Your voice, my dear girl – your *accent* – don't ever try and lose it!'

'It's all right for you to say that—'

'I know!' he said, showing the flat of his hand. 'I know *exactly* what you're going to say.' He leaned closer to her, their faces almost touching. 'A bow has more than one string. *You* may always *pay* to have your voice trained. Whereas *I* am stuck with mine! *Would* that I could speak in your tongue. A true cockney voice can *never* be assimilated . . . no matter *how* excellent the actor.'

'What bollocks you do talk at times, Wellington,' said Gerald Fairweather, chuckling and sipping his drink. 'What tripe spills from that gob of yours.'

'Mock as you will, Mr Fairweather, but please do not give an example of *your* cockney voice . . . I beg you.' He turned to the girls and curled his lip, mouthing the word, 'Ghastly!'

By the stove and spooning coffee into a pot, Flora was amused by Gerald and was beginning to warm to the man. 'So, how did you manage to persuade your father in the end, Mr Wellington?'

'I purposely made myself ill, in India. Which is where I was sent – urged by Pater. Urged to sail off and work on my great uncle's rubber plantation. I can't tell you how awful it was.' He leaned back and became thoughtful. 'Mater did a very good job of persuading him that I was not cut out for the work of a labourer. Not that I actually worked out in the fields, as was the suggestion. Once home, with a touch of diarrhoea, he suggested I should take up from where I had left off, much to my relief.'

'And where was that?' asked Fanny.

'Do you *really* want to know?'

'Of course. What's more, you can't wait to tell us. Go on then . . . off you go.'

He sighed in his usual way and shook his head slowly. 'Where does one begin?'

'Try the beginning,' said Albert, more comfortable in their company now than when they first sat down to eat.

'Let me see . . .' Herbert leaned back, gazed at the ceiling, and began. 'Before the dreadful India trial, I attended St Edward's, Oxford where most of the boys were the sons of clergymen. Drawn there, no doubt, by the Romanesque chapel which joined the classrooms, library and dining hall . . . and the headmaster's residence. There was a small theatre, of sorts.' He paused before murmuring, 'I was a rather lonely boy—'

'Cut the spiel, Herbert ducky, and get to the point . . . or close to the end of your beginnings at least. Otherwise we shall be here till midnight.'

Refusing to even look at his companion, Herbert withdrew his pipe and tobacco from his inside pocket. 'I suppose you could say that I was influenced by English films which one could see in most cinemas for a few pennies. It was all part of my study programme. I looked to the audience and their rapture, or lack of it, with respect to the performance of actors. I had to know, you see, which actors kept them in rapt attention.'

'Not that Herbert would ever consider aping another,' tormented Gerald.

'There were quite a few theatre clubs in London of course, staging new plays in brief runs and this really was where I learned my art. Most times I sailed through the auditions. I suppose you could say I was most influenced by Ronald Colman, an Englishman who saw fit to emigrate to Hollywood. There was quite an exodus of actors to America, I fear.

'But we still have our Peggy Ashcroft, Laurence Olivier, Ruby Miller and so on and so forth.' Lowering his eyes from the heavens, he smiled faintly at Fanny who had started him on this course. 'At present I am engaged by manager Julian Frank, to appear in *The Unfailing Instinct* – a music-hall curtain raiser. Four weeks on tour: Manchester, Liverpool and Brighton and all for a pound a week. Is it any wonder I return to the fold quite broke?'

'Laurence Olivier. Now there is a good-looking geezer,' said Beanie in her best cockney. 'And a really good actor.'

'You think so?'

'It's what they say so—'

'It's all very much in the eye of the beholder. He was quite good in *The Ghost Train*. We toured together after its success in London. Dear Olivier . . . he does try so. He tripped on stage you know, slid precariously towards the footlights. Rather embarrassing all round but then of course it's not all bright lights and stardust. Indeed no. I've played in the dingiest of places with the best of people, but that is the actor's life. From West End to poor settlement houses, public baths, piers and town halls. Battersea, Ilford, Deptford and Camberwell. Superb training grounds which exercise the memory and extend one's range. I go where the need is great, it matters not. It's the smell of the greasepaint.'

Gerald began to clap heartily, a facetious attempt to bring an end to all that he had heard so many times before. 'And I smell the coffee.' He looked across to Flora who had her back to them. 'Don't suppose there's a thin slice of Christmas cake going begging, Cook?'

'Well, if you think you can manage it, Mr Wellington, I shall cut you a slice.'

'Not Wellington, my dear,' said Gerald.

Turning to face them, she replied, 'Oh? I could have sworn it was you, sir, trying to change the subject to stop them probing into your professional world. I'm sure you must get fed up talking about it.' She hoped so.

'Would that it had been I who so rudely interrupted,' said Herbert. 'Alas, Mr Fairweather will try anything to get the attention. Even in my family home as a guest—'

'No,' said Gerald, correcting him. 'I will try anything to stop you bathing in the limelight. There's a huge difference.'

'I was asked about my life, Gerald, and I was merely obliging. But still . . . if you must be centre of attention—' he said, leaning back in his chair.

'Not at all, Herbert. I would just rather not be bored to death on Christmas Day.' He smiled broadly and glanced at the others. 'Anyone for cards?' The room fell silent as each of them waited for Herbert's reaction. Beanie saved the day.

'So where d'yer live when you're not in residence, Mr Wellington?'

'Oh please, call me Herbert. Wellington sounds rather formal in these surroundings. Outside of course, when I am in the public eye, then I would expect you to be proper.' He reached across the table and patted her hand. 'But not here and especially not today.' He leaned back in his chair again, inhaled slowly and let out a relaxed sigh. 'It is so good to be home. And as for where I live . . . in a tiny London garret in Maida Vale, along with my contemporaries. Well not all of them, naturally. Gerald here prefers Islington.'

'It's not a preference, Herbert, it's a necessity. I don't receive a family allowance, let's not forget. I make my own way in the world – unashamedly.' He waited for a sarcastic retort – it was slow in coming. 'And besides . . . I happen to like Islington. It may not be as fashionable as Maida Vale, but it does have a more . . . *bohemian* mood.'

Roaring with laughter, Herbert almost fell off his chair. 'Bohemian? Are you mad?'

'No. But you wouldn't understand so—'

'There's nothing *to* understand, Gerald. Now if you were to be living in say . . . Bloomsbury.'

'Old hat, dear chap,' returned Gerald, twisting the knife. 'You are very much out of touch.'

'Well,' said Fanny, sensing the tension beginning to rise again. 'All I can say is what do it matter where you live so long as you're 'appy. And Gerald looks that.'

'And what would a scullery maid know about anything?' The sneer was back on Herbert's face.

'Parlour maid, actually.'

'Oh I say! Pardon me, Miss Parlour Maid! Please do excuse me for getting it wrong.' He studied her face deliberately. 'And what does a parlour maid do other than fuck the bootboy in the bed of her employer?'

'Now now now, Mr Wellington. There's no call for that!'

'Well, you might not think so, Cook, but then, you did not come across the pair of them behaving like street hounds. It was a sight I would not like to experience again.' He fanned his face, 'I feel quite ill at the recollection.'

'You've got a nerve!' shrieked Fanny. 'Them that live in glass 'ouses—'

'Yes I know . . .' He flapped a hand indicating that he found her tiresome. 'Fetch a bottle of whisky from the cellar, girl, and be quick about it.'

'Excuse me but it's her day off!' Beanie's flushed face matched her temper. 'You're not s'posed to even be here. You, Mr High and Mighty Wellington, are an interloper!'

'Oh dear. Another troublemaker. Get these people out of here, Cook, before we shall have to see them carried out. Send them to their rooms . . . and yourself for that matter.' He shuddered theatrically. 'I can't really bear to be around people from low rank.'

'Oh for Christ's sake, Herbert, show some respect!'

'Would that I could, Gerald, love. But look who I am surrounded by . . . a scrounger and . . .' he waved a hand dismissively at the rest of them.

'Oh it's my turn now, is it? I'm to be insulted too!'

'I'm not insulting you, I am merely speaking the truth.'

The sudden crashing of Gerald's fist as he banged it down on to the table startled them all. 'It's the same old story every time! You ruin a perfectly good day!'

Herbert leaned across the table and into the face of his friend. 'I should go to the lavatory if I were you. You are full of—'

'Shut up!' snarled Gerald, stopping him in his track. 'Shut your filthy mouth before I shut it for you.'

Furious, Herbert showed a clenched fist. 'I think an apology is called for, wouldn't you say?'

'Not from me it isn't.' Their faces were so close now as to be almost touching.

'Come on, come on,' said Albert. 'There's no need for this. Shake 'ands and make up. We've all 'ad a drop over the odds and you got through a bottle of champagne all by yerself, Mr Wellington. That's what it is, too much alcohol.'

'Who gave *you* permission to speak?'

'Permission? I've never needed permission, Mr Wellington, and I certainly ain't gonna start with you. I should get yourself up to bed. I think you need to sleep it off. You might regret—' Before Albert could utter another word, Herbert's fist caught him on the cheekbone and with such a mighty blow that it sent him sprawling across the room.

Fanny was quick to his defence. She grabbed the remains of the chicken and pushed it into Wellington's face, with juice and giblets trickling slowly down his front. 'I'm only sorry the parson's nose is bigger than its arsehole 'cos that's where your 'ead deserves to be!'

Grabbing her by the collar of her new white blouse, he almost strangled her and when Gerald stepped in to help, Herbert all but used Fanny as a weapon as he flung her on to him. Everything on the table went crashing to the floor and chairs were flying in all directions. Bedlam erupted as each of them dived in to stop Gerald from killing his chum. His hands were round his throat and he was squeezing with all of his strength.

'He's not worth hanging for,' said Flora, gazing down at the unconscious Herbert Wellington lying flat on his back and out for the count. 'He's nothing but a drunk – an ill-tempered drunk.'

'I know,' whispered Gerald, breathless. 'And I swear that one day I will hang for him. He wants to die laughing.' His face pinched, he shook his head slowly, 'I always, *always* rise to the bait.' With that he left the kitchen, collected his things and went without another word.

'Well, there we are,' said Flora, disgusted by their behaviour. 'They say there's nothing stranger than folk and the more different types I see, the more I believe it.'

'Not us lot though, eh Cook? We know who we are and what we're about. It's the sodding upper classes . . . and it's not strange *I'd* call 'em!' Fanny was still on the floor her voice all of a quiver and she could no longer control her emotions. She began to cry. 'My Albert 'adn't done nuffing wrong. Herbert 'ad no cause to punch 'im like that.'

'That's all right, love,' said Albert, an arm around her shoulder as he helped her towards the armchair by the fire. 'He'll come round soon and when he does I'll smack 'im on the nose and knock 'im out agen.'

'You'll do no such thing,' said Flora, tidying some of the mess. 'Between us we'll carry him up to the morning room and shut him in there to sleep it off. Disgraceful . . .' she said, tut-tutting. 'I'm glad his mother wasn't here to see it. That woman doesn't deserve the men in her life. She's kind and she's thoughtful and if you ask me husband *and* son take advantage of her good nature!' She glared at the unconscious young man lying at her feet. 'Shame on you!'

'He's spoiled our Christmas day,' grouched Beanie, not fully taking in what her mother had just said.

'Wasn't even invited indeed. I think we should leave the brute where he is and go out.' She glanced at her mother. 'We could all go to—'

'No!' snapped Flora cutting in before Beanie let the cat out of the bag. 'We won't all fit into my mother's tiny sitting room. Think yourself lucky that you've bin invited, my girl.'

'Ah, don't snap at Beanie, Cook,' said Albert. 'She ain't done nuffing wrong. We'll do as you say and get him upstairs and out of the way. Then we can muck in and clear things away. Me and Fanny are goin' for a nice walk to St Dunstan's Church to put the holly wreath she made on a grave and then back 'ere for a nice quiet time by the fire. We won't be lonely or that.'

'Well, I think that's very nice of you,' said Flora, calming down and filling the large butler sink with hot water. 'We should all take a leaf out of your book Albert, and tend the graves of them who left no one behind. Yes,' she murmured, 'we should all do a bit more.'

'You do enough, Cook. You make this place like a real home for all of us.'

'Yeah,' said Fanny, still a bit shaken. 'You look after the living who've got no one who particularly cares about 'em.'

'Oh come on now, Fan,' said Albert, 'you've got your sister over South London. You could 'ave gone to 'er for Christmas, you know you could.'

'We're all getting a little bit morbid,' said Flora. 'Come on, we'll have—'

'A nice cup of tea!' chorused the others, knowing her better than she knew herself. Tea was the answer to all upsets as far as Flora was concerned. Within minutes they were back in good humour and laughing at the horrid Herbert Wellington who was snoring like a drain.

4

The excitement of Christmas behind them, with all of its ups and downs, Flora, on New Year's Eve was busy yet again. The Wellingtons were entertaining the relatives from Newmarket and there were twenty-eight guests to feed as well as the family of four above stairs. Herbert had decided to stay at home, knowing where his bread was best buttered. And now, in the library with Tobias, he privately commended himself on his shrewd decision. His father was in a chivalrous mood, not unusual after time spent with the uppity in-laws who annoyed him by *not* flaunting their wealth. Grace's family had been wealthy for centuries and were used to it by now and wouldn't know how to show off if they wanted to.

The father to son talk, as Tobias had put it, was to please himself more than Herbert. He was feeling a little downcast and didn't like it. Not that he would ever succumb to this fact, not even to himself would he ever admit that he was anywhere close to being an underling. Looking every bit the lord of the manor, leaning back in his leather chair, his legs crossed he puffed at his pipe.

'Now you've obviously put two and two together,

Herbert,' he said, rather grandly, 'with regard to my wealth and so on.' With eyes narrowed, considering the pros and cons, he kept his son in suspense. 'Not that I blag on about it.' Another deliberate pause. 'How old will you be this coming year, twenty-five . . . twenty-six?'

'Something like that, Father, yes.'

'Quite. Well then, all the more reason for our tête-à-tête. Now then, this garret in Maida Vale . . . All very well as a young bachelor's flat but for a young man of your age and standing, I think a house might be more appropriate. What do you say to that?'

Herbert was, on this rare occasion, speechless. Was he hearing correctly? Was his father offering to buy him a house? He could do no more than gaze, mystified, at the man. His father certainly was in a good mood but . . . a house . . . a house of his own?

'I can see you're a bit stumped, old chap, let me explain . . .' he chuckled, giving him a fatherly wink.

Usually at this point – when alone with his father – Herbert would find some excuse to leave. A long-drawn-out and incredibly boring explanation was about to be delivered. 'May I pour myself a tiny brandy, Father? After all, it's so seldom we have a chance to be alone in the library like this?'

'Man to man you mean? Yes . . . well you have your mother to thank for that.' He coasted a hand towards the drinks cupboard. 'Help yourself and pour one for me while you're at it. It's a bit early in the day but then what the eye doesn't see . . .'

'Mother's eye you mean?' Herbert knew very well

who he was referring to. Any opportunity to put down Grace, and Tobias grabbed at it. This was nothing new.

'Ah, you're more astute than I imagined; you've noticed it too.'

'Of course I have,' he said feigning a look of disdain, and handing over a glass of brandy. In truth he couldn't care less. They were hardly a loving couple and he wouldn't have wanted it any other way. The vulgarity of parents behaving as if they were in love was obscene in Herbert's eyes. 'It's all this business of her joining the Suffragettes.'

'Rejoining,' said Tobias, eyebrows raised. 'This is her second round, old chap. She's trying to reap a second youth – a second time,' he sighed. 'It's the ungainliness of it all. Women chaining themselves to anything that doesn't move. God alone knows why?'

'To be more like men, do you think?' said Herbert, scratching an ear and wondering how he could pilot his father back on track. 'I dread to think of the tantrum from Sarah, once she knows you're going to buy your son a house. She'll want to be treated as an equal. Perhaps it's not an idea we should pursue, I should hate it if you were to quarrel with her. And quarrel she will, make no mistake, Father.'

'She can bloody well scream the odds for all I care. It'll be a good lesson for your mother. The sun shines out of your sister's backside where she's concerned. She's ruined the girl. Given in to every damn, *considered*, whim.'

'You don't have to tell me. Not that I ever complained when Sarah was given whatever she wanted no matter the cost.'

'You mustn't blame your sister, Herbert. A female, no matter how young or old, will take what is offered. It's your mother you have to thank.'

'So you said.' Herbert, with brandy to his lips, leaned on the mantelshelf above the roaring fire. 'So . . . the house?' He tried his utmost to sound casual over something that had truly excited him.

'Women must be harnessed,' muttered Tobias, caught up in his own thoughts of how he had let his dark lady of the stage slip tragically from his life. 'Give them slack and they get up to all sorts of madness. Which is why . . .' he said, eyeing his son and sipping his drink, 'I asked you in for a chat.'

'Oh?'

'The house comes into it, naturally. I would not have mentioned it else wise. But a house without a woman at the helm couldn't work. They have their uses and it's a foolish man who doesn't see that. Now if I were you, I would draw up a list of the females you've been overly fond of and mark the one who is best at organising. That's what you'll need. A woman to see to the running of the house and so on.'

'*Marriage?*' gasped Herbert. He hadn't expected this. 'You expect me to marry someone in order to run this house you're offering to buy? Really, Father, you go too far at times,' he said, chortling.

'You're not getting any younger, Herbert. It's time you were settled. It'll please your mother no end . . .

and she'll need persuading to part with some of her inheritance.'

'Oh now you do tease me. *Mother* purchasing a house, for *me*? Would that she would,' he scoffed. 'No. If we are to see this thing through I'm afraid the shekels must come out of your pocket, Father.'

'Ah, well, yes, but . . . an updated Will is about to be drawn up. Naturally I shall bequeath most of my estate to you, being my only son and heir. Obviously your mother will have been overly generous with your sister, which means that some chap or the other will marry into money. Our family money.' He shook his head slowly. 'You know your sister as well as any of us. She'll likely marry a penniless artist or musician.' He leaned back in his chair and sniffed. 'You take my point, Herbert?'

'Not exactly, Father. But then I don't have your quick brain and I am the first to admit it.'

'Best have as little in your mother's pot as possible?'

'Ah!' he drooled, as if he hadn't already seen the plot. 'Clever. Very clever.'

'And if her darling daughter does have a tantrum . . . well, she can bloody well fork out for her as well. At least that way the house will be in your sister's name before some blighter comes along to carve off what he can.'

His mind working like a finely tuned machine, Herbert wanted the best out of this most unusual fatherly mood. 'Well, even if she did agree to fork out there'll be other costs involved, furnishing it and so forth. I suppose I could give up my career and get a proper job. But then as you know I've not your head for figures nor am I as astute when it comes to dealing with business people. I suppose I could apply for work in a shop,' he glanced furtively at his father's reaction: his frown was back. 'A gentleman's shop, obviously. Savile Row perhaps?'

'I beg your pardon, Herbert, but no son of mine will serve in a shop, no matter what or where it is.'

Point scored. 'Is there an opening in the bank, is that what you're getting at? A clerk. I could manage that.'

'No. No, I don't see us working for the same company. I should stick to what you know best. You appear to be doing rather well. Working alongside notable actors. I wouldn't mind one or two of them at the dinner table. Perhaps a fashionable playwright or two. Maybe a famous director.'

'So you think that Mother would lash out for decent furniture?'

'Good heavens, no.' He sipped a little more brandy and a faint smile was barely recognisable. 'I suppose my coffers can afford to be a little depleted. We must keep up the family name, after all.'

'Indeed,' said Herbert, wondering how he should best react. A bit of snobbery always helped where his father was concerned. 'Well, it sounds too good to be true, that is of course, if Mother spares me from where the middle classes seem to be merging, and the humiliation of those dreadful residential estates, with houses shoulder to shoulder.'

'God forbid a Wellington would ever sink to the

depths, m'boy,' said Tobias, standing bolt upright. 'So there's the deal, Herbert. Get yourself married and you'll be the proud owner of a house in the suburbs – Hampstead or perhaps Highgate, furnished modestly but in good taste. Your own taste, naturally.'

'Sounds idyllic, Father. A dream come true. But . . . sadly . . . I have yet to meet the right person. And as you say, one would need to find an efficient woman. One who could see to things. These days they are a rare commodity.'

'Well then, we shall have to write ourselves a list. What about the Waterston girls for instance? They're from good stock and not too unattractive.'

'Oh, please, Father . . .' groaned Herbert. 'Spare me those two dreadful ladies at least.'

'Well,' said Tobias, striding towards the door. 'I've said all I've to say on the matter. I must now brace myself for your mother's cousins, aunts and uncles. Thank the Lord your grandfather chose to stay in India.' With his hand on the doorknob, he stood regal. 'Find yourself a wife or continue to live in your garret, penniless.' With that he left his son to mull it over. But there was hardly any mulling to do. Of course Herbert could, as one or two of his acquaintances had done, marry to keep up appearances, but the very thought of touching a naked woman intimately repulsed him. He was going to have to plan his life very carefully to ensure that he got exactly what he wanted. One thing he did know, in this gender war which seemed to be growing, he would always remain the private man and keep his sexual preference under wraps . . .

The foolish Valerie Arkell Smith came to mind. This woman should never have married in the first place, to his way of seeing it. To give up her child for adoption and allow herself to live and dress as a man did nothing for the cause. Had she have been honest enough *not* to have changed her name and identity, more lesbians would have followed in her footsteps and furthered the crusade. In crossing the gender divide she was not alone, unsavoury stories of female-to-male cross dressers were littering the newspapers. It was all a little too grubby for Herbert who had immediately cut ties with the woman he might otherwise have admired for coming out into the open.

After an extremely busy and exhausting day of looking after the guests, Flora, having let the young people go to a local and lively tavern, sat by herself in the kitchen staring into the flames of the fire. Beanie had done her best to persuade her mother to go with them, but she was having none of it. She was more than tired, her feet ached, the muscles in her legs were throbbing and besides which, New Year's Eve had never really meant that much to her. Christmas was the time to celebrate and she had had a lovely time, all things considered. Now all she wanted was to be in her bed and wake up to the sound of church bells at dawn ringing in her new year. She had no desire to wait up until midnight to see the old year out. The trouble was that other people tended to think that people should not be alone on this night of the year. For this reason and this reason only she did feel a little on the lonely side.

When the clock on the landing above struck eleven she stretched, yawned and decided that it was time for her to sink her head into her feather pillow. The sound of laughter on the stairs seemed to be getting closer and when she heard footsteps coming down into the basement she prayed that this was not going to be a request for supper for thirty. It was Sarah Wellington and her brother Herbert who descended upon her.

'Cook! You're all by yourself,' said Sarah, in high spirits and flushed from drink. 'Where is everyone?'

'Out celebrating. It is New Year's Eve, after all.'

'Of course they are.' She turned to her brother and giggled. 'Be a lark if we could find them. Much more fun than upstairs. What say we go find them, Herb?'

'You'd have a job,' said Flora, knowing exactly where they had gone. 'It won't be one public house they'll visit tonight. A tavern crawl is what I heard.' She didn't want Herbert spoiling Beanie's New Year the way he had almost ruined their Christmas Day. 'You look a little more sober this evening, Mr Herbert. More sober than the last time I saw you below stairs.'

'I know, I know,' he said, bowing humbly and in a theatrical manner. 'I ask your forgiveness, Cook. I behaved intolerably and apologise.'

'Granted,' said Flora, her face serious. She would make the most of this. 'It doesn't fare well on the family name when you behave like a common drunk.'

'How so right you are, Cook . . . and wise. May I presume that I am in favour, once again?'

He never had been in her favour but she refrained from saying so. 'I very much appreciate you taking the trouble to come down and say how sorry you are, Mr Herbert. You may take it that I bear no grudge. Now if it's supper you're after, the larder is full. You'll find cold meats and cheese on the second shelf, bread in the—'

'Tut-tut!' he said, showing the flat of his hand. 'We did not come down to be served. We merely—'

'Oh, shut up Herbert.' Sarah slumped down in the other chair by the fire. 'Take no notice of him, Cook. He spends too much time with bloody actors. I'm sure he forgets who he is half the time.'

'Oh would that I could!' groaned Herbert, brushing a hand across his forehead. 'I sometimes wish I too had been born in the backstreets, Cook.'

'So what did you want then, Mr Herbert, if it isn't food?' She was too tired to listen or watch him perform.

'A bit of fun, Cook,' said Sarah. 'Where do you think your children might be now?'

'My children?' Flora knew her meaning but she was biding time. She didn't want these two to find Beanie, Fanny and Albert. They deserved a break away from the Wellingtons, no mistake.

'Oh, you know what I mean, and if they were your children you'd have every right to be as proud as punch. They're lively and fearless apart from all their other qualities. Creeping out after dark and off to jazz clubs . . .'

'Well yes, but that was only the *once* and they got a good grilling over it. It won't happen—'

'Oh, Cook! Don't be such a killjoy. Fun is something

we should all have once in a while, especially when you're young.'

'I dare say.'

'And as for the new girl, Beanie, my friends thought she was beautiful. One chum gave all three of them a lift home just so he could have her by his side.' A smile swept across Sarah's face. 'You can imagine how he felt when she chucked him. The women are usually all over him. What a lark!'

'Which was probably the reason why she would have nothing more to do with the gentleman. Beanie's a pretty girl and no doubt has had many admirers before starting work here.' She had and Flora knew it. 'I wish I could tell you where they might be this evening but I don't know. If you'll take my advice you won't venture out into the back and beyond at this time of night. You'll have your purse snatched or pockets picked. Rogues smell wealth from a mile off.'

'But we go to taverns all the time, Cook,' purred Sarah. 'From the bawdiest tavern to the best jazz clubs. A little of everything does you good.'

Bored with it all, Flora could see she was going to have to throw in a couple of taverns where they might find what they were looking for. If they bumped into Beanie and the other two, then so be it. 'You could try Kate O'Connor's in Salmon Lane or Mick Murphy's in the High Road. Or the Rising Sun in—'

'Yes, yes,' interrupted Herbert, 'I know where that is.'

You would, thought Flora. It was a popular tavern where men dressed as women and women as men.

'There'll be plenty of singing there tonight, I've no doubt.'

With that information the two of them bade her goodnight and happy new year. There was more than one reason why brother and sister were in search of Beanie. Earlier, in Herbert's bedroom, with the door closed, they had been talking and he had told all their father had said, except for the small matter of the gift of a house. Sarah, seizing the opportunity, agreed that he should find himself a wife. A liberated young lady though she was, the shame of having her friends betting that her brother wasn't all he should be, had caused her much embarrassment and more than once. He could go to prison should he ever be found out, and that thought made her blood run cold.

'Find yourself a ragged girl and coach her in the same way as in Bernard Shaw's play, *Pygmalion*,' had been her off-the-cuff reply and Herbert had seized upon the idea. Concentrating on grooming a 'lesser mortal', he could continue his secret lifestyle without anyone guessing. During their animated discussion on how it would work beautifully and be such a lark, Sarah mentioned Beanie from below stairs as a fine example. Again, Herbert, who lacked new ideas, pounced on it. The family scullery maid! Perfect!

He could have her trained to mix in high society and she would be forever grateful to her wonderfully kind husband. So much so he may never have to touch her. They would have separate bedrooms, naturally, as all part of her training. This was a gem of an idea that his nincompoop sister had come up with. At last, within the world into which he had been born, he would enjoy exaltation. His faked concern over human welfare and the alleviation of suffering of the lower classes would be received with applause.

After a brief tour of the taverns Sarah finally spotted Albert in the midst of a small crowd of lads, laughing heartily. Pushing their way through, she and her brother were as much home here as any of the locals who were done up to the nines and very much in a Christmas mood. By the time Sarah reached Albert, he was in full voice and hadn't seen her approach. Herbert slipped away to another corner where Beanie and Fanny were enjoying a group singsong by the piano. Fanny spotted him first and gave him a wink. 'Fancy you coming in 'ere, Mr Herbert,' she said, a little tipsy. 'Slumming 'cos it's New Year are yer?'

'My dear girl . . .'

'*My dear girl* . . .' she mimicked, teasing him. 'You're so bleeding posh, Herbert, it's a wonder you show yer face in 'ere.'

'I show my face,' he drooled, 'to all and sundry. An actor learns to be at home in all places and with all people.' He showed an actor's smile and glanced at Beanie who was taking no notice of him whatsoever. She looked lovely, there was no denying, not even from Herbert, should he be asked his opinion. Her hair was pinned back and up into a pleat with loose curly strands falling around her face, her eyes almost matching the deep blue hat with matching wide band of silk ribbon and small clutch of tiny silk flowers. Beneath her new unbuttoned blue coat, she wore a soft grey and blue striped blouse with her grandmother's silver cameo brooch at the collar and tiny earrings to match. Her black ankle boots, polished to look like new, were gleaming beneath her dark blue taffeta skirt.

'Gonna buy us a drink then, are yer? It being the new year?'

'It isn't quite,' he said. 'After midnight who knows . . .' he added, unable to keep the patronising tone from his voice.

'Ah, right,' Fanny cut in, 'I'll keep you to that. Drinks after midnight then. You're a saintly man all right,' she said, giving him a seductive wink, 'I'll give you a kiss that'll make you wanna bat different in the future.' This did no more than to cause him to inwardly shudder. The very thought of it!

'Actually,' he said, reaching out and taking a glass of ale from his sister who was at the bar and used to his stingy ways, 'you assume quite wrongly, Fanny my dear. I have friends and I have lovers. Friends are strictly male and lovers strictly female. Although, having said that, the females are carefully selected.' He held up a hand as if to stop her protesting but she had already become bored and he need not have bothered. 'I'm not saying that I only look to my own class, naturally.' He floated a finger, discreetly, towards Beanie. 'Now *there* is someone I could be taken with. Very much so, in fact.'

'Oh, right,' grinned Fanny, not believing a word of it but finding the vision of him and Beanie walking out amusing. 'Well you'd best get in quick then, 'adn't yer? Treat 'er to a double brandy, me old cock and she'll be too glassy-eyed to recognise yer.' With that, Fanny threw back her head and gave a hearty laugh. 'You never stop being an actor, do you Herbie? You must fink us lot 'ave sawdust for brains. If you're not as queer as folk think then I'm a brass farving.'

Disgusted by her coarse delivery he sighed deliberately and turned away. As a natural actor and trained by the very best of people he had to fancy himself what he would have others believe. He wove his way towards the small group in which Albert was holding court with Beanie listening. Certain that his presence would be more than appreciated, him being something of a celebrity, Herbert entered the arena, smiling. But Albert was in full flow and no one was going to stop him.

'Half an hour sooner and I would 'ave got in. It was Wembley Stadium for Christ sake! The Wembley cup final! They should 'ave known that thousands would 'ave turned up. Ticket touts, that's wot it was about. Under the counter ticket. I mean I ask you – a cup final – Bolton Wanderers and West Ham United. What did they expect? Thousands of us turned up and thousands were not only disappointed but bloody angry. They climbed fences . . . course they did. Bound to.' He paused while he swallowed some beer. All this talking was making him thirsty.

'They never really stormed the barriers though, Albert, surely not. That was the press 'aving a field day, wasn't it?'

'No, mate,' he said, licking his lips. 'There was a lot of casualties. Hundreds of blokes invaded the game. Stormed the blooming barriers and then Bolton Wanderers go and beat West Ham by two goals. West Ham should 'ave won. Would have done too if—'

'Sounds more dramatic than any play I've been in,' said Herbert, rudely interrupting to get the limelight. 'But there we are, it's all over and done with. Now tell me . . . did any one of you manage to see that marvellous play, *The Sea Urchin* at the Strand earlier this year?'

This strange question was certainly a show stopper. Here was a man from another walk of life interrupting a football story to ask about a West End play? Herbert either took their silence to mean that they were interested or he was once again, as so often happened, bulldozing his way through. His presentation, his stance, his expression, had somehow intimidated this otherwise unyielding group of East Londoners. 'Peggy O'Neil was a star! I wish that at least one of you had been there to enjoy a brief reminisce of a fine play. The playwright on this occasion did us proud.' He looked from one to the other of them, smiling as if he meant it. 'How strange the world of theatre is. He has always been, I modestly confess, a fan of *mine* . . . and here I am . . . turning the tables.' He looked up to the heavens, still smiling, and shook his head slowly. 'And to think I turned down a part in one of his plays.'

'This is Herbert,' said Beanie, bringing him down from his heights. 'He's the son of our boss. Me, Fanny and Albert, that is.' She then turned to Herbert and grinned. 'Did you manage to get a ticket to the big match at Wembley then?'

'No. Football matches aren't exactly the place that actors—'

'Of course not,' said Beanie cutting in. 'Bit like us lot . . . we'd find the sort of play you're talking about a bit on the boring side, I expect. Horses for courses.' She turned to Albert and sniffed. 'Right. Time for the next tavern. We'll leave you lot to Herbert. He knows a lot of actors. Gonna be famous one day, ain't you, Herb?'

Furious with this underling putting him down in public, Herbert used all of his will-power not to bark sarcastically back at her. If he was to appease his father and get his house, he would need the little cow to agree to marry him. It was a trump of an idea and he was not going to let it slip through his fingers. He would simply have to show respect for the cockney until marriage contracts had been signed, when he could then treat her like the servant she was. She would be excellent in her natural role as obedient servant, wife, once she had been trained according to Bernard Shaw's novel idea.

'Yep,' said Beanie, enjoying herself. 'Herbert will be a very famous actor – one day.'

'Oh never famous, Beanie. Just happy in my work. And as for football . . . of course we would love to have the time to go but you know . . . Directors are very hard on us. They work us like dogs and for peanuts.'

This little speech did the trick. The group relaxed

and almost felt sorry for him. There was a slap on the back from the eldest in the group. 'Never you mind, old son. Give us the nod when you've got a bit of time between shows and we'll get you to the best match going. Now then . . . what's your poison?'

If only we knew, thought Beanie. 'There you go, Herbert. We leave you in good company. Enjoy yourself and –'

'No no no, my dear!' His power was to the fore. He had to win her over. 'It is you and Fanny . . . and of course Albert here, that I came in search of. That *we* came in search of. Sarah had this bright idea of finding you and spending New Year's Eve in your company. A thank you for putting up with me and that dreadful man, Gerald . . .' he waved a hand in the air '. . .what ever his name was. A hanger on, I'm afraid.' He was addressing his audience once again. 'A bit part actor who wishes to rub shoulders with those of us who are further up the ladder. Couldn't get rid of the pest. He caused a terrible row . . . a bit of a punch-up in fact.'

'A punch-up?' voiced one of the group, amazed. 'I never thought your lot went in for punch-ups. Thought you was too posh for that.'

'Oh please, don't let the accent fool you. We are all the same under the skin, my friend. I, unfortunately, have been cursed with this dreadful upper-class inflection. Don't judge me for it,' he whimpered pleadingly.

'Come on,' said Albert, taking Beanie's arm. 'Let's find Fanny and get on the move. I've 'eard enough.'

Had it not been for Sarah working on Fanny in

order to keep her there, Herbert would have been left high and dry. Instead of them leaving the public house she had managed to get a table in the corner of the packed tavern and there was nothing Albert or Beanie could do about it. They were going to have to put up with utterly boring Herbert, and on New Year's Eve!

The sense of being trapped soon left Beanie. Herbert's acting ability stretched far and he managed to not only talk in a normal voice but bring his accent down and lose the twang and . . . actually enjoy this impromptu part. This is how he saw it. He was merely a player in a production of his own making. He asked Beanie about her childhood and managed to look and sound sympathetic when she gave a new version of her past. The roles were being reversed. She was now the actress and in fine fettle. She had all three listening with watery eyes.

'Mum was devastated when she heard that dad'd been killed in the war. He never came back and he was never found. Blown to smithereens was the story. Mum was ever so sad over it but then, just as she was coming out of her black mood which lasted a good five years she heard from one of his mates that he never was blown up.' Beanie paused, enjoying herself. She had them leaning forward and listening.

'The man meant well. But once he broke the news that dad never was killed but legged it to America with some wealthy woman, changing 'is name and identity, that nearly finished her off. She went into a deep depression and then one day, when I came 'ome from school . . .' she dabbed her eyes with her new Christmas handkerchief, '. . . all I could smell coming out of our little house was gas. Then when I opened the door and looked through to the kitchen I saw her legs. I knew what she'd done. I knew she'd put her head in the gas oven.'

'Oh . . . you poor sweet, dear, thing,' said Herbert, taken in by her performance.

'I 'ad to go and live with an aunt after that. My dad's sister. She never knew about dad legging it and I never told 'er. Which really made it worse. She kept goin' on about Mum having been seen out with other men. Called her all sorts of names. Said she should 'ave bin content to be a war widow . . . should 'ave bin proud of it. That her husband had died fighting for 'is country and all she could do was go out with other men. She said that Mum killed 'erself 'cos no man would take 'er on and marry 'er.' She raised her lovely blue eyes to the ceiling. 'Never mind, Mum, in heaven, we know the truth and that's all that matters.'

By now, tears were rolling down Fanny's sorry face and Albert was a little more than watery eyed. They had actually believed this story. Sarah however, showed no emotion. Looking from one to the other, she spoke in a quiet caring voice. 'Go up to the bar, there's good chaps. I think Beanie needs a few private moment. I'll stay with her. Get the drinks in, Herbert, and make them shorts. Brandies all round I would have thought.'

Having little choice, Herbert agreed quietly and led the other two away, leaving Sarah and Beanie alone. 'I do not know, Bea,' said Sarah looking directly into her face, 'how I managed not to burst out laughing! What a rocking performance. And what a cracking tale. Where did it all come from?'

'Oh . . . so you saw right through it then? You kept a straight face though. I was watching yer.'

'I know you were. And I was watching you.' She began to chuckle.

'Be careful . . . they'll see us laughing and that'll only upset Fanny. She'll think that we're making fun of 'em.'

'Don't be such a nincompoop. I'm cheering you up, aren't I? Telling you that your mother's in heaven and you'll be with her one day.'

'They wouldn't go for that. We're not simple, you know . . . just 'cos we work in the kitchen. Don't mean to say we've not got a brain.'

'No, I know,' said Sarah, ashamed. 'I can't help it, Beanie—'

'Call me Bea, everyone else does.'

'I can't help being the way I am, Bea. It's the way we've been brought up, Herb and I. I've seen other families, not as . . . well you know . . . wealthy as us – and they seem so much more relaxed about things. My father is so ruddy irritable all the time!'

'Maybe he's got good cause to be irritable. Work and that.'

'No. I don't think it's that. What about your father? Is he a jolly sort? Easy going?'

'He probably was, yeah.' Beanie looked into Sarah's face and shrugged. 'He was killed during the war. At the beginning. I was only nine.'

'Oh you poor thing. But you must remember him . . . surely?'

'No. He was in the navy so away at sea for most of when I was little. My granddad told me all about 'im though. Even showed me a picture of 'im in uniform. He looked really nice.' The photograph that Beanie had been shown was the son of her granddad's friend, borrowed for the cause.

'So, did your grandparents bring you up?' Sarah was talking to Beanie as she had never talked to anyone before. Her friends, herself included, only ever talked on a superficial plane.

'Not really, no. It was me, my mum and grand-parents all in a two up two down. They were always there from the beginning though, so I s'pose they helped bring me up, yeah.'

'It sounds cosy,' said Sarah, sipping the remains of her drink. 'Very cosy and loving.'

'Yeah. It was.'

'And now?'

'And now I've chosen of my own free will to be a live-in maid. I'm happy, they're happy . . .'

'Really?' Sarah cut in. 'Honestly happy working below stairs?'

'Of course. We're like a family down there. Well . . . you 'ave to be to make it all work. But yeah . . . it's good. And Cook's like a mother to all of us.'

'And you don't miss having a father?'

'No. Never even thought about it. Why – would you be lost without yours?'

'Hardly,' said Sarah smiling and rising. 'Come on, we'll join the others.'

The raucous laughter above the din of chatter and the plonking of the piano keyboard was creating a magic atmosphere in the tavern but while Sarah had been bonding with Beanie her brother Herbert had found himself in dangerous waters. He had a knack of antagonising all and sundry. This time it was a young man from Essex who had brought his fiancée into this part of London knowing a good time was guaranteed. Accompanying him were two stevedores from the London docks where he too was employed as clerk.

'Far be it from someone like myself to correct you, sir,' voiced Herbert, 'but I did *not* infer that your friend was anything other than a beefy young man.' The one thing that Herbert did lack was the ability to stop acting at the right time. Pressing a hand to his chest and tilting his shoulders forward he sported innocence. 'I am no more than a man of the stage. Would that I had your wit. I express what the playwright puts to paper . . . whereas *you*, sir . . .' he clasped his hands together and raised his eyes to heaven. 'You, dear boy, have a masterly way with words. Wit is in the eye of the beholder and I behold.' At this point he bowed majestically and at this same point he felt a sharp pain to his jaw as he went flying through the little space between himself and others who had already sensed trouble and had backed away.

Miraculously there was hardly a broken glass or bottle as he came crashing to the floor, his arms flailing. In this part of the world a punch-up was quite normal and the people simply stepped aside. But this was a little more than normal. Herbert had looked too long at one of the men and had made no effort to try and hide his lust. Not that that was a problem in itself but he was a queen on the prowl to their way of thinking. Before he could even think about heaving himself from the floor, two strong arms linked with his and hauled him up, dragging him to the door, out of which he was thrown to land with another bump on the pavement. 'Methinks you do protest too much, sir!' was his damning statement. The men he had assumed to be a couple were still in the doorway.

'And *me* thinks that you won't see this new year out, mate!'

'Stay out of this part of London, old cock, if you know what's good for yer! And thank yer lucky stars it's New Year's Eve! You've bin spared!'

'I shall never be deprived of my birthright! I was born here, sir!' He thumped his heart with a hand and left it there. 'I have lived for most of my life in East London whereas you . . . you are an interloper. Go back to Essex I say!'

The two men looked at each other and weighed up the odds. Should they give him a good beating now and spoil their evening or not bother. They decided on the latter.

Herbert decided to depart while the going was good.

On his way back to Beaumont Square he cursed his father for making such a ridiculous suggestion. Marriage indeed. And as for his sister Sarah proposing the common girl from below stairs . . . he shuddered at the thought of himself courting the cockney. Arriving at number ten, swaying from the effect of his double whiskies, he came upon the cousin from Newmarket, Digby Morton.

'Good heavens, Digby old boy, you're not going out *there*, are you?'

'I thought I might find a tavern more lively than upstairs, Herbert. I'm afraid the aunts and uncles are reminiscing, yet again.'

'Well, be it on your own head, Digby,' said Herbert showing the flat of his hand. But I beg you, please do not say that your cousin did not warn you.' He stretched an arm forward and pointed a warning finger at the streets beyond the square. 'It is a hellhole out there! A snake-pit! Far be it from me to advise a cousin five years my senior.'

'Six, Herbert. I should splash some cold water on your face before you present yourself. You are already very drunk.' With that, Digby Morton made his leave.

'Haven't you forgotten something, dear boy?'

'I think not, Herbert!' Digby did not look back.

'Are you not going to wish me a happy new year? A year filled with offers and lead parts?'

'Goodnight, Herbert!'

Leaning on the door of number ten, Herbert felt nothing but despair for his cold cousin from Newmarket. "The man hath no soul . . . and one can do no more than find it in one's heart to forgive his lack of passion. Would that I, for one solitary day, may be less fired with such *intense* feelings.' This he voiced while pulling on the highly polished bell ring. It was Flora who came to the door. She looked at him but said nothing. Her expression should have been enough. Standing aside, she waved him in the way her mother used to wave in her father when he had had a good night out at the pub.

'Oh, Cook. *Dear* Cook. What an angel of mercy you are.' He stumbled past her and made his way, swaying from side to side, to the wide and winding staircase from whence came overly loud conversation and laughter. 'Oh to be in the house of the home. Such joy! Such recompense! Such—'

'Is there anything I can get for you, Master Herbert? Perhaps a large glass of water? It's a wonder you haven't collapsed on the way home. I fear you might have had one or two over the odds.'

'My dear woman, the only thing you can get that would make this New Year's Eve complete, is an early night. It pains me to see you at my beck and call.'

'I shouldn't worry about that. I intend to stay awake and see the year in myself.'

He turned slowly to look into her face. 'Well of *course* you would. Of course of course you would! What *was* I thinking? And no doubt you would rather see it in with a handsome man lying beside you but . . .'

'Begging your pardon, Master Herbert, but I shed my corset for no man!'

'I was thinking of your husband, madam. For do you not wear a gold band upon your finger?'

'I do sir, you are quite right. I apologise.' With that, Flora turned away and left the drunk to himself.

'Cook, don't go . . . please . . . I have something to tell you . . .'

Stopping in her track she looked back at him and waited. Certain that anything he had to say would be a waste of time. 'Well then, Master Herbert, what is it?'

'You promise not to tell my parents?'

'If I must.'

'Say it for me. Say you promise.'

'I promise.'

'I was set upon by two bully boys and brutally beaten. And worse then that . . . I was thrown out of the tavern as if I were a common drunk. Thrown, Cook! Tossed into the gutter.' The drink getting the better of him, he began to sob like a baby. Still Flora could hardly tell if this was another of his acting fiascos or whether or not he was truly upset. Moving closer to him, she stroked his hair as he sat crumpled on the staircase.

'You make trouble for yourself, lad, that's the nub of it. You drink too much too fast and then go and provoke people. What about your sister? Is she still in the tavern? I saw you going out with her.'

Blotting his face with his sparkling white handkerchief he nodded. 'The scullery girls are there too and that wretched bootboy.' He took a long slow breath and seemed the better for it. 'It was partly his fault and

partly the fault of that vulgar girl who goes by the name
of Fanny. They deem fit to mix with the very *lowest*
of the *low*.' Having shifted the blame from himself he
felt better for it. 'Women . . . are at the bottom of
everything. I shall *never* marry, Cook. It is a woman's
business to get married as soon as possible and a man's
to keep unmarried as *long* . . . as he can.'

'I should turn in as soon as possible if I were you,
Master Herbert. You don't want to collapse in front
of your guests above stairs.'

He was not listening. 'I shall have a word with
mother. Sack the lot of them is what I say.' With
that he turned away and climbed the stairs without
a bye or leave.

'I shouldn't go into the drawing room if I were you!
You're in no fit state –'

Flapping a hand at the silly woman he continued
up to where the laughter was coming from, wondering
what he might recite for the guests and inwardly
scolding himself for deserting a sinking ship. How
could this motley crowd enjoy themselves without a
professional entertainer? He would recite something
from the great master himself – Shakespeare!

Back in the kitchen, Flora poured milk into a small
saucepan, ready for her cocoa. She would sit by the
fire and let the old year go and welcome the new
by herself. Of course Beanie would rather be out
with the young people having a lively time and why
not? She thought back to when she was her age and
again Tobias Wellington came to mind. Her memories
though no longer held romance, especially since she

had just had another small run in with his son – Beanie's half brother. At least the two daughters of the man were together and for some strange reason Flora gleaned some small pleasure from that. After all she had nothing to offer Beanie on this special night. Other than her grandparents the child had no relatives that she knew of, Flora having been an only child. *If only* was running through her mind now. If *only* her Prince Charlie had meant all he had said long ago when they would meet in secret and after they had made love. She had truly believed that he loved her and foolishly believed that one day they would be man and wife – that he would seek a divorce. But she had no regrets where her daughter was concerned. She loved her more than she imagined she ever could love a child and her only sadness right then was that Beanie was at that age when wings were strong and the desire to explore other territories, stronger. No doubt she would fly away in a year or two to find adventure or to settle down and be married. Whichever way it turned out, one thing was for certain, Flora was in for a lonely life unless she did something about it. But what could she do? Walk around with a banner advertising for a friend for company?

Pouring the hot milk into her own blue and white mug she realised that her melancholy mood was due to the time of year and not from the laughter from above that she had heard when opening the main door to the drunken son of the no doubt drunken father upstairs. Back in her chair by the fire, she asked herself silly questions since there was no one else around to talk to and not caring if someone should arrive and hear the ramblings of a lonely woman.

'What would the consequences be, I wonder,' she murmured, half smiling, 'if I were to go up there and announce the news to the family that there were not two heirs to the Wellington fortune but three? Would Sir be shocked or pleased that his other daughter was living under the same roof? And how would Grace Wellington take it?' Glancing at the clock she was surprised that it was no later than eleven o'clock. Still an hour to go. The tapping on the basement door took her by surprise. Had Beanie realised that she badly wanted her there? Wasting no time she turned the key in the door and opened it, only to find Lenny the gardener standing there with a small Christmas rose in a small terracotta pot.

'This was meant for a Christmas present, Flora, but it hadn't flowered you see so I didn't think it good enough. But look 'ere . . . this rose came out just this afternoon.'

Touched by his thoughtful ways, she ushered him in and pulled another chair up to the fire. Ten years her senior, she could have seen him as a fatherly figure but she didn't. He was a friend. A trusted friend. 'You shouldn't have come out on such a cold night, Lenny. There's snow up there ready to come down again or my name's not Flora Brown.'

'Brown, eh,' he said, warming his hands by the fire. 'Well, well, I never had you down for a Brown.' He scratched his head, a well worn habit. 'I don't know why but I thought you would 'ave 'ad a more unusual name if you take my meaning. Nothing wrong with Brown but no ... I would 'ave said you were a Turner or Baker ... something like that. Know what I mean?'

Laughing at his way of thinking and his serious expression she was very pleased that he had deigned to show his face. Yes, company was what she had been craving and the lack of it had made her a touch melancholy. 'Why don't you light your pipe, Lenny, make yourself at home? Would you care for a bit of supper?'

'No.' He shook his head. 'I shan't stop to see the new year in. I wouldn't do that. I dare say you prefer to sit by yourself at a time like this.'

'I dare say I would not! But if you would rather be in your own little place then –'

'I should cocoa,' he said, lighting his pipe. 'It's a bit on the lonely side if you know what I mean. Not that I mind my own company but certain times ...'

'It's nice to hear another voice in the room. Yes, I know what you mean and I'm pleased you came and I'll be even more pleased if you stay till midnight.'

'Oh well, in that case I will,' he said. 'In that case I will.'

'Did you want to play a game of cards?' she said, wondering what on earth they would talk about if they did nothing else but sit looking at the fire.

'No, I'm not in the mood if you know what I mean. I'm more'n happy to just sit. If that's all right with you. My late wife was deaf you know, so I'm used to just sitting. But then I never was one for conversation. You never know what to say at times, do you?'

'That's very true. So how long have you been on your own then?'

'Let me think now . . .' He closed his eyes and counted under his breath. 'Yes, I should reckon it must be that by now . . . a good ten years, maybe eleven. She died peacefully, thank the Lord. I managed a nice little funeral tea. She's buried in a tiny churchyard in Globe Road. That's what she wanted, yes it was very nice. All of her family came, you know. Mine too. Lovely turn out.'

'Oh well then, that was all right,' said Flora, quite comfortable in her armchair and in his company. 'I take it you never had children. Because I've not heard you mention any, have I?'

'No that's right. On account of her being deaf. She didn't wanna trust herself not waking up when she should. That kind of thing. And what with me being out at work all day and sometimes working overtime. She was worried about that.'

'And what about you? Did you miss not being a father?'

'No . . . what you don't 'ave you don't miss. No, I'm not one for regrets. What about you? I mean to say you never even married, girl, did you? It must 'ave been out of choice because you're a handsome woman. I will say that and I don't mean nothing by it. Take it as it was meant – an honest to goodness bit of truth. A compliment if you like.'

'I shall take it as a compliment. And thank you for saying so. You've got brothers and sisters then?'

'Oh, yes, I've got brothers and sisters. Not all of 'em

are still alive but mother 'ad ten altogether so . . . there we are. What about you?'

'Only child.'

'Ah . . . um. Shame that. Still . . . there's a reason for everything. Perhaps you were meant not to 'ave family to fuss over, eh?'

'Who knows, Lenny? Who knows?'

'Mmm. What about if I treat you to see a moving picture one of these days? You'd like that, would you? 'Cos a soul has to have an alternative to work, you know. Bit of leisure, if you get my drift.'

'Well that would be very nice, Lenny. Very nice. I'll buy some sweets for us to suck and you can pay for the tickets.'

'Nothing in it, mind. I'm a bit older than you and apart from not 'aving much money I've got no sex neither. All that died with my first wife. No sense, no feeling, eh,' he chuckled, not in the least bit embarrassed. 'I've got a friend, mind you, now he's more your age. Works in the canning factory; lovely fella. So if ever you fancy going out . . . you know . . . for a change of company and a bit of romance . . . I think you'd like 'im and I know he'd like you. Yes, you're a handsome woman and a good cook. What more could a man your age want, eh?'

'Oh, I wouldn't know about that.' So easy in his company, she was very tempted to break her confidence of over twenty years and pour out her whole story.

'And you know that daughter of yours is the image of you. She is that. Not the eyes so much but she's got your features.' He said this so matter-of-factly and without blinking an eyelid that Flora wondered if she had ever let it slip. She was flabbergasted.

'Well . . .' she mumbled, once she'd found her voice. 'I can't lie to you, Lenny, and I shan't deny my own child. But how on earth did you know?'

He threw back his head and laughed at her. 'In our neck of the woods and you ask me that?' Shocked by this, Flora felt herself go cold. Did everyone know?

'A mate of mine worked at the clay pipe factory before they closed it down . . . and course . . . with that job went the little house in the court yard. I only popped round there once or twice before they moved but I must 'ave spotted you 'cos I recognised you the minute you walked out into that garden out there. He soon filled me in . . . but I never told 'im where you was working now. No. I'm not one for gossip. You want people to know, you'll go and tell 'em yerself. That's 'ow I see it. Fancy another cup of cocoa? My round.'

Still in shock, although not angry or hurt by it, Flora nodded. 'Yes please. And you'll find some shortbread in the biscuit tin. I take it you don't know who the father is too?'

'Oh no. No, we didn't discuss your personal business. No. He just 'appened to mention you 'ad a daughter called Beanie, that's all. Can't remember now 'ow it came out. Shall I fetch the tin in or put a few on a plate?'

'The tin'll do.' What a strange world this was, thought Flora. Everything had changed within the last fifteen minutes since he arrived. He knew the secret. Had known it all this time. And it didn't matter. Her mind was beginning to turn over. 'Would you like to know a secret, Lennie? But it could shock you.'

'Not really. I like a nice even sort of life. That does me.'

'Well, I'm in a mischievous mood now – don't know why – so I'll tell you. I want you to know who Beanie's father is.'

'Go on? You sure about that? I mean, it takes a few seconds to tell and then you're stuck with me knowing for a lifetime. If you stop on as Cook, that is.'

'It's Mr Wellington.'

The sound of the biscuit tin hitting the stone floor made her smile.

'Love a duck,' he said, 'love a blooming duck. Well . . . now . . . you have shocked me. Does his missus know?'

'No, Lenny, she doesn't. Pick up the biscuit tin, make the cocoa and come and sit down. I'll tell you the whole blooming story.' And tell it she would. She surprised herself at how happy she was to have a trusted ear. Yes, Flora was ready to tell her mate everything.

5

The atmosphere in the tavern at ten minutes to midnight was building up in a crescendo. Without the worry of Herbert causing trouble, Beanie, Sarah, Fanny and Albert were in high spirits, singing and dancing along to the piano man with the rest of the crowd. The atmosphere was magic. When Digby Morton, this being the third tavern he had checked, stepped into the open doorway it was Beanie who spotted him first and who waved him over. She was at the time managing in the very limited space to do the charleston with Fanny and Sarah. Digby's first reaction was to step back outside. Crowded places and especially noisy taverns were not high on his list of pleasures, but Beanie was not going to let him off the hook. Pushing through others who were in full swing she arrived in front of him, smiling and a little tipsy.

'Don't be put off by the noise, ten minutes and it'll be over. Come on, Mr Morton . . . let your hair down!' She grabbed his arm when he made a polite show of declining the offer. 'Come on, sir. Your cousin Sarah's the odd one out in this place. I bet she could do with a bit of support. Come on . . . please . . . just this once. Once in your lifetime. Do it for Sarah.'

Looking through the mass of moving bodies he managed to catch Sarah's eye and she was smiling at him. Smiling radiantly and looking happier than he had ever seen her. 'I shall come in, but I ask you not to force me on to the dance floor. I would much prefer a quiet corner, if anything.'

'Quiet?' said Beanie, giggling. 'A corner, yeah . . . but never quiet.' She took his hand and pulled him through, touched by his bewildered expression.

True to his word, Digby Morton found himself a chair in a corner, content with the gin and tonic which had been thrust into his hand by his cousin Sarah. But at one minute to midnight when the music and dancing stopped and a circle of overly happy people formed, he showed no resistance to being pulled up from his chair to join in. With Sarah one side and Beanie on the other he crossed his arms and held their hands and appreciated the silence that gradually came as they waited to hear the chimes of the town hall clock followed by a heart-rending chorus of 'Auld Lang Syne'. Surprising himself, he did not retreat back into his corner when the sound of exuberant voices filled the tavern as folks wished one and all a happy new year. The brushing of a kiss on cheeks he found easier than he imagined but when he came face to face with Beanie in the midst of the turmoil he did no more than look into her face and she did no more than smile back at him shyly. Then surprising himself, he took her by the hand and led her outside into the street. Again with no words passing between them, they walked hand in hand towards the small gaslit green in Sidney Square.

'If the air is too cold for you we could always—'

'No,' said Beanie, stopping him mid-sentence. 'It's not too cold, and I like it here. It's where I sometimes come when I need to be by myself. Not all the benches are safe to sit on though,' she said, giving one of the four wooden slatted iron benches a shake. 'See what I mean?'

'Which one do you recommend?' he said, quietly chuckling. 'If any?'

'The one over there in the corner by the lamplight. It's usually taken at any time of the day or night but it's New Year's Eve and everyone's celebrating. Which brings me to somefing which has been puzzling me.'

'Why I am here and not in my country house, celebrating?'

'Tch. I might 'ave known you could read minds as well.'

'As well as what?' he said, gazing at her face in profile under the lamplight. Her lovely, honest face.

'Nothing in particular. So why did you choose to spend a time like this in this dump of a place? Mixing with working-class people when you could be done up to the nines at some ball or the other?'

Taking his time to answer, he said, 'Why do you call it a dump of a place? The humour is rough and coarse but there is always laughter. It's steeped in history. The Romans swam in the river as did the Saxons when they arrived. The best of poets, playwrights and novelists have found a wealth of material and great architectures have left their mark. Whereas, in my country house I am surrounded only by my own arable land – glorious though the sunsets are – it does not compare to the riches of this small area of London town.'

'Oh right . . .' said Beanie, feeling less conscious of the class gap between them. 'I can see what you're gettin' at. Us lot can't wait to get out into the fresh air and cornfields with all them poppies and your lot come down to London for the buzz and 'istory.' She shrugged as she smiled into his earnest face. 'Funny old world innit?'

'I'm one of the fortunate ones in that I am able to enjoy both worlds.'

'But if push came to shove . . . where would you choose to be if you couldn't come and go as you please?'

'I can't answer that, I'm afraid. I've not given it any thought.'

'Well never mind that . . . off the cuff . . . go on . . . country or town?'

'Town.'

'West End or East End?'

'East.'

'Never,' said Beanie, giggling. 'Never never never in a month of Sundays would someone like yourself be 'appy living in Stepney. That's a bit of pie in the sky, Mr Morton, if you don't mind my saying so?'

'I don't mind your saying so if you don't mind my telling you that you're quite wrong. My cousin Grace and second cousin, Sarah, choose to live here and not at Laversham Hall.'

'That's true,' murmured Beanie, thoughtful. 'That shows you really . . . how different we are. I'd love to

live in the country and so would most East End people.
Do you mind if I ask you another question?'

'So long as you don't mind if I decline to answer.'

'All right,' she said, trying to find the right way to
present her question. 'It's just a little thing but . . .
well . . . people from your walk of life, do they hold
hands as a matter of the right thing to do, never mind
who they might be walking along with? Providing they
know who they are, of course. Only round this way,
it's sort of different. We don't do that unless you're
walking out wiv someone. I only ask because you're
not the first that's done that. One of Sarah's friends
took me out for a drive in 'is car and a walk round a
park and he took my hand as well. I never knew quite
what to make of that, but since you've done it as well
I s'pose it's gentlemanly manners. I expect that's what
it must be.'

She turned her face slightly towards his to see if
his normal serious expression was back. It was but
for reasons that never entered her head. Could it be
that the seemingly unemotional Digby Morton might
be falling for her? 'Well . . . Mr Morton?'

'I can't remember the question, Miss Brown,' he
said, amused by her honesty. 'I have a feeling you've
answered it for yourself.' He withdrew his gold watch
from his waistcoat pocket and leaned back in order to
see it more clearly under the light. 'I think we ought
to be getting back to the tavern before tongues start
to wag.'

'That's true,' she said, up from her seat in a flash.
'Let's be getting back, then.'

Taking his time, Digby rose and once again took her hand, pleased that she seemed far more relaxed now that she believed she had the answer to why he was holding it. Walking slowly along in silence, one question in particular kept forcing its way into his mind: Why had she been drifting in and out of his thoughts since the very first time he set eyes on her in the drawing room of number ten?

The excitement in the tavern over, the happy revellers were pouring out with small groups going their separate ways to various parties. Singing could be heard echoing through the backstreets and beyond. Celebrations were beginning all over again. Invitations had been bandied around the tavern, all and sundry were welcome to any of the parties, including Sarah and her friends. Sarah as always, had managed to break through the class barrier and was all for stopping out until dawn or when people dropped exhausted into their beds. Having done her utmost to persuade Fanny and Albert to go with her, she finally gave in to their refusal and linked arms with a handsome young man, a market vendor who sold popcorn.

Walking slowly back to number ten, in Fanny and Albert's footsteps and with Beanie by his side, Digby Morton was quiet and thoughtful. Beanie wasn't sure whether she was meant to make conversation or not. She finally did what she wanted and stopped thinking of social manners. 'Did you enjoy your dinner this evening, Mr Morton?' she said, unable to think of anything else to say.

'I did. Did you have a good Christmas?'

'Oh yeah, well in a way I did. Master Herbert and a pal of 'is butted in and spoiled things a bit. And once they'd filled their bellies and drank too much, they started to argue and a fight broke out.'

'And did he and his pal stop overnight?'

'They did, Mr Morton. And what's more they weren't expected, still it's none of my business. I felt very sorry for his friend. Master Herbert was so rude to him. Couldn't blame Mr Fairweather for up and leaving like that. Never even said goodbye or anything.'

'So they spoiled your Christmas,' he said, looking straight ahead, not even glancing at her.

'Not really. We 'ad a lovely time in the end.'

'Better than if you had gone home to your relatives?'

'I'm not sure how to answer that. So if you don't mind and you won't fink I'm rude, I shan't.'

'As you wish,' he said, glancing furtively at her face and wondering if he might kiss her lightly on those angelic lips.

'I take it you want to be treated the same at the table tomorrow, Mr Morton – no meat and no fuss?'

'Of course. Why would I want it any other way?' He turned his head slowly and looked at her closely, waiting for an answer and could not help the sensation that swept through him as the light from the gas lamp spilled over her lovely face. 'Unlike my cousin, I do not change with the weather, Beanie.' This was the first time he had called her by name. 'I have never eaten meat and I have no desire to. I'm sure there are certain foods that you dislike.'

'You're not on trial for not liking meat, Mr Morton. I was just checking, that's all. Or as my mother used to say, making polite conversation.'

Digby went quiet. She had mentioned her mother almost in the past tense. This girl, to his mind was clever. She gave nothing or very little away when it came to her personal life which caused him to want to know more. Drawing closer to number ten, he could see that the lights in the drawing room were on and from the sound of the piano his dreadful Aunt Maud was playing her party piece, which in itself was bad enough, but what usually followed was a poetry reading from Lord Tennyson's works which she never managed to get right. She always read as if broken-hearted.

'I imagine you must be very tired,' he said at last. 'I do hope your room is at the very top of the house. By the look of things the family festivities are not yet at an end.'

'Oh no. I'm too excited to be tired. It's a new day of a new month of a new year and I can feel it. It's in the air, Mr Morton. That "something special" that you can't see or touch but you know is there . . .'

'Yes,' he said, 'I know exactly what you mean.' He was thinking about something quite different. Love was on his mind.

Arriving at the ornate iron gate he bade her goodnight and politely brushed a kiss across her hand, his head slightly tilted so that their eyes would meet. 'Thank you for your hospitality,' he all but whispered, leaving her in a state of heavenly bliss as she walked down the steps into the basement.

Seeing her mother as snug as a bug by the fireside with Lenny the gardener warmed her heart. She had not been alone on New Year's Eve after all. Albert and Fanny were sitting at the table. 'Something smells good,' Beanie said, peeling off her coat. 'Smells a bit like mince pies to me, Cook.'

'Yes,' said Flora, 'I always put a few in the oven at this time and on this new day. And they always go faster than the ones I bake on Christmas Day.' She looked slyly at Beanie and winked, the sherry had taken effect and she was more relaxed than she had been in a very long time. 'Of course, you wouldn't know that . . . this being my first Christmas spent with you.'

'That's right, Cook,' returned Beanie, winking back at her discreetly.

'Best mince pies I've ever tasted.' Albert was already biting into one and checking to see how many more were left on the plate. 'You won't wanna be eatin' them, Fanny love. They'll make you too fat to get through that pantry window next time we get locked out.'

'Very amusing, Albert,' said Flora, giving him the evil eye, daring him ever to do such a thing again.

'Well, everyone,' said Lenny. 'I'm gonna love and leave yer. I like your company but I don't like your hours. I'm off 'ome.' Pulling himself out of his arm-chair he patted Flora on the shoulder. 'Thanks for a lovely evening. Best new year I've 'ad in a long time. We must do it again, sometime.'

'Oh, so we've got to wait a full year, have we?'

'Well no, not really, but I can't just come and go in the evenings as I please. You might be busy down 'ere or pleased with your own company.'

'If you're passing, Lenny, whistle down the basement. If I open the door I open it, if I don't I don't. How does that suit you?'

'Just the ticket. Good night all and Happy New Year. God bless the lot of yer!' With that he left the way he came in, via the servants' door instead of the tradesmen's entrance to the side of the house. Lenny had moved up a notch.

'So,' said Flora, prising open the lid of the cocoa tin, 'by the looks on your faces a good time was had by all.'

'It was smashing, Cook.' Albert helped himself to another mince pie. 'Silly arse came and went, but this time we never let 'im worry us, did we, Fan?'

'Worry? I should say not. He can come to the tavern when we're there any old time. Free entertainment he is. You want a ringside seat when he's around. He might as well wear a placard round 'is neck: Kick my arse, I'm a snooty git!'

'Tut-tut, Fanny! Your language gets worse. And I do wish you wouldn't use that expression. I don't like it.' Fanny went to say something but Flora raised a hand in protest. 'Just settle down all of you. You've had a lovely evening and it's time for bed, after your cocoa. We've an early start tomorrow. Madam wants a full breakfast served at eight thirty. Thank the Lord they're not stopping for lunch. I'm still aching from top to toe from this evening's meal.'

'Last evening, Cook,' said Albert, grinning. The effect of drinking seemed to be wearing in rather than wearing off. His face was bright red and his eyes glassy. 'It's a brand new day!'

'Yes, all right. I take it you do all want a nightcap?'

'Yes please, Cook,' said Beanie, slumped in a chair with her feet on the fender and warming her toes. 'I was just wondering . . . should I do the hot water bottles now . . . before any of that lot up there turn in?'

'Gracious me,' said Flora, stopping in her tracks, 'that had quite slipped my mind.'

'Gawd, you don'arf look worried, Cook.'

'Albert, I am not implying that I'll lose sleep over it. I lose sleep over no one or nothing. Take away my soft pillow and eiderdown and that would be a different matter.'

'I'll start filling the bottles now,' offered Beanie, 'Won't matter if we've not warmed 'em first, will it?'

'It will. Take that kettle and tip a little of the warm water in each of them.'

'I do know that, Cook. I 'ave done it before. But I don't see why I can't just put hot water in instead of scalding hot water. They won't crack if I do that.'

'Oh, do as you think best. Who am I to tell any of you what to do? I'm only the cook after all. Albert, give Beanie a hand, there's a good chap.'

'No, it's all right. I'd rather do it by myself. I wanna

sober up before I lay me 'ead on a pillow or else the room'll start spinning. Up and down them stairs a few times'll bring me round. I knew I shouldn't 'ave had that last gin. Everyone was so generous in the tavern. Kept buying us drinks.'

'Mmm. No doubt they'll be all the more sorry in the morning when they find there's no money in their pockets to get them through the week.'

'Oh Mum, stop being a killjoy!'

That slip of the tongue brought silence from both Beanie and Flora. But the roar of laughter from Albert broke the tension. 'Now that is going too far, Bea, girl! Poor old Cook don't want us lot for children. I shouldn't fink so!' He put his arm round Flora's waist and squeezed her fondly. 'It would be nice though . . .'

'For you maybe!' said Flora, thanking the Good Lord under her breath. Another slip like that could be their downfall.

'What do you say, Fan? Wouldn't she make a lovely muvver!' The only response from his sweetheart was her low snoring. Fanny had fallen asleep in the old armchair.

'Oh Gawd, looks like I'm gonna 'ave to carry 'er to bed.'

'I beg your pardon, you'll do no such thing. Leave her be till the cocoa's ready then we'll wake 'er. Such carryings-on. If them upstairs were to see you doing such a thing we should all be sacked. Going into her bedroom indeed. I don't know what the world's coming to, the way you young people behave. In my day . . .'

Leaving her mother to preach to Albert, Beanie went into the scullery and filled the stone water bottles, hoping that she might bump into Mr Morton . . . He would be leaving after breakfast the next day and she'd be too busy below stairs to even think of a way of seeing him to say goodbye. She knew it was silly and romantic but their time together in Sidney Square and the walk back from the tavern had been just wonderful. It hadn't mattered that it was cold and it wouldn't have made any difference if it had been raining cats and dogs. In his company she had felt so different. It was almost as if her heart had a will of its own. It had positively been pounding and she was now feeling gloriously happy.

Carrying two of the water bottles, one under each arm, she went upstairs hoping for that glimpse of him. The holiday season at an end, he might not visit for twelve months or more and she may not be working below stairs in this house by then. Anything could happen in a year.

Arriving on the landing by the open doorway of the drawing room she looked in slyly to see Digby standing by the marble fireplace listening to his cousin by marriage, Tobias, talking politics. Pausing for a few seconds was risky since the house rule was that, unless serving in the dining room, servants should not be seen – they were to be invisible. Her risk paid off, for almost as if by intuition, Digby glanced her way and for a couple of seconds they looked at each other before she disappeared up the next flight of stairs and into the master bedroom. On her return she saw that the drawing-room door had been closed. It didn't matter now as far as Beanie was concerned. She had got her wish, she had seen him and he had seen her. That was all she had wanted.

Lying in her bed that night before this wonderful day came to an end, she brought Mr Morton to mind and relived every second since he appeared in the tavern doorway. She recalled the first time she saw him in the dining room and again in the library. She remembered it all as if it were a film which she could run over in her mind whenever she wanted. If she never saw him again, that would be enough – her memories would last a lifetime. There would be no sad parting and if he were to leave before breakfast it wouldn't matter, she had him in her heart and in her mind. It was enough.

By 11 a.m. on New Year's Day, most of the house guests had left number ten and the kitchen below stairs was spotless. Needless to say, all of the staff were exhausted and Flora for the first time since she could remember was in need of a vitality nap. With the others going about their chores in the usual manner, a little slower than usual, she made the excuse that a migraine had been brought on by the late night. No one minded or cared. With Cook out of the way they could all stop for twenty minutes and put their feet up. But the vitality nap was going to have to be put off. The library bell had jingled and when Fanny went up to answer the call she was greeted by Mrs Wellington who seemed a little more serious than usual. Thankfully it was Cook she wanted to see. The dread that had not quite left her was that Herbert had split on them. Had he done so, it would surely have meant instant dismissal. Using the master bed while the family were away would bring serious consequences. Relieved that she and Albert had been spared, Fanny arrived back in the kitchen, unruffled.

'Mrs Wellington wants a word, Cook.' She spoke in such a calm voice and with a smile on her face that Flora imagined Mrs W had good news to impart. Perhaps on this very first day of the year she was about to offer a pay rise for each of them. Her own tiredness held off; she went upstairs and into the library. The touch of worry in Grace Wellington's face put Flora on her guard.

'Ah, Cook,' she said, managing a warm smile, 'come and sit down, you must be exhausted. The breakfast was excellent and the family guests left praising the excellent running of this household, not to mention the superb dinner served yesterday evening.'

Flora smiled and nodded, then sat on the small armchair opposite her employer. 'We all pulled together, Madam, and I must say I would hate to lose any one of them. We work together as a good team and look out for each other. Which to my mind is how it should be.'

'I couldn't agree more.' Grace was smiling but that hint of worry was still clouding her eyes. Something was wrong.

'I asked you up, Cook, because . . .' blushing she waved a hand, '. . . I know it's silly of me but I purposely chose the wireless myself from Harrods and, well, I believe I was more excited about that than any of the presents I had bought for the family.' She was still blushing and avoiding Flora's eyes.

'Wireless, Madam?'

'Ah,' said Grace, going cold, 'my instincts were right. You know nothing of it?'

'Well, I have been very busy due to the entertaining right up to Christmas and then what with the New Year guests—'

'Cook, please! I have no intention of criticising you and obviously you are in the dark. Allow me to explain.' She sat up straight, placed her hands in her lap and composed herself. 'I wanted to give all of you something for below stairs that would bring you pleasure while you worked. I do know how hard you work, please believe that.'

'Thank you, Madam. That means a great deal to me and I know the girls, and Albert and Lenny will be pleased when I pass on your appreciation.'

'Quite so. This wireless . . . am I to take it you know nothing of it?'

'Yes, Madam.'

'I see. Then we have a very serious problem on our hands, Cook. Very serious indeed. You see . . . here on this low table in the library as a surprise . . . I left a special gift for below stairs. I hadn't gift wrapped it but there was a card and I had tied a pretty ribbon around it. The envelope with the card inside was marked clearly. I had inscribed the words: *A gift to be enjoyed by each and every one of you from Tobias and Grace Wellington. A special thank you for your devotion and especially for Christmas week.*' At this point Grace raised her eyes to meet Flora's and their minds instantly were one. The wireless had been stolen.

'That was very kind,' said Flora, 'and I see the point of your calling me in. On one hand I'm flattered and on the other deeply worried. But . . . with my hand on my heart I can tell you that if it has gone missing, the blame is not with any of your staff.'

'I see,' said Grace, a little disappointed. 'Could this mean that there was a visitor or two while we were away?'

'If you mean did anyone from below stairs bring strangers into this house, the answer is no. Quite definitely, no. I would never allow such a thing and if I believed you thought otherwise, Madam, I would rather pack my bags and leave.' Flora's anger was rising. Was she being accused of something here?

'But if the only ones to be here from Christmas Eve until our return—'

'We were not the only ones here, Madam,' Flora interrupted, sharply. She knew exactly who had taken that wireless.

'How so?' Suddenly the tables were turned and Grace was on the receiving end.

Normally Flora would never tell tales out of school but reputations were at stake. 'Your son returned on Christmas Eve with a friend. They joined us below stairs for Christmas dinner and soon afterwards the friend left. Master Herbert disappeared on the morning of Boxing Day and returned in good time for your homecoming and New Year's Eve.'

'I see,' said Grace, unable to hide her frustration with her son. 'I had no idea, so you can imagine . . .' She turned away from Flora's gaze and shuddered. 'I apologise for thinking the worst.'

'It's understandable, Madam, and I must say I'm relieved that any suspicion is not directed below stairs.' A strained silence hung in the room and for the first time since she had met Tobias those many years ago, Flora felt an overwhelming sense of shame. Here she was in the same room as his wife whom she had never once given any thought to, apart from resentment, when she should really have been shouldering guilt. She had known from the start of their romance that he was a married man. 'At least it wasn't your son who took the wireless just for the fun of it.'

Grace frowned. 'You think it was this friend, then?'

'Well, the wireless wasn't there when I went into the library to tidy up a few hours after he'd left. They had been in there the night before, drinking and smoking. Up until then I hadn't been in the library so I can't say precisely when it disappeared. But what I can say is that no one from below stairs left this house between your leaving and your son arriving so—'

'Please, please don't go on,' said Grace. 'It's obvious what has happened and it wouldn't be the first time. Did you happen to catch the name of this friend?'

'I did: Gerald.'

'I thought as much. Gerald Fairweather.' Standing up Grace managed not to shed a tear but the grief showed in her eyes and face. She went to the window and murmured, 'Where did they sleep?'

'Master Herbert in your room and his friend in Master Herbert's room.'

A long sigh of relief escaped from Grace as she looked to heaven and silently thanked God for it. 'Well at least we know now what happened to the wireless. I'll trust you not to tell the others and I shall see to it that another will appear in the kitchen sometime during the next week.'

'Very well, Madam,' said Flora, rising. 'Is there anything else I can do for you?'

Closing her eyes tightly, Grace summoned every bit of will-power but she could not help her tears. 'Oh, my dear Flora, you have no idea the heartache one's son can cause.'

'I can imagine, it's not easy being a mother. Our emotions are for ever being pulled one way and then another.'

'Indeed,' she murmured, sitting down again. 'A mother weeps while the father smiles happily in a world of his own making.' Then, looking up as she recalled Flora's words, she said, 'You have had a child?'

'I have,' said Flora, a new determination sweeping through her. Why should she deny it? She was proud of Beanie and loved her as any mother would and more. 'It's not something I speak of and if you could find it in your heart to drop the matter, I would be the better for it.'

'Sorry, my dear. Of course.' She looked away,

embarrassed. 'We never think of the heartache others are going through. Too wrapped up in our own misery, I expect.'

'I must say that it's not once crossed my mind that you might be less than happy, Madam. If you are, you certainly don't wear your heart on the sleeve.'

'Thank you, Flora, that in itself is comforting.'

'Was there anything else, Mrs Wellington?' Flora was beginning to feel the need to get out of that room and below stairs where she knew what was what. This familiarity was making her feel edgy.

'Do you know, that's the first time you've called me by my name.'

'Yes and I apologise for it. Maybe it was because you called me Flora instead of Cook.' Barriers, momentarily were down.

'There's nothing wrong with calling me Mrs Wellington, Flora. In fact, I think I would prefer that to "Madam". In fact, if I am to be this open and honest, I would prefer it if you called me by my Christian name. Yes, I would be more comfortable if you were to call me Grace and I were to call you Flora. But my husband would never have it that way, isn't that strange?'

'Not so strange . . . not really. I admit I've not been in domestic work before coming here so wouldn't really know much about what is and what isn't the done thing but, really, I don't give a monkey's what we call each other so long as the machine is oiled and efficient.' This made Grace laugh and her laughter brought a smile to Flora's lips.

'You make us sound like a factory, my dear. Would you care for a glass of sherry?'

'Well,' she said, glancing at the grandmother clock, 'I suppose we could call it lunchtime . . .'

'No. We'll call it medication. This business of the wireless going missing has upset both of us, has it not?'

'Well, yes . . . Thank you, I would like a small drop of sherry. And as far as making this house sound like a factory, I suppose that's because I worked so long in one . . . old habits die hard. But I will say this for it, you get an insight into the way men think and behave.'

'Working in a factory you mean? How interesting,' said Grace, pouring their drinks and wanting to know more. 'In what way?'

'Well, you said your husband would rather have you called Madam instead of Grace, and really, that sums up men. They have to call the shots. It's not so much what he wants you to be called but, more importantly, he must be the one to lay down the house rules.'

'Well, I agree wholeheartedly with regard to men having to call the shots, as you so aptly put it, my dear, but this business of "Madam" comes from his background, I fear.'

Flora, by now, was enjoying discovering more about the man she thought she once knew. 'Wasn't a royal prince, was he?' she smiled.

'Goodness no,' chuckled Grace handing Flora her drink. 'Quite the opposite in fact; his roots, my dear, are in Bethnal Green.'

The look of astonishment on Flora's face caused

Grace to throw back her head and laugh. 'I know, it's hard to believe but it is a fact. I shouldn't laugh but it is rather ridiculous. By trying so desperately to appear as if he were born with a silver spoon in his mouth he makes it blatantly obvious that he was not.

'I've given up trying to explain that servants must be treated with the highest respect. After all, we live under the same roof and you are bound to see things that we would not wish to have spread around, my son's behaviour for instance.'

'That's very true,' said Flora, wondering what might happen if the shoe was on the other foot. Grace seemed to have read her mind.

'Equally, should one of the staff have personal problems I should be the first person they turn to. But oh, no, Mr Wellington will not have that.'

'I can see why you'd think that way and I have to revert back to my theory of well-oiled machines. If your chambermaid is distraught you might not get your bed made up as well as it should be.'

'Something like that, yes. But men will be men and Mr Wellington will be Mr Wellington. I can't tell you how much he loathes the women's movement. Which, instead of putting me off, simply fuels my passion.' Her expression had changed from when Flora had arrived in the library. It was relaxed, glowing in fact, and there was a sparkle in her eyes.

'All men loathe the women's movement, it's why we must support it the best way we can.'

'Indeed, Flora. I couldn't agree more. Actually there is a march planned for a week today.'

'Yes, I'm looking forward to it. Of course I shall only be able to spare an hour but that's better than ten minutes.'

'You?'

'Yes, Mrs Wellington.'

'Oh, please, do drop the formality while we're alone like this. Call me Grace.'

'Yes, Grace, I shall be parading through the street holding my banner. And, had I more time, I'd be the first to gatecrash the publishing house.'

'Goodness me,' she smiled, topping up their glasses. 'So you too are part of the movement. I had no idea. How wonderful.'

'Quite a few domestics and factory girls are suffragettes, Grace. We have more to complain over, don't forget.'

'Well yes, I suppose you do.'

'I was never bothered about getting the vote. Politicians are all from the same can if you ask me, but fair pay for women, myself included, is why I joined in the first place.'

The conversation continued in the library for an hour or so, sometimes the two women agreed on certain things and other times they debated. The time simply slipped by. More importantly – they had bonded. Two women, separated by class, had spent time together as if they were from the same background. Never mind that their daughters were from the same blood.

The sound of the door handle turning stopped their conversation momentarily. Guessing it could only be the master of the house – or his son – Flora lowered her head. She would take no chances should it be her former lover. To be recognised now would be catastrophic. It *was* Tobias. He looked directly into the face of his wife and behaved as if Flora was invisible.

'Well? Do we know who the thief is?'

'We have a good idea, Tobias, I think it best if you and I talk later.' She was trying to give him a message: the blame does not lie below stairs.

'Ah, so one of your trusted staff *is* a thief. I might have guessed things were running a little too smooth-ly.'

'Tobias, please give me a few more minutes with Cook.'

He checked his pocket watch and raised an eyebrow. 'Very well, but once you've finished your chatter, perhaps you would be good enough to send the culprit to my study.'

'Yes, Tobias, I shall be very happy to do so.' She was thinking of Herbert and how shocked her husband would be to have him enter the study and not one of the servants. She hid her smile.

'Will he be surprised that one of your son's friends could do such a dreadful thing?' said Flora, her voice almost a whisper.

'He will pretend to be, my dear.' Grace went quiet, picturing the scene. 'But Herbert will no doubt put on a performance he has played out on stage. He does have talent, I will say that for him, if only he would put it to good use.'

'And you don't consider being an actor worthy of your son?' Flora thought it right down his street.

'Oh, it's nothing to do with him being a thespian, my dear. It's the melodrama that goes with it, and the company he keeps. But there, you don't want to hear all of that.'

'It must be disappointing,' said Flora, 'not being close to your only son. Unless my presumptions are wildly wrong, you are a bit on the sorry side?'

'Your presumptions are spot on, my dear. Not that it's always been this way. Up until his first part in a professional stage play, he was always by my side, when he was at home that is. He kept out of his father's presence as much as possible. But Mr Wellington tried his best to develop Herbert's strong, masculine side . . . He sent him to India believing he would return home a man.'

Had Flora not been the one to remark on the time Grace might have said too much. Never before had she opened up in this way and she had only scratched the surface. Any longer in Flora's company and she might have confessed that all was not as it appeared to be and that given the courage she would ask her husband to leave or go herself.

Flora on the other hand, kept her cards very close to her chest. It wasn't in her nature to open up her personal life, she had spent too many years keeping secrets and she could hardly let anything slip in front of this woman. The same woman whom Flora had caused to be so hurt and humiliated when she had walked into her parents' house in Brick Lane to discover that

Tobias had not only been cheating on her, but had made another woman with child. And while Grace Wellington had stood in the sitting room, staring into the crib which held the half sister of her own children, Flora had been upstairs hiding.

As she was leaving the library, Flora heard Grace all but whisper, 'Don't be surprised if I should come down to your quarters one day for a friendly chat by the fire.'

'You're welcome anytime, Mrs Wellington. And you may trust that all we've spoken of in this room will go no further.' With that she smiled and left Grace to herself. Slowly walking down the staircase, Flora felt nothing but bitterness towards Tobias Wellington. She had learned much about him today. The sadness in Grace's eyes was heart-rending. Underneath her composure she was a disturbed woman and a good deal of the blame lay on Flora's shoulders.

On the landing she came face to face with Sarah Wellington who sported a mischievous smile. 'Hello, Cook. What shenanigans I missed on Christmas Eve, eh?' she laughed, and with that she took the stairs two at a time.

'Oh dear,' sighed Flora, 'I sense trouble afoot.'

When Flora entered the kitchen she was surprised to see that all three of her staff were in a state of euphoria, giggling and gossiping. 'I turn my back for five minutes and you skive,' she said, hoping everything was all right.

'Oh, Cook,' laughed Fanny, 'we've 'ad such a laugh. You tell 'er, Bea. I won't be able to for laughing.'

'Well?' said Flora, pulling on her apron. 'What's been going on?'

'Oh, nothing really,' said Beanie, shooting Fanny a black look. How could she tell half a story? And she dare not tell it all. 'Sarah was down here making us laugh, that's all.'

'Just as well she did come down,' said Albert, 'they only blooming well thought that one of us 'ad nicked a wireless. But we soon put 'er straight, eh girls?'

'And how did you do that?'

'Well,' said Beanie, 'we 'ad no choice but to tell 'er about Master Herbert's boyfriend being 'ere. Told her all about the punch-up on Christmas Day.'

'Come on . . . and the rest,' chuckled Fanny, forgetting herself.

'Oh, bits and bobs,' said Beanie. 'It's easy to make Sarah laugh.'

'She loves coming dahn 'ere, Cook, honest to God she does,' Albert chimed in.

'Until she tires of *you*, Albert, then it'll be another story. I hope you didn't say too much?' The room went quiet. 'Well? Has the cat got your tongues? Out with it!'

'Oh . . .' Albert flapped a hand, 'not much more to tell, Cook.' He nodded towards the clock, 'Time's running on. We'd best move ourselves if they're to get any lunch today.'

In their fervour of relating it all to Sarah, it came out that Albert and Fanny had been discovered in the master bedroom by Herbert and Gerald. Best that Flora should not know that they had told Sarah.

Satisfied that there was no more to it and that Sarah would by now be confirming the story which Flora had delivered to Grace Wellington, she quickly regained some kind of order in the kitchen and set them all to work. The underlying worry for Beanie was, would Sarah spill the beans on Fanny and Albert? It would mean the sack for all of them if she did. Worry taking over from mirth, Beanie grabbed her coat and slipped outside, heading for her favourite bench within the ornate railings of the Square. Here she could think things through and lose herself in nature, with the cold air and winter sunshine on her face. She meant only to be there for five minutes or so.

From the library window, where she had gone in search of her mother, Sarah caught sight of her new friend, sitting alone. When the door opened she turned around quickly and kept her back to the long narrow window, protecting Beanie. It was Digby Morton, her cousin. He, unlike the rest of the family, had decided to stop another day.

'Digby! Just the man. I'm longing to gossip and you're the only one I dare to mention it to. Will you listen? Please say you will? Just this once?'

'If it's to do with this business of the wireless . . .'

'No . . . no, that's only half of it. Crack a smile and I'll tell you,' she grinned.

'Go on, but be warned, I may well stop you in mid-flow or simply take my leave.'

'Oh, stop being so grown up and sit down.'

He checked his new wristwatch. 'Very well. Ten

minutes and I must be on my way, I don't want to miss my train.'

Taking his hand she led him to the settee and sat very close. 'You're not going to believe the goings-on here on Christmas Eve. That crafty brother of mine came home with his chum Gerald in tow. He had no idea that the staff were here for Christmas.'

'And?'

'And . . . he went into the master bedroom, with every intention of spending the night in there with you know who, and . . . he caught Albert the bootboy and Fanny the parlour maid cavorting on my parents' bed – stark naked!'

'Oh dear. Well, rather he had caught them than they had caught him and Gerald. Now about the wireless—'

'Well, that's just it. It was Gerald who pinched it! They had a scrap after Christmas dinner, below stairs. Gerald went off in a huff and obviously took the bloomin' wireless with him, isn't that too much?'

'And the staff are to take the blame? Yes, that *is* too much, Sarah.'

'Of course they're not, silly. Mother will tell Father and Herbert will get a talking to and that'll be the end of it.'

'Unless of course Herbert switches to one of his less than charming moods and tells what he saw in your parents' room.'

'Oh, he wouldn't do that. Not even Herbert would stoop so low . . . would he?'

'If he thought it would smooth things over for

himself, yes.' Standing up, he thought for a moment and wandered to the window. 'This could turn out to be a sorry day if we are not careful.' Looking down into the Square he saw Beanie, alone but not lonely. She had her face to the winter sun and appeared relaxed and he felt a strong desire to join her.

'Oh. What a damp squib you are, Digby. But wait. If he *were* to tell on them, they could tell on him and Gerald.'

'They would be turned out before they had a chance to utter a word of it. I cannot believe it probable that Uncle Tobias would entertain one of them in his study, speaking ill of his son. Where is Herbert at this moment?'

'In his room with a sign on the door: DO NOT DISTURB. I AM LEARNING MY LINES. Which of course means that he is sleeping. You know what a lazy devil he is.'

'Good. I shall go to him now before the fuse is lit.'

'Rather you than me. He'll be miffed to be caught napping. You know what a swine he can be when his feathers are ruffled.'

'I do indeed, but needs must.' With that he gave a hint of a bow and left the room. Luckily, on his way up to his cousin's room he met no one on the stairs. His mind was engaged as to the best way to deal with the dreadful young man whom he was unfortunate enough to be related to. On seeing the sign on the door, scrawled in pencil, he found himself smiling. He tapped on the door and as expected there was no answer. He tapped again and waited. He then turned the handle and entered his cousin's hideaway. As expected, Herbert was sprawled on his bed resting, but not asleep.

'Digby dear boy, do come in and close the door behind you. I have the most frightful migraine. Pull up a chair, dear chap, and I shall, if you can bear it, recite my lines of the play in which I am to be auditioned this very week.'

'Would that I had the time, Herbert. I fear I may miss my train to Newmarket if I stay one minute longer than I should. I am here to report the consequences of your coming home unexpectedly on Christmas Eve.'

'Oh, please dear boy, spare me,' groaned Herbert, a hand on his forehead. 'Those dreadful people below stairs caused me such pain and grief I cannot tell you.'

'I'll come to the point . . . Your friend accompanying you on Christmas Eve left this house in haste and took with him a brand new wireless set which was intended as a present for the staff.'

'Nothing you tell me will shock, Digby, I am used to people taking advantage of my generosity. Gerald begged to have a roof over his head at such a special time of the year; would that I had refused. I came all the way from Stratford-upon-Avon to grant his wish.'

'You *knew* he took the wireless?'

'I didn't know there was a bloody wireless. And frankly, dear boy, I couldn't care less. Better that *he* should have it than the plebeians. You surely agree with me on this one, cousin. I know we have our differences—'

'I do not. Furthermore, when you are called into Uncle Tobias's study, I urge you not to mention the "incident" in his bedroom.'

'Oh would that I could! Too, too, embarrassing for words, cousin. No, I must erase it from my mind.'

'I'm pleased to hear you say that, Herbert. For should you turn coat, if confronted as to how you dare come here with Gerald at Christmastime, when you imagined you would have the house to yourself, I shall personally box your ears and face *before* you go to your next audition.'

'What is this, Digby, what have you been drinking? You threaten your own—'

'It is not a threat, Herbert, it is a promise.'

Sitting up, Herbert paled. 'But you don't understand. If there is a worthwhile opportunity which has come out of this dreadful Christmas scenario, then I must clutch it with both hands. Sarah has persuaded Father that I should marry that awful scullery maid with the ridiculous name.'

Laughing at the very thought of it, Digby shook his head. 'Now you are going *too* far with your theatricals.'

'It is no laughing matter. If I am to be the owner of a house in Highgate then I must marry! That's what he said, I assure you. And this matter, cousin, is strictly confidential. *Strictly*, you understand. Mother knows nothing of this – as far as I know.'

'Good grief, you believe it. You believe that girl would marry you.'

'Of course she would, given half the chance! Oh

please, do relax, I have no intention of marrying that little minx. I dare say she put those two up to it, some kind of dare. Probably she dared them to sleep in the master bedroom. Oh, if only they had been asleep. It was a dreadful sight, believe me, Cousin. Copulating naked in my parents' room – it was disgusting! I shall never be able to wipe that scene from my mind.'

I could think of worse things, thought Digby. 'So why did Sarah choose Beanie?'

'Oh . . . *Beanie* is it . . . we are on first name terms? Tut-tut, Cousin.'

'Why that girl in particular?'

'Oh it was Sarah's idea! She insisted we could turn her into Eliza Dolittle. Bernard Shaw would sue me, I have no doubts about that. Stealing his idea and turning it into real life. And to think that I contemplated going along with it. I even went out in search of her yesterday evening. New Year's Eve of all times. What a blissful lucky escape. She stood out in the crowd flirting and cavorting with those ghastly men.'

'And if Sarah talks your father into insisting on this marriage?'

'Now you do torment me, Digby. My own dear beloved sister? Never!'

'But if she did and he were to be taken by the idea to the point of making it happen?'

'Well, at the risk of losing a house of my own in the very best part of London . . . I would very likely comply, dear boy – marry her and make my bed of nettles. Oh, God! The sacrifices I am obliged to make . . .' He dropped back on to his feathered pillows and laid a limp hand on his damp forehead. 'Try not to make a noise when you close the door behind you, old chap. There's a good fellow.'

'So am I to understand that you agree to tell your father that it was most likely your friend who took the wireless?' At least one thing had to be agreed before he left the room.

'*Wireless?* What is this obsession with a wireless?'

'The staff must *not* be accused of stealing it. You must—'

'Oh yes, yes . . .' Herbert raised his hand and waved him from the room. 'You'll box my ears *and* my face should I stand in defence of the dreadful Gerald Fairweather. You know it would make my day if he were to go to prison. It would really . . .' he smiled.

Digby left the room with the idea of putting off his return to Newmarket until this business of the theft was cleared up. He did not trust Herbert; never had. In fact he was probably the only person alive that he positively loathed.

Glancing out of the landing window he was a touch disappointed to see that Beanie was no longer on the bench. If he would only admit it, she was the reason for him considering a longer stay and not the stolen wireless. And then, he caught sight of Tobias coming furtively out of a tall elegant house on the opposite side of the Square. A house which, in its heyday, during the second half of the nineteenth century, had entertained the rich and famous of society: respectable men – pillars of society – but with dark, hidden secrets.

Bad times followed and although things had picked up in recent years, the proprietor of the House of Assignation, Lillian Redmond, was now too old and too tired to resurrect her jaded house interior to its former glory. Still, she had her regular customers and her small team of beautiful courtesans and that was enough.

From a window on the third floor, the old lady, with a slender, wrinkled hand holding back the French lace curtain, turned her focus from the girl who had been sitting alone to Tobias Wellington as he took the longest route home to his house across the tree-lined Square. So many times she had watched men arrive and depart incognito from her property and it had often amused her at the lengths some would go to avoid public exposure. But for some reason, which she had never quite fathomed, this gentleman from across the way saddened her. He had a lovely family and in particular a beautiful, serene wife. Why then did he spend so much time and money with her girls?

Lillian Redmond had lived in Beaumont Square for at least four decades and had come to think of it as *her* Square. From her window, with its bird's-eye view, she had seen many comings and goings, new owners moving in and old ones passing on. She had watched showy funerals with their flower-decked horse carriages driven slowly around the Square and she had seen the horse and cart funeral with its lone charity wreath.

Tossing crumbs to her darling pigeons on the sill

below, the woman eased down the window with the broken sash, not minding that one day she would be carried out feet first – in a red silk-lined coffin of the very best oak.

Taking off her coat, after her brief spell alone in the Square, Beanie was interrogated by Fanny in a humorous mood. 'Cook's out for your blood, Bea, skiving is what she said. Where you bin then? Come on, spit it out.'

'In the Square. Nothing wrong with taking five minutes off on New Year's Day is there?'

'In the Square all by yourself? Who plucked your 'eartstring down the tavern last night, then?'

'Mind yer own business.'

Looking slyly at Albert who was polishing shoes and boots, Fanny began to sing a little ditty: '*There's something the matter with Beanie Jane. She's perfectly well and she hasn't a pain; it's her favourite rice pudding for dinner again. Yes, something's the matter with Beanie Jane.*'

'Don't be ridiculous. I'm overdue for a half day off so if I like I can sit outside in the Square till it suits me.'

'I think not,' said Flora coming out of the pantry and carrying the flour bag. 'The laundry service is behind what with the Christmas and New Year holiday. We're all going to have to pull together and get the washing done. Sheets, pillowcases and towels. The copper boiler's going to be going all day.'

'Can't the guest sheets wait, Cook?' said Fanny, hoping today would be an easy one.

'Certainly not. In fact I would appreciate it if you and Beanie made a start on stripping the beds. And if you'll stoke up the boiler, Albert . . .'

'Everyfing back to normal then, eh Cook?' said Albert, a touch fed up with Flora's sudden industrious mood.

'Precisely. Work will always expand to fill the time. Remember that and you'll never be behind with your chores.'

Puffing out air, Albert was sulky. 'If we live our lives according to that little proverb, Cook, there'd be no time for leisure or pleasure.'

'That's where you're wrong, lad. A stitch in time saves nine. You can work that one out for yerself. Boiler?'

'It's not work that kills people off but the worry of it,' said Fanny, looking at Beanie and then nodding at the door. 'Come on. Let's get it over and done wiv.'

Following her out of the kitchen, Beanie said in a voice loud enough for Flora to hear, 'If it was up to me I'd leave the sheets where they are. They only slept in 'em for one night.'

Smiling inwardly, Flora had to admit to herself that Beanie was right. Really and truly, should the sheets be pulled back and the windows opened, no one would know the difference. 'The pillowcases must come off in any case,' she murmured. After they had gone about their duties, Flora had time to mull over all that had been talked about in the library. No matter how she reasoned the fact that Grace Wellington enjoyed a privileged life, she had to admit that she herself was happier and probably always had been. 'It's a funny old world,' she murmured, 'a funny old world.'

With the house quiet, Beanie and Fanny believed the Wellingtons to be either in their own rooms resting, or out of the house. Giggling and larking around as they went from room to room, whipping sheets off beds, they had no idea that Tobias, the master of the house, had come home and had been watching them from the landing – watching and enjoying. They were young and fun-loving and this house could do with more sounds of carefree laughter. So, taken with their light-hearted frivolity, he stole quietly down the short flight of stairs and stood in the doorway of the guestroom in which they were now playing pillow fight.

'You'll be in for it should Mrs Wellington see you,' he said, smiling at them.

Drawing breath, the girls froze on the spot. 'We was just 'aving a bit of fun, Sir. It won't happen again,' said Fanny. Beanie kept quiet, waiting to see if his smile was going to fade into a frown.

'So long as it doesn't become a habit,' he said, looking from Fanny to Beanie. 'You're a new girl, are you not?'

'I've been 'ere for getting on for three months now. I helped Fanny serve at table on New Year's Eve.'

'Ah . . . you must excuse my having not noticed. Too many in-laws at once. I take it you must be the scullery maid? Madam did mention it but I'm afraid it slipped my mind. Please accept my apologies.'

Out of the corner of her eye, Beanie checked Fanny's expression. She too was dumbfounded by the familiarity and friendly tone in the master's voice. Unknown to them, the reason for his good mood was that he had spent the last couple of hours in the house on the other side of the Square with a courtesan probably the same age as these two young ladies. Fanny, with her impish face and red hair amused him while this other girl, this new girl, stirred something in his memory – or rather someone. She reminded him of the girl from Brick Lane. The girl whom Grace had forced him, in her own sly way, to give up.

'Try to keep the noise down. Madam has had a tiring week and is resting.' He turned from them and went to the privacy of his study.

'Stone the crows,' whispered Fanny, in case he was loitering outside the room to catch them out. 'I've never known 'im to talk to any one of us before. I wonder what's fuelled 'is fire?'

The sudden crash as the wardrobe door flew open caused both girls to cry out. 'Shut the bleedin' door then!' It was Sarah Wellington, grinning from ear to ear.

Pushing the door shut with her foot, Fanny, with hands on hips, glared at her. 'That wasn't very funny, we could 'ave 'ad 'eart seizure over that!'

'Oh shut up, Fanny,' laughed Sarah. 'What a lark, eh? Father flirting with his maids.'

'Never mind that . . . jumping out of a wardrobe indeed!'

'Well, what's a girl supposed to do for fun in a stuffy

house like this? And what may I ask was Father doing in here, being so *nice* to "below stairs", as he refers to you?'

'He caught us larking around and it amused 'im,' said Beanie, matter-of-fact.

'Nothing amuses Father, Bea. Mind you, he does have a penchant for a young pretty face. Didn't pinch your bums, did he?'

'That's a terrible thing to say about your own dad!' snapped Fanny. 'You should be ashamed, Sarah.'

'Oh, listen to you . . .' she said, winking at Beanie. 'If any one of us should feel ashamed, it's you, Fanny. Sitting stark naked on poor Albert . . .'

'So what if I did? Albert's gonna marry me one day – we're saving up for it!' More laughter followed which brought the serious-faced Digby into the room.

'Oh, I might have guessed. Three girls playing the fool.' He closed the door on them and his footsteps could be heard on the stairs.

'I thought he'd gone to Newmarket,' said Beanie, blushing.

'Ah ha!' cried Fanny, 'now I know who's putting the glow in your cheeks. You're blushing!' Swanning around the room hugging a pillow, Fanny began to hum the tune from her earlier ditty.

'Digby?' gasped Sarah. 'You're trembling in your drawers over Digby? My cousin doesn't have a passionate bone in his body, I'm afraid you picked the wrong one there, Bea.'

'I never picked him or anyone. Fanny's just getting her own back, that's all.'

'Mmm . . . I wonder . . .'

'Oh, sod the pair of you!' snarled Beanie as she marched out of the room, leaving them to strip the bed. Stomping down the stairs, angry with everyone and for no particular reason, she didn't care who might hear or see her. She had had enough of this house and was going to insist that she took a half day off that very afternoon. She would go back to her old house and see who was living there. If it was empty she would find the landlord. She could move back in and get a job to pay the rent instead of having to live in someone else's house. She had had enough of serving the upper classes.

Angry thoughts continued to charge through her mind and by the time she arrived in the kitchen she was in a foul mood. 'I'm sorry, Cook,' she said, not sounding the least bit sorry, 'but I am due a half day off and I'm taking it today. Come rain or shine, I'm going for a long walk. I feel as if I'm locked up in a cupboard and can't spread my arms and legs.'

Albert looked from Beanie to Flora and expressed his shock with wide eyes. 'Careful, Beanie girl . . .' he said, in a fatherly fashion.

'Careful yourself, Albert!' She pulled on her hat and coat, grabbed her handbag and stormed out of the house.

'Stop looking so worried, Albert,' said Flora. 'She'll walk once round the block to cool off. Someone's ruffled her feathers, that's all.'

'So you won't be too hard on her then . . . when she comes back in? I mean this being New Year's Day?'

'No, Albert, I shan't mention a word of it.' If he only knew that Flora wanted to rush out after her daughter and hug her and tell her that everything would be all right now that their first Christmas away from the lovely little house was over and that they had taken a step forward.

'You're a good woman, Cook. A lovely person. I 'ope you don't mind my being so familiar but it had to be said.'

'Well, since we're by ourselves, Albert, no, I don't mind. I might be embarrassed though, should others be present.'

'Well, since that's not very often . . . D'yer mind if I say something else which is a bit on the personal side?'

'Well, that rather depends on what it is, Albert,' she said, measuring flour into her mixing bowl. 'But spit it out and get it over and done with, my shoulders are broad.'

'It's somefing my Granny Blake use to say, "Work must come first but always make time for pleasure."'

'And?'

'You should get out a bit more, Cook. Go to the pictures once in a while, or to see a show. The Hackney Empire puts on some cracking entertainment and the tickets are cheap.'

'You could be right, lad, but who am I to go with? Or would you have me sit by myself?'

'Well,' he said, scratching his neck and chancing his luck. 'Wot about Lenny? All he ever does is walk from 'is place to 'ere and back agen.'

'I'll think on it,' she smiled, folding back the sleeves of her white blouse. 'Now then, if this meat pie is to be ready for lunchtime, we must get a move on. And since the girls are not here perhaps you wouldn't mind slicing the onions for me?'

'Course I wouldn't. One more pair of Master Herbert's shoes to polish and I'm done.'

The sound of fast feet on the stairs leading down into the basement brought a sigh from Flora. What now, she thought, recognising the steps. She paused for a moment and waited for Sarah Wellington to come charging in.

'Where's Beanie?' she shrieked, her face displaying her mood. She was overly excited. 'She hasn't gone on an errand, has she, Cook?'

'Where's the fire?' said Flora in a calm voice. She was used to Sarah by now.

'Oh you'll never guess, what. Neither you, Cook, nor you, Albert. Not in a million years!'

Albert looked sideways at her and shook his head slowly. 'Go on then. We can't wait, can we, Cook?'

'Well . . .' crooned Sarah, sinking into the armchair and stretching her legs out. 'Herb and yours truly have just come out of Father's study. Having persuaded my brother once again that the girl I chose for him to marry is the right one, we presented the idea straight away and before Herbert could change his mind. And, to my amazement, Father said he'd think about it. Naturally, he put forward his concern of what some people might think but I argued the point and now, in the end he's given in.'

'Herbert is to be married . . . to a woman . . . ?' scoffed Albert.

'Well, he can hardly marry a man! Besides, he's left all of that behind him now. Behaving so soppily was just a silly trend. But the best of it all is . . .' She went quiet and looked from Albert to Flora. 'You are listening to me, aren't you? I mean to say, this *is* the best news of the year. and even Mother doesn't know yet.' She went quiet and then smiled. 'He's such a sly fox.'

'Dear, dear,' said Flora, 'he *is* your father, don't forget.' Sly fox was not the label she would pin on Mr Tobias Wellington. A lying, cheating, debauched swine were the words running through her mind.

'Not Father, Cook – *Herbert!* Earlier on, when we were discussing Father wishing him to tie the knot, he never mentioned a dicky-bird about a house in Highgate or Hampstead. Can you believe that . . . ? Mother is to buy him a house and Father will furnish it, *only* if he agrees to marry.'

'Yes,' said Flora, bitterly, 'I can quite believe it.'

'Mind you . . . as I said, Mother doesn't know anything about it, yet. She's bound to agree though, what mother wouldn't? Only too pleased to get him married off I would have thought.' She paused for a moment and then said, 'You agree with me, Cook, don't you? If you were his mother, you would want the same for him. Wouldn't you?'

'I suppose under the circumstances, and if I could afford it, I might do the same.'

'I knew it. I just knew it!' She clasped her hands to

her face, 'It's all so bloody marvellous, can you imagine the fun of it all!'

Flora couldn't but she held her tongue and plunged her hands into the flour and diced margarine, suddenly realising just how wealthy this family was.

'Just think of it . . . To take a girl out of the lower classes, someone used to buying second-hand clothes, and turning her into a beautiful lady dressed in finest silks and satins. Affording her the very best elocution lessons, teaching her deportment and manners . . .'

'Sounds like something out of a fairy story,' said Albert, returning Flora's smile of contention.

'Of course we shall have to move her in straight away, above stairs, I mean. Oh yes, and it must be a tightly kept secret. No one must know. Can you imagine . . .' again she drifted into her world of imagination '. . . introducing her into society once she's been properly trained and flaunting her as a member of a European royal family.' At this point Sarah burst into joyous laughter. 'What a lark!'

'I believe that in the play they thought the heroine to be a Hungarian princess,' said Flora, letting Sarah know that she could read and *did* read and knew that their idea was not exactly original.

'Oh, never mind that. This is going to be for *real*, Cook.' She leaped to her feet and paced the kitchen floor. 'Oh, where is Beanie? You must know where she's gone and how long she'll be?'

Scratching his head, bemused by the whole affair, Albert said, 'I don't think Beanie's gonna find it all that exciting, Sarah. In fact, if you were to ask my opinion, and I think both girls would agree with me, it's a daft idea.'

'Well, it might seem like a daft idea now, Albert, but once you know who the lucky girl is, you might think differently.'

A stony silence descended on the room.

'You surely don't mean Beanie?' said Flora at last.

'Yes! Now you see why it's so marvellous? Herbert and I chose Beanie! She's going to have everything she ever wanted – no more working in kitchens; no more wearing dull second-hand clothes. She'll shop in the finest stores, and dine at the swankiest restaurants *And*, she'll be my sister-in-law!'

Gripping the edge of the table, Flora felt as if she had been struck by lightning. She felt nauseous, giddy, mournful. With the sensation of icy needles shooting up from her legs and millions of tiny white lights flashing inside her head, she crumpled and collapsed on to the stone-tiled floor.

6

Tucked up in her bed the following morning and feeling like death, Flora could not understand why Grace Wellington had come into her room and with a gentleman she could only assume to be a doctor. Was she at death's door?

'How are we feeling this morning, Mrs Brown?' The man sounded as if he were speaking through an air vent. She couldn't answer him. Her head was thumping and she felt quite sick. 'A little better after a good night's sleep?'

'A bucket, sir,' she moaned, 'I need a bucket . . . hurry, please.'

'Ah.' He turned to Grace and said, 'I should ring for a servant, Mrs Wellington.'

'I beg you . . .' Flora's face was deathly white.

Pushing past the doctor, Grace pulled the chamber pot from under Flora's bed and placed it in front of her in the nick of time. 'This must surely be concussion, Doctor,' said Grace, not too pleased with his lack of urgency.

'It would seem so,' he said, pulling the small chair to the bedside. Placing a hand on Flora's forehead he asked if she had a headache. Slumping back into her pillows she just managed to nod in reply. 'Would you say it was an ache or a pain?'

Covering the chamber pot with a small hand towel, Grace left the room, wishing that it was her own personal doctor attending on the poor woman. Going downstairs and into the drawing room, she rang the servants' bell. It was Beanie who came to her call, worried but trying to hide her upset. 'Is Cook all right, Mrs Wellington?' she said, hating having to use the word Cook at a time like this.

'She will be after a day in bed. The doctor's with her now.'

'I know he is. What did he say was wrong?'

Taken aback by her urgent tone, Grace smiled kindly. 'It's nothing to worry about. No broken bones, a touch of concussion that's all.'

'Shall I go and see if she needs anyfing?'

'Presently, but not just yet.' She handed her the covered chamber pot. 'See to this and ask Fanny to fetch up a cup of weak, sweet tea for Cook.'

'Yes, Madam,' said Beanie, close to tears. She didn't want to go downstairs and she didn't want Fanny to take up the tea. She didn't want even the doctor to be at her mother's bedside. She wanted them all to go away so she could be with Flora and look after her as a daughter should. 'Do you fink that she might manage some soup at lunchtime?'

'We'll see. I shouldn't concern yourself over it, with one pair of hands short in the kitchen, you'll have more than enough on your plate. Cold meat and salad will be fine for Mr Wellington and myself . . . and Master Herbert, of course.'

'Yes, Madam.' Turning away, Beanie went below stairs wondering what could have caused her mother to faint. She, Fanny and Albert had had to work ever so hard the evening before, preparing and serving the meal without Flora at the helm, so there was no time for explanations. Then, at the end of the day, once the kitchen was spick and span, all three of them wanted nothing else but to drop into their beds.

'It's cold meats and salad for lunch, Fan,' she murmured, walking through to the wash house.

'Thank Gawd for that,' said Fanny while at the sink, scouring a pan. 'They'll want taters wiv it though, Beanie, won't they? Beanie! Where the bleedin' 'ell are you now!'

'Stop yelling,' said Beanie, coming back into the room. 'She never said anyfing about spuds, so I wouldn't bother. Doctor's up there with Cook and they reckon she's got concussion.'

'Oh, that's all right then. We won't be by ourselves when it comes to cooking dinner and that. Albert reckons it's lucky she never broke a bone. Went down with a right crash by the sound of it.'

Taking a small china teapot from the Welsh dresser, Beanie tipped in some hot water to warm the pot. 'I'm to take weak tea up for 'er. I wonder if she'll be able to manage a biscuit?'

'Put a couple on the tray in case.'

'So what do you reckon caused her to pass out like that?'

'I wasn't dahn 'ere, Beanie! Fancy asking me, I was stripping beds by myself!'

'Well what did Albert say, surely he must 'ave mentioned it?'

'He said somefing about it, yeah.' She was being evasive. 'There's beef and 'am in the cold cupboard. D'yer fink they'd want both?'

'Course. So what did Albert say then?'

'Oh, I can't remember. Stop going on about it. She only fainted for Christ's sake. Anyone'd fink she 'ad a heart attack by the way you go on.' Fanny had sworn on Albert's life not to say anything about this proposed marriage. He had been warned not to by Sarah.

'Where is Albert anyway?' said Beanie.

'On an errand for Master Herbert: shaving cream and blades. I know what I'd like to do with 'em. Cut 'is bleeding throat.'

'What's he done now?'

'You'll find out in good time. I'm never gonna get these pans up to Cook's liking. Albert bleeding burnt the bottom of this one.'

'Find out what in good time?'

'Oh, stop wagging, Beanie. I've got enough on me mind as it is. Get a tea towel and start drying this lot or we'll never get straight.'

'Excuse me for breathing,' moaned Beanie, grabbing a tea towel. 'Don't know what's got your goat up. If you ask me—'

'Everything tickety-boo in here?' Herbert had crept into the kitchen. 'Cook's making the most of it and stopping in bed all day. Would that I could perform on stage as convincingly as—'

'She's not acting!' snapped Fanny. 'Exhaustion is what's on my mind. We all work too bleeding hard if you ask me.'

'Well, yes . . .' he drooled, pulling up a chair, with an eye on Beanie. 'But what might someone like you do, Fanny, should you find yourself unemployed and with too much time on your hands?'

'That's not fair, Master Herbert,' said Beanie, 'coming in here and threatening Fanny with the sack when she's been working round the clock.'

'That was not my meaning, dear girl. What I actually meant to say was, how would a girl like yourself for instance, fit into another way of life? A world in which you would not have to dip those slender fingers into hot water?'

'I shouldn't want another way of life, thank you, I'm content with my lot.' Beanie deliberately clanked the clean porridge saucepan on top of the milk pan, hoping the din would see him off.

'Ah, but . . .' smiled Herbert, more oily than usual. 'What of fine clothes and exquisite jewellery?'

'There's nothing wrong with the clothes I wear and I've got a very nice gold-plated cross and chain, thank you. We don't want for nothing, do we, Fanny?'

'Speak for yerself.'

'I'll wager five pounds, Beanie,' drooled Herbert, 'that should a wealthy man propose, you would accept. Especially if that gentleman were tall, handsome and highly respected.'

Drawing breath, Digby Morton came to mind. Was Herbert Wellington paving the way for his cousin? Surely not. 'It would depend on the man in question. Are you suggesting that there might be such a person, Master Herbert?'

'Oh, please,' he swept a hand through the air, 'do drop the Master. Have we not socialised? Did we not enjoy each other's company in the tavern on New Year's Eve?'

'Well, is there? Is there, *Herbert*?' She had to know. Digby Morton had stayed on because of her . . . if only that were true.

'Answer my question first and then I shall tell you,' he smiled, trying to flirt.

'What was the question again?'

Sighing dramatically and raising his eyes to heaven, he spoke in a slow and deliberate tone. 'Would you marry a man above your station? Someone who would be prepared to groom you until you were ready to be taken into London society?'

'Depend who it was,' she said, wondering why he kept gazing at her.

'Well, you do have spirit and gusto, I will say that for you. Where are your parents, Beanie? Indeed, who are your parents? Are your relatives rogues and vagabonds; would you be prepared to leave them behind as you—'

'Herbert, do come up at once!' It was Sarah shouting from above; she was beside herself. Her father was in his study with Grace, putting forward his idea of marrying Herbert off to Beanie.

'I fink that sounds rather urgent, Herbert,' said Fanny, urging him to go.

'I beg your pardon, who gave *you* permission to be familiar? It is *Master* Herbert!'

'Oh, is that right,' said Beanie, 'well, where us lot are concerned, what's good for the goose is good for the gander!'

'How dull that you are a little on the boring side, my dear.' He released a long-drawn-out sigh. 'It's no good, I'm afraid, I can't possibly go through with it. Common we can cure, the voice we can train, grooming would not be a problem, but . . . boring comes from within. I'm afraid you would be an embarrassment amongst the literati.' He hauled himself out of the chair and left the kitchen, shaking his head.

'Sodding cheek!' barked Fanny. 'How dare he talk to you like that!' She picked up a carving knife. 'I'd like to chop 'is cock off!'

'What was all that about, anyway?' said Beanie, dropping into a kitchen chair. 'What *was* he on about?'

'I would tell you, Bea,' said Fanny, 'but Sarah made Albert promise not to say a word. She'll explain it all. It's all and nothing now in any case, thank God. You're better off wiv us, Bea. It would 'ave bin nice though, if he wasn't such a nasty, puffed-up, prat. A friend of my sister used to be a domestic in Hampstead. It was all right. They had their own little sitting room off their bedroom. Me and Albert could 'ave worked for you. It would 'ave bin lovely.'

Unwittingly, Fanny had just disclosed exactly what it was all about.

'You mean . . . Herbert Wellington was gonna ask me to marry *him*?'

Shrugging, Fanny opened up. 'Apparently it was all Sarah's idea. The family would rather he was married than 'ave a scandal. He is gettin' worse, I will say that. It's as if he's blooming well proud of what he is an' wants to flaunt it. I wouldn't fancy 'is chances in jail, they'd make mincemeat of 'im.'

'I can see all you're saying, Fan . . . but why me?'

''Cos you happen to work 'ere, silly. Any old working-class girl would do. Someone who'd jump at the chance of living a life of luxury. Sarah would probably 'ave suggested me, but she knows I wouldn't chuck my Albert for no one. You ain't got a fellar 'ave yer, so . . .'

'His parents would never allow it, I don't know what Sarah was thinking. They stick together that lot.'

'Well that's where you're wrong, Bea. By all accounts, his old man's bin won over and if I'm not mistaken, he's probably putting the idea to Mrs Wellington right now.'

'Oh . . .' Beanie sank down into a chair again when she should have been cracking on with her work. But her mind was running riot now. All the Wellingtons really wanted was a cover for their horrid son – a cover not a proper wife. So she wouldn't have to sleep with him nor kiss and cuddle. 'You did say Hampstead, didn't yer, Fan?'

'Hampstead or Highgate is what I heard.' Fanny didn't need Beanie to be sitting on her backside at a time like this, but if Beanie *was* considering the deal and might just pedal with the rest of them, she was best left to herself.

'Sarah said something about you having elocution lessons and that,' she added, to help sway her friend. 'That'd be a right lark.'

A warm glow crept into Beanie's heart. This crazy, absurd idea could very well be an answer to a prayer. Her mother could live a comfortable life and not have to work from dawn to dusk, as she had always done and they could spend more time together in a leisurely way, being daughter and mother. Going shopping together or to the tearooms whenever they fancied. Beanie was aware that compared to other women of her age, her mother behaved and looked older than her years and never allowed herself the tiniest bit of self-indulgence. She was only forty but behaved as if she had turned fifty. With money to spend on lovely clothes or a visit to the hairdresser's whenever she wanted, she would stand out as a beautiful woman. She may even find romance.

If she *were* to marry Herbert Wellington she had no doubts that she could stand up to him, she was a good match for his intellect any day. Her experience in the clay pipe factory would stand her in good stead. She had worked alongside men of all moods and personalities. The drippy Herbert would be putty in her hands.

'It's not as if summink like this happens every day,

Bea,' said Fanny breaking into her reverie. 'I would give it a good deal of thought if I was you. You don't wanna live a life of regret now, do yer?'

I don't, thought Beanie. I most certainly don't. 'It's worth thinking about, I grant you that. But don't keep on about it, will yer? I've got to weigh up the pros and cons. I wouldn't be able to 'ave any babies, don't forget and—'

'Course you would!' Fanny cut in. 'You wouldn't be the first amongst that lot to take a secret lover who could get you in the club. And Herbert could play the father figure. Who's to say it wouldn't be his kid? It'd be one in the eye for the gossips. Yeah . . .' smiled Fanny, thinking about it. 'That would really put the lid on rumours about 'im being a bit on the queer side.'

Arriving through the back door came Albert, frozen to the bone. 'I wish it would bleedin' well snow again and be done with. It's like a skating rink out there.' He shuddered and peeled off his icy cold coat, cap and gloves.

'Ne'mind, honey-bun, sit yerself by the fire and Fanny'll make you a nice, hot milky drink with a little drop of Cook's brandy in it. That'll warm the cockles of your 'eart.'

'It's not me heart that's hurting, Fan. It's my feet. My toes are numb to the bone. You're gonna 'ave to pull off me boots with care, otherwise me toes'll snap off, I swear it.'

Leaving Fanny to fuss over her sweetheart, Beanie made haste with the kitchen chores. She was going to have to impress Mrs Wellington from now on. If they wanted a scapegoat, she would oblige.

Grace Wellington had listened to all her husband had to say on the matter of wedlock and had asked for time to think it over. Of course she wanted to see her son married off and no longer her responsibility. She was fed up with the raised eyebrows from those women in her circle whose sons and daughters were bringing up young families of their own. The idea of marrying Herbert off in this manner was not ideal but it was a way out of an embarrassing situation. More importantly it would stop those people who were beginning to whisper behind their hands – some with a satisfied smirk and others with a self-opinionated look of repulsion.

Carefully thought out, this idea of her husband's, with one or two adjustments, could be the answer to her frequent sleepless nights, worrying over her son. She had no intention of purchasing a house out of her own capital and felt sure that unless Tobias had been squandering his money recklessly, he could afford to buy a property for Herbert. A house in one of the better London suburbs was absurd whereas a modest property in a less expensive area, Golder's Green, perhaps, would be quite acceptable. As for the idea of his model wife being Beanie . . . that was simply out of the question. The wedding itself would be a modest affair. Her dear friend Colonel Hugh Thurston and Miss Angela Bland came to mind. Their wedding, last April, took place in the Savoy

Chapel and had been applauded by society as the most tasteful of the year. This would do very nicely for Herbert and his bride-to-be.

Now, with a goal in mind, she must unload herself of the worst trepidation that had been troubling her for several weeks. For this, she would have to speak to Flora, her cook. The timing had to be just right to enable both women to slip once again into the relaxed mood they had enjoyed recently in the library. To go into Flora's bedroom now while she was unwell would be inappropriate, but to leave it until she was fully recovered and charging around in the kitchen, would be a little tricky. She decided to act straight away.

Knocking quietly on the bedroom door, Grace was pleased to see Flora looking a little more herself.

'I hope those three are pulling their weight down there, Mrs Wellington. I shall be back on my feet by the morning and much better for stopping in bed for the rest of the day.'

'Stop worrying, my dear. Herbert is eating out, Sarah has offered to give a hand and our only guest is my cousin, Digby. I'm sure below stairs will cope.'

'I feel such a fool,' said Flora, 'passing out like that. I don't remember hitting my head so I wouldn't think I've got concussion. Bit of a headache, that's all.'

'I should think it was the shock of hearing that your scullery maid is the chosen one,' she said, laughing. 'It's all moonshine, my dear, and nothing more. Push it from your mind.'

'Hogwash more like. It beats anything that I've ever heard. I can hardly believe your husband would go along with such a silly idea. Young people will come up with madcap plans, we all know that, but a grown man?'

'My thoughts entirely.'

'A marriage of convenience indeed. May the good Lord have been looking the other way, Grace, is all I can say on the matter.'

'Indeed. We both have good reason to object but all of that aside, it was quite outrageous. But there, Beanie will see the amusing side of it no doubt. Your daughter has much of yourself in her.'

Stunned, Flora could no more than stare at Grace. 'What's that supposed to mean?'

'Come, come, my dear. Brown is a common enough name I grant you, but Flora is not.'

'I wish you would get to the point, Grace, for my headache is the worse for it. What has my name got to do with anything?'

'I think you know the answer to that. And before you say anything, please, please believe me when I say I bear you no ill feelings. Quite the reverse in fact.'

'I don't know what this is all about,' said Flora, irritated. 'I collapsed. That's all I can tell you.'

'Yes . . . but we cannot ignore why you collapsed. We've come this far, Flora, let's not push skeletons back into the cupboard. It's not necessary, you have my assurance. I know now who you are and your daughter – Tobias's daughter.'

'I see . . .' murmured Flora. 'But . . . I mean . . . how did you find out and more importantly how long have you known? Did you know when we shared our first glass of sherry together and chatted as friends?'

'No, I hadn't put two and two together then.'

'And now you have. Well, don't lose any sleep over it, Grace, we shall have our bags packed and be gone by the morning. We have somewhere to go so you needn't feel obliged in any way. We'll move in with my parents. But I will say this and I'll say no more. I never knew who the master of the house was when I applied for this job. I lied about Beanie because we were both out of work and had to give up our little cottage. An unmarried woman with an illegitimate daughter in tow does not go down well at interviews, I'm sure you will agree.'

'I realise all of that, Flora, don't take me for a fool. My husband has caused enough damage to my self-confidence in the past without you, my new friend, adding to it. I am not a silly woman who sees only the sunshine, I promise you.'

'I realised that before now, Grace. But I have to know how you found out and how long you've known. Grant me that much at least.'

Grace drew breath and then spoke quietly, as if she were in confession. 'After I had been to the house in Brick Lane, I read my husband's journals and continued to do so on a regular basis. Without him being aware of it, obviously. Flora Brown was mentioned several times . . . along with others.'

'Well,' replied Flora, deeply embarrassed. 'I don't really know what to say to you and that's the truth.

But I will say this in my defence, I had no idea that Beanie's father went by the name of Tobias Wellington. I knew him as Charles. Prince Charlie is what we called him. Had I known that he was the master of this house I would never have taken a step near it. He told me that he lived somewhere in Westminster. Maybe you've moved since then?'

'No. We've been in this house since we were married, but my parents have a house in Westminster.'

'Well then, I expect that's where he got it from.' There was no more to be said as far as Flora was concerned. Leaning back into her pillows she focused on the window, hoping that Grace would leave her now to recover from this humiliating exposure.

'I can't really explain why I took an instant liking to you the moment you stepped into the library for the interview. I don't want to lose you, Flora, and I don't want to lose Beanie. She and Sarah, as you no doubt have noticed, have already bonded in a way. It may be pure coincidence but it does send a tingle down my spine, as if someone from a higher plane has mapped out a way for them to come together. They are sisters after all is said and done.'

Flora turned her face away. She was weeping. Weeping for all those years she had spent wondering about Tobias's family: where they might live; how many children they might have; if he ever considered the daughter he had left behind. 'I'm sorry . . .' she said, her voice broken and hoarse. 'I wouldn't blame you if you hated me, you don't have to try to be kind.'

'I don't hate you, far from it.' Grace was now having difficulty expressing herself. Her own emotions getting the better of her. 'Of course I was angry and hurt when I saw your newly born baby in that makeshift crib but—'

'Please . . .' said Flora, burying her face in her hands. 'Please don't ask me to bring that day back to mind. I was there, Grace, in the house. Upstairs . . . hiding. A very frightened and mixed up girl. I felt so sorry for you having to find out like that. I wanted to come down and say how sorry I was.'

'I didn't know you were there or I might have come up and talked to you. I wanted to know so much and Tobias is a compulsive liar. He couldn't tell the truth no matter how many times I asked if he was seeing someone else. He would simply look into my face and lie. The worst of it was that I *knew* he was lying but couldn't prove anything. He even made me the guilty party for being a nasty, suspicious person, when all the time I knew he was betraying me over and over again.'

'Well, it's all behind you now. Throw him out and be done with, is my advice.' Flora lay back on her pillow and closed her eyes. 'I'm sorry if I shock you but my head is pounding.'

'I shouldn't have disturbed you, I don't know why I did. But if it makes you feel better, Flora, I'm prepared to bring the whole thing out into the open . . . within these four walls, of course, *if* that's what you want. I know that Tobias is taking care of you both and that's how it should be.'

'Taking care of us?' murmured Flora, her eyes still closed. 'In what way?'

'He should have done more than simply finance you, I know, but at least—'

'Finance?' said Flora, pulling herself up on to her elbows. 'A hundred pounds as a pay off? A hundred pounds for me and Beanie to live on until she was old enough to go to school and I could go back to work? A hundred pounds to see she was fed and clothed right up until she was old enough to earn a living? By my reckoning, that amounts to five pounds a year!'

Deeply embarrassed, Grace could feel herself blush. 'I was under the impression that you were receiving regular amounts.'

'Well, I don't know how you make that out, but then, it's really none of my business what your husband chooses to tell you.'

'Indeed,' said Grace, now regretting that she had mentioned it. 'I expect you'll want to leave as soon as you're able. Both you and Beanie will receive your full month's pay. I can't blame you for not wanting to stay in this house now.'

'Of course I don't want to go,' whispered Flora, upset for this wretched woman. 'It's not for me to say, but I don't think you should leave this room until you've pulled yourself together. It wouldn't do for anyone to see you in this state.'

'I know,' said Grace, her handkerchief covering her face. 'I'm sorry. Just give me a minute to compose myself.'

'Take as long as you like. If it makes you feel any

better I don't bear any grudges. Why should I? I was young and naive but I should have known better than to let your husband bed me.'

'My husband . . .' murmured Grace, heaving yet another sigh. 'I don't think he is my husband any more, I hardly know him. Probably he is supporting another family. There must be another woman somewhere who sees herself as his wife – more children even. How can I possibly know?'

Flora laid a hand on Grace's arm. 'Why don't we keep this under wraps? We're the only ones that know, best we leave it that way.'

Grace leaned back in her chair, almost recovered. 'You may think this an odd thing to ask but . . . did he court you? Did he pretend he was single and fancy free? Did he not tell you he had two children?' She shook her head, mystified. 'Did he say he was unhappy? That he regretted marrying me?'

'At first I had no idea that he was married. He behaved like a bachelor who had fallen in love with a girl from a different class. Yes, he did say he loved me, but he said a lot of things which, looking back, was a load of twaddle. I was too young and too impressionable. He even managed to pull the wool over my parents' eyes – and they're canny, trust me on that.'

'What makes a man behave in such a way?'

'Who can say? And now that you know?'

'It doesn't matter any more. I don't love him, I don't even like him. I'm lonelier when Tobias is here than when I am by myself. It would take a man of philosophy to explain that to me.'

'No, I don't think it would,' said Flora. 'I don't think it would.'

After an hour or so of sharing gentle laughter and sorry tears Grace Wellington from above stairs and Flora Brown from below, agreed to keep their secret. Things would remain as they were and no one would be the wiser or hurt for it.

Once Grace powdered her face she went below stairs in search of Beanie. As ever, her trusted staff were busy and doing their best to manage in Flora's absence. Paying respect to Fanny, who was temporarily in charge, Grace surprised them all with her friendly tone.

'I can see you're busy down here, Fanny dear, but if you could spare Beanie for ten minutes?'

Rising to the sudden elevated position, Fanny straightened and bore a majestic expression. 'Yes, Madam, I'm sure we'll manage. I'll send her up directly she's scrubbed her hands.'

'Thank you,' said Grace, leaving them to it. The gentle smile soon dissolved when she came face to face with her cousin Digby on the landing.

'Ah, Grace,' he said, giving his usual hint of a bow, 'I was rather hoping to have a private word.'

'Oh, dear,' moaned Grace. 'Am I to presume then that you have picked up on the silly rumour that is sweeping through this house?'

'Would that it was a rumour,' he said, studying her face.

'Well, it is, Cousin. Another of Tobias's bizarre ideas. Just ignore it,' she said, shaking her head. 'I am about to put paid to the nonsense once and for all.'

'Then I shall not bring it up again.' Affording her a rare smile, he leaned forward and kissed her lightly on the cheek. 'Thank you for your excellent hospitality. I shall be out of your way shortly.'

'Oh please, Digby, out of my way? You're the only sensible one around here. Stay as long as you like.' She softened her tone, 'To please me . . . stay another night at least?'

His eyes no longer on her face but glancing over her shoulder, Grace turned to see that Beanie had arrived. 'I fear I must leave today,' said Digby. 'I've urgent business in Newmarket,' he added, loudly enough for Beanie to hear.

'Digby, old chap!' Tobias appeared suddenly from his study. 'It looks like Mr Churchill's sticking to his guns, a shilling off income tax as from this coming April!'

'Really? And from where did this news come?'

'It's in *The Times*, old chap, listen to this.' He unfolded his newspaper and read; '*It is now firmly believed that Mr Churchill may well forgo the raising of the Sinking Fund to save him ten thousand pounds which will pay for the shilling off income tax.* What say you to that . . . eh? Come on . . . I can see you're stumped!'

'Not at all, Tobias. I still hold that the three and a half million pounds he started his task with was fiction. Under the old order, any surplus goes automatically to the discharge of debt. And as we know, since the

Armistice, over six million of the taxpayers' money has gone the same way.'

'Oh bosh,' said Tobias, a touch arrogant. 'You read the wrong columns, sir!' With that he disappeared back into his study.

'We'll be lucky if we see sixpence off income tax,' said Digby, taking his leave and nodding politely at Beanie on passing.

Having taken Beanie into the library and closed the door, Grace brought up the subject of the plot which her husband and Sarah had hatched to marry off Herbert. She said that it was a silly bet between father and daughter, no more than a ten-shilling wager that, for a house, Herbert would marry the first girl he set eyes on that day. Beanie, in so far as she could make out, had been that girl.

Angry that she had been the butt of their frivolity, Beanie stretched to her full height, her chin proudly to the fore. 'Sarah did come below stairs and get her knickers in a twist about something of the sort, Madam, but I took it for what it was – a New Year's Day prank. Obviously they could not wait until April Fool's Day. But having said that, I wouldn't marry your son for all the silk in China. No insult intended, Madam. And as a matter of interest there's another who's won a place in my heart and myself in his. But I would ask you to keep that to yourself, Madam, please.'

'Of course, Beanie,' said Grace, realising that the girl's pride had been hurt and not believing for one minute that there was a suitor in the wings. 'We'll say no more about it.'

'Thank you, Madam.'

'Good. Now then, I must get on. I have to do some work on the annual housekeeping budget, and I can tell you that there will be a raise in salary for all of you below stairs, and possibly there will also be a small bonus. You've all worked extremely hard this past few weeks.'

'Thank you, Madam, but I don't think I had best say anything about that below stairs. Best if it came from you, I wouldn't want to put Cook or Fanny out.'

'Quite,' said Grace, 'I was forgetting myself.'

'Will that be all then, Madam?'

'Yes, that will be all,' said Grace, noticing that she really did have the same shape and colour of eyes as her daughter, Sarah.

When Beanie had gone, Grace sank down into her elbow chair and cursed her husband. The self-opinionated man was the bane of her life. It was time to consider her own future happiness. Once Sarah had found herself a husband, Grace would begin divorce proceedings against Tobias. Herbert would never marry, sooner or later the poor chap was going to have to face up to his father and admit it.

Also, there was the important matter of Tobias's accounts. If neither Flora nor Beanie were receiving his financial support then where was the money going?

Below stairs, things were relatively normal. Except

that Sarah had rolled up her sleeves ready to fill in for Flora whichever way she could. 'Okay, chaps,' she grinned, 'I've greased my elbows. What can I do?'

'Bedrooms please,' said Fanny, giving her the job she most hated. 'Beanie can go with you—'

'Oh, not beds . . .' said Sarah, wishing for a more interesting task.

'So . . .' said Fanny, slicing cold meat, 'you expect your parents to get into an unmade bed and wivout any sheets and pillowcases, do you?'

Sighing melodramatically, Sarah clicked a finger and thumb at Beanie. 'Come, slave, we have our orders!'

'We'll pop in and see 'ow Cook is while we're at it.'

'No need. Mother was in there for an hour. Cook's now having a doze by all accounts.'

Going upstairs, Sarah asked Beanie if Herbert had proposed yet and what might her answer be. Beanie told her straight. When she got herself married it would be for love and not money. The question of whether she could learn to love Herbert did not come up. Sarah simply shrugged it off and said. 'Come on, we'll make a start on Herbie's. He's still in here, learning lines.'

Arriving at his door, Sarah pressed a finger to her lips. 'Listen,' she whispered, giggling. Pressing an ear to his door she motioned for Beanie to do the same. From within they could hear Herbert clearly as he strode around the room, reciting his lines

for a play adapted from Robert Louis Stevenson's
Kidnapped. His Highland accent was fiercely over
the top.

'*Why David, the innocent have aye a chance to get
assoiled in court; but for the lad that shot the bullet,
I think the best place for him will be the heather.
Them that havenae dipped their hands in any little
difficulty . . .*'

At this point Beanie burst out laughing and Sarah
was quick to clap a hand over her mouth. 'Stop it!'
she hissed. 'If he hears you he'll be furious.'

'*. . . For if it was the other way round about, and
the lad whom I couldnae just clearly see had been
in our shoes, and we in his I think we would be a
good deal obliged to him oursels if he would draw the
soldiers.* Oh for Christ sake! Who in their right mind
would write such drivel?' The thud of the manuscript
hitting the door made things worse. Neither of the
girls could stop themselves from laughing, muffled
though it was.

Composing herself, Sarah cleared her throat and
spoke in a loud affected voice. 'How dare you, sir!
How dare you speak ill of our own dear Robert
Louis Stevenson! Off with your head I say! Off!
Off!'

Suddenly the door was wrenched open and a
red-faced, furious Herbert stood before them. 'Sarah!
Of all people to mock and torment and interrupt me
when I am in rehearsal. My very own sister! My very
own flesh and blood!'

'I'm sorry, Herbert,' said Sarah, keeping a straight

face. 'I got carried away. I er . . . I was er . . . in a school play and . . . yes, it was the very play that you are reading from and you were so convincing, so I played my part on cue. Sorry.'

'Sorry?' he boomed, still in rehearsal mode. 'You take a man from his work and all you can say is sorry! Be off with you – be gone!'

'We've come to make your bed, Herbert.' Desperate not to laugh, Sarah bit the inside of her cheek.

'*You*? Taking on the role of a scullery wench?'

'Well, yes . . . Cook's ill in bed and—'

'A cook prepares food, she does not make beds!' He then turned on Beanie. 'Dear *God* . . . don't tell me you've come here to accept a proposal made by my father on my behalf?'

'You should be so lucky,' said Beanie, laughing. 'Where's the play gonna be on then? I don't wanna miss it.'

'Dear girl, my closest friend, an author and playwright, is waiting at this very moment to hear from the artistic director at Sadler's Wells who is looking for plays to stage at the New Vic. This could well be a major breakthrough for a very talented young man who—'

'Yeah, all right. I only wanted to know where it was going on.'

'How dare you interrupt your betters midstream? Below stairs with you at once, do you hear?'

'I can't,' she said, 'I've gotta make the beds.'

'Oh, I see it all now.' He turned to Sarah. 'Mother

has asked you to shadow this girl . . . should anything else go missing.'

'Herbert . . .' warned Sarah. 'We know who took the wireless, don't forget.'

'I *know* who stole the wireless. I and no one else . . . except of course that skinny, gingerheaded, freckled-face boy—'

'Albert?' snapped Beanie. 'He did not!'

'And I say he did,' crooned Herbert, a sly smile spreading across his face. 'I saw the devil with my own two eyes. From my window I saw him slip out into the Square with his booty and walk furtively in the direction of the Mile End Road, before he stopped on the corner and spoke with a man wearing rough clothes and a check cloth-cap. Money and wireless were exchanged.'

'You're lying,' said Beanie, hating him more by the second.

'When is a lie not a lie . . . ?' he said brushing a hand through his thick dark hair. 'Fiction and fact go hand in hand . . . life and—'

'I'm gonna go below stairs this minute and fetch Albert up. You can say it to 'is face.'

'Oh please, spare me the melodrama.' He looked mournfully at his sister. 'Sarah, do take this girl elsewhere. Anywhere but where I may view her presence from my window. I have had quite enough for one day.'

'I will, Herbert, of course I will. But we can't leave it like this. Were you play-acting or did you see the bootboy with the villain?'

'It is possible, dear sister, that I dreamt it. Suffice to say that the bootboy looks and behaves far too shifty for my—'

'So you didn't see him?' Sarah knew exactly how to handle Herbert.

'I may have: I may not have. It matters not.'

'It matters a good deal!' snapped Beanie. 'You can't go round accusing people of stealing things. It's not right!'

'We are speaking of someone of low birth and rank. Someone who is less than a chap's servant. Now if you don't mind—'

'You rotter,' said Beanie. 'You couldn't care less about anyone but your own self. Now take back what you accused Albert of or I shall go straight to Madam and tell her what you said!'

'Oh, how very tiresome. Would that one of the two of you had a grain of intelligence and a touch more sense of humour. I was *joshing*, dear girl.' With that he gave his accustomed drawn-out sigh and shut the door in their faces.

'Come on,' said Sarah. 'Let's see to my parents' room and that will be that.'

'What about Mr Morton's?'

'Digby? Oh he left thirty minutes since, back to Newmarket. Come on, I want to get out of this house and you're coming with me.' Pulling her by the arm they went into her parents' luxurious bedroom and talked about Herbert while making up the bed. Sarah still had the notion that Beanie would be good for her brother, and that the life she would live, were she to marry him, would be good for her. Beanie said nothing, she gave a polite nod now and then as if she were listening and interested. She had Digby Morton on her mind. Either he hadn't bothered to go in search of her to say goodbye or he had, but couldn't find her.

Smoothing the heavy gold silk-brocade bedspread with the flat of her hand, Beanie couldn't help but wish that she and her mother could enjoy the luxury that the Wellingtons took for granted.

'Oh dear,' sighed Sarah, gazing out of the window. 'One day he will be caught out and all hell will let loose.'

'Who are you talking about now?' said Beanie, joining her.

'My father.'

'What of it?' said Beanie, catching sight of him across the Square and to all intents and purposes, behaving quite normally. 'What about 'im?'

'You see that lovely, grand house behind those double gates? *Double* wrought-iron gates mind, not single, like ours.'

'Yes,' said Beanie, 'of course I see it . . . so?'

'Well, what do you think happens in there – what sort of people do you think live there?'

'Same as the ones who live 'ere,' said Beanie. 'The rich and bored who can't fink of nuffing else to do but jump out of wardrobes and scare a poor maid to death.'

'Well, you are wrong,' drooled Sarah, deliberately holding back her secret. 'I'll give you three guesses.'

'I s'pose you're gonna tell me it's a whorehouse – a brothel.' Beanie showed a look of indifference. 'Well . . . is it?'

'No, actually. It is a House of Assignation.' She tilted her face sideways and raised an eyebrow which did not go unnoticed by Beanie. This was her party trick from when she was very small.

'How long 'ave you bin practising that then?'

'Practising what?'

'Raising one eyebrow without the other.'

'I didn't even realise I was doing it.' She nodded towards the house and grinned. 'A House of Assignation under the cover of a girls' finishing school. It's so outrageous, just like the woman who runs it.'

'Fancy up the name as much as you like – it's still a brothel. Who cares anyway?'

'Oh dear,' sighed Sarah, spreading out on the bed, 'you are so frank, Beanie Brown. I wish I hadn't told you now, but sent you over on an errand to give a note to the proprietor – Lillian Redmond.'

'Why?' said Beanie, taking a small silk cloth from the bedside table and shaking it.

'Because it would have been more fun. I could have written on the note that you wanted to work there.'

'Well she would 'ave soon found out that I wasn't one for all that, thank you very much. Now then, Sarah, give us a hand or go away. You'll get me in trouble, I've got work to do. Fanny'll scream blue murder if I don't get a move on.'

'I'll take you over the Square if you like. Old

Lillian is a hoot, she's in her seventies but still looks gorgeous. Can you believe that?'

'No, I can't. She's not still at it, I hope?'

'No, silly. She is the *Madam*. Oh, but you should see her clothes, Beanie, they are perfectly wonderful. Flowing silks and lace in vibrant colours. She lifted her frock once and showed me her French drawers. A little red silk skirt hung over her stockinged legs, with clusters of black ribbon roses and divided with tiny jet buttons. "You must always gild the lily no matter what," she said.'

'God. I 'ope she's no one's grandmuvver; the very thought of it.'

'Queen of London's high society is our Lillian. Only the very best of gentlemen may cross her threshold.'

'So, she's made a packet out of it then, clever cow. The very best of gentlemen usually 'ave the very best of wallets if I'm not mistaken.'

'Exactly.'

The penny suddenly dropped. 'You don't mean that your father . . . Mr Wellington . . . ? Surely he wouldn't visit a place like that?'

'Wouldn't he? And before you ask, no, Mother probably doesn't know.' She waved a hand to show her indifference. 'They keep up the charade of a happy couple, mind you. They should have divorced years ago – it is a loveless marriage.'

'Well,' said Beanie, dropping on to the edge of the bed. 'You 'ave shocked me. And Mr Wellington really does pop through the Square and into that house?'

'Yes. Mother knows he goes with other women, he always has done. I don't miss a trick. Obviously she doesn't know that I know and I'm certain she hasn't a clue that he spends a fair amount of time over there. I am informed by my dear old friend, Lillian, that he has six ladies on his list and serves each in rotation.'

'Stone me . . . that's shocking. I'm really jolted by it to tell the truth. I never thought that your kind did things like that.' She shook her head in disbelief. 'You're kidding me on, aren't you? It was a joke, wasn't it?'

'No, every word is true. Don't cast me in the same light as Herbert, he tells stupid lies daily. He lives in a world other than ours is all I can think. Now you know why I am in and out of this house like a yo-yo. It's the only way I can keep a balanced mind.' Brightening up, she said, 'Come on, go and get yourself wrapped up and we'll do a bunk.'

'I can't do that,' said Beanie, taking the lead. It was all right for Sarah, she didn't have to worry about keeping a roof over her head. 'I'm needed below stairs.'

'What if I come down and give a hand?'

Moved by Sarah's need of company, she shrugged. 'We'll see 'ow the land lies before making plans. It's not fair on Fanny and Albert otherwise. You go down while I pop in to see how Cook's faring.'

'Will do,' said Sarah, rushing off. Since Beanie had joined the staff the atmosphere in the house had altogether changed. Whoever or whatever was responsible didn't matter. One thing Sarah was certain of: her mother was more relaxed – happy even.

Gently turning the doorknob, Beanie pushed open the door into Flora's bedroom. Seeing her mother sleeping peacefully, she closed it behind her and went to sit at her bedside. She brushed a few strands of hair from Flora's face and then leaned forward and kissed her gently on the cheek. 'Is everything all right down there,' murmured Flora, half asleep, half awake.

'Yeah. We're all filling in for you, Mum, even Sarah. She fancies 'erself as one of us, I reckon. Who'd 'ave thought it, eh?'

'We're not so poor,' said Flora, yawning.

'I know.'

'Don't you even think about marrying that dreadful Herbert Wellington,' said Flora, yawning again.

'Last fing in the world I'd do. But I wouldn't mind walking down the aisle with Mr Digby Morton.'

Quietly chuckling, Flora pulled the bedcovers up around her neck and snuggled her face deep into her pillow. 'Don't forget to close the door behind you, love.'

'Course not. You 'ave a really good rest while you can.'

'I fully intend to, Bea.'

Smiling down at Flora, Beanie held back her tears. Her tears, had they come, would not have been from grief but love. A warm comforting sensation was sweeping through her. Yes, they had done the right thing in coming to this house, it felt almost like home. Yeah, thought Beanie, that's what it is about number ten Beaumont Square. It feels like home.

7

Throwing caution to the wind, once lunch had been served, Beanie had left a note for Fanny and Albert, who had gone to lie down for a well-deserved rest. She'd scribbled that she would be gone for only a couple of hours and would make up the time that evening when *they* might like to get away from the house for an hour or so. Wrapped up warm against the chilly, bright day, she met Sarah, as planned, at Wapping Station. From here they would go to the lively tavern on the riverside, the Prospect of Whitby.

Linking arms and giggling like schoolchildren playing truant, they stole through the alleyways and courtyards, coming out into Long Row where some of the shops were open and others had their shutters down. This was a clear indication as to which of the shopkeepers could not afford to close, festive season or otherwise. A tiny pawnbroker's was dimly lit; the tinker, ever hopeful that pots and pans had been burned over the holiday period, had his shutters open and hanging above the small dusty window were second-hand teapots and kettles. Standing in the doorway of a tiny grocery shop was an old Jewish man looking up at the sky as if he were reading it like a map. 'I think you could be lucky, girls.' He spoke with the tone of a market trader. 'More sunny intervals.' Lowering his eyes, he smiled at them. 'You want a nice slab of cheesecake to take home? It's cheap, but that don't mean to say it's poor quality.'

Patting her tummy and sporting an expression of having eaten too much over Christmas, Sarah shook her head. 'Another time,' she said, quickening her pace and encouraging Beanie to do the same.

'What about some lovely Hamisher cucumbers?' he called after them. 'I've only just opened the barrel today – crisp as a lettuce! – take a dozen for the price of ten and split them between your mothers.'

'Another time!'

'Another time?' he replied. 'Another time and I could be dead! You want them or you don't want them? Don't mess me about!'

On reaching another shop, with a glow of light coming from the rear, the girls, still quietly laughing at the grocer's antics, stopped and looked in through the window. It was a photographic studio with a display of framed photos on view. Some dusty and old-fashioned of unsmiling family groups, but mainly modern families dressed in the latest fashions, which no doubt would have been hired for the day. There were also a few portraits of proud middle-aged ladies and gentlemen, sitting or standing as if frozen in time.

Across the dusty, plain window, etched in green and gold, was the sign: POTTS STUDIO – FAMILY PHOTOS

AND OTHERS. 'Others', in this case, meant naughty pictures. Although the girls could see no further than the display in front of them, Mr Potts, from within, could see them very clearly. Trying to make out whether they were window-shoppers or had heard about his discreet and heavenly studio room on the first floor, he sucked on his bottom lip and wondered whether to throw caution to the wind and switch on his special lighting.

Half sure that he might be looking at two potential and exemplary models, he chanced his luck and swivelled two ornate full-length mirrors around to reveal two posters of voluptuous young ladies in silk underwear. Then, he flicked a couple of electric switches, bathing the rear of the shop with spotlights. He then went through the motion of examining a group of family photos, spreading them out on a table.

Not altogether ugly, with narrow brown eyes, a nose like a mellowing plum and thick lips, Mr Potts cursed himself for not having trimmed his beard as perfectly neat as he would have done this morning, had he have known that two lovely young ladies were going to peer through his window. Christmastime and bank holidays were always touch and go where customers were concerned. Glimpsing his reflection in an oval gilt-edged mirror on the wall, he ran a hand through his thick, reddish-grey hair which curled around his pink silk necktie. He looked all right, all things considered. At least he was wearing his old and trusted green frock-coat, unbuttoned to show off his new blue and red waistcoat. He wasn't sure about

the pink silk necktie but, since he could see from the
corner of his eye that the young ladies were entering
his studio, there was no time to whip it off.

'We thought you was shut and then the lights came
on,' said Beanie, excited about this place which had
an old-curiosity-shop feel to it.

'Well,' said Potts, pouting his lips and considering.
'Strictly speaking, the studio is closed. Although you
are welcome to view my work while I continue with
this job here.' He glided a hand through the air, arched
his body and tipped his head down. A gesture to show
an obedient servant at their command. This technique
was well-practised and had for a few years rewarded
Mr Potts with a good income. Running a photographic
studio, to his mind, was far more secure than rushing
from one disaster to another snapping photographs
which an editor might, or might not, purchase for
his newsprint. Younger photographers were popping
up like dandelions on wasteland hoping to scoop that
sensational picture. This very private business of Mr
Potts was also far more lucrative and with less local
competition. His dream was that one day he would
be the proud owner of a successful studio in the West
End of London.

'We wouldn't want to disturb you,' said Sarah,
politely. 'But my friend and I were thinking of taking
up modelling.'

'Were we?' said Beanie, barely audible. She caught
the look of encouragement from Sarah and said no
more. If nothing else they were in for a bit of fun.

Smiling, he turned his back on them and continued

with the work in hand. 'I am never disturbed by a pretty face and certainly not by two. Please feel free to admire all portraits and group pictures.' He allowed a short pause and then said, 'It's a photographer's dream to have attractive girls like yourselves walking into his studio.'

With raised eyebrows the girls looked at each other, flattered and each with the same thought: *He wants us to model for him.* Not known for beating about the bush, Sarah responded to his invitation. 'How funny that you should say that, that's exactly why we came in. Of course, it depends how much you will pay us and how . . . naughty . . . you want us to be?'

'I don't recall saying anything about naughty,' he said, knowing they were hooked. All he had to do now was reel them in with as little bait as possible.

'How much?' remonstrated Beanie, not taking this 'lark' of Sarah's seriously. 'And before you answer, don't forget we're not backstreet whores. We are from good families,' she said, trying to imitate Sarah's well-bred accent.

'I'm not saying you are from bad families. But if we are speaking of breeding, you, my dear, are from below stairs and your friend, above. Now tell me I am wrong.'

'Gosh,' said Sarah. 'Are you saying that I'm worth more than Bea?'

'No.'

'And what about you, Mr Potts – above or below?' said Beanie, enjoying the silly banter.

'I am . . .' he said, thinking about it, '. . . I am on

the landing, between the devil and the dark blue sea.
I pay half a guinea for a pose such as you see here . . .'
he flapped a hand at the posters of the scantily clad
models.

'And if they wore no brassiere?' said Sarah, excited
by the prospect of being utterly bad.

'Three quarters of a guinea.'

'And no drawers?'

'A guinea. And before you ask . . . not a penny
more whether you shave off your beards or not. Not
all my clients want a photo of women who are bald
below.'

'And if we pose together – two guineas?' said Sarah.

'Between you,' said Potts, reeling them in.

'Each,' said Beanie. 'Two guineas each or we go
elsewhere.'

Potts nudged his spectacles to the bridge of his
nose and cast a photographer's eye over them. 'I
would need to see the goods before I commit,' he
said, stern faced. 'We shall adjourn to the studio
upstairs.'

Saying no more, he marched to the front of the
shop, locked the door and pulled down the blind. He
then turned off the spotlights and swivelled the piece
of furniture, turning it back into an innocent mirror.
'Follow me please,' he said.

Beanie looked at Sarah with a question in her eyes.
What have we let ourselves in for? Shrugging, Sarah
motioned for them to follow.

'I know all about the white-slave trade, Mr Potts,'
said Sarah, bravely.

'Well then, you must tell me all about it one day,' was his reply.

Arriving in the studio room, both girls were astounded. This was really special, more like backstage at a theatre or music hall, than a photographer's studio. There were different scenes painted on canvases of all sizes. On a long clothes-rail hung a range of costumes: beautiful gowns, exotic drawers, ragged frocks, silk and velvet cloaks . . .

'I never expected anyfing like this,' said Beanie, her eyes wide.

'My clientele are many and varied, I cater for fancies. A most distinguished gentleman, whose name I shall not mention, owns the long red-sequinned feather. He will only purchase a photo of a well-rounded naked woman, wearing his feather where it tickles his fancy. His fancy being her fanny. If you are shocked by such things perhaps you should leave.'

'So you want us to strip off our clothes?' Sarah was now beginning to lose her nerve.

'Not for the moment, thank you. I should like to scrutinise you through the eye of my camera. I shall expect many facial expressions and poses.' He looked over the top of his glasses at them. 'You may be beautiful to the naked eye but you may not be photogenic. Please remove your hats and coats.'

Again, Beanie and Sarah found themselves looking at each other and wondering if they *should* leave now. 'Well,' said Sarah at last, there's no harm in having our picture taken . . .'

'I shall not photograph you, I wish to see you

through the eye of my camera, to appraise your features.'

'Oh, right,' said Beanie, linking arms with Sarah and posing. Sarah's response was to cross her eyes and screw her nose.

'Well,' said Potts, looking through the lens of his brass and wooden camera. 'I am an accomplished photographer, so I dare say I could do something with the two of you.' He emerged from under the black cotton camera hood. 'But we need a theme.'

'Dancing girls . . . ?' suggested Beanie, 'we could kick our legs high without bloomers on?' She couldn't believe she said that.

'No. Nipples, bellies and fannies are the order of the day. That or something not done before.'

'What actually happens to the photographs?' said Sarah, warming again to the idea.

'They will not be printed as postcards to be eyed by all and sundry. They will be in a private collection, photographs for my clientele and no one else. But unless we can come up with a theme, ladies, I'm afraid your bodies, as lovely as they must be under your frocks, are not as plump and juicy as one might like.'

'We need to think of something really erotic,' said Sarah.

'Exactly, but I have a notion that it is not going to come from any of the three of us here today. I wish I could be more helpful but there we are. You are pretty girls but not voluptuous women . . .' a salacious smile spread across his face.

'Blooming cheek,' said Beanie, flicking at a lazy bee,

which had woken too early from its winter sleep. 'We could get work in magazines, I bet we could!'

'You and a million others, my dear sweet girl.'

'I'm not a girl,' she said, flicking at the flying insect once again. She hadn't noticed Sarah backing against the wall. 'We're young women, and I think that what we could do . . .' She was trying desperately to come up with a novel idea. Two guineas was half a year's salary for a scullery maid after all. And he would pay this to them for a day's session in his studio. 'What about poor and ragged . . . ? Has anything like that ever been done, Mr Potts?'

'It wouldn't work, too sordid. Try and think of beautiful things . . . heavenly scented women in—'

'Mr Potts!' By now Sarah was flat against the wall, terrified. 'There's a bee in this room!'

'A what?'

'Can't you hear it buzzing, Mr Potts? There is one, I tell you!'

When the bee came at her again, she hoisted up her skirt and petticoats in a vain attempt to swat it away. Alas, she simply made the bee more angry as it got itself caught up in her lace-edged silk petticoat. Her panic and fear seemed to excite Mr Potts as beads of perspiration covered his forehead. Back underneath his black camera hood, he caught the magic moment as both girls were fervently trying to remove the bee from Sarah's drawers.

The piercing scream which came from Sarah stimulated Mr Potts into a state of fervour. His only wish at that moment was that he had been born rich, with

sufficient funds to purchase something that would
only ever remain a dream: a moving picture camera.
Making the most of this unique opportunity, he made
no attempt to go to the girls' aid. If only it were a
wasp inside her drawers, he fantasised, for the wasp
will sting more than once. Beanie, throwing caution
and decorum to the wind, pulled up Sarah's skirt and
petticoats and threw them over her head, revealing her
silk-knickered rump.

Pulling down Sarah's drawers and seeing the telltale
mark on her bum, she dropped to her knees and
attempted to suck out the bee sting. This was Potts'
moment of greatest opportunity if he could act quickly.
Striding from his camera to Beanie, he grabbed the
hem of her skirts and flung them across her shoulders.
He not only had Sarah's peach-like bottom to snap but
Beanie's rump which sported patched cotton drawers
and loose elastic.

With their backs to him, Sarah still crying and
Beanie still working on the bee sting, they were so
absorbed that they had no idea that Potts was record-
ing the scene. A scene which could either secure a
future of riches for them both or damning public
disgrace. Mr Potts could see the guineas piling up.
Lasciviously pursuing his task, the photographer could
not believe what he was seeing through his viewfinder.
The sucking over, the girls had crumpled to the floor,
with Beanie comforting her distraught friend. Their
skirts awry and their knickers showing – one at half
mast – this was the crest of his wave. This was utopia!
'Never before has this happened . . . never . . . never

in a lifetime could an artist hope to catch one beautiful girl kissing the arse of another beautiful girl, such sensuality . . .' he gasped, flashing his camera one more time.

'You never did take pictures of us like that?' said Beanie, shocked.

'If you did,' murmured the injured Sarah, 'we'll want at least three guineas each.'

'Three guineas each if you agree to do another session for me.' Potts slumped down into his chair and shook his head slowly. 'You did it, girls,' he said, 'it has been many months since I have experienced such arousal.' Closing his eyes, he put his hands together in silent thanks.

Beanie and Sarah could not believe it. Three guineas each? This *was* a dream come true. Beanie could buy nice clothes and Sarah could be a little less dependent on her parents. 'We'll do it,' said Sarah. 'When do you want us to come again?'

'In three days' time. By then I will have developed my pictures. If you accept your fee today then these will be my property to do with as I will. But, if you have a change of heart once you see them, we'll call it a day. Agreed?' Slipping a hand inside his waistcoat pocket he pulled out a small pillbox, removed a pill and swallowed it.

'The world could be our oyster, ladies,' he smiled. 'Depending on your good selves we may print only photographs for my special clients or we may mass-produce them . . . postcard size. I leave it to you to decide how rich you wish to be.' He slipped a hand inside his frock-coat and pulled out a small wad of banknotes and counted out six pounds, handing three to each girl.

'Guineas, Mr Potts,' said Sarah. 'You said guineas. Three shillings more each, please.'

On their way back to Beaumont Square, the girls had talked non-stop, and agreed that they would not want photographs of themselves produced as picture postcards. Images in plain brown envelopes for his lecherous regular customers would keep them out of the public eye. What they hadn't considered, and which Mr Potts was very well aware of, was that not only the male species would want a copy of these exclusive photographs, but women too. Once the girls had gone he clasped his hands together and thanked the poetess Sappho of 600 BC who was reputed to be homosexual and to have started the ball rolling; her birthplace Lesbos, the cradle of lesbian love. Whether the two girls who had walked into his life were indeed lovers, he cared not – the photographs would certainly imply it and that was all that mattered.

Back at number ten, things seemed to be going smoothly below stairs and Fanny and Albert were in a nice, loving kind of mood. 'Ah,' said Fanny, getting up from the chair by the fire. 'Just in time to peel the spuds for dinner, Bea.'

'Let me get me coat off.'

'Where did you go then? To the Prospect or Ship's Anchor?' said Albert.

'Neither.' Beanie spoke before thinking. She knew what was coming next and had to think quick.

'Oh, so where did you go then?' Albert looked from Bea to Sarah. 'You never did just go for a walk, I know.'

'We stopped in a small tearoom and had cream buns,' said Sarah, 'and we got talking to a couple of lads who told us all about life inside the post office. It was fascinating.'

'Well, now that you've 'ad a fascinating time,' grinned Fanny, 'you'd best go on upstairs and see what your father wants. You're to go to 'is study the minute you get back.'

'Am I indeed?' sniffed Sarah. 'Well, I shall have a cup of tea first.'

'I wouldn't if I was you. It was Herbert who came down wiv the message and he 'ad that smug sort of look on his mush. Best get up there straight away, Sarah my girl, if you know what's best for yer.'

Sarah caught the look of concern in Beanie's eye. Surely no one had seen them going into the saucy photographer's? Without a word passing between them both girls were thinking the same. 'Well if I must, I must,' said Sarah, turning to go, her mind working overtime to come up with a credible story. It wasn't too difficult. Her mother's birthday was coming up and she was looking for a nice frame for a photograph she'd chosen from the family album. Reaching the top of the first flight of stairs and deep in thought, she came face to face with her brother.

'Oh, the happy wanderer returns,' he said, grimacing.

'Hello, Herbert,' grinned Sarah. 'How's tricks?'

'You ask *me*?' he said, an astonished look on his face.

'Yes, Herbert, I ask you. Why shouldn't I?'

'Mmm . . . Father would like to see you in his study.'

'I know, Fanny told me. You know my friend Fanny . . . the parlour maid?' She winked at him and left him shuddering.

Standing in front of the study door, she took a deep breath and imagined herself about to go on stage and deliver lines of fiction as if they were fact. She tapped lightly on the heavy mahogany door and waited.

'Come in.' By the tone of her father's voice he was certainly in one of his supercilious moods.

'Hello, Daddy,' she said, popping her head round the door. 'You wanted to see me?'

'Yes, Sarah. Close the door, come and sit down. It's time for a father to daughter chat, I fear.'

'Oh . . .' she said, worriedly. 'I haven't done anything wrong have I, Daddy?'

'Firstly,' he said, tapping his fingers on the desk between them, 'drop this business of calling me Daddy. It has always been Father and I see no reason to change it now, especially as you are a young lady and not a child.'

'Of course, Father, I don't know what came over me.' She smiled at him sweetly. 'Whatever is wrong?'

'In short, I do not like the idea of a daughter of mine cavorting with scullery maids. Especially when that scullery maid lives in this house!'

'Oh?' murmured Sarah, her acting ability to the fore. 'But as you thought it all right for her to marry Herbert, I thought—'

'That was all pie in the sky. I was overcome momentarily with the idea of getting your brother married off. Now I couldn't care less what he does with his life. But you . . .' he said, clasping his hands together and looking over the top of his reading glasses, '. . . are a different matter. If you are so friendless as to mix with cockneys for company, then we must consider sending you to a finishing school. Rather late but better late than never, wouldn't you say?'

'Well, that sounds fun. The one across the Square you mean?'

'No . . .' he said, averting his eyes. 'I was thinking of Paris. The Johnston-Smythe's have recently sent their two daughters to a perfectly good place, the name of which has escaped me for the moment. There you will learn how to be a lady and be groomed in all the social graces and prepared for marriage to a gentleman of the upper class.'

'Oh, I would much rather go across the Square, truly, Father,' she pleaded. 'I would miss you and Mother and Herbert too much if I were to go abroad. And I've seen the ladies who board in that elegant house and they seem so happy and energetic and—'

'Sarah, I don't know anything about the house across the Square! If you say it is a finishing school for young ladies, then so be it. But it is not a finishing school which I wish you to attend. It's far too close to home.'

'For comfort, you mean?' She was beginning to enjoy herself. 'I suppose it is in a way. I mean, I wouldn't be able to misbehave would I? Not with a perfectly good view of it from the library . . . no perhaps you are right. Although I would like to get an idea of what a finishing school is all about. Could you arrange something with the lady of the house – sorry, the headmistress of the finishing school – that may help me? Maybe I could spend a day over there. What do you think?'

Stumped for an answer and looking flummoxed, Tobias remained silent, now drumming his fingers on the desk. After what seemed like an age he said, 'You really don't like this proposition, do you?'

'What proposition, Father?'

'Attending a finishing school – in Paris or else-where.' He could see no other way out of this tricky situation other than to let his wayward daughter think she'd had her own way. 'So we'll drop the matter for the moment. On the question of mixing with those girls below stairs, I stand firm. People of our class do not behave as if they are from the slums. And I can only imagine that when you were out socialising with them and mixing in bad company, going from tavern to tavern, you did not behave in a ladylike way. Your slang vocabulary of late has not gone unnoticed.'

'Oh Father,' purred Sarah, enjoying herself, 'you really are a stuffed shirt, you know. What on earth would Grandmother Wellington say if she could hear you now? Let's not forget that *she* had to scrub floors in order to see you at a decent school. Never mind Grandfather, God rest his soul.

'Didn't he slave over a sewing machine until his back was bent permanently? Now then, Father, how would you have felt, if as a lad, living in the slums of Bethnal Green, you were made unwelcome at a friend's house whose father had risen from the gutter and lived in a house like ours?'

'Sarah, I really do not have the time or inclination to listen to your views on social issues. The past is the past. It is the present that counts and I will not have you mixing with scum!'

'Poor Grandmother,' sighed Sarah. 'I can only pray that you were never this disparaging with her. We do hear of children rising above their parents of course.'

'Stop being melodramatic, Herbert is more adept at it than you. Speaking of whom . . . this silly idea of him marrying that girl has been quashed.' Tobias was feeling very uncomfortable. His daughter seemed to have the upper hand.

'Well, I shouldn't think anyone else will have him. Not that she was in the least bit interested anyway.'

'By she, I take it you mean the scullery girl, Miss Brown?'

'Yes, Father, that is precisely who I mean.' There was a short silence, broken by Sarah. 'Am I to take it that you've said all you have to say?'

'No, indeed not. You, my girl, must learn a lesson. You are not to leave this house for one week and you are most certainly not to ever again venture below stairs. Is that understood?'

'And if I do?'

'Your allowance will be stopped.'

'Well then,' said Sarah, rising, 'I shall have to be let out, shan't I? So that I may earn my own living. I could always get a job scrubbing floors at the children's home.' With that she smiled at her father and left the room, leaving him to try and fathom out what had gone wrong. Hadn't he been a good father? A good husband? Swivelling his chair around he gazed out of the window, across the Square to the House of Assignation where he could escape from all things unsavoury.

'Her mother has spoiled her and turned her into a brat. That's the nub of it!' His anger rising, he cursed Sarah for showing him no respect and cursed the day that the new girl stepped over his threshold. Before then, Sarah had not exactly conformed to his rules and he knew that she often went to jazz clubs in the West End. But at least there she mixed with her own kind. Pulling on the servants' bell he determined there and then to sack the scullery maid for changing an organised house into one of turmoil. Herbert had blamed the Christmas Day fight with his dear friend on the scullery maid. He also said – but could not swear – that he believed her to be the one who stole the wireless.

The quiet tapping on the door brought him from his thoughts. 'You rang, sir,' said Fanny giving a hint of a curtsy. She knew how to please him.

'Yes I did, Fanny. Send the scullery maid up will you, please.' The expression on his face was dour.

'I shall probably speak with each of you individually about this business of the stolen wireless.' He looked up at her, 'Well off you go, we haven't all day to waste.'

'Yes, sir,' she said, backing out and closing the door between them. She had a strange feeling of dread. If Beanie was to be sacked for going out when she shouldn't have, even though she had been out with Sarah, what would happen to her and Albert if they were found out? And what, she wondered, had he meant by needing to see each of them over the stolen wireless? Everyone knew who took it.

She went below stairs worried for Beanie but more so for herself and the man she loved. To her surprise she came face to face with Mrs Wellington who had been in the servants' quarters checking that things were running smoothly without Cook.

'Ah, Fanny,' said Grace, smiling, 'just the person. Shall we go through this evening's menu? We've only one guest for dinner, Miss Partridge. She's quite an old lady and eats very little but is somewhat fussy.' This was an understatement. The woman had been Grace's Nanny from the time she was born until she was a young lady. Cantankerous best suited Miss Partridge. Cantankerous – with nothing to lose. At the age of eighty she was obviously of a mind that she could do and say whatever she liked. Clearly, she was enjoying this last phase in her life and making life hell for her butcher, baker and everyone else who came into her happy orbit.

'Will that be all, Madam?' said Fanny, preoccupied.

'Is anything the matter, my dear? You look rather pale.'

'No, Madam, but Mr Wellington has asked that Bea go up to his study.' She answered Grace's questioning eyes by adding, 'He doesn't seem at all pleased.' Her face turned from pale to pink. She was blushing.

'I see. Did Mr Wellington give any indication as to why he wanted to see Bea?'

'Well, not really, but he did say he would most likely see each one of us over the missing wireless.'

'Oh, did he now?' Her mood changed swiftly to anger but as always she remained in control. 'Well, I shouldn't worry Bea for the moment. I'll pop in to see Mr Wellington and let him know how busy you are.'

'Thank you, Madam, so I shouldn't say anything at all?'

'No, no,' said Grace, waving it off as unimportant. 'Give me ten minutes with Mr Wellington and then come to the library. I've just a very short list of food items that Miss Partridge can and cannot eat, or *won't* eat,' she said, smiling.

'He wouldn't . . . Mr Wellington, I mean . . . he wouldn't think that one of us pinched the wireless, would he? I mean, that would be stealing from ourselves, wouldn't it, and none of us would do a thing like that. We're not thieves.'

'Of course not, dear, it's just a fly in the ointment. I'll go and have a word.' With that she turned and strode towards the study, cursing Tobias for tainting this New Year. Throwing open the study door and closing it behind her, not so gently as she normally might, she glared at her husband.

'What on earth is going on, Toby? I've seen Sarah close to tears after a few minutes with you and then my maid shaking in her shoes. Is this going to be one of those days when you imagine yourself to be king of the castle?'

'Oh dear. It's that time of the month again, is it?'

'Toby! How dare you' – she turned away embarrassed – 'I can hardly believe you would say such a thing.'

'So Sarah was in tears . . . how interesting.'

'*Close* to tears.'

'You would never have believed her upset had you been in here a few minutes ago. Perhaps it is she who should have gone on stage, not the West End theatres, mind. No, low-class music halls more like. She's under a bad influence mixing with your servants and the scullery maid is the worst.'

'Ah,' said Grace, pulling up a chair. 'So this is why you've summoned Beanie. Are you about to sack her? First Sarah and now the young maid. Are you tired of female company, Tobias, is that it?'

'Don't be ridiculous, I suggested that Sarah might like to think about a finishing school in Paris. There was no more to it than that.'

'I see. And am I to pay those exorbitant fees as well as purchasing a house for Herbert in one of the most expensive parts of town?'

'The house was just another attempt at bringing our children into line. Although they are hardly children they certainly behave in a childish manner. But, it would appear that your son has made up his mind to remain a confirmed bachelor. It's a trend that's sweeping through young people at the moment. Let's hope a passing phase.'

'Really? So my maid will remain my maid and not become my daughter-in-law – how sensible. And Herbert will get over this fad of preferring the company of gentlemen to ladies—'

'Grace, please, I do not like your tone nor your inference!'

'And I do not like yours! This high and mighty act does not impress me one iota. What is it, Toby? Are you finding this festive season a little on the stifling side? Missing your workplace are you? Too many days spent at home for your liking . . . ?'

'Oh dear . . .' groaned Tobias, running a hand through his hair. 'Well, I suppose Herbert had to get his ideas of being an actor from somewhere.'

'Oh yes,' said Grace, livid. 'Indeed. Were you not on stage acting out your part when I first set eyes on you?'

'That was a school play, we were expected to take part.'

'Perhaps you were expected to, and not chosen, but that doesn't mean you are not a natural thespian. After all, your lies over the years could fill volumes. I hardly take notice any more when you try and explain your coming home late. In fact, I no longer listen, Tobias. I don't even feel repulsed by the stench of alcohol on your breath and the odour of stale, cheap scent on your clothes. I don't feel anything, Tobias, because I do not care any more.'

Peering at her as if she were a complete imbecile, Tobias said, 'Are you unwell, my dear? Or have you taken to drinking gin below stairs?' This last remark was a mistake, a very big mistake. Not only was he using his normal form of attack in defence of himself, but turning the tables on her. He was the one who drank gin with whores. He was the one who had, throughout their marriage, spent most of his social hours away from home or in his study.

'I'm going to ask you something that I used to ask many years ago,' said Grace, 'Why did you marry me?' The room went silent and Tobias looked very much a man lost for words. 'Yes, I thought that would silence you. You had an answer months after we were married, do you remember? An answer that became a stock phrase: "I felt sorry for you." Do you remember saying that, Toby? You should, my dear, because you said it more than once, and always with an enigmatic smile on your face that I could never quite fathom. Did you mean those words or was it an attempt at humour? Not that it matters now – none of it matters now.' This was hurting her more than it was hurting him. Dismay showed on her face but it was pain she felt in her heart. Dredged-up misery which she believed she had put to bed.

'You're just upset about this business of Herbert bringing his friend back over Christmas, I expect. You really aren't as broad-minded as you like to make out, Grace, my dear. Our son is the way he is, and there's

nothing we can do about it. I have tried. God knows
how I have tried.'

'Purchasing a house for him, you mean?'

'Trying to get him to marry was the intention, as
well you know.'

'But you don't have the funds, Tobias. Surely, then,
the intention was for it to come out of my account?'

'What difference does it make – your account;
my account. We are married, Grace, what is yours
is mine!'

She sank back into her armchair and paused. 'Of
course it is. And what of the cost of Sarah's finishing
school?'

'Well . . . yes, that too. But that idea has been
dropped, let her go her own way and make her own
mistakes. I dropped the idea as soon as the ungrateful
girl questioned it. It's a pity, mind, I think she would
have benefited from it. But there, I cannot argue with
you and your daughter on every single good idea
I have.'

He had turned things around once again, laying the
blame at her feet but Grace did not take the bait this
time. He was confirming her beliefs on the kind of
man he truly was. It was not her imagination; it never
had been. 'I recall a time,' she began, 'just two or three
years after we were married, when you had once again
turned your back on me in bed. The next morning,
whilst preening yourself in front of the mirror, I asked,
as I had done many times before, if you were seeing
another woman. I wonder if you recall your answer?'

'Hardly, my dear.' He scratched under his shirt

collar and sighed. 'But do tell me. What did I say that has obviously bothered you for the past two decades or so?'

'You said: "My dear, you are barking up the wrong tree." I asked which tree I should bark up, and you said – as you swanned out of the bedroom – "I have found myself a handsome homosexual."'

Bursting into laughter, Tobias looked genuinely amused although a little pink in the face. 'Did I really say that to shut you up? Goodness me. Good gracious. And you believed it?'

'No, of course not. How could a lovely young newly-wed think such a thing of her handsome husband? But it never quite left my mind completely. I couldn't quite understand at the time why a man would say such a thing if there was not a shred of truth in it. You might have said, "I've found myself a whore . . . a married woman . . . an innocent young girl from Brick Lane . . ."'

'Oh, I see,' he said, rubbing his eyes with the tips of his fingers. 'This is what it's been leading up to. Well, get it off your chest, say what you have to.'

'Not at all,' smiled Grace, 'there's no need. No need whatsoever.'

The tone in her voice was a give-away, she was up to, or on to something. But what? Her husband's mind was racing. Why, after all these years, should she bring up the girl from Brick Lane? There had been so many others, but then of course, she hadn't found out about those . . . as far as he could tell.

'Am I to take it then that your insinuations are a way

of pointing the finger of blame for our son's sexual preferences, on to me?'

'You may take it whichever way you like, my dear, I am certainly not losing sleep over it, nor will I. Shall I tell my maid that you are ready to see her?'

'Oh God no, not now. Frankly I don't care who pinched the bloody wireless!'

'Ah . . . the wireless . . . so you weren't going to sack her?'

'Possibly. Should she have managed to convince me that my own son was lying, then I may not have. Yes, I may have given her a second chance, but it would have gone with a strong warning: Keep away from Sarah and remember her place – *below* stairs.'

Outside his study, with the door closed, Grace paused for a moment as a sense of great relief swept through her. The more she found out about her husband the less she wanted to know. But the time had come, yet again, to look into his accounts. Not his diary or journal, that was all much the same as it had been over the years. Checking his bank statements was something else and now quite urgent. All this talk of spending large sums of money on the children was out of character, even though the intention was for *her* to make these investments and not Tobias. She had to know the truth as to why he was behaving as if he were a millionaire and worse still, a philanthropist. Her worry was that only the bankrupt or insane might behave in such a way. She hoped it was insanity and felt not the slightest twinge of guilt for having thought it.

A sense of isolation swept through her as she stood on the landing wondering whether to go to her sewing room, where she would be alone, go and find Sarah or Herbert for a short but friendly chat to clear the air, or go to the top of the house to see how Cook was faring. She decided on the latter. There was no doubt about it, in the company of Flora Brown, she felt as much at ease as if she had found not only an ally but a friend . . . and Tobias knew nothing of it. If he did, he would try to put an end to this new friendship as he had done with so many others in the past. He despised the suffragettes and to keep the peace she had at first stopped going to meetings, but more recently, having rejoined, had kept her cards close to her chest. She had learned how to achieve what pleased her, the freedom to think for herself and do what she wanted without constant criticism from Tobias.

Always have a good friend who listens well, had been something her mother had once said and something Grace had not forgotten. That she should find someone like Flora Brown, from a completely different background, was a bonus. Working-class women were worldly and shrewd. They had to be to come through struggles that she could only imagine. She felt she could trust Flora with her secrets. Slipping into Cook's bedroom once again, Grace was pleased to see her sitting up in bed and looking better.

'I was just about to have a wash and get dressed, Mrs Wellington,' said Flora, feeling guilty at staying in bed all day. 'I'm sure the girls are managing but another pair of hands will not come amiss, I dare say.'

'From what I can tell, Flora,' said Grace, bringing them back on to first name terms, 'they are enjoying this unexpected responsibility. I should make the most of it and stop right where you are.' Glancing at the small alarm clock and seeing that it was by now six-thirty, Grace felt it appropriate for them to have a glass of sherry. For this she would either have to ring the servants' bell or fetch a decanter and glasses from the library. She decided on the servants' bell, knowing that should Tobias see her fetching and carrying (as he would put it) for their cook, he would create merry hell. 'Would you like one of the girls to fetch some tea or something a little stronger, sherry perhaps?' said Grace.

'A glass of sherry would be very nice, Grace. Purely medicinal, of course.'

'Well, of course, my dear,' chortled Grace, enjoying herself.

'Someone's in love,' said Fanny, scraping dripping into an enamel baking dish. 'Meet someone on your walk with Sarah, did yer, Bea?'

'Yes and no.'

'Ahhh,' crooned Albert. 'I thought she came back in a more than happy mood. Come on then, give us the low-down.'

'I would, Albert, if I thought you could keep it to yerselves.'

'Oh, thanks very much,' said Fanny shoving the dish

into the hot oven and peering at the roast chicken. 'If we can't trust each other down 'ere, Bea, who can we trust?' She shut the oven door with a bang.

'No I mean, *really* keep it to yerselves. In fact, never to mention it again, not even to me unless I bring it up.'

'Blimey, gal,' said Albert, scratching his head. 'What *'ave* you been up to?'

'Well, the thing is,' she said, checking that no one was coming down the stairs, 'it involves someone else who would be in even worse trouble than me if it was to come out.'

Intrigued and wanting to know more, Fanny pulled up a chair. 'Come on then, out wiv it.'

Looking from Fanny to Albert, Beanie had second thoughts. 'Well . . .'

'Well, my arse!' said Fanny. 'You can't change yer mind now, can she, Albert?'

'She can do what she likes, it's a free country.' He was deliberately offhand. A ploy which always worked on Fanny so why not Bea?

'But we're like family now. If you can't trust us who can you trust?'

'That's true,' said Beanie. 'Well, if you cross your hearts, I'll tell you. But you must swear that you won't ever mention it in front of Cook, or anyone come to that.'

'We swear,' said Fanny, crossing her heart. She then glared at Albert who was more dumbfounded than anything else. 'Cross your bleeding 'eart, Albert Henry, or she won't tell us!' Albert, as if in a trance, did as he was told. In truth, he was worried as to what they were about to hear.

'All right,' said Beanie, smiling now. 'Where d'yer think I got this from?' She pulled up her skirt and took her three guineas from her knickers pocket and showed her fortune in the flat of her hand.

'Blimey,' said Albert, agog.

'You never did nick it, Beanie?' said Fanny, scared.

'No, I never! It's my wages . . . for being a model.'

'Oh yeah,' said Albert, 'and what sort of poses did you do then?'

'Well,' said Beanie, smugly, 'as a matter of fact all I did was show me knickers, back view. Not bad, eh? Three guineas for a flash of me drawers.'

'You sure that was all you 'ad to do?' Fanny, with her back to Albert gave Beanie a look to say, I'll have some of that but don't let on.

'Disgusting!'

'Albert Henry,' said Fanny, laughing at him quietly. 'I do believe you're blushing. But I agree with you on this one. It's disgusting, bleeding disgusting.' She turned back to Beanie and winked with a smile.

'I take it this 'appened while you was out with Sarah? She'll see you in deep trouble, my girl, if you don't watch your step.' Albert had taken on a fatherly role. 'I'm gonna 'ave to 'ave a word with that young lady.'

'You will not!' scowled Fanny. 'We made a promise. Sarah would never trust Beanie again if she knew she'd told us and Beanie would never trust us again if we were to tell Sarah we knew all about it.'

'All right, all right,' said Albert, a little uncomfortable with all of this. 'Keep your shirt on.'

'So you agree then, this is our secret?' said Beanie, with an eye on Fanny who was stabbing a finger into her own chest as she mouthed the words, *I'm coming next time!*

'Well, I can't say I approve of it,' said Albert, 'and I wished you 'adn't told us, really. You've made us an accessory to the facts. Let's 'ope you don't get caught out and me and Fanny don't get pulled into Mr Wellington's study for questioning.'

'They won't find out, Albert, don't be so bleeding dreary. Three soddin' guineas just to 'ave the pictures taken? Do that once a week and Beanie could end up buying 'er own little 'ouse. If you ask me, I fink you should go and pose, Albert Henry. You're an 'andsome devil with a lovely body and a beauty of a cock.'

'Fanny, I don't find that amusing!' Albert slammed a closed fist on the table. 'That kind of disgusting talk could turn me right off you!'

'Oh,' said Fanny, placing her hands on her hips. 'That sounds a bit masculinist if you ask me. If I remember rightly, on Bea's first day here, you said she had a nice arse. Well, didn't you? So when I say you've got a beauty of a cock, you shouldn't get uppity!'

'Ah . . .' he moaned, flapping a hand, 'you twist everyfing to suit yerself, Fanny, that's your problem. I just don't fink you should say that sort of fing in front of Beanie. In bed, yeah, but not in public.

'I mean, it's different for men,' said Albert, his virtu-ousness fading a little. 'I mean, when we're excited, it's a bit difficult to hide it, if you know what I mean.'

'Well, you say that, Albert,' Beanie continued, enjoying this wicked talk. 'But I don't see men walking round London with their dicks behaving like water diviners when a gorgeous woman passes by or at the Lido for that matter. And be honest, bathing costumes are getting skimpier. Last summer I saw girls wearing bathing costumes that only came down to the bottom of their bums. Every bit of their legs was showing . . . right up to—'

'Yeah, all right, Bea, that's enough.' Finding a quick way to stop this embarrassing chatter, Albert rubbed his hands together and scanned the kitchen. 'Everything tickety-boo then, is it?'

Coming out of Flora's bedroom, Grace walked slowly downstairs wondering whether she should, as her friend had suggested, confront Tobias outright over his spending.

Caught in the act of deliberating outside his study door, she blushed as it suddenly flew open and he appeared in the doorway. 'Grace . . . whatever are you doing hovering on the landing? Not more problems, I trust?'

'No, no, my dear,' she said, smiling at him sweetly. 'Actually I was just coming to see if you would like a tiny snack brought up. You hardly touched your lunch, and dinner won't be served for a couple of hours yet, below stairs being short staffed . . .'

'Well, that's very sweet of you to think of me, Grace, but I can't say my appetite is up to much just now. I think a good, long, brisk walk should see to it. This business of Sarah going off the rails—'

'Oh,' said Grace, cutting in, 'hardly off the rails, dearest. She's just a little short of chums at the moment, that's all. Most of her London friends live in Chelsea and even further, so I shouldn't fret too much over her using the girls from below stairs to fill the gap.'

'Well yes, if you think so, my dear,' he said, fiddling with his gold albert. 'Usually women are more up on these things.' He checked his pocket-watch reflectively, 'I should think I'll be gone for an hour and a half, back in good time to join you for an aperitif.' With that he kissed her lightly on the cheek and left.

'It's bitterly cold, dear, I should wear your thick scarf if I were you!' she called behind him. He continued down the stairs, showing a hand in acknowledgement. 'That's right dear . . . off you go . . .' she murmured to herself. 'Take as long as you like.'

Going into the library she watched through the window as he walked away out of her sight and then gave him a few minutes in case he'd forgotten his umbrella. Once satisfied that it was safe for her to go into his study, she took a deep breath and told herself to be calm and not to rush. If she was to find out the precise state of his financial affairs, then she had to be in control of her faculties.

In the stillness and solitude of his study, Grace pulled the key to his bureau from the small silk pouch which she kept under her wraps. The fact that he had believed, long ago, that he had mislaid his spare set had been a small triumph. Pushing everything and everyone else from her mind, she pulled the box file marked Accounts from its place at the very back of a deep drawer. Then, with a mixture of dread and fervour she unclipped the box file.

8

It was a week before Beanie had the chance to get two hours off work and go with Sarah to Potts Studio to see how their pictures had come out and to establish an ongoing business arrangement. They were going to tell him that, while they were prepared to show off their bottoms and continue the theme which had excited him, they must always have their faces away from the camera.

Happily discussing this on their way to the studio, they had no idea that Herbert had seen them leave the house together and was trailing them, to see exactly where they went and who they were meeting. He blamed Sarah for his mother turning down the idea of purchasing a house for him and she was in his bad books. At the bottom of this contentious mood, which he often found himself in, was the ever shadowing horror of his own failure to be a successful actor.

Although, given an audience and footlights, he could carry off a part in a stage play, he didn't know the meaning of tact or humility, but only false pride which his father had instilled in him. As a boy, Herbert had also been browbeaten into believing that he had to be tough and strong. These characteristics, going against his true nature, had produced a crushed man who was for ever trying to prove himself one way or another. His pompous behaviour was sadly a cover for his dire lack of confidence.

However, the qualities which Herbert had had to suppress were essential in the world of theatre. He had more than once ignored a director, upset producers and insulted costume designers, not to mention those who had to sweat and toil with the more menial work backstage. In short, he had become an actor only to be hired if there was no other character actor available – his opportunities were severely limited.

By the time the girls reached Long Row and Mr Potts' shop, both were excited and bubbly. The prospect of being paid to have fun was giving each of them a sense of freedom for different reasons. From her three guineas, Beanie had bought herself some fashionable black ankle boots with a lavatory-pan heel and a nice warm cardigan for her mother. Explaining how she had come by the money hadn't been as difficult as she thought. Her white lie had gone down well and Flora was not in the least bit surprised that both she and Sarah had been asked to sit for a photographer. She had asked that she might see the photograph as soon as it was developed and Beanie was quick to tell her that it wasn't allowed to be seen by anyone until it was actually published in a magazine.

As far as Flora was concerned, her daughter was the loveliest looking girl in the world and she could see why she would be chosen as a model for an advertisement. She thought that three guineas for one sitting was rather a lot of money, but since she had no idea of the publishing world, she embraced it and was very proud of her Beanie. Sarah, on the other hand, kept quiet about it. The thought of trying to explain it to her father made her blood curdle.

Going into the shop they saw Mr Potts in an altogether different light. In a fatherly manner, he was making a great show of affection for two miserable and cross looking children, who under their nanny's supervision were to have their picture taken for the family album. The seven-year-old was dressed up in a crinoline frock which was decked with ribbons and bows and on her feet sparkling white socks and black patent shoes with silver buckles. The ten-year-old boy was wearing a matching light blue frock-coat with tight fitted pantaloons and a white-frilled shirt. His shoes were identical to his sister's and his hair, although short and straight, was equally perfect.

Seated side by side on small throne-like chairs, neither of them would show even the merest hint of a smile. Instead of strangling them, Potts simply played along with it all, winking at the children when the nanny wasn't looking and giving personal compliments to the nanny which the children couldn't hear.

Turning from the children he had repositioned, for the umpteenth time, he came face to face with Beanie and Sarah and asked them to please go upstairs into the waiting room. Nanny seemed very impressed that he had a waiting room and wondered if she might go up there too.

'Oh no,' said Potts, pandering to her vanity. 'You're

much better off with me. We have air circulating down here and light coming in through the window. It's a little on the dark side up there,' he said, 'but these young girls . . . they don't seem to care. Whereas a lady of your station . . .'

A gentle smile, a slight shake of the head and a delicate flutter of the hand was his answer. She would stay in her padded chair and wait patiently and as saintly as one could under the circumstances. The children were little brats, but they were her charges after all was said and done.

Having the upstairs to themselves, Beanie and Sarah investigated every nook and cranny and were forever amused or wonderfully shocked by pictures of women in all kinds of clothes and positions. The most amusing was one of a woman with dark hair – a fat, nude woman. With legs wide open, she sat on a battered old chair by a fruit stall counting oranges into a brown paper bag. Nestling between her thighs was a huge mass of ginger curls with a perfect parting. Amidst the variety of others, were nude women chained up, nude women in a bath, nude women dancing together and even one of a nude woman sitting on the lavatory pan eating a bunch of grapes. The striking thing was that Mr Potts had been telling the truth on their first visit. Plump women of all shapes and sizes were obviously in demand – the bigger the better.

'Ah,' said Potts, having finally seen the back of the spoiled children, 'I see you've been admiring my work. This is my very latest . . .' He pulled a large print of a woman on a bicycle with black hair and blue eyes, wearing nothing but a pair of voluminous pink bloomers. Her perfectly round breasts were like big balloons.

'So, you are three days late but better late than never. Anything is better than having to deal with children and nannies, bless their dear sweet hearts. What is it to be, then – photos or postcards?'

'Photos,' said Sarah, positively.

'Less is more,' added Beanie. 'Our pictures will be unique, so you'll get more gold sovereigns for 'em and less chance of being arrested.'

'You could say that,' murmured Potts, keeping his thoughts to himself. Forever conscious that he could be snarled by the police, he had so far managed to cover his tracks very well. It was true that the boys in blue did raid photographic studios through-out London but fortunately for him they focused on wealthier areas, such as Hampstead and where wealthy businessmen lived in abundance and were always on the lookout for the next new set of photos. Here in this dingy part of the East End, the police were too busy with more serious crimes to come poking their noses into little photographic studios.

'I'm quite pleased with the results of our first ses-sion,' he said, going over to a tall, wooden apple storer which he had converted for his own use. Pulling out the third brown envelope from the second rack, he considered the girls again. If they were here to push up their fee he was going to have to give in, but how little he could get away with was the question. These pictures had already been shown to one of his exclusive and very rich clients who wanted to purchase a set straight away. Naturally, he was making him wait – a ploy that always worked.

'I thought that today we might perhaps try an artistic pose . . . semi-nude. What do you say? Nothing on other than a pair of drawers, stockings and a suspender belt.'

'You haven't seen our bosoms, Mr Potts,' smiled Sarah. 'We may be padded up for all you know.'

Blinking at her supposedly tormenting remark, he said, 'As for the pose . . . I should think if one of you were to take on the role as wicked tutor and the other of naughty student?'

'With our faces *away* from the camera though,' said Beanie, nervously.

Potts deliberated for a few moments as if considering this and then slipped the photos from the envelope and spread them out on his table. 'You may be a touch jolted by these, most ladies new to modelling are when they see themselves as I have caught them with the eye of my camera.'

'Stone me blind!' Beanie was more than jolted, she was shocked out of her life. 'You can't sell them to people!'

'Gosh,' said Sarah, looking closely at one of herself with her drawers at half mast. 'Is that what I look like from that angle? Goodness . . .' she began to giggle, quite chuffed with herself.

'You can't sell these, Mr Potts,' said Beanie going pale. 'You just can't.'

'Good,' he said, pandering to her. 'Exactly the

response I would have expected. It takes a little while for new models to get used to the idea, the idea that this isn't really you, but yourself as someone else. If that doesn't make sense to you now it will later, when you have more experience. Did you enjoy spending your three guineas?'

Sarah was too absorbed in the pictures to register anything he was saying. 'Bea . . . you look stunning in this one. Look!' This was one of her on the floor with her clothes awry and knickers showing. 'It hardly looks like you!'

'It blooming well does look like me and I'm not 'aving people see that my knickers are patched and baggy. No, I'm not 'aving that. Take that one out, Mr Potts!'

Relieved there was a different reason for her modesty than he would have thought, he obliged and put that picture to one side for the time being. 'I believe,' he said, studying the natural pose of Beanie sucking out the sting from Sarah's bottom, 'that this is one of the most perfect photographs I have ever had the pleasure of taking. You are a natural, Miss Brown . . . and so too are you, Miss Wellington. With me guiding you, I believe you could reach the height of modelling. I can even see you in moving pictures. In short, ladies, you could become quite famous.'

'Oh . . .' purred Sarah, examining another shot of herself. 'I'm not keen on that one, my nose doesn't look like that, it's much smaller, Mr Potts. Have you been touching it up with a fine brush?'

Would that I could, he thought. 'It's the light my dear, any collector would see that straight away. Although, I can't say I agree in any case. You are equally as stunning in this as the others.'

'Can you do that, Mr Potts?' said Beanie scrutinising another one. 'Can you tart 'em up with a paintbrush? 'Cos my boots in this one look as if they need a good polish and I know I polished 'em before I came out that day.'

'Mmm . . .' he said, squinting at the picture over the top of his glasses. 'Easily remedied. I can blacken a boot, lighten the hair, colour the eyes. But what I cannot do with the brush is what Mother Nature herself makes perfect. She, in her wisdom, created two beautiful ladies to perfection. Would that I were her husband.'

Laughing at his strange way of thinking, the girls were becoming more and more enthralled, seeing themselves in a light which would shock their mothers. 'I fear you do flatter too much, Mr Potts,' chuckled Sarah. 'I grant you that Beanie is stunning to look at, but I'm nothing special.'

'Ah, how wrong you are. It is the eyes and the expression in your eyes which will bring out the devil in the male species. With those eyes, my dear, you could lure a king who would, without hesitation, give over his kingdom to possess a work of art, such as either of you two ladies.'

'Actually, Mr Potts is right, Bea, look,' said Sarah, showing one of them both facing the camera. 'The eyes – we've got the same eyes.'

'Similar,' said Potts, 'you cannot have the same eyes.'

'Oh, you know what I mean.'

'You're bloomin' well right. We 'ave 'an all! Or 'ave you bin at 'em as well wiv your paintbrush, Mr Potts?'

'Indeed no, would that I were so talented. You flatter me.'

'I wish I had your curly hair too,' said Sarah, 'and the colour. Yours is rich and dark whereas mine is . . .' she shrugged, disdainfully. 'Well, no colour at all, really.'

'Which women would die for,' said Potts. 'I would hazard a guess that your father is the one with raven hair and your mother the one with the beautiful dark blue eyes. Now tell me I am wrong.' He was addressing both girls.

'*My* father has dark hair, Mr Potts, and dark blue eyes. So you are both right *and* wrong. I'm unable to speak for Bea of course.' She spoke in a soft tone, believing as she had always done, that her new friend was an orphan.

'*Your* father?' said Potts, surprised. 'Are you telling me that you are not sisters?'

'Course we're not,' said Beanie, 'and you know full well we're not. Why else would you 'ave pointed out that I was from below stairs, with my accent, and Sarah from above with hers?'

'Did I say that?'

'Yes you did, Mr Potts, so stop pulling our legs. We'll pose for you agen, no fear. So you don't 'ave to try and smooth talk us over.'

'Obviously not,' he said. Saying they looked like each other had simply rolled off a tongue so used to flattering customers. But a very good idea was now taking shape in his mind. They actually could be taken for sisters, and sisters posing together in this way might add a new sort of customer to his clientele. Someone 'up there' had waved that rare and wonderful magic wand over him on the day these two strolled into his world. Through the lens of his faithful camera, which forever gave him new ideas, he could see the sisters – naked.

'Yes,' said Sarah, arranging the photos into a neat little pile, 'I think we're worth more than three guineas each a sitting.'

'Do you?' he said, knowing she was right. There was more to them than pretty faces and peach bums. 'Well then, I may not be able to afford you after all. How much did you have in mind?'

Before Sarah had time to think about it, Beanie butted in, her mind on other things. 'You called me Miss Brown and Sarah, Miss Wellington . . . so you must 'ave known we wasn't sisters. I think you tell lies, Mr Potts, and if we're to work together I think you should be a little less devious.'

'My dear girl, have you been as honest as you deny my good self? Did you for one second believe that I would trust the names you gave, when you first came, not to be pure fiction? No one in this business – models nor customers – gives their true names. I have no problem with this, but I do have a problem with your calling me a liar. I flatter, occasionally, to boost an ugly woman before I turn her away, but I do not lie.'

'Oh stop it, you two!' Sarah turned to Potts and sported a huge and genuine smile. 'I think our business arrangement is going to run very smoothly. I think we are worthy of five guineas a sitting. You may print five of each pose which will give you a handsome profit. Yes or no?'

Sinking down into his captain's chair, he said, 'Have I a choice?'

'Of course you have. Find a pair like us who will fit the theme that you adore so much.' She knew they had won this man over and that he would not wish to lose them to a more lucrative deal in the West End.

'Five guineas it is,' he groaned, cupping his face with a hand. He thanked the good Lord she had not asked for twice that amount, which he would have agreed anyway. After all, it was a simple matter of arithmetic. He would charge his wealthy clients sixty guineas a set instead of forty.

'Let's get to work then. Please strip off your clothes, ladies, and remember I have seen more nude bodies than you have had hot dinners, so no need for any embarrassment.'

Horror-struck, Beanie looked to Sarah for support. Surely she would refuse to bare her breasts and bottom? But Sarah was already disrobing. She knew her friend was staring at her but thinking only of the guineas piling up, she avoided eye contact. Watching her friend slowly undoing the tiny glass buttons of her frock to reveal her white, silk bodice, Beanie was filled with shame. Her underwear was not silk nor satin, it had been mended here and there and it was elastic which held her drawers up and not a nice satin waistband with pearl buttons.

Close to tears, she looked to Mr Potts for sympathy. 'I can't do it,' she all but whispered. 'I'm sorry, but I can't do it.'

'That does not surprise me. With a man present, how could such an inexperienced girl as yourself undress? I shall leave the room and when I return I expect you will have wrapped one of those silk housecoats around yourself.' He looked from the much-relieved Beanie to Sarah, who by now was removing her petticoats. Mind you, this girl had removed her clothing for a lover or two – lucky devils.

'I'm really not sure we should be doing this, Sarah,' said Beanie, making sure that Mr Potts had left the room. 'Maybe we should count our blessings and leave now?'

'Three guineas has now increased to five and who knows how much in the future?' She unfastened a stocking and carefully rolled the delicate silk down her leg. 'No one who knows us will ever see those photos. Just silly old men or sad, ugly ones who can only dream of touching a beautiful woman's soft flesh. We're doing them a service, Bea, why should only the handsome and rich have all the fun? My father would never be content with a photo.'

'I suppose you 'ave got a point there,' said Bea, with her back to Sarah as she removed her coat and began to take off her blouse. 'And the money'll mean that my mum can 'ave an easier life.' This was the second time she had slipped up.

'What does your mother do for a living?'

'Oh, she works up North in a mental institution . . . in the laundry room.'

'Why up North?' Sarah was now taking off her brassiere and not in the least bit concerned that Beanie could see her small firm breasts. 'Does her family come from there?'

'Yeah,' said Beanie, slipping off her skirt, 'well . . . one of 'er sisters went there when she left the children's home and stayed. Mum joined 'er about five years ago while I stopped with my Nan and Granddad over Bethnal Green way.'

'Well, there we are then. You can be her saviour and I shall buy myself some freedom. A rented flat in Kensington would do very nicely. That is, of course, if we continue to come on a regular basis. I don't think Mr Potts would want one of us, it's both or nothing.'

'Time is running on, ladies,' called Potts from below. 'You have one minute and I shall be up and at my camera!'

'Oh Gawd,' said Beanie, unfastening her suspender belt quickly and rolling down her thick, woollen, black stockings.

'It's not that I don't love my parents, I do. But I need to break away. Does that sound selfish. Bea?' Turning to look at her, wondering why she had gone quiet, she saw that Beanie had her drawers tangled around her boots.

Laughing at the comical sight, Sarah told her that she should have taken off her boots first and then her knickers. Especially since they were new boots and still not worn in. 'Silly thing,' said Sarah, 'let me help you.' She was by now naked to her drawers. 'Sit still, while I unbutton your boots.' The sound of Potts coming up the stairs caused Sarah to rush which made things worse. She tugged at Beanie's knickers

'What's this?' he said, instantly aroused by the sight of one nearly nude girl on her knees, trying to pull off a pair of baggy drawers from the other. Losing no time he was at his camera, and taking pictures. Getting into a state, the girls were laughing and ended up all but rolling around the floor, still trying to disentangle Beanie's knickers. Potts could not believe his luck, this was better than the first session!

Leaving the studio with no thoughts of consequences, the girls linked arms. 'Your drawers are a scream,' laughed Sarah, 'they'll end up in a museum one day.'

'Oh, no, they won't. They're gonna be chucked as soon as I've had time to go out and buy a lovely set of underwear – no more baggy pants for Beanie Brown!'

'Yes, but you mustn't throw those away, Bea. You have to keep them for when we go to see Mr Potts. They're all part of the theme: you in rags and me in silks. I can see it all now. He's a shrewd man, but who cares so long as we can keep on pushing up our fee?'

'I suppose so,' said Beanie, seeing the sense in it. She was also thinking about her mother. Flora would certainly want to know what was going on if she suddenly saw her daughter in fine clothes and even finer underwear. 'I might 'ave to keep some fings in your room, Sarah, if that's all right?'

'Yes, I had thought about that. We mustn't leave any clues, you know how nosy Fanny is and we daren't let her find out what we're up to.'

'Ah . . .' said Beanie, pulling a sorry face. 'I've already told her and Albert. She wants to come with us one time wivout Albert knowing. He didn't fink much of what we're doing.'

'Oh dear, you really are going to have to learn to keep your private life private, Bea. We can't let Fanny in on this. But not to worry, I've just thought of a marvellous idea. One that will line her purse and keep us in with Lillian across the Square.' Thinking about it, Sarah started to laugh. 'It'll be such a hoot.'

Beanie didn't think so. 'She wouldn't do something like that . . . Fanny selling her body . . . ? Never!'

'She wouldn't have to. I know that Lillian has three old gentleman visitors with pots of money who want no more than to sit on a bed with their shrivelled-up bits covered while a lovely girl sits in her underwear on a chair and listens for an hour while they go on about their past history from boyhood.'

'Blimey,' chortled Beanie, 'what peculiar people walk our streets. I seem to be discovering more and more since we became friends, Sarah. I s'pose you're gonna say I've lived a sheltered life agen.'

'Well, you have been a little sheltered, that's true, Bea . . . but you're a quick learner.'

Before going into the studio, Herbert assumed the role of a lecherous male with a lust for pornography. His acting ability his best asset, he entered the shop ready to give a convincing performance. He already had a very good idea what this place was about and why his sister and the below stairs girl had been in there. Too much of his precious time had already been wasted, but he was prepared to spend as long as it would take to get on the right side of the owner of this place. He needn't have worried, his type to Potts was honey to the bee. Herbert, if nothing else, reeked of wealth.

'Good day to you, sir,' said Potts, his usual affectation to the fore. 'How may I be of service?'

His well-practised art of coming straight to the point threw Herbert. He had imagined a guarded and more shabby shopkeeper to greet him. 'I . . . er . . .' mumbled Herbert, his rehearsed lines worthless. 'I would like to purchase some photographs which I hear you may have tucked away under your counter. If I am mistaken, then I apologise and will leave henceforth.'

'Well . . .' said Potts, wondering how much he might charge this one. 'In a sense you are mistaken but then again you're not completely wrong. I do not keep photos under the counter, as it were, but you may like to view my studio above stairs where I can offer works of art.'

'Indeed I would,' said Herbert, his confidence returning.

Leading Herbert to the staircase, Potts waved a hand. 'Please go up, you can't possibly miss it, excuse me while I lock the shop door. Private viewing, I consider, should be just that. We don't want a grumbling grandmother coming in with her precocious grandchildren.'

'Indeed not,' said Herbert, a touch effeminate and momentarily letting slip his masculine pretext.

After turning the key in the door and pulling down the small blind, Potts allowed himself a moment or two for speculation. Which photos of his male nudes should he present to the sissified gentleman? More importantly, how high might he push the price? Deciding to play it by ear, he went upstairs taking on a slightly different persona . . . a touch more effeminate, perhaps?

'Ah . . .' he said, sporting a tone of indifference. The man was gazing at the nude woman in chains. He may not be, after all, what he seems. 'That is not a particularly good example of my work, and I am the first to admit it. The theme however is rather popular.'

'I'm sure it is, sir,' said Herbert, 'but for my part, I find it rather crude. There are fat gruesome women and there are lovely young ladies. I much prefer the latter.' He smiled benignly at Potts who returned the gesture.

'Well . . . as a matter of fact I do have something which I am certain would please you . . . my latest collection. New Art is the correct terminology. As yet, they have not been viewed by anyone other than myself. I can offer you sir, photos of not one lovely young lady but two, posing together. For this privilege of being the first to view I must ask you to lay, if you would, a five-pound note on the table. Should you not purchase I shall accept the five pounds and say no more. Should you, on the other hand, wish to purchase, then the five pounds will become part of the total cost. For a set of pictures of this quality I ask sixty guineas. Expensive for this neck of the woods, I agree, but low-priced in comparison to extortionate West End studios . . . as I am sure, sir, you will appreciate.'

'Indeed,' said Herbert, 'but I would rather not, if you don't mind, lower my standards by having to lay five pounds on the table. I am here to purchase, sir, and if you have new work in the mode of which you have suggested, I shall place a cheque for sixty guineas on your table this very day.'

'Mmm . . .' said Potts, feigning hesitation. It would not do to appear too eager. 'I take your point and I beg your pardon, sir. A gentleman of your standing is obviously to be trusted.' He bowed briskly and went to his apple storer to retrieve the photos of Beanie and Sarah. Holding the envelope to his chest as if it were an adored child of his own, he sighed. 'You will excuse me for taking this moment to vaunt, but I am a very proud pictographer. These, sir, epitomise the art of photography.'

'I consider myself privileged,' purred Herbert, aping the fellow's bow.

Sliding the pictures from the envelope as if they were made of the most fragile silk, he laid them on the table and then slid the tips of his fingers gently across the set to display them in order of sequence. The one of his sister crying out with her knickers down and Beanie sucking her rump, showing her own patchwork loose drawers, was the first to meet his eye. Though truly shocked he covered it well.

'Highly amusing,' he scoffed, looking from one to the other until he had seen the full set. Sliding them back into the envelope, he asked, 'How much would sir be asking for the negatives?'

Potts was stunned. He hadn't anticipated this. He made a quick mental calculation and then said, matter-of-factly, 'Six hundred guineas would be a fair price, sir.'

'Pounds,' said Herbert. 'I will pay five hundred pounds and no more.'

'You drive a hard bargain, sir, but since you are a true gentleman, I shall say no more. Five hundred pounds it is.'

Triumphant that he had created a theme for his models which would line his purse over the next year or so until others copied him, he went off to collect the negatives from his safe. He had, after all said and done, a far better roll of film in his camera from today's sitting, or rather, falling, as the case happened to be. For the next set of pictures he would insist on six hundred pounds and was confident that this new client would pay up.

'All I ask is that you do not hand these negatives over to another photographer who would likely print thousands which will of course render your set worth-less. These pictures are unique in that they are—'

'Yes, yes,' said Herbert, tired of this man. 'They are the one and only set.'

Slipping the negatives into the brown envelope with the photos, he pushed them into the deep inside pocket of his overcoat. 'To whom shall I make the cheque payable?'

'Potts Studio,' he said, leading the way to the stairs and to his desk where pen and ink were waiting.

Once the cheque had been handed over and a receipt given, the men shook hands, with the promise of meeting again the following week to view the new set of photographs of the same two models. Unlocking the front door, Potts strolled on to the pavement with Herbert and looked up at the sky. 'I believe we may be in for snow,' he said, not giving a toss one way or another. 'I should drive carefully,' he added, looking along the long narrow road for a sign of his customer's motor car.

'Oh, Mr Potts,' said Herbert, a smile of triumph on his face which he could not disguise. 'I did not drive here, I walked. And now I shall take a tram to my bank to stop the cheque you have in your possession and place these photographs in their vaults. You should choose the girls who come in to model for you more carefully.'

'Sir . . .' said Potts, appalled, 'I trust you jest . . .'

'You may trust as much as you deem fit, sir. And should you imagine for one second that you may come in search of me, I shall hand over the photographs to the police. I trust you will destroy the latest set of negatives. No one likes going to prison. Good day to you.' With that, Herbert turned away with every confidence that the man would swallow this bitter pill and learn a lesson from it.

Having been born and bred in this part of the world, there wasn't much that could shock Mr Potts. He had built up his little business from nothing. He was a man who had had to beg for a living as a child and sleep rough under tarpaulin in Covent Garden, eating discarded fruit and raw vegetables to ward off starvation.

To him, the likes of Herbert Wellington were easy meat when it came to retribution. Without any difficulty, he could easily hire a couple of ruffians on the cheap to frighten the silly fellow half to death if he so wished. On the other hand, should the photographs be lost to him forever, he had his second set of pictures taken that day. He doubted that the girls would ever show their faces again and were more than likely in cahoots with this upper-class twit whose cheque he crumpled in a cold hand, knowing it was worth no more than the paper it was written on. Another man might have been filled with fury and taken a cosh to Herbert, but not Mr Potts. He was too clever by half. He would mass produce the new photographs as postcards and at least quadruple his earnings to make up for his loss. Both girls would be drooled over . . . by at least a thousand men.

Returning to the kitchen at number ten, Beanie looked a little flushed and Albert picked up on this right away.

'If you've bin where I fink you've bin, Beanie girl, you're heading for trouble,' he said.

'Well,' said Fanny, keeping on the good side of her man, 'be it on 'er own head, Albert, that's what I say. Best we don't get involved.' Turning her back to him, she grinned and gave Beanie a wink.

'I'll be all right, Albert. I'll be careful, promise.' She went over to him and kissed him lightly on the cheek. 'Fanks for worrying over me though. Now then, why don't you two take a break, Fanny? What needs doing?'

'Shred the suet and soak the dried fruit. It's spotty dick with custard tonight. Mr Wellington's favourite. Cook said she'd come down in a couple of hours to organise us.'

'Oh good, she's feeling better then?'

'Seemed all right when I took her up a cup of tea. Mrs Wellington's in there wiv 'er now as it 'appens. She's being really kind to 'er.'

'I am a bit tired as it just so 'appens,' yawned Albert. 'Awake at half past five this morning, I was. Don't know why. You coming up, Fan?'

'Gimme ten minutes and then I'll creep in if it's all clear. Master Herbert's out and so is Mr Wellington, so it's only Mrs W to worry about.' She turned to Albert and frowned. 'Blimey you do look all in. Don't you go falling asleep before I get up there, will yer?'

'I'll try not to, love, I'll try not to,' he said, staggering out and still yawning.

'He was as perky as you like before you suggested that break. Poor sod, keeps goin' till he drops. So . . .'

beamed Fanny sitting herself by the fire, '. . . did you put in a word for me?'

Beanie joined her by the fire, her feet on the fender, wriggling her toes. 'These boots are gonna take a lot of wearing in.'

'Don't change the bleedin' subject. Did yer or didn't yer?'

'I talked to Sarah about it and she thought it was a bit too risky, all three of our mugs out there showing our altogether. And before you start cursing 'er, she's come up wiv an even better idea for you. Something entirely different that'll earn you as much as we get, if not more. I'd rather do that myself to tell the truth.' She gazed into the flames of the fire and wondered if she should swap with Fanny and let her go to have pictures taken of her in her bloomers.

'Come on then, half a story's worse than none. What did Sarah say?'

Beanie then recounted almost word for word what Sarah had said and watched as Fanny's little face lightened up. It sounded all right to her and all she had to do was go across the Square. The fact that it wasn't a finishing school for young ladies didn't surprise her. 'I always thought them girls looked a bit too much on the glamorous side.'

'So what d'yer reckon then . . . you gonna nip over there with Sarah once it's dark? I'll keep Albert occupied playing cards. P'raps he'd like to see the back of you for an hour, anyway? Tell 'im you've got an 'eadache and need a nice walk in the cold air. That should do the trick.'

'I don't 'ave to make excuses to Albert, thank you very much. We're not married, yet. And even when we are I intend to keep a little bit of my life to myself.' She stood up and stretched. 'I'll go up and give 'im a little cuddle to keep 'im in a rosy mood. I'll leave you to arrange it with Sarah then, shall I?' She got as far as the kitchen door and then turned around. 'Did he give yer three guineas again?'

'No,' said Beanie, 'he gave us five each and all because I got me knickers tangled round me ankles.'

Fanny's faced dropped. 'You never took your drawers off, Bea?'

'Yeah, but it's all right. Only six of 'is special clients from rich parts of London'll see the pictures; that's the deal.'

Fanny's expression remained as her worry deepened. 'You sure you're doing the right thing, Bea?'

'No, but how else am I ever gonna get out of this bleedin' life? I don't wanna scrub sinks, lavatories and spuds all me life, now do I?'

'I s'pose not,' she murmured, leaving Beanie to herself.

Creeping up the staircase, Fanny was suddenly aware of how quiet the house seemed. There was a deathly kind of hush as if someone had died. She shuddered, murmuring, 'Another bleedin' ghost walking over me grave.'

When she reached the attic rooms the sound of the door into Flora's room opening stopped her short. She came face to face with Grace Wellington. 'Is Cook all right? I just came up to see if she wanted anyfing and to tell 'er that we're all tickety-boo down below.'

'She's fine, but still resting. I should take a twenty-minute break yourself, Fanny. You're looking a little pale, it's all this extra work I expect. I'm very grateful for the way you've rallied to the cause. Well done.'

'That's okay, Madam. It's not only me that's pulling the extra weight. Albert and Beanie are as well. And it's no 'ardship, just so long as we know that Cook'll be back at the helm in a day or so.'

'Oh, sooner than that I imagine. She's all but ready to leave her sickbed, but I insisted she stay for a while longer.' With that, Grace smiled at her and went down to her bedroom. She too was in dire need of some privacy and a soft pillow to cry on. Having taken the plunge and examined Tobias's financial affairs she had been horrified to see that over the years, not only had he spent every penny he earned *and* his savings, but had had loans from more than one bank and had put up the house as collateral. Any cheques which had been paid out were for bills, the rest had been withdrawn directly from their bank in cash. Worse still, he had on one or two occasions forged her signature when it suited him. Corresponding amounts which he had paid to one of his several banks had been withdrawn from hers. In short, he had managed to secure one of her cheque books and had been using it. He had also forged her signature on documents when securing two loans.

She could, of course, make appointments to see the managers at those banks from whom he had borrowed, but her only reward would be a scandalous court case which would probably see her husband in prison for forgery. She had shared all this with Flora who listened intently so as not to miss anything but even so, she could see no way out of Grace's dire predicament. The only conclusion she could reach was that Tobias was certainly leading a double life and somewhere there could even be a second family to support. There was no evidence in his files of him playing the stock market and losing out. What neither woman had taken into account was that he did have a serious addiction: women – expensive women. Women who were much closer to home than they could ever imagine. Not only had he been paying exorbitant prices for their services at the House of Assignation but he had been lavishing them with expensive gifts, living out the life of the millionaire they believed him to be.

Whatever the reasons, Grace had to forget all of that and concentrate on how to maintain her dignity and not lose her house to the bank. She was not broke by any means, but if she did not act soon, she would within a couple of years be selling off her family heirlooms and living in a much smaller house. Flora's words had been encouraging, but forceful. Grace must turn to her family for financial advice, and she must do it immediately. The only person that Grace could trust to keep the dreadful secret was her cousin, Digby Morton.

Lying on her bed and going over all that had been said during her private time with Flora, she could see that the advice this astute working-class woman had given was the right course to follow. With renewed energy and determination, she went to the library and locked the door behind her. At her own writing desk she penned a notelet to her cousin:

Dearest Digby,
There is a matter of utmost urgency that I must
speak with you about in private. I cannot express
anything in this letter for fear of it getting into
the wrong hands. This, my dear, will show
how distressed I am. Please come as soon as you
possibly can.
   Your cousin,
    Grace

At the dinner table that evening it was very much a case of all things being well. Herbert was in a particularly good mood; Sarah, still buzzing from her time at Potts Studio, and Tobias a touch more lordly than usual. Grace, having had much experience at covering her feelings, was managing a relaxed face, where inside she was filled with rage. To an outsider this would appear a close, privileged, family scene.

'Well,' said Sarah, 'I think that all things considered, the girls and Albert have turned out a very decent spread, don't you agree, Mother?'

'Yes, dear,' said Grace, 'we're very fortunate.' She would like to have said more but knew that Tobias or Herbert would be in like hounds had she overly praised the staff. The low, baiting chuckle from her son she ignored. Tobias did not.

'Well may you josh, Herbert. If you lived here

permanently as I do and did a full day's work, five days a week, you might not think it so funny. Always one of those bloody people from below stairs wandering around the house, when I come home. You are only here for short spells—'

'Indeed, and no doubt you would be too, Father, if only Mother would release you. I don't know how all of you put up with it. We should move to a house with proper servants' quarters.'

'Release, Herbert?' said Grace, topping up her glass of wine. 'You make me sound like a jailer.'

'Come come, Mother dear. You know what an old rogue Father is, given half the chance he would have a little place of his own. Lots of husbands do, you know.'

'Quite so,' sniffed Tobias, 'and so do sons. When you start paying your way, *then* talk of us moving to a larger and more expensive house.'

Grace shuddered inwardly at her husband's dictatorial tone. Herbert's pathetic attempt to please Tobias had as ever been turned against him. By now he should be used to it. His father from the very beginning criticised every single thing he did, every childish painting at the nursery school, and every school report. Not once did Grace ever hear him speak to his son with compassion or understanding, giving encouragement or praise. If anyone was responsible for the way Herbert had turned out, it was his father.

In a more normal mood she would have tried, as ever, not to take the side of her son but today she was not in a normal mood. Not caring what Tobias would say, she slid her hand across the table and squeezed Herbert's hand.

'Herbert doesn't tease me, Toby. And his suggestion of you having your own place was hardly idiotic. It's a grand idea in fact and one we should have executed years ago.' She looked slyly at Tobias, who was by now glaring at her.

'Think of all the trouble it would have saved you, dear. Running about all over town when your clients could have come to you.'

'Will you not have staff to fetch and carry for you, Herbie?' said Sarah, deliberately breaking in before her father retaliated. She knew exactly what her mother was getting at. 'Once you're married and in a house of your own? If ever you do marry, that is.'

'Oh dear,' said Herbert, touching the corners of his mouth with his napkin. 'We have dared to make fun of Sarah's working-class chums, Father. When will this passion for the people below stairs fizzle out, one wonders? You really should widen your horizons, Sister.' He looked from her to Tobias, 'I take it your offer to send her off to a finishing school was met with disdain?'

'Herbert, dear,' said Grace, her anger not totally subdued. 'Stop trying to side with your father. You should have learned by now that it never works.'

'Actually, Herbert, I didn't fancy going off to France. I did make an alternative suggestion, did I not, Father?'

'Your sister does not want to further herself, Herbert. Now leave it at that.'

'Well, no, that's not strictly true. I wouldn't mind going over the Square, and it would mean I wouldn't be here at mealtimes. Most of the young ladies are resident from what I can make out, and I'm sure it must be a very good finishing school, Daddy. It seems very lively with people coming and going all the time. And the tutors are all men, Daddy. I see only gentlemen going into the house, so that should please you; no sissy or feminist women to influence my young mind.'

'What are you talking about, dear?' mused Grace. 'There isn't a finishing school in this Square. Whatever gave you that idea?'

'It's what I heard, somewhere. The best finishing school in London, is what someone said. Have you not heard that, Daddy?'

'I have not. Why are you sniggering, Herbert?' Tobias was shifting uncomfortably in his chair. 'Is something amusing you?'

'Indeed it is, Father. Have you not noticed a change in my sister? She deigns to call you Daddy these days.'

'Oh, that. It's just another of her passing fads. No doubt it is in style at the moment, personally I loathe it, but there we are. I'm too old-fashioned, I expect.'

'On the contrary, I think you're a modern man, Father,' teased Sarah. 'I mean to say, you're not anywhere near as drab as some of my chums' fathers. And there's a much lighter spring in your step than in theirs. Especially when you go out for one of your long walks. I expect that's what it must be. The exercise.'

'They say that exercise and rest fortify body and mind and with that in mind, it's been a long day so if you will excuse me . . .'

'It certainly has, Mother,' sneered Herbert, 'I too am ready for a good rest after all of my exercising today, I feel as if I have walked for miles. But then I suppose, taking all the back streets into consideration, I have done.

'I meandered into Wapping today, such a ghastly Dickensian backwater. I can't think why the authorities do not insist it be pulled down and rebuilt. What say you to that, Sarah – or is it one of your favourite little hideaways? I must say I was rather shocked to see you there, but then, you were with that dreadful girl you wanted to marry me off to.'

'I beg your pardon, Herbert,' snapped Tobias, 'but I think you must have been mistaken, your sister would not think of going to a place like that – Wapping indeed! Whatever can be there to interest any of us around this table? Furthermore, Sarah has been told not to go out socialising and unless she has disobeyed my orders, you are, as usual, confused.'

'Why not ask her, Father?'

With all eyes on her, Sarah, going pink, could not deny it. 'Yes, I was there actually. I wanted to see how the very poor managed to live and I asked Beanie if she would be my guide so that—'

'Is that so, young lady, and did I not also order you to stop socialising with the scullery maid?'

'Yes, but this was to be the last time. I truly wanted to see Wapping and it was even worse than I thought. It made me realise how lucky we are . . .'

'Oh,' groaned Herbert, raising his eyes to the ceiling. 'What is to become of you, Sister? Wasting time going in and out of the dirty little places that masquerade as shops and stores.'

'*Shops*? I should think the people living there are too poor to buy anything or too drunk to need anything other than a disgusting pillow and old blanket.'

'Well that is what I thought too, but there are shops and there are *other* places. A pornographic photo studio, for instance. Is that not true, Sarah?'

'I have no idea, Herbert. I was more interested in where people live . . . the conditions of the poor and so on. I'm writing a thesis on the East End of London actually – The Working Classes.' She turned to Herbert and grinned. 'So you see it was not I who was wasting time today, it was you. Snooping around following people when you should be learning your lines, you do have a part in a play to rehearse, do you not?'

'Would that I had the energy or interest to listen to Sarah's drivel, Father, but I am completely burned out. It may have appeared to my sister that I was following her today, but alas I was not. I too was researching, for certain characterisations. I have received a manuscript from my agent – an adaptation of one of Charles Dickens' stories.

'I'm afraid I am obliged not to divulge more than that at the moment. But I did find just the character to imitate, a certain Mr Potts. I managed to get into conversation with him . . . it was most rewarding.'

Standing up, he kissed his mother on the cheek and bid them an early goodnight. He then turned to Sarah and said, 'If you can spare a few moments, do come to my room, Sister. I managed to retrieve from Mr Potts some photographs which you might find interesting.' Stunned into silence, Sarah could do no more than stare at her brother as he swaggered out of the room.

Had Tobias not had his mind on other matters he would have given Sarah a lecture on what was expected from the children of men in his position. 'Oh, and by the way,' he said, offering Grace a rare smile. 'I've arranged to visit Miss Partridge, tomorrow.'

'Nanny?' Grace could hardly believe this.

'Yes, Grace, your Nanny. It was arranged on her last visit but slipped my mind until this morning when I glanced at my diary. The old girl hasn't prepared a will,' he said, 'and I agreed to help her out, look over her to see that she does it correctly. It's quite a complicated procedure.'

'A will? Surely not? Whatever can she own that's of any value?' said Grace.

'Well, exactly my dear. That is what I asked her. But it seems she owns that dreadful old rambling house she's been living in all these years, left to her by an uncle, apparently. Who would have thought it? She lives like a hermit without two farthings to rub together and yet she is a woman of property.' .

Grace was horrified to think of him going to see

her. This sudden interest in Miss Partridge was totally out of character. Could he possibly have designs of wheedling his way into her will? She could not take her eyes off him, as if she was trying to read his mind. 'Perhaps I could come with you just for the ride?'

'No, no. She wouldn't want that, Grace. Leave the poor woman with some sense of dignity. Two of us helping her fill in a form? I hardly think so.' He had, yet again, managed to make her sound foolish. 'Of course I shall advise her to sell the house and go into a suitable retirement home near the sea.'

'You talk Miss Partridge into something?' said Sarah, 'I doubt that, Daddy. I doubt it very much.' Grace was not the only one who suspected his motives.

'Well, there we are, my dears. It just shows how wrong you can be, she listened with great interest. But we shall see, I shan't push her into anything she doesn't want to do.'

No, thought Grace, you shan't. Because Nanny does not like you and never has done. Maybe the clever old thing was out to prove something. 'Well, try and not confuse the poor old dear and remember to give her my love.'

'Well, I shan't be home for lunch or dinner tomorrow, by the way,' said Sarah. 'I'm meeting up with some chums in Covent Garden and then we're going on to Sophia's place. It's her birthday and we're going to celebrate.' Sarah was eager to get away from the table. She had a score to settle. Herbert obviously had seen her coming out of Potts Studio and she needed to know what he had been up to. His interference in her life alone was enough. But to torment her over it at the dinner table was evil.

'Covent Garden?' barked Tobias. 'More material for this book you are supposedly writing? Good God, it will be the meat market next! And no doubt you'll celebrate in some seedy jazz club?'

'That's right, Daddy. And it's going so well that soon I shall be needing a typewriter. Oh and I think the writing desk in my room is too small, I shall need a desk as well.'

'Really?' He looked from Grace to Sarah. 'You are somewhat rather demanding today, Sarah. We do not have unlimited funds, since both you and your brother deem fit not to earn your own living.'

'Oh, I shall buy my own equipment from the fees I will get for the articles I'm writing by hand.'

'Articles,' said Grace. 'How interesting, darling. On what subject?'

'The rights of women. There will be three altogether: The right not to have to sell one's body to eat; the right to choose whether one may work in the City, no matter the class; and the third, which I can't wait to scribble – the right to see all brothels boarded-up for good.' She was lying through her back teeth to try and get the message across to her father, who was shifting in his seat and looking a touch uncomfortable.

'Well, I think that's very commendable, dear,' said Grace. 'I should very much like to read them once—'

'Oh no, Mummy. I would be too embarrassed. Let's wait until an editor has cast an eye over them first. In fact, let's wait until they're published.'

'Are we to presume that you have been commissioned to write for a particular journal?' said Tobias, worried.

'Yes, Father, you may presume that. *The Link*. The editor is a friend of Sophia's. We'll be discussing the material over lunch. If I pull this off, I shall write another on the evils of prostitution and the procuration of mistresses. Must dash . . .' With that she was up from the table, out of the door and off to have words with Herbert.

'How very tiresome,' said Tobias, the worries of the world on his shoulders, 'your liaison with the suffragettes must have made an impression on the girl at an early age.'

'Well, at least I have something to be proud of then. It was not for nothing after all.' Her look of satisfaction was reciprocated with one of hostility from her husband. 'Perhaps I shall withdraw from the cause and let the young take the baton, leaving me with time to look into other matters of interest. What do you think?'

'What other matters could possibly interest someone like you, Grace?'

'You'll find out in the fullness of time, Toby, I promise you.' She smiled a little too smugly for his liking. He shifted in his seat, clasped his hands together and closed his eyes.

Charging into Herbert's room without bothering to knock, Sarah found him, as usual, lying on his bed, resting. 'How *dare* you follow me!' she barked. 'You are insufferable!'

'Oh, do shut up, Sarah. I have done what I have done for the good of our family name. And that, my dear girl, is an end to the matter.'

'What do you mean, you sly, evil, swine? Done what for the good?'

'Secured from Mr Potts those disgusting pornographic photos of you and that slut from below stairs.'

'They are not pornographic, they are artistic! Of all people, *you* should have seen that! Did you buy them from him . . . is that what you're saying?'

His face broke into a broad smile and he began to chuckle. 'I gave him a cheque he could not refuse and then went to my bank immediately to stop it.'

'And the pictures?'

'In safe keeping. In the vaults of our family solicitor, marked private and confidential.' Herbert, it would seem, could not manage to ever tell the complete truth. The photographs were in the vaults of the bank. Mention of the family solicitor would worry Sarah even more. 'I shouldn't return to Potts if I were you. When I left him he was in a particularly ugly mood. To quote him precisely: "If those girls turn up here again they'll get their faces slashed."'

'You complete and utter bastard liar!' she hissed.

'If you would be so kind as to close the door quietly behind you, Sarah, I am trying to think.' He sighed heavily. 'Would that I was miles away from here.'

Slamming the door behind her as hard as she possibly could, she stormed into her room, flung herself on the bed and punched the mattress and then the pillow, imagining it was Herbert's face under attack. Once she had exhausted herself, she lay back and thought how to get back at him. This modelling work she had found without searching had been the answer to a dream. Her dream of freedom from her father, with his silly outdated house rules. It was almost as if he had something to prove to the world when the world couldn't care less. Apart from Beanie, her friends were from well-connected families, and their fathers were giving them freer rein.

Realising that neither she nor Beanie dare go back to the studio in Wapping, she tried to think of other ways in which she might earn her own living. She had never been top of the class at school and had found most lessons painfully dull and boring. The only subject in which she stood out as a talented child were the art classes. The mere mention of it to her father, many years ago, had been met with ridicule: 'No daughter of mine is going to try her hand at being an artist.' When she had asked him which profession he would have her successful in, he had given her one of his condescending looks, saying, 'Marry young and marry well.'

Her mind went back to Potts Studio. If she could only lease such a place and employ girls like herself and Beanie to pose for pictures, that would be seen as art and not pornography. Surely such a place would be very cheap to rent. She thought about her girlfriends who, like her, were wandering through life aimlessly, hoping to find something that would fulfil their hopes and dreams other than marriage. They would be willing to pose for her, it would not only be a joy but earnest and rewarding in other ways too.

'The Wapping Girls,' she whispered, enjoying the daydream. Sitting up, a new dawning rushed through her – if Mr Potts could set himself up then so could she. It had, after all, been she and Beanie fooling around that had given him the idea of two naughty girls together. Dashing out of her room in search of her mother, she could hardly contain her excitement. She found her in the library looking through her own bank statements.

'Mummy!' she cried out, her face flushed with enthusiasm. 'I *know* what I want to do, at last I know what it is!'

Slowly turning to gaze at her adorable daughter, Grace smiled gently. 'Go on, my dear . . . before you burst a blood vessel.'

'I want to be a photographer. Not an ordinary family photographer . . . more in the line of New Art. All I would need is the equipment and a loan in order for me to lease a small place as my studio.' Falling to her knees and laying her head on Grace's lap, she pleaded with her not to say anything to her father or brother, whom she knew would only put a damper on it.

'I can't see anything wrong with your idea, Sarah,' said Grace, a touch preoccupied. 'But funds might be a problem . . .'

'A problem? But it wouldn't be thousands of pounds, a few hundred, that's all.'

'Indeed . . . but a few hundred to spare, let alone on a venture that might not take off, is out of the question. In a year or so things might look different.'

'But a year is a lifetime!'

'Well, it might seem that way to you now but it's just a moment on life's clock. Really, you must learn to be patient. We may have to sell Laversham Hall in any case, to boost our funds, but until then you must wait.'

'Sell Laversham Hall? But that's your family home?'

'Yes dear, I know. But we seem to use it much less now that you and Herbert are adults and—'

'Mummy, you can't sell it, you simply can't. You were brought up there, your roots are in Suffolk.'

'No. They were, but since I married and your father and I were given this house my roots are here. You were born here, my dear. This house is my world, I would rather sell the house in the country than number ten.' She placed a gentle finger under Sarah's chin and tilted her face, to look at her. 'But if you *really* preferred it we could possibly move to Suffolk and put this place on the market.'

'No, not this house!'

'Well then, that's settled. Things change, dearest, and we must adjust along the way. Now run along and see if below stairs are back into their usual routine. I imagine that Cook is back to normal by now but we don't want her to overdo it.'

In an entirely different mood, Sarah left her mother, wondering what had happened to make her think about selling one of the family homes. Surely her father hadn't bought Herbert a house without telling her? Or maybe he had been overspending across the Square? Something bad had happened and because of it they were going to have to let go of their lovely house in the country.

Alone again, Grace telephoned her family solicitor to let him know her intentions. Naturally, the deeds of the house were with him and he was the best person to deal with the sale. Pleased though he was to hear from her, he was, as most solicitors seemed to be, very busy. Because of this he hadn't really registered the intonation in her voice. Once again she was in for a shock: Tobias, some ten years back, had taken a loan on the house, a mortgage. Five years later, he had secured another loan. The solicitor ran through dates and amounts as if she knew all about it and just needed a reminder on when and how things had transpired.

Her first reaction was to keep quiet – say nothing, go along with all he was saying – but already in a state of anxiety, she found it impossible at one point even to speak. She was on the brink of collapsing into tears.

'Please . . . give me a moment . . .' was all she managed to say before taking a very deep breath and composing herself. Her solicitor by this time had realised that something was wrong. He waited patiently for her to explain, and explain she did – everything poured out. Right back to the Brick Lane revelation to the present day when Tobias was as unfaithful as ever and with more than one lover. She also told him of their financial state of affairs and he was, quite frankly, shocked. Grace had shocked a solicitor.

His parting question was, 'What do you want to do about it?'

'I don't know. I haven't really had time to think, let alone plan. Laversham Hall must be sold of course and the debts paid. Whatever's left over will have to be paid to banks for various loans that Tobias has taken. Taken in my name as well as his own, you see. So unless I want to see him going to prison for forgery, there isn't very much else I can do but sell and pay up.'

This man had come to know Grace more and more since she had turned twenty-one and had inherited the family house in the country which had once been the home of her great-grandparents. 'Things can't possibly be that bad, Grace?'

'They can, I'm afraid . . . they are,' she said, unable to stop the tears. 'I believe that I am going to find out more and if that is the case we may be close to bankruptcy.' All went quiet, she could almost touch the anger coming down the line. 'But,' she said, swallowing, 'I have written to my cousin, Digby Morton.'

'Good,' said the gentle man, cutting in. 'He will come to your aid, I'm certain of it. There might be a clause written in though, my dear, and I cannot say I would blame your cousin if he were to insist on it.'

'Yes,' said Grace, 'I know exactly what you mean. If I am to file for a divorce it must be before Digby disburses a loan. Otherwise what proof is there that Tobias will not . . .' At this point she found it impossible to go on. So distraught she could not utter one word.

'Grace?' His tender voice made her feel worse. 'Grace, I shall hang up now while you compose yourself. Please feel free to telephone whenever you need to, God bless.' With that, he put down the receiver and left Grace with the dialling tone competing against the pounding of her heart. She had said it. Spoken the word out loud. After so many years of thinking it, she had now voiced it and to her solicitor of all people: Divorce.

Telling Beanie that their brief time of adventure in Wapping was at an end was easier than Sarah imagined. Together, sitting on a bench in the Square, wrapped up against the cold January air, they talked as they had never talked before, Herbert being the first topic of conversation. After explaining what had happened, Sarah confessed that although she had always loved her brother, because he was her brother, she had not always liked him. As children, he had ruled the roost and had sometimes got her into trouble by telling tales out of school. She blamed her father for it. He had always bullied Herbert with words rather than action, which always had him crying into his pillow.

Beanie also opened up. She broke her well-kept secret, begging that Sarah would never tell anyone. She confessed that she had never known her dad. The story of him being killed during the war might not be true but simply a concoction by her mother and grandparents for the sake of their reputation. Sarah's response was to simply shrug it off, saying that she might have in the long run been better off without a father. For as far back as she could remember, Tobias had caused her mother no end of grief and it hadn't gone unnoticed.

'Promise me, Sarah,' said Beanie, guilty that she had broken the secret, 'promise me you won't ever let on to anyone and especially not to my mum. She don't even know that, for me, the penny dropped years ago, when I was fourteen. I wanted to find out more about where he was killed and where he was buried. Mum wouldn't talk about it and that wasn't like her. So I soon put two and two together and it never took much to find out more. My mum never was married.'

'So you don't even know who he was . . . is?' said Sarah, intrigued by her story which by comparison was far more interesting than her own. 'He might be alive and well for all you know?'

'So what if he is, I'm not bothered, what does it matter? He must 'ave left Mum as soon as she knew she was pregnant so . . . no . . . I'm not bothered. Would you be?'

'I'm not sure,' said Sarah, honest and sincere. 'I think I might want to know . . . I think.' She looked sorrowfully at Beanie. 'And there I was complaining about my brother when you don't have one at all. It must have been lonely, Bea, was it?'

'No, not really. Not so I can remember. But I will say this about your brother in his defence. He might 'ave done what he did for your sake, getting them photos out of Potts' hands to save you getting into deep water. Maybe he's the sort who can't express their feelings and it comes out wrong. Take Christmas Day, all the blame for what 'appened was put on Herbert and it even seemed like he caused the trouble. But who was it who nicked the wireless and who was it who goaded 'im about 'is boring stories? Bloomin' Gerald wot's-'is-name.'

'I suppose you could be right, I would like to think so, Bea. It's not been all that easy for him. What with the way he is and everything. Father was horrid to him when he was a boy . . . and then he sent him off to India when he didn't want to go.

'Well . . . all I know is that when I'm ready to open my photographic studio I won't let Father stop me. I really won't.'

'What are you talking about, Sarah? *Your* studio?'

'That's right, Bea, in a year or so I'm going to do it. Not like Mr Potts, though. Rude but not crude, if you like. New Art. Mother's going to finance it.'

'Sarah, that's brilliant! I'd love it if you did that, it would be fabulous!'

'See, there's two sides to everyone,' said Sarah, lifting herself from the bench seat. 'I'm not just out for a lark, there *is* a serious side to me.'

Wanting to know more about it, Beanie linked arms and strolled with her, back to number ten, not caring who saw that they were best friends. Because to her mind they were, even though Sarah lived above stairs and she worked below. Parting company, Beanie was greeted by a not too happy Fanny.

'You're gonna bleedin' well get the sack you are, Beanie Brown. Never mind who it is you keep on skiving off wiv. That won't 'old no water when push comes to shove!' Fanny was a little on the jealous side.

'I was only out there for ten minutes, that's not gonna crack the day, is it?'

'No, but what if you was seen from an upstairs window? Sarah'll get it in the neck an' all. They don't want 'er mixing wiv the likes of us.'

'Well, she won't be for very long if you ask me. I reckon she'll be off soon, doing 'er own thing. The modelling come to an end by the way. We can't go back there no more.'

'And why not, may I ask?'

'We just can't, that's all and I can't say I'm that sorry,' murmured Beanie, pouring herself a cup of tea. 'I think we went off the rails a bit there. It all seemed to 'appen so quick we never 'ad time to reason the consequences. We could 'ave got into so much trouble.'

'And over the Square? You're not gonna tell me that's off as well. I was banking on earning a few more quid, you raised me 'opes, Beanie Brown.'

'Do what you want, Fanny,' said Beanie, carrying her tea to the fireside. 'I'm not yer keeper. I don't think you should though. Think about it . . .' she said, gazing into the fire, '. . . getting paid for sitting with 'ardly anythin' on in front of a dirty old man.'

Slamming a few pots and pans about, Fanny went quiet before saying, 'Gone a bit holier than thou, ain't yer . . . wot's brought all this on then? You was full of it not so long ago, no holds barred is what I thought!'

'I know, but what if Albert found out? You'd lose

'im, Fan, I know you would and so do you, really. Money in the bank or not. A bloke wouldn't want 'is sweetheart to do things like that, especially not your Albert.'

'It could change our lives,' grouched Fanny, 'all that money I could put by. Don't wanna be at everyone's beck and call all our lives – me and my Albert – what kind of an existence would that be?'

'Not as bad as some 'ave got,' said Beanie, still gazing into the fire. 'I don't reckon it's what you've got so much as 'ow happy you are.' She went quiet, then murmured, 'It's a funny old world.'

'Well it won't be bleedin' funny if you don't get yer arse off that chair and get cracking. Cook and Albert'll be in from the markets shortly and I ain't 'aving them goin' on at me for slacking. Especially when it's you that's slacking and not me.'

'I'll get on in a minute. Stop goin' on.'

'Anyone'd fink you was born above yerself,' she grumbled, 'the way you go on. Born wiv a silver spoon in yer mouth, was yer?'

9

After two days deliberating as to whether to confront Tobias over her findings, Grace decided against it. She would follow her instincts, instead. This was not the time for an explosion and things might get worse if she opened up too soon. The outcome might be disastrous and she still had Sarah and Herbert to think of. Her husband would not be able to deny the truth this time. With the evidence laid out before him, he would, she felt sure, do as he had always done and turn things round to place the blame on her shoulders, accusing her of forever hounding him. She would wait for her cousin, Digby, to arrive – he was due that very afternoon. He was a sensible and reasonable man, and she would follow his advice. All of these things were going through her mind in the calm of the library, the room she loved so much and would so dearly miss, *if* the house was to be sold off.

When her cousin's motor car pulled up outside the house, it was Beanie who spotted him first. Collecting the lunch tray from the morning room, she had a clear view of the gleaming black motor car and its driver. Thrilled to see him again, she stepped back for fear of him spotting her gazing at him. He hadn't been in her mind every hour of every day, but he had been there at night before she drifted into sleep, and he had been there again in the morning, when she awoke.

Telling herself she was being silly, she straightened and became as prim and proper as a servant should when greeting a visiting member of the family. It was Fanny who answered the door and told him where he would find his cousin, Mrs Wellington. Hearing his footsteps on the stairs, Beanie froze on the spot and not until she heard the door of the library open and then close again did she relax. Enjoying the wonderful sensation sweeping through her, she walked slowly down below and showed an ordinary face.

'I'm going to have to have a word with Albert,' said Flora, as she came into the kitchen carrying a sack of potatoes. 'He should have brought these in and tipped some in the spud box for us to use before he went out.'

'Well it is his half day off, Cook,' said Fanny, a touch miffed by her grumbling about her beloved.

'That's as may be, but he could have done this little job for me first.' Looking from Fanny to Beanie, Flora wondered what had got into the pair of them. Something was in the air. They weren't nattering to each other, nor were they skiving or sulking, no doubt she would get to hear of it soon. Meanwhile she had her own work to do and her own dreams to dream. Now that Grace Wellington knew that Beanie was Sarah's half sister as well as her friend, she wondered if her daughter might, one day, have an easier life.

When Digby arrived in the library, his face set and

looking terribly concerned for his cousin, he held out his arms and Grace fell into them. 'Nothing is as bad as it seems, my dear . . .' he said, searching her face.

'I do hope you're right, Digby,' she said, hugging him tightly.

'I know I am. You remember grandfather's saying, "If there's a problem then we must throw money at it?" He never did of course, but then there really hasn't been much of a problem so far. We should take comfort from that.'

'Indeed we should,' she said, smiling. 'So, am I to presume you know something of what's been going on? You mentioned money and problem in the same breath.'

Digby took a few moments before answering, trying to find the best way of telling Grace that he had always been concerned over the way her husband lived his life. Any fool could see that his outgoings must surely be more than his income. 'Tobias has a taste for the good life, has he not?'

'Ah, I interpret that to mean . . . his seeing other women?' said Grace, not embarrassed by it but bothered that Tobias's behaviour had not gone unnoticed. And if Digby knew, who else might?

'Well, yes, I suppose that is what I mean.'

'Yes. And I am ashamed to say that I've known for a very long time that Tobias is unfaithful. I blame myself in part for this dreadful mess. Tobias has been spending as if he were exceedingly rich, which he is not, and flaunting money, which was not his to flaunt.

'In short, my dear cousin,' said Grace, turning her back to him and close to tears, 'he has forged my signature whenever it suited him and it suited him quite often, apparently. This house and Laversham Hall have been mortgaged. I do not have adequate funds to pay off the debts. Cash has been withdrawn from my account too, my signature forged. I'm afraid this is not a recent thing, Digby, it's been going on for years.' She turned to face him and shrugged, 'My children were no more than a few years old when he took a mistress and made her with child.'

'Grace, are you sure you want to tell me all of this?' said Digby, deeply embarrassed by this uncharacteristic admission of a marriage going wrong from the very beginning.

'I have to, Digby,' she said, offering him an appealing smile, 'and I'm sorry that you are the one I have to turn to but—'

'Oh for goodness' sake, Grace. If the tables were turned and I were in trouble you would be the one I would call upon, but then you know that.' Pushing a hand through his hair, he looked bewildered by it all. 'It's just that it's . . . well . . . a bit of a shock hearing it all at once.' A worried smile spread across his face. 'To say the least.'

'Yes, I suppose so but you spoke as if you knew?'

'Well, yes, some of it, but not so much the very personal side of your marriage. I had a good idea that Tobias may have strayed now and then and that you might have financial difficulties.'

'But how could you possibly know that? How could you even guess that we were deeply in debt?'

'Because Nanny, Miss Partridge, came to see me soon after her visit here.'

'Really?' All of a sudden new thoughts rushed through her mind. Did everyone around her know – and if so for how long? Right back to when she found out about his illegitimate daughter? Worse still, did others know more than she did . . . might there be still worse to come?

'I seem to have been living in a transparent world, Digby,' she said, gripping the back of an armchair and taking a deep breath. 'How long have they all been gossiping, I wonder?' she said, easing herself into the chair. 'And what did Nanny have to say?' murmured Grace.

'That things in this house were not all they appeared to be. That Toby was living like a king with an income of a prince and if he were to continue, he would end a pauper.'

'I see. Well, I can't say I'm not disappointed that Miss Partridge chose to go to you, Digby, instead of taking me aside as she always used to and giving me a good talking to.'

'I believe she realised that you knew what was going on,' he said, boldly telling the truth.

'How funny,' murmured Grace, 'you of all people and Nanny, who has always been like a mother, imagined that I would shrug off growing debts and forgery had I known earlier what was going on?'

'No, that isn't what I said, Grace. But can you

honestly look me in the face and tell me that you haven't turned a blind eye for too long? That you haven't been an easy touch?'

'Yes, as a matter of fact I can.' Rising from her chair she strolled to the window and looked out, thinking back to the day when she insisted on going with Tobias in the hansom cab, twenty years ago. 'You see,' she said, gazing down at the Square, 'it wasn't so much a blind eye I turned . . . but my entire back. There is a subtle difference. I knew and I believed that if I said nothing and waited, he would eventually come to me with the truth and we could start afresh. But he never did, in fact things worsened. So I flew from the gilded cage, as he will refer to my life, and I enjoyed some freedom of my own.' She turned and looked at her cousin. 'And you may rest assured, Digby, I did enjoy myself. I flirted with another kind of life and once it was over I was content to let him go on with his way of life. By then he had all but killed the love I once had for him. I hardly cared what he did or who he saw.'

'But you had no idea that he was vastly over-spending?'

'Not at the time, no, later perhaps, but never as much as this. And certainly not forgery and theft.' She went to her small writing table and withdrew her silver cigarette case. She had started to smoke again.

'Well,' said Digby, 'I can and will help you sort out the finances but I think you should consider a change, Grace.'

'What kind of change?' she said, drawing on her gold cigarette holder.

'Well, you must surely have thought about selling one of the houses, I can't imagine you wouldn't have.'

'Yes, but which one? Should I hide away, a lonely woman in too large a country house, or continue living here, knowing that all of our so-called friends are sniggering? Sarah's of the age when having fun is top of the list and London is the place for that. And as for Herbert . . . well he hardly makes enough to keep on the room in Maida Vale. He obviously will opt for staying in London too, here in this house, with all its memories and bad atmosphere.' She turned once again to the window overlooking the Square.

'All of this is pure conjecture, of course,' she continued, 'abstract reasoning. I don't even know if, once all debtors are paid, we shall have the funds to live in *either* of the houses.'

'Ah,' said Digby, 'so it is blacker than you've painted so far and worse than Miss Partridge imagined?'

'Would you like to see for yourself?' She pointed to a military chest. 'There's a very thick file in there. Toby doesn't know I've taken bank statements and legal documents from his bureau.'

At last Digby had heard the worst of it from his cousin. He had had his suspicions but she had now confirmed the way things really were. Imagining the worst, on his journey down from Newmarket, he had considered two or three options. One was that he would purchase number ten Beaumont Square and that Grace would live in Laversham Hall. This, obviously, was not something she wanted and quite rightly so. To live mostly by herself in such a house in a remote part of the countryside would not suit his cousin.

'No,' said Digby, looking at his cousin's sad face, 'I shouldn't like to look at your personal papers, Grace, there's no need, but I do have a proposition to put to you. Are you in the mood for listening now or shall we break off and have some tea?'

'Oh, Digby, I am so sorry, my dear, and after that long journey, too.' Grace was up in a flash and ringing the servants' bell. 'You see,' she said turning to him, 'this isn't like me, is it?' There was no response. 'Digby, it isn't, is it?'

'I'm sorry, Grace, I was thinking of something else, what did you ask?'

'It doesn't matter,' she said, smiling. 'What were you thinking?'

'That I should love to live in this house. It's far too big for one person, I know, but those attic rooms and the guest bedrooms . . .' This was no act to help her take the bitter pill of having to sell to her cousin, he was thinking about all sorts of things. 'Do you realise just how big this house is, Grace?'

'I've not really thought about it.'

'Let's have our tea and then go from room to room and imagine how it might be changed.'

'But why would we want to—' The soft tapping on the door stopped her. 'Come in,' said Grace, straightening her shoulders and relaxing. The mask was back on.

'You rang, Madam?' It was Beanie. She was aware of Digby looking at her but wasn't certain as to whether she should acknowledge this. She could feel her cheeks burning and that familiar rapid beating of her heart when she was close to him.

'We'd like some tea and . . .' turning to Digby, she asked if he would like a snack.

'Tea will be fine,' he said, his eyes fixed on Beanie.

'Thank you, Madam,' she said, giving a hint of a curtsy before leaving. Once the door was closed again, Grace slouched back into the soft-cushioned chair. 'Oh dear, this is going to mean five good, hard-working and loyal people out of work, Digby.'

'Not necessarily. Do they not have homes to go to?'

'No, well, the gardener of course, he doesn't live in. But the others . . . I expect relatives will board them until they find other positions. Oh dear, I feel as if they're part of the family, especially Beanie the scullery maid.'

'Really, why do you single her out? They all appear efficient and courteous.' The mention of Beanie's name caused a small surge of emotion to rush through him.

'Yes, but she is different, my dear, very different.' Shaking her head, hardly able to believe what she was about to tell him, she sighed heavily. 'That young lady, Digby, is Sarah and Herbert's half sister.'

'What? Now that really is absurd, Grace,' he said,

hoarsely. Clearing his throat, he continued, 'You are under more stress than I imagined.'

'I know it sounds impossible but it's true. It's an incredible story but I do assure you that she *is* Toby's daughter. What's more, I've become quite close to her mother, my cook, Flora Brown. The girl from Brick Lane.'

'Grace, you can't possibly be serious.'

'It's true, I tell you! Isn't it mad? Isn't it quite, quite, mad?' She was close to becoming hysterical.

'But I don't understand. What on earth does Tobias think he's playing at?'

'Oh, he didn't bring her here, Digby. And before you ask, Flora did not come here with the intention of bringing it out into the open. She didn't know that this was where he lived and believed him, at the time, to be living in Westminster. He had told her his name was Charles. She and her family nicknamed him Prince Charlie. Can you believe that? It's so absurd, more absurd than a trashy, badly written, romantic novel, wouldn't you say?'

'I wouldn't know, I've never read one.' He turned away from her, deeply concerned for himself and his own feelings. 'You have truly shocked me this time, Grace, well and truly. I didn't even know the girl was your cook's daughter.'

'No, neither did I for a while. How it came out doesn't really matter. I've been reading his journals for twenty years, on and off. The girl from Brick Lane was mentioned by name occasionally. I eventually put two and two together, then Flora and I had a heart to heart talk. Apparently she almost passed out in our bedroom, when she saw Toby, for the first time in the house, two or three months after she'd been working here.'

'Flora the cook was once Tobias's mistress – is this what you're telling me?'

'One of his mistresses, my dear,' she said, averting her eyes. 'Whether she is the only one to have had a child by him, I have no idea. Luckily, Flora and I see eye to eye about most things. In fact I can say with my hand on my heart, that she is a trusted friend now. The only true one I've found since my schooldays.

'Isn't that strange? Two women from different worlds, never mind her having been my husband's lover for two years. Maybe there is something wrong with me. Should I have slapped her face . . . ? Sent her packing . . . ? I don't know. It never occurred to me. It might have done all those years back when I walked into that house to find a baby in a makeshift crib. I dare say that was enough of a shock to last a lifetime.'

Digby, deep in his own thoughts, had not been listening to her. His eyes were glazed as he thought about this girl who had come into his life and found a place in his heart. 'Well,' he said, thinking aloud, 'at least the girl has Wellington blood in her and not ours.'

'Digby, whatever makes you say such a thing?'

'Nothing, nothing at all,' he said, realising he had lost the thread of their conversation. The soft tapping on the door was a blessing in disguise. Confused with all that he was hearing, he was lost for words.

When Fanny came in with the tea tray, Digby sighed inwardly with relief. He was all at sea and Beanie was the last person he wanted in the room right then.

'Thank you, Fanny dear,' said Grace, her face giving nothing away. The show of everything being normal came second nature to her. 'Just leave the tray on the table, would you, dear, we'll help ourselves. Is everything running smoothly below stairs?'

'Yes, Madam?' There was a quizzical expression on Fanny's face.

'Oh, I just wondered that was all. It's just that Beanie answered the bell and I don't know . . . I expected her to bring the tea, that was all.'

'She's peeling potatoes, Madam, did you want to see 'er about something then?'

'No, no, not at all. Thank you, Fanny.'

Once the door was closed again, Grace glanced at Digby. 'It's hardly fair, is it? Sarah's half sister scrubbing potatoes for our evening meal.'

Pouring their tea, Digby mentioned casually that he might like to get to know Beanie a little more, since she was family so to speak. Grace could see nothing wrong with that and trusted her cousin implicitly not to say anything. 'I am certain she does not know that Tobias is her father. So you'll have to be very careful—'

'So her mother hasn't told her, how interesting. It's all rather strange . . .'

'Is it though?'

'Yes, I would say so. She hasn't let her child know that her father is from a wealthy family. Never mind that it just so happens to be *this* family and that she's been living under the same roof as her father and her half sister and brother. Of course it's strange, Grace, any woman I know would have it out in the open and much earlier on in life. Financial compensation is what I'm getting at, Grace, or has Tobias seen to that side of things, is that where some of the money has been going?'

'No. He gave Flora a hundred pounds twenty years ago, after Beanie's birth and left it at that. Never to be seen again, except once or twice for a stroll in the park, according to his journal.'

'Good grief, the man is a worse rogue than I thought, he should have been paying maintenance, Grace. Had he have done so that girl would not, I assure you, be working in a kitchen as scullery maid. She has a good brain, a fine sense of humour and she's honest to all intents and purposes.'

'Goodness me, Digby, you have been observant, I hadn't realised you were so perceptive. What a dark horse you are at times, and, yes, I agree, he should have been giving an allowance of some sort. At least we'd know that some of the missing funds were well spent. Again, I have only myself to blame. I dismissed the girl and her baby all those years back and pushed them from my mind.'

'Well, perhaps you were doing both of them a favour without realising. Look at the way the girl's turned out.'

'Indeed. Sarah would do well to take a leaf from her book, not to mention Herbert. I almost wished the tables were reversed – that I was the girl from Brick Lane.'

Laughing softly at this he sat down and sipped his tea. 'You wouldn't last five minutes, Grace, neither of us would. If we were to change places now, we could not survive in their world yet they would take to ours like a duck to water.'

'Exactly. Maybe it's something we should both be more aware of.'

'This may surprise you, Grace, but it is something I've been thinking about, especially of late.'

'This is no time for a debate on politics, my dear. We've other things to contend with, don't forget; another time perhaps.' The look of anxiety was back. She was beginning to feel panicky about getting her life into some kind of order, frightened that she was on a downward slippery slope. All this talk of surviving in a depraved situation was getting to her. 'We mustn't look on the black side, must we?' she said, talking more to herself than to her cousin.

'No, in fact I shall let you into a little secret that may well lighten your mood. I think I might be in love.'

'Really?' said Grace, feeling too depressed to show enthusiasm. Under different circumstances, she would be blissfully happy for him. 'You must tell me more . . . later perhaps.'

'If I should propose marriage – and I am not saying that I shall – what do you think of St Dunstan's Church? Follow in your footsteps, so to speak.'

'Yes, dear, that would be lovely, continuing the

family tradition.' She brushed a hand across her fore-head, 'You will forgive me if I sound—'

'Or maybe a country wedding,' he cut in, 'that would be rather nice.'

'Yes . . . it would . . . whatever you think best.' She glanced at her wristwatch.

'I think perhaps I'll go for a short walk. I should like to think a few things through. Oh, and I may not be in for dinner this evening.'

'Really?' said Grace, surprised. 'Why ever not? You are not going back to Newmarket so soon, I hope?'

'I shall, hopefully, be wining and dining the girl I wish to marry. That is of course, if you agree to give her the evening off.'

Staring into his face, Grace was bewildered. 'I don't follow, Digby.'

'We need to get to know each other more. I'm talk-ing about your cook's daughter, Grace. That wretched girl, Beanie. I do believe she has stolen my heart.'

'Stop teasing, Digby. You hardly know her and besides, it's rather sudden, don't you think? You're just trying to cheer me up, I know it. You are such a sweet man.'

'And if I were to marry her, everyone could stay on here.'

'Oh stop it,' chuckled, Grace, 'you go too far. Be serious.'

'You could go on living here as if it were still your home. It's large enough for all of us and to be perfectly honest, I doubt that my wife and I would be here as much as we'd be in Newmarket. You know how much

I love that house. In other words I should like to buy this house from you, Grace.'

'Good gracious me . . .' Grace all but whispered. 'You really do have intentions on the girl?'

'Yes, I do.'

'Well, then, yes but I am truly shocked by this. Shocked but very happy. Why *am* I so very happy over it?' She laid a hand on her forehead. 'I seem to be swinging from one mood to another, perhaps I'm going down with something.'

'I can't see why you would be so shocked. Over the New Year holiday you were positively glowing at the dinner table when you boasted at having the best of all maids join you this year, and I was ready to agree with you. I've not met anyone quite like her before, Grace. She's so easy to talk to, bright and with a wonderful sense of humour, I saw that on the very first day I met her. I had called her into the library and told her that I only wanted vegetables for my meal. She outwitted me, I can tell you. Of course that's no reason to want to marry someone, I realise that. It's any number of things, like her face holds a certain expression that you can't quite fathom what she's thinking and yet you know she's thinking something quite profound. Remarkable, don't you think, for a scullery maid?'

'Digby, you really *have* fallen in love. My cousin Digby in love at last,' she said, her eyes shining. 'I think it's absolutely wonderful. How did it—'

He raised a hand to show he wanted to end it there. Then made her promise to put all he had said to one side for the present and reluctant though she was, she had to make that promise.

'Now then,' he said, straightening. 'Back to the reason for my visit. We've talked over the finances and I hope I've reassured you that there's nothing for you to worry over. We can sort things out and have your bank balance healthy again, but first things first, Grace. I have to advise you and advise you strongly, to bring out into the open the business of your cook and Tobias, before it leaks below stairs. It's been aired, don't forget, between you and your cook but once something is in the air it has a tendency to spread.'

'Oh dear, I had a horrid feeling you were going to say that. Well, it has to be dealt with sometime so why not the present? How shall we go about it?'

'Short and to the point. You must insist that the woman joins you and Toby in his study, to talk through the matter thoroughly.'

'Oh, it's all very well for you to say that—'

'I'll do more than say it to you, Grace. If you like I will talk to him.'

'Oh,' said Grace, closing her eyes with relief, 'if you only would . . .'

'Then it's settled, we should act straight away.'

'And you'll sit in with us when Flora comes up?'

'If that's what you want, of course I shall. Tobias will not be pleased but I hardly think this is the time to consider *his* feelings.'

*   *   *

That evening, after dinner had been served and the kitchen cleared, Flora and Beanie sat by the fire in the armchairs, resting their stockinged feet on small footstools. With the flames of the fire reflecting in the polished copper kettle and jugs, the room was warm and cosy and if Flora hadn't wanted to have a heart to heart with her daughter, they might well have dozed off. But, since her talks with Grace Wellington and the fear of something coming out at an inappropriate moment, she wanted to reveal to Beanie the truth about her father. No easy task, but Flora had also thought long and hard and knew that it had to be dealt with and soon.

Why this felt like the right time she had no idea, but there was a certain urgency deep inside, willing her to act now. Fanny and Albert had gone to the picture palace in the Mile End Road so this was a fine opportunity to talk in private.

Beanie, in a tired voice, asked Flora what she was thinking about as she stared into the fire. 'Just about the past,' said Flora, 'when I was your age.'

'Was it much different from now?'

'I should say it was, things never stay the same and I can appreciate that. But my goodness, when I think of Master Herbert creeping into this house with a man he was prepared to share a bed with . . . well, I was shocked by it. That would never have happened in my day.'

'Maybe it did, but you never knew about it,' said Bea. 'Don't forget that by living in this posh 'ouse and in this Square, we're rubbing shoulders with a different class of people. Maybe there is one rule for the rich and one for the poor. If that's the case, I'm glad we was poor.'

'We weren't poor, Beanie. If you want to make comparisons go for a walk along to Whitechapel and into the back alleys, there you'll see how the poor must live, or rather, survive. If they're not begging for food they're selling their bodies for it.'

'I know but that don't change the fact that there's a big difference between us and them above stairs.'

'Everything seems to be moving so fast,' said Flora, quietly, in a world of her own. 'We can hardly keep up with it. Telephones, the wireless, gramophones, motor cars pulled by engines instead of horses, electricity . . . and now there's talk of wirelesses being in every household one day, showing moving pictures just like you see in the picture palaces.'

'Nothing wrong with that, Mum, it's exciting.'

'For your generation, I suppose it is.'

'Stop talking like Gran and Granddad, they're always goin' on about the old days when you could 'ave a nice ride in a lovely hansom cab for the price of two cups of tea.' Beanie chuckled at the thought of it. 'I told 'em about Herbert Sherbet upstairs and they told me not to be disgusting.'

'Well then, that's your own fault, Beanie, you knew what you were doing by mentioning it. You're a little tormentor at times.'

'But they love me all the more for it, according to Granddad. I wonder what my other grandparents are like?'

'Did you miss having two sets of grandparents, do you think?'

'Course not, what you don't 'ave you don't miss. But I've never really understood why you never mention 'em, or avoid it when I've asked. Where do they live, for instance?'

'I never met them, so I couldn't say what they're like or where they're living. I was eighteen when I met your father, an impressionable age. Young and carefree and a touch on the naive side. How was I to know he was a married man?' Her stomach in knots, she waited for a reaction.

'You should 'ave asked.'

Turning slowly to look into her daughter's face, Flora said, 'That's not the sort of response I would have expected, Bea.'

'So . . . my guess was right. What did he do, love and leave you?'

'Something like that. Listen to me, I can hardly believe it myself and I can hardly believe you're being so casual about something so weighty.'

'It's a mystery and I like mysteries, and scandal. I bet it was scandalous?' She grinned saucily at Flora. 'Stop being so serious over it. Who was he, then? And don't give me all that about 'im being a royal prince – Prince Charlie. I might 'ave believed it when I was tiny—'

'To me that's what he was, at the time. But I was taken for a fool and I've no one to blame but myself and what's more . . . I've no regrets, none whatsoever. If I hadn't 'ave fallen in love with the man I wouldn't be sitting here with you, would I?' Squeezing her lips together, Flora tried not to let her emotions get the better of her.

'If it's too painful you don't 'ave to talk about it. I don't really care who he was, Mum, so long as you're all right about it. I was only pulling your leg, it really don't matter. You loved 'im and that's all that counts.'

'It's the master of this house,' she blurted out, cut and dried.

'Oh yeah . . .' chuckled Beanie, 'and I'm a white witch.'

'It's the truth, Bea. *He* is your father. But I swear to God I never knew this was his place when I came for the interview or I wouldn't 'ave stepped over the threshold.'

'Stop telling fairy stories, Mum. Tell me the hard gritty truth, I can take it.'

'I just did, Bea. I was courting him for two years, right up until I gave birth to you. Then he vanished – more or less. I saw him once or twice after that but it was never the same. I knew in my heart he was going to give me up.'

Staring into Flora's face, Beanie felt sick. 'Mr Wellington? You had a love affair with *Mr Wellington*? *He* was your Prince Charlie?'

'Yes. You remember the night that you, Fanny and Albert went out when I told you not to and I had to answer the master-bedroom bell?'

'Of course I remember but what's that got to do with anything!'

'Listen and you might find out!' snapped Flora.

'You think this is easy for me? Well, it isn't so you just listen or leave.'

'Mum . . .' whimpered Beanie, '. . . you just told me that that man upstairs who pays our wages is my *dad*, how d'yer expect me to feel?'

Gazing into the fire and shaking her head slowly, Flora continued. 'When I saw him from behind his newspaper in that bedroom, I thought I would keel over. He never recognised me though, thank the Lord. We would have been turned out into the street, make no mistake.'

'Of course we wouldn't, would we? That wouldn't be right.' She leapt up from her chair causing it to fall over and crash on to the stone-tiled floor. 'You've bin slaving down 'ere for 'im and 'is sodding family and drippy friends when all the time he was the one that walked out on yer! His wife walks around in fabulous clothes and expensive jewellery while all you've got is a uniform and a set of best clothes. Best clothes that they wouldn't even use to wipe their noses on!'

'It's the way of the world, Bea. It's always been that way and no one's ever gonna be able to change it. Now calm down and act a bit more ladylike'

'Ladylike! Me, a scullery maid? I'd be accused of rising above me station!' Picking up the chair and crashing it down by the fire she clenched her fists tight. 'The *bastard*!'

'Stop it, Beanie, that kind of talk'll get us nowhere!'

'I don't want us to get anywhere. Right is right and you and me shouldn't 'ave to be working in *my* father's basement from dawn till dusk; scrubbing, cooking, fetching and carrying!'

‘Maybe you're right and maybe not, but I'll tell you this much, I don't envy that poor woman upstairs!'

‘*Poor* woman, how do yer make *that* out?'

‘Never mind for now, I've said enough. I'm not made of stone. I'll repeat what I said and let that be an end of it for the time being. I do not envy Mrs Wellington and I would not be in her shoes for all the tea in China. I would rather be down here with you than upstairs with that man!'

The look of anger, distress and frustration on Flora's face stopped Beanie from saying anything else. Something in this household was not right, even she had picked up on that, but for her mother to say she wouldn't swap places with Grace Wellington, then things must be worse than she could ever imagine. ‘I'm sorry, Mum,' she murmured finally, taking her place next to Flora by the fire. ‘I don't know the full story. I'm acting like a kid.'

‘No you're not, Bea. Let's leave it for now, I will tell you more once my stomach's settled down a bit.'

The sudden jingle of the servants' bell in an otherwise silent room made them both jump and then smile over it. ‘God, it feels like the devil 'imself's just summoned us,' said Beanie, a hand on her beating heart.

Flora could see it was the bell linked to Tobias Wellington's study. ‘Shall we ignore that?' said Flora, not knowing quite what to do.

‘No, I'll go.' With a hand on Flora's shoulder she bent down and kissed her on the top of her head. ‘I love you more than anything in the world, Mum, and I don't care who or what my dad was. A coalman or a king, you loved 'im at the time you fell for me and that's all that matters.'

'Bea . . .' said Flora, panic showing in her eyes, 'you won't say anything up there, will you? You could do so much damage. Wait till you know everything, eh?'

'Course I will, stop worrying.' Leaving Flora to herself Beanie stopped in the doorway and turned round. 'Mum?'

Flora looked up at her child and waited. 'Yes, Bea, what is it, sweetheart?'

'See . . . you never did lie to me, did yer? My dad *is* rich and all rich people 'ave got a bit of royal blood in 'em, ain't they? Or so they like to think.'

Chuckling quietly, Flora turned away from the flames of the fire to look at her lovely daughter. 'If the royalty 'ave blue blood we'll 'ave to wait for Prince Charlie up there to die to find out, won't we?'

'No, I'll stick a pin in 'is arse when he's least expecting it.' With that, Beanie, in a strange kind of mood, went above stairs, not quite as subservient as usual, And usually she wasn't as subservient as she might be.

Knocking gently on the door of Tobias's study, she felt her stomach churn. Digby Morton was in the house after all and she felt sure she could smell his scent.

Stepping cautiously into the room, a scared rabbit waiting to see if the fox was about, she could hardly believe how shy she felt again on seeing Digby seated on a soft leather high-backed chair, legs crossed and looking more handsome and strong in character than ever before.

'You rang, Sir,' she all but whispered, addressing the master of the house who was seated behind his desk, leaning back in his chair. Grace was in another soft chair. All eyes were on Beanie.

'Yes, I did,' he said, clearing his throat and looking extremely serious. 'Would you be so kind as to ask Cook to come up?'

'Why?' she spoke without thinking. Her immediate thoughts were that they were going to be horrid to her mother.

'I don't see that that's any of your business, young lady,' snapped Tobias, under pressure and in a bad mood.

Remembering that Flora had begged her not to say anything out of order, Beanie raised her chin and kept her mouth shut tight but the hard stare she gave this man who had run out on her mother was enough to melt ice. 'No, Sir. It's none of my business, Sir. Was there anything else, *Sir*?'

'I would say if there was, you impudent girl. Now get out of here and do as you're told.'

'Yes, Sir. Of course, Sir,' she continued, backing out and bowing humbly as she closed the door behind her.

'Make sure she's out of this house by the end of the week, Grace. *That* is what comes of allowing your daughter to mix with staff, respect goes flying out of the window. Familiarity breeds contempt, I've always said so. Now, I am proved right.'

'Oh, I don't think she was being contemptuous, Tobias. She was trying her best merely to behave like an obedient servant, I'm sure of it.' Digby glanced furtively at Grace and returned her knowing smile.

'Well, think what you like, Digby, you always do. A cock and bull story trumped up by that bloody woman downstairs and you've both fallen for it. I can hardly believe this of either of you.'

'Would that it was a cock and bull story, Toby. Sadly it is not. You should take some time out to read your own journals, if nothing else but to jog your memory.'

'My memory does not need jogging, Grace. I have seen this woman already, don't forget. And you can take it from me she is the last person on earth I would have had an affair with. She's a bloody cook for God's sake. A fat and very *plain* cook.'

'She is slightly plump and has not the time to visit beauty parlours. Don't be so facetious, it's out of character. And as for seeing her, that was just the once I believe, when she came into our bedroom in answer to the bell and you had on your reading glasses. Since then she has studiously kept her distance from you. That hardly sounds like someone trying to win you over.'

'I did not say she was trying to win me over, Grace, I implied that she had been working on the weaker side of *your* character. We'll see both her and her daughter out of this house before breakfast, you may trust me on that!'

'Speaking of her daughter, did you not see that she has almost identical eyes to Sarah?'

'No, Grace, I'm afraid I don't make a habit of gazing into the eyes of scullery maids.'

'Well, I don't see why not, you've gazed into many the eye of a prostitute, if I am correct in my speculation as to where my funds have disappeared to.'

Tobias turned to Digby and shook his head slowly. 'I do apologise for all of this, old chap, but once your cousin has the bit between her teeth, we none of us can talk sense into her. I would get out of here and pour yourself a brandy in the library if I were you.' He managed to smile but was clearly masking pent-up anger and aggression.

'Thank you, but no. I can see you are deeply embarrassed but is it not wise, under the circumstances, to clear the air, once and for all?'

'The whole thing is a farce which is best left to theatrical producers. I can see now where Herbert gets his obsession with acting from, I've a mind to put a stop to this nonsense before it gets out of hand,' growled Tobias. 'If I thought for one minute that—'

The second tapping on the door stopped him short. Coming into the room, Flora smiled courageously at Grace and was met with a supportive nod. 'You wanted to see me, Mr Wellington,' she said, keeping a serene tone to her voice.

'Well, yes and no, Cook . . . yes and no,' he said averting his eyes, as if he were studying some trifle on his desk. 'It's all deeply embarrassing and no more than a wager which had got completely out of hand. My wife here believes that somewhere along the way, in the long forgotten past, you and I knew each other, in a, shall we say, intimate way,' he scoffed. 'To put an end to her somewhat overactive imagination, I thought it only proper if you were to come in here and defend your good name.'

'Defend it, Mr Wellington?' said Flora stepping a little closer to him. 'Defend *my* good name? Why on earth would I have cause to do that when I have spent the past twenty years working from dawn until dusk in order to keep my child and myself from being homeless?'

'Exactly my point,' he said, shaking his head disdainfully. 'I can only apologise for my wife who—'

'Apologise for your *wife*? I think you've got the thing the wrong way round, haven't you? I think that it's Grace who deserves an apology – from both of us. From you and I, *Prince Charlie*. Or should I say Charles from Westminster? I should raise your eyes if I were you, take a good look at this face of mine. Older and suffering from wear and tear it may be, but it is the same face, and the eyes that you so often lied into are still the same eyes.'

Lifting his head slowly, he looked at her and his face paled. He was speechless. Dumbstruck because he had been found out and this time no lies or defence tactics would get him off the hook. 'Good grief . . .' he muttered, shocked to the core.

'I don't think I need to stay, do you? Unless of course, you want to know how our daughter has managed to come this far without a father and without financial support? Come this far, Mr Wellington, and not once gone off the rails. She's a lovely girl and you, sir, have missed out on her growing up. She's not only lovely but intelligent and not without compassion. She has, after all, been working long hours below stairs and at your beck and call. Please do not think for one moment that you have any claims on my child.'

She turned to Grace and said, 'We'll pack our bags immediately, Madam.' Then turned finally to Tobias, 'I may only have been a girl from Brick Lane, Mr Wellington, but my flesh and blood is as good as yours any day, my morals far better and my conscience clear. Good day to you, sir.'

Leaving all three of them astonished and lost for words, she turned around and walked out of the study. Once in the hall, she smiled broadly, a smile that came from deep inside. The tears rolling down her cheeks were not from grief, anger or misery – she had had her moment. The moment she had been waiting for since the day she saw him in his lavish bedroom, smarmy and high-handed. Clenching her fists she closed her eyes and thanked her guiding spirit for bringing her to this place . . . she felt a surge of happiness course through her body.

Before going into the kitchen she patted her eyes dry and composed herself ready to face Beanie, who had probably been worried sick as to the outcome of the family meeting. She had sat by the fire using every bit of her will-power not to go above stairs and support her mother and could see, once Flora returned, that she need not have worried. The expression on her mother's face was one of calm serenity.

'It was all right, then?' she said, returning Flora's smile.

'It was, Beanie, it was more than all right. I may be wrong but I have a feeling that Mr Wellington will be packing his suitcase shortly.' She didn't want to tell her then that they would be leaving that night to go to her parents' house where they would have to lodge until they found suitable employment and accommodation. 'Now, if you can manage it, I would rather forget the whole thing for now and get on with my work, this larder's in a bit of a two and eight. Later on, you can come into my room and I'll spell it all out for you. Can you manage to wait?'

'Course I can. Has he found out who we are?'

'Bea . . .' warned Flora, chuckling. 'It's not something for questions and answers, we need to sit down with me talking and you listening. Now, I'll ask you again – can you manage to wait?'

'I said I could, didn't I . . . so it all came out then?'

Giving her daughter a hug, she reminded her that she had her smalls to wash and dry by the fire in her bedroom. She then went into the larder and threw herself into work she always tried to put off: sorting and tidying, shelves and cupboards, and labelling bottled fruits. She had to do something to use up her energy, the adrenaline still pumping through her veins. Tidying cupboards seemed exactly right.

An hour or so later, Flora was still knee-deep in pots and pans in the pantry while Beanie was reading a paperback by the fire. With Fanny and Albert out, the only sound, apart from Flora shifting things about, was the crackling of the coal fire to which Beanie had added a couple of small thin logs courtesy of Lenny the gardener. It was a homely scene and catching a glimpse of her daughter looking very cosy, she wondered if she had done the right thing by speaking out so boldly. Had she not said she would be packing her bags and be gone by the morning, there might have been a slim chance that Mr Tobias Wellington would go elsewhere. She could only speculate on the mood above stairs at that moment. Her worries, though, were to be calmed because Grace was on her way down.

'Ah, Beanie,' she said, pleased to see that she was still there, 'I wonder if you would be so good as to pop into the library. Mr Digby is in there and he might like a little supper. Would you mind?'

Once Beanie had gone above stairs, Grace popped her head round the door of the pantry and asked Flora if she would join her by the fire. At first she was reluctant, not because she did not wish to be pulled away from her task in hand but she felt as if all had been said on the matter and wanted to put the lid on it.

'I'm not sure if I can say anything to appease you, Grace,' she said, washing her hands in the butler sink. 'I can only say that I'm very sorry to have been the cause of all this trouble.'

'I'm not here for an apology, Flora, I'm here to congratulate you.'

Joining Grace by the fireside, she gave her a quizzical look. 'On speaking up, you mean?'

'Indeed. You were quite wonderful, to the point and positive. I wish I could be more like you. But there, it's never too late to learn or change, is it?'

It took no time at all for the two women to get into their usual easygoing conversation, except that this time, it was Grace doing most of the talking. She had no intention of mentioning Digby's designs on Beanie but she did want to explain the way things were going to be and that she wanted Flora to stay on. She told of her cousin's plans to purchase the house from her and rearrange it under the guidance of one of the best architects in town. When she asked if Flora would agree to stay on, if she were offered a small suite of rooms in the attic, she was met with an expression of sheer disbelief.

'Of course,' said Grace, 'it can only be a bedroom, bathroom and kitchen-cum-parlour, but at least it would be your own little place.'

'But you need those rooms up there,' said Flora, mystified. 'A bedroom for Fanny, a room for Albert and another for Beanie. Because it must go without argument that if—'

'No one is to be sacked. The plan for this basement is to convert it into a self-contained flat. It would be for a married couple and that's something we would have to speak to Albert and Fanny about. But that's—'

'But the kitchen is down here?' said Flora, interrupting. 'The kitchen, pantry, everything. There's no room, Grace. I don't know what your cousin can have been drinking today but . . . it's just not possible.'

'The kitchen, my dear, will be moved to the first

floor, which makes very good sense. Closer to the dining room but not too close.'

'Oh, I see what he's getting at . . . It wouldn't be the first grand house to go down that road. Modern thinking is what I hear on it. Well, well, our Mr Digby is not as unsociable as he likes to make out.'

'My cousin will live mostly in Newmarket, but obviously we shall see more of him which pleases me no end. We've been more like brother and sister than cousins for as long as I can remember.'

'Well, I never did . . .' Flora simply could not believe that such changes could be made. A little suite of her own? 'What's the catch, Grace?' she said, giving her a cheeky smile. 'Not your old man, I hope?'

Laughing, Grace shook her head. 'What a thought. Tobias going from my room to yours!'

'Well, all I can say,' said Flora, chuckling, 'is that your cousin, if he really means to do this, is a knight in shining armour. But what of your husband – where does he fit into all of this?'

'We must wait and see, time will tell.'

Knowing exactly what she meant – that divorce was in her thoughts – she nodded, knowingly. 'They that dance must pay the fiddler, my dear Grace.' Glancing at the clock, Flora frowned. 'Beanie's taking her time, what's she doing up there?'

'Talking to Digby, I expect,' said Grace, giving nothing away. 'I suppose I had better see what kind of a mood Toby's in. He's been walking about like a bear with a sore head ever since our little meeting.'

'I should think he is, the fool,' said Flora going to

the basement door, believing she had heard footsteps coming down into the area. Peering through a pane of glass in the door, she saw two men loitering above and looking as if they were about to come down. 'Who the dickens are they?' she murmured.

Joining her at the back door, Grace peered up at them, 'I've no idea.'

'If they knock, I'm not too sure whether we should open the door to them.'

'Oh, stop being silly, Flora,' scolded Grace, studying them through the window. 'Someone selling something, I should think?'

'I doubt that very much,' said Flora, turning the key and opening the door. She didn't have to ask what they wanted, they were in first.

'Mr Wellington live 'ere, love?'

'He does, and who might I say is asking for him?'

'Never you mind about that. We was just passing, that's all, pals passing by.' With that both men went back up the steps and away. Back to Mr Potts' studio to report that they had found the house and the man. These rogues working for Mr Potts looked more like fish-market porters than hardened criminals, but inside their overcoats, in large purpose-made pockets, were weapons of the crudest type.

'I wonder . . .' said Grace, apprehensively. 'Whatever could they want with Tobias?' She returned Flora's look of unease and shuddered.

Checking the clock on the mantelshelf, Flora shrugged. 'Whatever can be keeping Beanie?'

'Keeping Digby company. Sarah's out and so too

is Herbert for that matter. We mustn't blame him for wanting people more his age around him.'

'But Beanie's not quite twenty-one, Grace, and Digby would be turned thirty, I imagine?'

'Only just, my dear. And you really shouldn't worry over my cousin. He is the most trustworthy person.' With that she leaned forward and kissed Flora lightly on the cheek. 'Goodnight, my dear, and thank you again for being so frank with Toby. You managed to cut right through whereas we probably would have beaten about the bush.'

'I'm a firm believer that if there's anything to be said then it should be said straight away, while the iron's hot. Goodnight, Grace, I hope you manage to sleep.'

Turning to face Flora, Grace looked all but mystified. 'How could you tell that I was dreading a long, sleepless night?'

'It stands to reason. Your world's been turned inside out *and* upside down. How could you expect to switch off as usual? Take a strong sleeping draught. Sleep will do you more good than harm, it'll all look quite different tomorrow, I expect.' With that, Flora sat herself down by the fire and waited for Grace to go. She had had enough, more than enough. Working-class people were much easier to deal with. As lovely a woman as Grace was, she certainly lacked common sense at times. To Flora, the very idea of putting up with a husband who behaved the way hers did for so many years, was criminal. Never mind finding out this late in life that he had been fiddling her bank account.

So immersed in her thoughts, Flora didn't hear Beanie coming into the kitchen. When she did appear in front of her with a curious expression on her face, she was startled. Her own belief of remaining calm while all else fell about her, could last only so long.

'You were a long time up there, I hope you weren't getting the third degree?'

'Course I wasn't, we were chatting about everything and nothing. He's so nice.'

'Oh, is he now? Well, all I can say is don't trust that lot as far as you can throw them. Stick to your own kind, Bea, and you won't go far wrong.'

'I don't agree,' she said sitting down and unbuttoning her boots. 'He's considerate and kind. He's gonna take me to see a play at the Aldwych Theatre, *It Pays to Advertise*. It's 'ad good reviews. According to Digby the *Daily Mail* said it was a play of a thousand laughs. You wouldn't think he had a sense of humour looking at 'im, but he does.'

'Taking you to see a play? Mr Digby Morton?'

'Nothing wrong in it, is there?' said Beanie, pulling off a boot. 'He joined us down the tavern on New Year's Eve so why shouldn't I join 'im at the Aldwych? You're too old fashioned, Mum, that's your trouble. People don't worry so much about classes mixing the way they did in your day. Us cockneys are in vogue, anyhow, according to Sarah that is.'

'In my day, indeed? I'll have you know my days are not over yet, my girl. But I am ready for my bed having said that. Don't bolt the door or we shall have another clowning if they can't get in through the door.' She leaned forward and kissed Beanie's forehead. 'Don't burn the candle, Bea. We're to be up early tomorrow.'

'What . . . earlier than usual?'

'No, but . . .'

'Well, then?'

'Oh, I don't know. I'm too tired to think straight, and I've had more than enough for one day. Goodnight, sweetheart.'

Climbing the stairs, Flora wondered if the world was changing a little too fast for her. Here she was, in a grand house, on friendly terms with her employer and her daughter being taken to see a play in the West End by a rich man. Never mind that she had given the master of the house a piece of her mind and then been congratulated for it by his wife. Well, if this was the way things were going, she would go along with it. Worse things happened at sea. If she had an inkling of what the following days held, she would not be sleeping this night.

If they thought Herbert horrible, they had seen nothing of his worst side yet.

10

In the wee dark hours of the next morning, Herbert staggered in a drunken state through the gate to number ten and kicked over an empty garden plant pot which had been placed in the middle of the step. Cursing aloud, he picked it up and was about to toss it on to the front garden when he saw that there was a note inside. Holding it under the lamplight he read: *Mr Wellington, we came to collect something from you for Mr Potts. We will be back.* Not really taking it in, he slipped the note into his pocket and managed to focus on the door lock and turn the key.

Staggering up to his room, the words *We will be back* swam through his pickled brain. 'One too many cocktails, dear boy,' he muttered. 'Gerald bloody Fairweather. Driving you to drink, Herbert, love. Pushing you over the top.' A huge grin spread across his face. 'At least that's what he intends . . .'

Arriving in his bedroom, he kicked the door shut with the heel of his shoe and dropped on to the bed, out for the count. In a more sober state he would have realised the possibility of a good beating contained in those few threatening written words.

Even though Potts the photographer wanted the

pictures back and especially the negatives, he would not be too bothered. Cheeky girls were two a penny but an original theme, such as Beanie and Sarah had presented him with, was unique. He could always pair up two of his regular models and repeat the bee-stinging sequence. But of course he had to make an effort to try and get back his photographs from the idiot who had duped him, or have his hired help give him a hiding, as a warning to keep his mouth shut.

Waking at mid-morning with a pounding headache and no memory of how he had got home from the Soho jazz club, Herbert poured and drank three glasses of water from the jug on the table next to his bed. Into the third glass he popped an effervescent. Then, lighting a Turkish cigarette, he sat up in bed and wondered how he would get back at Gerald for humiliating him by having a boy of seventeen at his heel. Perhaps he might go to the depraved Islington, to Gerald's bedsit, and demand that he return the wireless and pay back his debts. He owed Herbert three pounds six shillings. He might then offer to waive the loan and forget the wireless if he threw out the angelic boy while he was there to witness it. *Yes*, thought Herbert, *that is exactly what I shall do*. The obnoxious, pathetic smile was back on his face. The trouble with Herbert was that he was a lonely soul with no one to talk things through with.

His fragmented memory of the previous evening still on his mind, he recollected the note in the plant pot. The note had mentioned Mr Potts, he felt certain of it. Searching his pockets he found what he was looking for and read it again. 'My God,' he declared, a hand against his face, 'the devil is after me and all for a bunch of disgusting pictures!'

Resolved to go straight to the bank and retrieve the brown envelope and have it ready for the rogues when they returned, he stood up, brushed himself down and ignoring all else, left the house, turned out of the front gate and crashed into Flora, causing her wicker shopping baskets to fall across the pavement. One of the baskets containing nothing else but new-laid eggs from the market.

'You idiot of a man!' screeched Flora. 'Why can't you look out for other people?'

His eyes doleful, his expression one of contempt, he looked from her furious face to the ground. 'Have the bootboy clean that immediately. Before the flies pounce for a feast.' Saying no more he strode away, head high.

'That man will meet a bad end,' murmured Flora, picking up the groceries and provisions. 'I'll strike him myself one of these days so help me!'

Hearing the commotion, Beanie popped her head out of the basement door and called up to her mother asking what had happened. 'Tell Albert to come up please,' was the sharp reply. 'And yourself too, with buckets of hot water and the yard broom.'

'Blimey,' said Fanny, coming into the kitchen with the dirty crockery piled on to a breakfast tray. 'She's in a mood, Albert. You'd best get up there sharpish.'

'I know what this'll mean. She won't be in any kind

of a mood to let me take the afternoon off,' said Beanie, collecting the cleaning equipment.

'Why should she?' Fanny eyed Albert and pursed her lips. 'Why should you 'ave an extra afternoon off when we was turned down last week? All we wanted was to go and see my sister and 'er family.'

'Will you move yourselves down there!' Flora again.

To everyone's surprise, once all was calm in the kitchen again, Flora showed no reluctance at Beanie slipping away. She had had a while to think about Digby Morton wanting to take her daughter to the theatre and had warmed to the idea. After all that had been said above stairs with regard to who was who below, he, in his own way was endorsing his acceptance of her being part of the family, and that was fine by Flora.

Looking out of the tiny back window into the garden that afternoon, she watched as Lenny pushed his fork into the cold hard flowerbeds and turned over the heavy earth. Soon it would be time for planting his early spring bulbs and she wondered if she and Beanie would be there to see them in bloom. With his cap and his old garden jacket on, Lenny resembled a character out of a comic book. Ready for a cup of tea herself she pulled up the latch of the window and called him in for a break. His answer was a thumbs-up, he was ready for a cup of Flora's tea and one of her fairy cakes.

'So where 'as Bea gone off to then?' asked Fanny as all four of them sat round the kitchen table enjoying their tea break. 'She was a bit evasive if you ask me.'

'Well then, I expect she'd rather we didn't know.'

Flora would give nothing away. 'We live together like a family but that don't mean to say we can't 'ave a private life.' She looked from Fanny to Albert and winked at him. 'Who knows what you two get up to when you're by yourselves?'

'Now then, now then,' warned Lenny, 'no telling the truth and shaming the devil in front of me, that only leads to arguments. Take as you find and keep the peace.' He sipped his tea, leaned back in his chair and enjoyed his break. Lately, he had seen a slight change below stairs. Nothing that would shake the world but something that was gradually fuelling his confidence. Respect was being shown.

Once upon a time he simply came and went, the gardener getting on with things outside. But Flora had pulled him into the fold and treated him as if he was the head man, on account of him having been working at number ten the longest.

'Well, I couldn't agree more, Lenny,' said Flora, 'I couldn't agree more.' She caught Fanny's eye. The girl was smiling at her, smiling warmly.

'If young Beanie's got a secret boyfriend who are we to expose the girl?' said Lenny. 'Good luck to 'er is what I say. Love ain't no bad thing. It beats bad feelings, don't it?' The atmosphere in the room went nice and calm as each of them considered their own personal feelings on love: To Flora it meant enjoying the company of a good friend and companion; to Fanny it meant a good roll in the hay with Albert; to Lenny it was being there in that room with people to talk to instead of the brick wall of his lodging-room.

'What did 'appen out there earlier on, Cook?' said Albert suddenly. 'Did someone knock into you or did you trip on that wonky pavement? 'Cos if you did trip I fink it's time we complained about it.'

'No,' said Flora, looking at him over her teacup, 'I never tripped. It was Master Herbert rushing about as if nobody else had a right to be in the streets. Much more of him and he'll feel the flat of my hand against his cheek.'

'Now then, now then,' said Lenny, showing the flat of his hand, 'we'll have none of that sort of talk at the table, thank you.'

Finding it impossible not to laugh at him, they kept it to warm chuckles. 'D'yer know what, Lenny?' said Fanny, giving his cheek a squeeze. 'I love you like a dad, we all do. What would we do wivout you, eh?'

'Well that's exactly what I was thinking meself, someone's gotta keep order. I was thinking I might write up a list of do's and don'ts – that sort of thing. What do you all say to that?'

What could they say other than to agree? 'Your writing's all right then is it, Len?' asked Albert, tactfully.

'Well no, it's not, and that's just what I was thinking. Maybe you could give me a couple of lessons, Flora? 'Cos I know you can write.'

'And so can I!'

'No need to shout, Fanny,' advised the gardener, 'so, well then . . . you can all take it in turns to give me a little bit of your knowledge. Not that I *can't* write, I can write my name and that sort of thing, but there's always room for improvement. You should all think about that.' With that he placed his cup in the saucer, stood up and strode back out into the garden, his garden.

In a small and friendly tearoom not far from the Aldwych Theatre, Beanie and Digby sat at a table for two, comfortable in their surroundings. Each of the tables was covered with a white damask cloth with the centrepiece being delicate wax roses in a small round cut-glass bowl. The china cups and tea plates were the prettiest Beanie had ever seen, pale primrose and decorated with tiny blue flowers.

Having discussed the matinée performance of the comedy, *It Pays to Advertise*, which they had thoroughly enjoyed and having had a friendly argument over which of the actors, Tom Walls, Arthur Finn or Ralph Lynn, had amused them most, they were engrossed in conversation on a more personal level, which had been deliberately instigated by Digby. The rights of all people from lower-class families to royalty. Each of them putting across their views, at length, and disagreeing every now and then, they realised finally that they were saying much the same thing but from different viewpoints. More important than the nature of their conversation, they were enjoying themselves.

'We should do this more often, Beanie,' said Digby, unable to take his eyes off her open and honest face. 'If you'd like to, that is?'

'It's not a case of like or not. It's whether I can get the time off. Cook's very strict on that sort of thing.

I was lucky that she let me come out this afternoon,
I'm not due a day off for three weeks.'

'Yes, Beanie but—'

'Digby,' she said, butting in, 'do you fink you
could call me Bea? Now that we've become friends?
Everyone else does.'

'Beanie sounds too formal for you?'

'Yeah. I s'pose that's the word I was searching for,
formal.'

'Well, Bea, what I was going to say before you interrupted,' he said, smiling at her, 'with regard to your
being lucky to be let out by Cook . . .' he narrowed
his eyes and paused, searching for the right words.

'Well get on with it then. What?'

'It's very personal. *Very* personal.'

'Oh is it now? Well you've got me wondering now,
so out with it. We'll be 'ere all day at this rate and
then I *will* be in trouble.'

'About Cook . . .' He looked into her deep blue
eyes, hoping to get the message across without spell-
ing it out.

'What about her?' said Beanie, cautiously.

'I'm very close to my cousin Grace and—'

'You was in the study when it all came out,' sniffed
Beanie. 'So . . . what of it?' Her hackles were rising
and a new expression was on her face: stubbornness.
'It's all right, Digby. You 'ave to get used to the idea
of the private life being under scrutiny when you do
domestic work and live-in.'

Annoyed with himself for being so tactless he wasn't
sure whether to apologise or simply get on with it.

He decided to be more like her and not beat about the bush. 'Well, couldn't we manage to use the fact that she's your mother and wheedle another afternoon together? Next week, perhaps?'

'You must be joking. She'd give me the biggest talking to yet if I so much as tried just once to use our being related for my own ends. Don't even think about it, Mr Morton.' Her switching to calling him by his surname was a defence tactic. Now that he probably knew everything about her, that she was an illegitimate child, all feelings for him had to be quashed.

'Well, maybe if I were to approach her?'

'And why would you want to do that? I'm sure you're a very busy person with having to look after your estate and all that. Why should you have to speak up for me – why would you want to?'

'No reason,' he said, taking her hand and bringing it to his lips while looking deep into her eyes. 'No reason whatsoever, Bea.'

That touch, that look, that gentle kiss on her fingers sent delicious waves of ecstasy rushing through her body and soul. So much for quashing her feelings about him. She couldn't speak or smile. She simply returned that loving expression in his eyes and on his face. Seconds ticked by as they sat, holding hands and looking into each other's faces, until he cleared his throat finally and spoke in a husky voice, 'I think I may be falling in love with you.'

A few days later, with the photographs hidden away in his room, Herbert was interrupted while practising his lines. The sound which seemed to be filling the house was horrendous. Coarse laughter was only usually heard in bawdy music-halls. Popping his head round the door he saw the vulgar girl with the silly name and his sister hugging each other.

'Do you think it possible,' he said in a forced tired voice, 'for you to keep your good tidings to yourselves and use the Square if you must squawk like crows?'

'Oh come on, Herbert,' said Beanie, finding her voice. 'Don't be such an old stick in the mud.' With that she stepped closer to him, looked directly into his face and then landed a kiss on his cheek. 'One day you'll realise why I did that.'

'Oh dear,' droned Herbert, 'are things really coming to this? Off with the pair of you, off I say!' Closing the door in their faces and back in the privacy of his room, he covered his face with his hands, overcome with an emotion he couldn't quite fathom. Had the scullery maid managed to break through his barrier?

Sitting on the edge of his bed, he gazed down at the floor, aware of just how lonely he was. 'Would that I too could behave like a baboon,' he mumbled. 'Would that I could.' He then lay on his bed, crossed his legs, his hands behind his head and wondered if perhaps he spent too much time on his own. He also wondered how differently things might have been if he had stood up to his father during his adolescent years. Sarah, after all, had found a way round it, and with her wily ways had always managed to do what she wanted. Of course she had himself to thank for it, hadn't he been the guinea pig while she sat observing from a corner, watching and learning from his mistakes? Yes, thought Herbert, Sarah has much to thank me for. 'But you'll never acknowledge such a thing, will you, sister of mine?' he murmured with a drawn-out sigh before closing his eyes for a catnap.

The tapping on his door was, whether he would admit it or not, a welcome intrusion into his silence. 'Not you again . . .' he groaned on seeing his sister standing there with the scullery maid.

'Herbert, we have something to tell you.'

'Go on,' he droned, 'get it over and done with.'

'Cousin Digby and Beanie here, our scullery maid, are to be engaged! What do you say to that?'

'Good God!' He all but reeled back in shock.

'I told you!' laughed Sarah. 'My bet, I think. You owe me threepence, Beanie Brown!'

'What, pray, was the bet?'

'That you would say, Good God.'

'I see. Am I to take it then that there is to be *no* engagement between a member of our family and a member of the domestic staff?'

'No, Herbert, you are not. They *are* to be engaged!' With that, Sarah grabbed Beanie's hand and they ran off full of the joys of spring.

'Can it be true?' said Herbert, leaning on the doorframe. 'A common scullery maid to marry into the family? Surely not – Father would be devastated.' He went immediately in search of Tobias who had shut himself in his study away from it all. The door was locked but Herbert was persistent.

'Father, please do not lock me out of your life when

I am surrounded by ghastly people and horrific news. I beg you—' Suddenly the door flew open.

'Shut up, Herbert, and get yourself in here before anyone else tries to crash in on me.'

'Oh my God,' groaned Herbert, dropping into a chair. 'It *is* true. We are to be made a laughing stock, what is to become of us, what—'

'Shut up!'

This snapped order stopped him short. Had everyone lost their sense of dignity? 'Oh, please, sir, do not take your anger out on me. I must go, I have a deadline to meet, I must learn my lines by—'

'Shut up, Herbert,' snarled Tobias. 'Do not say another word. Do not moan or groan dramatically. Do not turn this crisis into a melodrama.'

Wounded yet again at being barked at, Herbert lost his voice and yet he could stop this dire thing from happening. He would see the girl scorned and ejected from his parents' house in an instant. And he would be killing two birds with one stone.

'Don't be too fretful over this, Father,' he said, caringly. 'I shall, in my own way, put a very abrupt end to this nonsense. Naturally I shall be discreet, you have my word.'

'Would that were possible,' he said, a hand clasped to his head. 'Would that were possible.' He sank into the chair behind his desk. 'I'm afraid there's more to it, Herbert.' Glancing at the door, his eyes filled with terror. 'I did turn the key, did I not?'

'You did, Father, of course you did. Now then . . .' He had assumed the tone of an adult comforting a child. 'What more could there possibly be that could bring a frown to your brow? Have I not assured you that I have the answer? I would have been gratified had you smiled and perhaps thanked me.'

'Of course I'm gratified, Herbert, your support is most welcome. Yes, it does lift a father's heart when his son and heir is so close to him.'

'Close? Oh . . . I do believe that's the nicest thing you've ever said to me.' His face creased and for the first time since he was a little boy, Herbert was genuinely moved by those few words. He managed not to cry this time.

'Of course we're close, have I not said so before now? Have I not shown by my actions that all I ever wanted was to be a good father? Why else do you think I've been a little on the strict side at times?'

'But you have never praised me,' said Herbert. 'Not once did you ever look at any of my drawings or my stories or anything that I did. I thought you never liked me, or were horrendously disappointed.'

'Disappointed, of course. I'm sure all fathers are, about one thing or another. But we'll leave that aside for now and hope that you might come round, eventually. You have a choice and I can only trust that you will choose marriage and not prison. Now then, you had best brace yourself for some shocking news.'

'*Worse* than this marriage proposal?'

'In a way, yes.' Tobias scratched his ear and thought of the best way to explain his past. 'You see, going back to what we were just talking about – your not wanting to be married and so on . . .'

'This has something to do with it?' Herbert was genuinely frightened. 'I'm the cause of—'

'No, no! I was referring to my wanting to set the right example. Right from when you were no more than three or four years old. When you'd had a good spanking for playing with dolls and dressing up in your sister's clothes.'

'A whipping, Father. You whipped me for it and more than once.' Herbert was speaking very quietly now. Subservient. Almost as if he were that child again having to face this dictatorial man in his study.

'Yes and a fat lot of good that did. Well then, you'll see why I tried a different way round it. A man has natural urges, Herbert. If he sees a beautiful woman he wants her. I wanted to set you an example, through my behaviour. And that's why I had mistresses. You can see that surely to God, a moron would see that!'

'Yes, of course I see that.'

'Well, there's the rub. I managed to fertilise a lovely looking young lady . . . much to my regret. She was a clever wench, aroused me so much . . . got me so excited. Well, you can guess the rest . . .'

'You've got a woman pregnant? At your age?'

'Excuse me, Herbert, but I am only in my late forties, hardly an old man. Besides, as usual, you read it wrong. I'm talking of a very long time ago, when I was full-blooded.'

'And this baby, was it male? Am I not your only son – is this the shocking news?'

'No, thank God. Another son like you and I should

think I would have run for cover in some far and forgotten place. No, Herbert, it was a girl.'

'Then why bother to worry over it? It's the past.'

'Yes, but sometimes the past has a habit of creeping up on one and in this case becoming the future. That scullery maid below stairs is your half sister.'

Tobias, wishing to place himself in the best light possible unfolded the story, slowly, and, naturally, cast blame on Grace when he arrived at the episode of her insisting on going with him to Brick Lane. On and on he went, until his son could take no more. Rising from his chair, Herbert spoke in a broken voice. 'I have something to show you, Father, something which has kept me awake many a night. Please excuse me for two minutes.'

When he returned, he made sure to lock the door behind him before he spread out the photographs of Beanie and Sarah, the connotations of which turned his stomach. To him their skylarking was deeply insulting. He sat down and watched as his father, with a look of horror on his face, examined the photos closely to make sure that the face of the girl who was baring her rump was indeed his daughter. 'Where in heaven's name did you get these . . . these . . . ?' he asked Herbert.

'I followed the girls because I had to know what it was that Sarah saw in the wench from below. Once they had left the photographic studio I went in and retrieved these. I made believe I was a collector who wished to purchase. I gave the photographer a huge cheque and went immediately to the bank and cancelled it.'

'And when may I ask did all of this happen?'

'Very recently,' said Herbert, beginning to feel, for the first time in his life, ahead of his father.

'And there have been no consequences? No one coming in search of them, no threats of violence should they not be returned?'

'No,' he lied, 'you have nothing to worry over on that count.' He had already made light of the rough-looking men who had called in search of him. This was *his* heroic act and he wasn't going to let his father interfere. He and he alone would see this dangerous and life-threatening business through to the very bitter end. 'I have the photographer over a barrel, Father. I threatened to go to the police if he made a fuss, exposure is what I used to blackmail the rogue. I had intended to burn them but thought better of it. Other than the photographer, my eyes are the only ones to have seen them, up until now of course.'

'I see.' Tobias straightened and a certain look of nobility was back on his face. 'Would you be so kind as to ask your mother's cousin to come into my study, Herbert? We'll see what he thinks of that girl now.'

'But Father, I beg you be a little more cautious. If the scullery maid is . . .' he could hardly bring himself to say the words, '. . . related to us, do you not think it best to simply send her away and say nothing to Digby? We could put them on a boat to China,' he scoffed, enjoying his moment in the sun.

'Don't be so damned ignorant! Bugger your cousin Digby, I'm more concerned with Sarah learning from this. It's never too late too learn from one's mistakes, young man. You might do well to bear that in mind. No, we'll have it so that both Sarah and Digby will be pleased to see the back of that bloody girl!'

'Well, if you think so but I have to say—'

'Don't waste your breath, if these pictures were to get out into the public domain we would be ruined. Society does not forgive something like this, neither does it forget. Do as I ask, Herbert, and let's put an end to it. Surely this will have the girl and her wretched mother packing their bags. Then, and only then, shall we burn this work of the devil.'

'Wretched mother? Good Lord.' Herbert was, once again, truly shocked. 'You can't mean that, Father, Surely not? Cook was your lover, she is the girl from Brick Lane.'

'Never mind all that now, fetch your cousin and then get back to your manuscript.' The tone in his voice dared his son to argue. 'This is a matter to be resolved by Digby and myself.'

In a state of confusion and wishing he were in his little garret, away from all this, Herbert went below stairs, where he knew his cousin would be, and ordered him to his father's study with no explanation; which of course amused Digby more than offended him.

Once his cousin had left the kitchen, Herbert turned on Beanie. 'I should pack your bags *now* if I were you.'

'Herbert,' cautioned Sarah, 'don't cause trouble now.'

'Cause trouble? Really, Sarah, tut-tut. Here in this basement, surrounded by the worst of all women and you tell *me* not to cause trouble?' He placed a finger under her chin and said, 'Such a pretty face, Sister. Why not put *that* to the camera next time, instead of your arse?'

The room went quiet. Beanie was flummoxed and Flora shocked. Fanny and Albert simply looked at each other, fearing the worst, that everything was about to come out with regard to Sarah and Beanie posing for the naughty pictures. Pushing her face close to Herbert's, Sarah whispered, 'If you've done what I think you've done, I'll kill you.'

'Tut-tut, Sister . . .'

'Have you handed anything over to Father?' she demanded, not caring who heard.

'Time will tell, my sweet, time will tell.' With that he flounced out of the kitchen, calling behind him, 'Tell your half sister and the hag to pack now.'

Waiting for the bomb to explode, Flora glanced at Sarah but by the expression of fury on her face, the weight of his passing remark about half sister had not sunk in. 'How dare he!' screeched Sarah. 'How dare he interfere in my life.' Furious, Sarah stormed out of the room on her way to her father's study.

'What did that drip mean by half sister?' said Fanny, puzzled.

'I don't know and I don't care,' said Beanie. She had other things to concern her and was so worried over the photos she felt sick. She knew that Herbert had retrieved them, of course she did, but both she and Sarah believed he would have destroyed them. But it would seem they were wrong and he had been more devious than they thought. Now they would be shown to Digby and she wished she was dead.

'But it is a peculiar fing to say,' murmured Fanny.

'Well, he's a peculiar sort of chap,' said Flora, 'anyhow, enough of this, we've got work to do.'

Dropping into a chair, Beanie, her head clasped in her hands, could only just manage to stop herself crying. 'He's so horrible. I wish someone would kill 'im and be done with.'

'That's a dreadful thing to say, Bea,' said Flora, thinking the same thing. 'I don't know what this is all about but if they've something to tell Mr Morton about you and Sarah or anything to do with us down below, it'll be like tipping dirty water down a drain. He's not the sort to listen to gossip.'

'I still don't know why he said it,' said Fanny, shaking her head. 'Half sister?'

'Never mind that now,' said Albert, piping up. 'Who was he referring to when he said "the hag"? He'd better not 'ave meant my Fanny!'

'No, that's not what he meant, Albert,' snapped Flora. 'Now leave it be.'

The room went quiet, deathly quiet and still, until Beanie turned very slowly and looked at Albert and Fanny. 'Mum had a love affair years ago with Mr Wellington. I'm his daughter.'

The instantaneous, raucous laughter from both Fanny and Albert filled the kitchen and could be heard on the first floor. Warming to the heartening sound, and finding this funnier than her best joke, Flora started to laugh too. They had just been delivered a well-kept secret that was explosive and they hadn't believed it. This *was* the joke of the year!

'Do you know what I think?' said Flora, blotting her face with a tea towel. 'I think that Master Herbert came down here by order of his father. I can hear it now: "We'll have no mixing of the classes in this house! Fetch your cousin from the basement this minute!"'

Crashing into her father's study, Sarah was even more livid to see embarrassing pictures of herself under the eye of three men: Digby, Herbert and her father. 'How dare you look at those without my permission!' she screeched, slamming the door shut. 'Herbert, give them to me this minute!'

'He will do no such thing, young lady, and you will mind your manners. You have disgraced the good name of this family as it is.'

'Good name of this family, Father?' She drew back, looked at him and smiled facetiously. 'The good name of Mother, don't you mean? After all, Herbert has a certain reputation, I have modelled for a photographer of New Art, and you habitually visit Lillian Redmond's House of Assignation where I believe you have not one paid prostitute on the go, but four or five!'

Neither chapel nor church had been as silent as that room right then. Turning to Digby, who had the slightest suggestion of a smile on his face, she said, 'If anyone is to take blame for these, it's me. I dragged Bea into Potts' studio and the whole thing started off as a bit of a lark. A bee happened to wake up too early and got under my skirts and into my drawers. The seedy photographer, not wasting a good opportunity, snapped us in that position.'

'Why are you telling *me* all of this, Sarah? Should you not be addressing your father?'

'It would be a waste of time. And the only reason I am excusing myself is because of Beanie, I don't think you should banish her from your life. There . . . I've said all I have to say.' Avoiding her father's fierce eyes, she turned round, opened the door and, about to slam it shut behind her, heard Digby call her quietly by name.

Standing silent and proud, she turned to him and waited to hear what he had to say. He picked up one of the photographs and tapped it on the palm of his other hand. 'This one is particularly good, both you and Beanie *are* quite photogenic. I should like to sit down with you at some point and discuss your idea of starting up your own studio of New Art photography.'

A smile spread gradually across Sarah's face. 'Thank you so much for seeing the photograph in the light it was meant, cousin Digby. And thank you for the compliment, I shall pass it on to Beanie straight away.'

'Before you go, Sarah, I believe there is something your father wishes to say to you.' Digby looked at Tobias. 'The girl from Brick Lane?'

'Here we go,' groaned Herbert, 'no doubt she will shriek it from the rooftops. Let me tell it for you, Father, to spare you the embarrassment.'

'Do what you damn well want, it would seem that anyone may have their say in *my* private study with no thoughts on what I may think.' He glared at Digby, in particular.

Herbert, once again, assumed the role of father superior himself as he turned to Sarah, gave her a certain look of sympathy and then said, 'That awful commoner from below stairs is a child born out of wedlock, the mother of that wench is also one of our domestic staff. Cook.'

'Good grief,' said Sarah. 'Cook is Beanie's mother . . . how fascinating.' She looked about her at the silent faces. 'Is that it?' she said, addressing Digby. 'Is that what you wanted my father to tell me?'

'Part of it,' he said, smiling openly. 'There is more. Your father is also Beanie's father, therefore she is your half sister.'

Sarah's jaw dropped and she gaped, stunned, at her cousin. 'My God . . .' she all but whispered, '. . . my sister . . . ?' She turned to Tobias. 'Father?'

'It's true, yes. I was a little on the wild side in my younger days.' He avoided saying that he was married at the time and that both Digby and herself were small children. 'But there we are, I shall pay them off and that'll be the end of it. Thankfully we found out in time, before your cousin got too carried away with his silly notions of marriage; we'll hear no more on that matter at least. Always the silver lining, what?' he smiled, believing that that was that.

'On the contrary, Tobias, we shall be hearing much more on it. I shall bring the engagement forward, if my future wife agrees of course.' He turned to Sarah and smiled.

'I hope you're as pleased as I am about this, Sarah. You have a sister which you richly deserve.' He then turned to Herbert, 'You too, Cousin. I should embrace it rather than disgrace it. She does like you, you know, despite your pretentious nature. That's the thing about Bea, she sees the good and ignores the bad in a person.'

Suddenly the door of the study slammed shut. Sarah had left without asking her father's permission to be excused and was on her way to the basement, running so fast she was in danger of tripping over her own feet. Bursting into the kitchen, she stood dead still and stared at Beanie, tears rolling down her face. 'You're my sister,' she said, in a whisper.

The room went deadly quiet with all eyes on Sarah. 'You're my sister!' she shrieked. She pulled Beanie up from her chair and hugged her, then waltzed her round the room.

Laughing and crying at the same time, Beanie and Sarah danced round the table and then out of the door and up the stairs and into Tobias's study, waltzing round the chairs, rejoicing and embracing this scandalous bit of news! Then, leaving them open-mouthed and somewhat stunned, the girls ran down the stairs screeching and laughing and not caring if the entire Square could hear them.

'I knew there was sumfing about them two right from the start,' said Fanny, jabbing the air with a finger and then downing her third glass of sherry. 'I said them two could be sisters, didn't I, Albert?'

'No,' said Albert, never one to miss the chance of

tormenting his beloved while giving himself the time to take this shocking thing in.

'I bleeding well did, Cook, and he knows it!' She sniffed and took another sip of her drink. 'It frightens 'im 'cos I've got a sixth sense. I always know when sumfing's gonna 'appen. I said only this morning—' Three loud thumps on the front door stopped her short. 'Who the bleeding 'ell's that trying to knock the 'ouse down? I'm not answering it,' she said, pushing her luck.

With all the commotion going on, it was Herbert who answered the door.

'Mr Wellington?' said one of the men.

'No. Who shall I say is calling?'

'Pals of Mr Potts,' said the other, straight-faced.

'Really? Well, I can only imagine it is my father you are in search of, but he is away on a very long business trip to India. I personally have not had the pleasure of knowing a Mr Potts.' He then all but closed the door in their faces. But they were not going to be put off so easily, a foot was firmly placed between door and frame. 'We want the pictures, Mr Wellington, or the price agreed on the sale – in cash.'

'I have no idea what you are talking about,' said Herbert, standing boldly before them, chest forward, shoulders back. 'Should you show your faces in this Square again I shall have my men march you to the nearest police station. Am I making myself clear?'

'Your men?'

'Obviously Mr Potts did not tell you that I am a chief officer at Scotland Yard. You may give your employer a message. Tell him the photographs have been destroyed and the girls in question will not be modelling for him again. Furthermore, should you persist you will end up in jail and Mr Potts' studio will be closed down henceforth.'

'Ah,' said one of the men, 'that does throw a different light on the matter.'

'Indeed. Now if I were you I would forget all about this particular mission and not come within five miles of my home again. Do I make myself clear?'

'You most certainly do, Sir,' said one, backing away. 'Absolutely crystal clear,' said the other. With that, Herbert closed the door firmly on the retreating thugs and commended himself on a fine performance.

'Well done you!' beamed Sarah. '*Brilliant* performance, Herb. Magnificent!'

'You think so . . . you should take the trouble to see me on stage, sister, you have seen nothing yet. Where is the *half* of a sister, may I enquire?'

'With cousin Digby. They're going out for a walk, isn't that romantic?'

Shuddering, Herbert could think of nothing less romantic. 'How very proper. Do tell Digby to come to my room on his return. If he is to be married there are certain things he should know about married life.'

'Oh, and you're the man to tell him I suppose?' she said, grinning.

'Sarah, dear girl, one has friends in the acting profession and one has friends. Some are single and some married. When working together as closely as we often do, touring the country, staying in dull hotels, we

have time to talk intimately. You may take my word
for it. I have much advice to pass on.' With that he
went back to his room, a touch more confident than
usual. He knew that his performance on the doorstep
had been a triumph. He hadn't needed Sarah to tell
him that it was truly magnificent!

From the window of his study, Tobias saw Digby and
the scullery maid, hand in hand on the park bench in
the Square and it fuelled his anger. 'It's incestuous.
This whole bloody family is *incestuous*.' Maybe the
time had come for him to slip out of their lives forever?
Slumping down in his captain's chair, he thought more
on it. He had toyed with the same idea several times
over the years. This world that he was part of did
not suit him. Grace's family, even though born into
money, had no real sense of style, they lived as if they
were ordinary people. He thought about his dark lady
of the stage – the only woman he had truly loved. The
only woman who had turned the tables on Tobias and
left *him* heartbroken.

In this reflective mood, he wondered if perhaps he
had been wrong in not leaving Grace years ago. He
and his lover had suffered much heartache and for
what? He imagined how happy they would be now,
had he not put his family first. Of course, there had
been lovers after her but none of them had pulled at
his heartstrings. Turning it all over in his mind he
could find nothing to look forward to. Hadn't Lillian
Redmond mentioned, more than once, that she was
considering moving away? Without his sanctuary at

the House of Assignation, what joy was in store? The dark clouds were gathering and he really didn't want to be in this house when the thunder roared and the storm exploded.

Collecting his thoughts, he made up his mind there and then that the time really had come and that he was ready to be courageous and finally leave his wife and join his true love. He had thought about it so many times that it now seemed his fate rather than his fancy.

Leaving number ten Beaumont Square in the wee dark hours of the following morning and for the last time, Tobias Wellington walked away, ready as ever he would be to cut the ties which had all but strangled him. He hailed a cab and ordered the driver to drop him at London Bridge.

Paying the driver and adding a generous tip, he stepped on to London Bridge and strode purposefully towards his destiny. It was dark and it was cold but a sense of coming freedom warmed his soul.

Arriving at the place where he would once have met his secret love, he leaned on the handrail and looked down into the dirty old river. This was the place where he often came when in a pensive mood. Smiling, with no other vision in his mind than his dark lady of the stage, he climbed on to the railings of the bridge and with his arms stretched wide, called out her name as he sloped forward and the wind rushed past, before the River Thames filled his lungs. Tobias Wellington was happy in his belief that he would join his true love who had thrown herself into the river at this very spot all those years ago. The poor girl had believed foolishly that she had been the only lover in his life.

The news of the suicide was indeed shocking and the only person who was not totally appalled by it was Grace. This was just the sort of cowardly act her husband was capable of, his timing was bang on. Now, when the going looked tough he had bowed out and left her to face the music. She had found the suicide note which he had left on his desk for all to see. The words were meant to make everyone feel deeply guilty and heavy-hearted, especially Grace. But she did not feel guilty or heartbroken. Yes, she felt a heavy sense of loss and of being alone but the note had even managed to quash that emotion. Tearing it into the tiniest of pieces she had thrown it away before anyone else had the chance to read it.

A few weeks after the funeral and by herself in the library, Grace felt very much alone in her changed circumstances and wondered if she was as strong as she had always believed. Both Sarah and Herbert had taken their father's death badly, each of them saying that they never really got to know what he was really like. They would discover with the passage of time that this was the fault of Tobias and not themselves. He had conducted himself as if he were an officer and a gentleman, of sorts, instead of a loving husband and father.

The sound of the doorbell ringing brought Grace to her senses. She closed her eyes and sighed loudly, 'Not another sympathiser, please dear God, let it not be someone else here to cry on my shoulder.'

But this time the caller had not come to see her especially. It was Herbert's friend, Gerald Fairweather. Ill at ease, with the stolen wireless tucked under his arm, he managed a sorry smile when Fanny opened the door to him. Without a word passing between them she showed him into the drawing room and went to fetch Herbert who was lying on his bed, as usual.

'I've come to return the wireless and to pay you back the three pounds I owe you,' said Gerald, deeply embarrassed.

'Three pounds four shillings, I believe it was,' said Herbert.

'Well I only have three pounds to spare at present but I shall fetch the rest another time.' He stood awkwardly, waiting to be invited to sit down.

'Very well. If you would be so kind as to place the wireless on the calling-card table.'

'Certainly,' said Gerald, his eyes lowered. 'I was sorry to hear about your father, Herbert. Very sorry indeed. If there's anything I can do . . .' He turned to face him only to see that his friend was on the brink of tears. 'Herbert, my dear chap . . .'

'It's perfectly all right,' murmured Herbert, a handkerchief to his eyes, 'I'm being silly. Please take no notice of me.' Turning his back on Gerald, he began to cry. From somewhere deep inside, emotions were surfacing. 'Thank you for calling,' he just managed to say.

Taking a grip on himself, Gerald walked towards his friend slowly and put a caring arm round his shoulders. 'It's all right,' he whispered, 'there's no shame in crying over your father. No shame whatsoever.'

'I'm going to miss him so much, isn't that ridiculous? He was horrid to all of us and especially me . . . and you . . . but I did love him, Gerald, and do you know what . . .' he looked into his friend's grief stricken face, '. . . I think he loved me, too. When I was a little chap, three years old or so, he was only trying to make me less soft. That's why he beat me, he told me so. We were in his study you see, talking, just Father and myself, and he wasn't preaching or anything like that. We were talking man to man.'

'Well then, I'm glad of it. You should have contrived it long ago.'

'I didn't contrive it, Gerald. It was he who called me in. He was terribly upset about something and I can't remember what it was but he called me in. He wanted someone to talk to, you see, and he chose me, his son. Wasn't that rather sweet?'

'Come on old luv, let's get the both of us a brandy, I think we need it, don't you?'

'Yes, I think we probably do.' He put a hand to his forehead, 'But Mother needs me, she's terribly upset, I should really be with her.'

'Well, then, we'll both go and sit with her. Now dry your eyes and stand up straight, like a man. For your father,' he said, smiling. 'For that miserable, strict old sod of a father.'

'Now really, Gerald,' said Herbert feeling happier for seeing him. 'You shouldn't speak ill of the dead, especially not when it's my father.'

'I wasn't, Herbert,' he said, 'I was being honest.'

*　　*　　*

Once a respectable enough time had passed after the suicide and life was more or less getting back to normal, plans already made between Digby and Grace with regard to his buying number ten were brought out into the open. The plan to convert the basement had not only shocked Fanny and Albert but thrilled them, they could hardly believe it was real; they were to have the basement to themselves. Beanie and Digby, once married, were to have the second floor and Flora was to have the attic rooms. Grace after much thought and trepidation had decided that it was time for her to have a complete change. She no longer wished to live in this house with its unhappy memories.

As it happened, two houses in the Square were being sold, a smaller but similar house to the one she had grown so used to and the larger house opposite. After much deliberation, Grace chose the lovely, smaller house. Before moving in, it was to be stripped, refurbished to modern taste and redecorated. Here she would live with Sarah and Herbert.

Sarah, still intent on opening a New Art photographic studio, with Digby as her silent partner, was subdued. The shocking death of her father had forced her to act in a more adult way. The house in the country, Laversham Hall, was to be let until the complicated business of finances had been sorted out.

All in all, with those changes forced upon the family and those which had been undertaken out of choice, life didn't seem so bad after all. Herbert was the only one who hadn't quite spoken up as to what he truly wanted and now, bracing himself to speak with his mother on a delicate subject, he knocked quietly on the door of his father's old study.

Upon entering he relaxed immediately at seeing his mother surrounded by piles of files and official papers, but looking very tired. The dreadful atmosphere that pervaded that study when his father was alive had dissipated. 'Oh, Herbert dear, will I ever sort out this mess?' sighed Grace. 'Some of these files go back twenty years and more.'

'Well, you know I'm always here to help if I possibly can,' he said, pulling up a chair. 'You don't have to do everything yourself.'

'Probably not, darling but . . .' She leaned back in her chair and rubbed her eyes. 'I think it's something I have to do, for myself if nothing else. I wasn't really complaining, I need to do this and I'm not sure why, I suppose it's a laying of the ghost.' She smiled at him.

'Mother, I've been doing quite a bit of serious thinking in that room of mine,' he said, wringing his hands nervously. 'And I was wondering, once we've moved into the new house on the Square, how would you feel if we took in a paying guest?'

'Paying guest? Really, Herbert, there would be no need for that, we're not completely ruined. Whatever made you think of such a thing?'

'Well, it wasn't so much the rent being the reason, it's just that I know someone who would be a perfect house guest and is in need of a room in a nice house, where he can be amongst friends.'

'Gerald?' said Grace, all knowing.

'Yes, Gerald. But you mustn't be a silly old thing and worry over it if it isn't something you feel comfortable with.'

'You would like Gerald to live with us as if he were family, and how does he feel about that? Is this something that you've come up with yourself or have you spoken to him about it?'

'Well, yes I have,' he said, blushing. 'You see – and this really is the difficult bit – for you, I mean. He suggested that we ought to share a rented flat, which of course I turned down.' He checked his mother's reaction from the corner of his eye and waited. 'We would share bills and the rent and so on . . .'

'I think that's a much better idea, Herbert. I don't think it would work as well if we were all under the same roof. No, I don't think I would feel comfortable with that.'

'But you wouldn't mind if we shared a flat?'

'You mean if you were to live with Gerald? No, darling, I wouldn't mind. Try and keep it as respectable as possible, if you see what I mean. Nothing is gained by flaunting your lifestyle, it simply makes matters difficult. Be discreet is what I'm trying to say.'

'Of course, Mother. Am I not always discreet? Discretion is my middle name and because of this I may tell you with my hand on my heart that no one except yourself, of course, has the remotest inkling of the way I feel about things, about Gerald for instance. Have you not seen with your very own eyes how forceful and masculine I have become around the house?'

'Well, yes, but you know, you don't have to be anything but yourself. And I know, Herbert, I know as your own mother should indeed know, that you are a very good and kind person deep down. Just be yourself, darling, it really is that easy.' Her emotional strings were being pulled yet again as her sad son sat before her, shoulders slumped and eyes downcast. This was a difficult conversation to have for any mother and son but once this bridge had been crossed, things would be so much easier. Grace was confident.

'Suffice to say that I love you as dearly as ever and I will go along with whatever makes you happy. Equally, to be fair, you might take notice of what I've said. Just live your life and let others live theirs.' Herbert covered his face with his hands and began to cry.

'Darling . . .' said Grace in a hushed voice and reaching across the desk to stroke his cheek. 'It's all right, really it is.'

'I know,' said Herbert, wiping his face with his handkerchief. 'I just wish we could have talked more before now. You don't know how tormented I've been and for such a long, long time . . .'

'Herbert,' said Grace, taking her hand in his and looking directly into his face. 'I'm not one for speaking ill of the dead but I am going to say this, just once, and we'll agree never to touch on it again. Your father was a dictatorial man, he had a strange power over all of us. But he is no longer with us and we have the opportunity now to start afresh, to live our lives the way *we* choose. Your father has gone for good, Herbert, and his harsh rules with him.'

'I know what you mean,' he said, managing a weak smile. 'Father put the fear of God into me ever since I can remember. I tried *so* hard to please him.'

'Do you think I don't know that? Others couldn't see it but I knew why you behaved like a bit of a know all. You were trying to impress the unimpressionable. But that's over now, it's all over, we can each be what we are.'

Letting out a long and heavy sigh, he shook his head slowly. 'Thank you, Mother, I feel as if a huge weight has been lifted from me. If you don't mind I should like to go to the library and pour myself a large brandy.'

'Why should I mind?' smiled Grace, her face close to his. 'You may do as you please providing you do not upset those around you. You are a fully-grown man, Herbert, never forget that.'

Standing by the door, his hand gripping the brass knob he turned to her again and said, 'Things are going to be all right, aren't they?'

'Yes, Herbert, things are going to be all right. The planned changes are very exciting, really. We are moving with the times and I for one, am ready for it.'

Below stairs, Lenny the gardener was keeping Flora company during his tea break. In his favourite chair by the fire, Lenny was deep in thought. So deep that Flora thought he might fall off the chair. Sleeping with your eyes open is what she called it.

'A penny for 'em, Lenny,' said Flora while rolling some pastry for a fruit pie.

'I shall miss sitting 'ere by this fireside,' he said, not

one for beating about the bush. 'If you ask me it's a daft idea. Why can't things stop as they are?'

'Because it's the age of change, that's why. Most houses on this Square are being converted if they haven't been already, flats for medical students mostly. Besides, you can sit by my fire in the attic, can't you, once it's all done and dusted.'

'I shouldn't think so, won't be the same, stuck up in the attic. You should 'ave turned the idea down flat.'

'Oh, so we won't be seeing much of you then, only in the garden while you're working?'

'Well, no, I shall come into the new kitchen for a cup of tea. Will there be a fire in this new kitchen then?'

'I expect so, most rooms on the first floor have a fireplace.'

'Well, that's where I'll sit then. So that's all right.'

'I'm pleased we've got your approval,' said Flora. 'We'd have left everything as it was if not.'

'Would you . . . ? Well, there you are. I've never been one for sticking in the mud, not really. Wouldn't mind another cup of tea . . .'

'Well, you know where the teapot is. Anyway, I should think there'll be a boxroom in this house, somewhere, that'd suit you.' She knew exactly where it was – in the attic. 'All you need is a place to lay your head down.'

'What, here in this house? Oh no, I don't think that'd be right. No we don't want to go rocking the boat, I'm all right where I am in my lodgings. But then again if it's suggested by the man who's gonna be my boss sooner or later, Mr Digby, then I should have to agree, shouldn't I?'

'Yes, Lenny, I would have thought so.'

'Well, then, that's settled. I shall go above stairs if and when I'm told to. Did you want a cup of tea then?'

'Yes, please. Do you mind if I say something on the personal side, Lenny, while we're by ourselves?'

'Well I can't answer that till I've heard what it is. But go on, I don't 'spect it be too bad. You're a fair woman. I doubt you'd—'

'Lenny, do you mind or not?'

'I said so didn't I?'

'It's just that I wanted to say that you've been a good friend for me, good company. And I want you to know I appreciate it, it means a lot when you're on your own.'

'Well, go on then, what was the personal bit you wanted to say?'

'That was it.'

'Oh . . . fair enough. So we're mates then?'

'That's right. But then—'

The sound of the basement door opening and the laughing and talking between Sarah and Beanie stopped their little parley. 'You'll never guess what, Cook . . .' Sarah pulled off her hat and slumped down on to a chair. 'Never in a million years will you guess . . .'

'I wouldn't bank on it after all that's happened here of late. Spit it out then.'

'Shall I tell her or will you, Bea?'

'I will.' Beanie knew her mother inside out and the only way was to be short and to the point. 'I told yer Sarah and me had posed for a photographer, didn't I?'

'You know full well you did,' sniffed Flora, waiting.

'Well, Sarah's bin inspired to start up her own New Art studio with Digby as a silent partner.'

'Is that it?' said Flora, knowing full well there was more to come. They had their knickers in a twist over something or she wasn't a cook.

'Digby's bought the second set of pictures off Mr Potts . . . the ones that me and Beanie posed for and he thinks they're excellent,' said Sarah, glowing.

'I see, well, let's have a look at them then.'

'Well . . .' Sarah looked at Beanie and waited.

'Go on then,' grinned Beanie. 'She can only rip them up and give me a backhander.'

'Oh, I see. Rude pictures were they?' enquired Flora.

'New Art,' said Sarah, drawing the package out of her coat pocket. 'Not rude, Cook. New Art.' She eyed Beanie for her approval before passing them over.

'Get it over with for Gawd's sake, give 'em to 'er!'

Easing them out of the packaging, Flora looked at each of them with no hint of expression or reaction. She then handed them across to Lenny. 'See what you think . . .' she said, keeping a straight face.

'Well?' Sarah looked anxious but Beanie was smiling. If her mother was in the least bit disgusted they would know it by now. It was time for a little teasing . . .

'They're worth a lot of money,' Beanie shrugged, 'but I think we ought to chuck 'em in the fire.'

'They're very good as a matter of fact,' said Flora. 'I never realised you had it in you . . . action pictures they are, not silly poses. If you'd 'ave posed half naked for the camera I might have ripped them through the middle.' She showed a serious face. 'They're very good indeed, well done the pair of you.'

Lenny on the other hand, having seen just one, was shocked. 'You can't let anyone see these,' he said, passing them back to Flora. 'You'll get locked up!'

'Course they won't,' sniffed Flora. 'I would 'ave done the same in their shoes – when I was a younger woman. Oh yes, I had just as fine a figure and good looks as this pair, if not better.'

'It's pornography.' Lenny turned his back on all of them and staring into the fire, shook his head. 'You don't wanna get mixed up in that kind of a thing.'

'We're going to lock them away until I'm up and running with my own studio. Mr Potts knows of a vacant shop not far away, we might be able to lease that. He was offish at first but we explained about Herbert, posing as the police officer in his attempt to protect my innocence and the family name, and he rocked with laughter.'

'Yeah,' said Beanie, 'he might not 'ave bin laughing if Digby hadn't coughed up though. Mind you, he was good wasn't he? Got the price right down. See, he's getting the idea already. He'll be turning into a Flash Harry before we know it, with a stall down Petticoat Lane.'

'It's a changing world, Lenny.' Flora pulled up a chair next to his by the fire. 'The times are changing and we must change with them.'

'Not me,' he said, positively. 'Oh no. I shall watch, mind you. Watch you all making mistakes and running before you can walk. I shan't interfere, but don't come to me crying when it all gets too much. There's nothing wrong with the old ways. Nothing whatsoever.'

Across the green, at her window, Lillian Redmond, a woman who had been born before her time, was watching as another family moved out of the Square. As a young lady, she would have been very much in tune with these new times . . . these Roaring Twenties. Her pastime of watching the gradual shifting sands of this genteel place in the heart of Stepney was beginning to wane. It was time for her to retire. Time for her to board the windows of her House of Assignation. Time to say goodbye to Beaumont Square.

SALLY WORBOYES

DOWN STEPNEY WAY

In the turbulent East End of London in the thirties, Jessie
Warner is growing up . . .

Emotions are running high in Stepney, with Blackshirts
marching through the streets and the Jewish community
under threat of violence. In the midst of this, Jessie
discovers a family secret and turns to her mother for
answers, but Rose is reluctant to reveal the past – for
there is something that Jessie must never know.

In Bethnal Green, Hannah Blake is being forced by
her cold-hearted mother to join the Blackshirts, despite
deep misgivings. Next-door neighbour Emmie knows of
the darkness surrounding Hannah's wretched past, but is
bound by a vow of silence not to reveal it. And meanwhile,
Emmie's son Tom, chipper and handsome, has just fallen
for a blonde girl he wants to bring home to meet Emmie
and Hannah. Her name is Jessie Warner . . .

The first of a new trilogy, DOWN STEPNEY WAY
is a vigorous, lively and honest novel, full of atmosphere,
depicting London in the thirties: the families, the traders,
the docks and factories, and the Blackshirts.

A Coronet Paperback

SALLY WORBOYES

KEEP ON DANCING

Rosie Curtis is devastated when her brother Tommy is viciously murdered after dabbling in the criminal underworld. Not only is her carefree existence suddenly over, but without Tommy's support, her dreams of becoming a dancer are shattered. Powerless to avenge her brother's death, Rosie throws herself into saving a local music hall from closure and planning a musical spectacular, despite the misgivings of her family.

But when Rosie comes face to face with her brother's slayer, she realises she must stop at nothing to see the criminals punished. While she fights to stage her show and put Tommy's killers away for good, her brother's smiling face appears in her thoughts, telling her to keep on dancing . . . can she find the strength without him?

A gripping vibrant East End saga, *Keep On Dancing* portrays the drama of everyday life with compassion and humour.

A Coronet Paperback

SALLY WORBOYES

WHITECHAPEL MARY

Suddenly and tragically orphaned, Mary Dean must find an extra source of income if she and her young brother are to escape the workhouse. The matchbox factory where she works pays poorly and she is desperate. Tempted by the lure of the House of Assignation, Mary accepts an invitation and becomes a courtesan in the exclusive establishment. Her very first client, Sir Walter, is entranced by her beauty and innocence; he insists that she be his and his alone.

But another threat lurks in the shadows. Mary's neighbour, a midwife, righteous in her hatred of prostitution, holds the key to a menacing secret – the identity of the terrifying Whitechapel murderer . . . the infamous Jack the Ripper.

Mary has no idea of the peril she has placed herself in or the intentions of those who surround her. Who can she trust . . . if anyone?

A Coronet Paperback

SALLY WORBOYES

WILD HOPS

It is 1959 and emotions are running high in the Kent
hop fields, where the harvest is traditionally picked by
East Enders on their summer break. Picking by hand is
becoming a thing of the past as mechanisation takes over.
The Armstrong family – Jack, Laura and their daughter,
Kay – are devastated by the news. Far from the bustle of
Stepney, the hop fields offer hard work but fresh clean air
and lively social gatherings around the campfires.

While Jack leads the protest against the machines, Laura
Armstrong is otherwise preoccupied: will this mean the
end of her seasonal love affair with the farm owner,
Richard Wright? And what of Kay who, on the brink
of womanhood, craves adventure and creates turmoil
when she and the handsome gypsy lad, Zacchi, meet
in secret?

As tensions grow between the East Enders and the local
Romanies, it becomes clear that this summer will change
lives for ever . . .

'Sizzles with passion' *Guardian*

A Coronet Paperback